Also by Kate Jacobs

The Friday Night Knitting Club
Comfort Food

KATE JACOBS

Knit Two

HODDER

First published in Great Britain in 2009 by Hodder & Stoughton
An Hachette Livre UK company

First published in paperback in 2009

1

A CIP catalogue record for this title is available from the British Library

ISBN 978 0 340 91848 7 (B)
ISBN 978 0 340 91849 4 (A)

Typeset in Plantin Light by Hewer Text UK Ltd.

Printed and bound by CPI Mackays, Chatham ME5 8TD

Hodder & Stoughton policy is to use papers that are natural, renewable and
recyclable products and made from wood grown in sustainable forests. The
logging and manufacturing processes are expected to conform to the environ-
mental regulations of the country of origin.

Hodder & Stoughton Ltd
338 Euston Road
London NW1 3BH

www.hodder.co.uk

Beginner

Seeing a pattern doesn't mean you know how to put it all together. Take baby steps: don't focus on the folks whose skills are far beyond your own. When you're new to something – or you haven't tried it in a while – it can feel impossibly hard to get it right. Every misstep feels like a reason to quit. You envy everyone else who seems to know what they're doing. What keeps you going? The belief that one day you'll also be like that: Elegant. Capable. Confident. Experienced. And you can be. All you need now is enthusiasm. A little bravery. And – always – a sense of humor.

I

It was after hours at Walker and Daughter: Knitters, and Dakota stood in the center of the Manhattan yarn shop and wrestled with the cellophane tape. She had spent more than twenty minutes trying to surround a canvas Peg Perego double stroller in shimmery yellow wrapping paper, the cardboard roll repeatedly flopping out of the paper onto the floor of the shop and the seeming miles of gift wrap crinkling and tearing with each move. What a disaster! The simpler move would be to just tie a balloon on the thing, she thought, but Peri had been quite insistent that all the items be wrapped and ribboned.

Gifts, smothered in bunny paper or decorated with cartoonish jungle animals, were piled in a mound atop the sturdy wooden table that was the focal point of the knitting store. The wall of yarn had been tidied so not one shelf – from the raspberry reds to the celery greens – was out of hue. Peri had also planned out a series of cringe-inducing guessing games (Guess how much the baby will weigh! Eat different baby foods and try to determine the flavor! Estimate the size of the mother's stomach!) that would have caused Dakota's mother to shake her head. Georgia Walker had never been a fan of silly games.

'It'll be fun,' said Peri when Dakota protested. 'We haven't had a Friday Night baby since Lucie had Ginger five years ago. Besides, who doesn't like baby showers? All those tiny little footie pajamas and those cute towels-with-animal-ears. I mean, it just gives you goose bumps. Don't you love it?'

'Uh, no,' said Dakota. 'And double no. My friends and I are a little busy with college.' Her hands rested on the waist of her deep indigo jeans as she watched Peri pretend not to fuss over the job she'd done. The stroller looked like a giant yellow banana. A wrinkled, torn banana. She sighed. Dakota was a striking young woman, with her creamy mocha skin and her mother's height and long, curly dark hair. But she retained an element of gangliness, gave the impression that she was not quite comfortable with the transformation of her figure. At eighteen, she was still growing into herself.

'Thank God for that,' replied Peri, discreetly trying to peel the tape off the yellow paper so she could redo the edges. Whether it was operating the store or designing the handbags in her side business, she approached everything with precision now. Working with Georgia had been the best training she could ever have received for running a business – two businesses, really. Her own handbag company, Peri Pocketbook, as well as Georgia's store. Still, Peri felt she had done a lot to keep things going since Georgia passed away, and now that she was pushing thirty, she was beginning to feel a desire to move. In what direction, she wasn't sure. But there would be no more Walker and Daughter without her. Of that she was certain.

Sometimes it wasn't very satisfying to work so hard for something that essentially belonged to someone else. It was hers but not really hers at all.

For one thing, Dakota had seemed less and less interested in the store during the last year or so, grumbling on the Saturdays when she came in to work, typically late and sometimes appearing to simply roll out of bed and throw on whatever clothes she could find. It was quite a change from her early teens, when she seemed to relish her time at the shop. And yet there were brief moments when her world-weary attitude would disappear and Peri could see the whispers of the bright-eyed, wisecracking little kid who loved to bake and could spend hours knitting with her mother in the store's back office or the apartment they had shared one floor above the yarn shop.

The shop was located on Seventy-seventh and Broadway, just above Marty's deli, amid boutiques and restaurants in Manhattan's Upper West Side. Only a few blocks from the green of Central Park, and the cool of the Hudson River in the opposite direction, it was a lovely part of the city. Oh, certainly there was lots of noise – honking taxis, the rumble of the subway underneath the streets, the sound of heels on the sidewalk and cell phone conversations swirling all around – but that was the type of commotion that had appealed to Georgia Walker when she moved in. She didn't mind the beeping of the Coke truck at five a.m. bringing supplies to the deli on the street level. Not if it meant she got to live right inside the action, showing her daughter the world she had barely imagined herself growing up on a farm in Pennsylvania.

Of course, now Peri lived in the upstairs apartment that had been Georgia's and the back office was no more. The wall had recently been blown out to make a separate showcase for the handbags she designed and sold; each purse was individually displayed on a clear acrylic shelf mounted onto a wall painted a deep gray.

The change to the store had come together after much discussion with Anita and with Dakota, and they'd consulted Dakota's father, James, too, of course, though mostly for his architectural expertise. But it made financial sense: Peri had turned Dakota's childhood bedroom in the apartment into an office so there was no need to tally up receipts in the shop anymore. Why waste the store's valuable real estate? And there *had* always been the understanding – with Georgia and with James and Anita after Georgia died – that her hand-bag business would have the chance to flourish. She had reminded them of that while purposefully avoiding the one ultimatum she knew everyone most feared: She would leave the store if she wasn't able to remodel. The concern hung in the air, and she saved voicing it unless it was absolutely necessary.

After all, what would happen to the store if Peri left? Anita, who had turned seventy-eight on her last birthday though she still looked just barely old enough to collect Social Security, certainly wouldn't be about to take over. Though she continued to arrive two days a week to help out and keep busy, as she said, Anita and Marty spent a lot of their time going on quick trips, by train or car, to wonderful country inns in New England and in Canada. Those two were on a perpetual vacation, and Peri was happy for them. Envious, a little bit. Definitely. Hopeful that she'd have the same thing someday. And if that legal department coworker her pal KC kept mentioning was half as cute as he'd been described, who knew what could happen?

And then there was Dakota, who had nearly finished up her first year at NYU. It wasn't as though she could step in to run the store – or that she even seemed to want to do so anymore.

Not everyone wants to go into the family business.

Peri's decision to work at the yarn shop, and create her own designs, had not been popular within her own family. Her parents had wanted her to become a lawyer, and she'd dutifully taken her LSAT and earned a place at law school, only to turn it down and leave everyone guessing. Georgia hadn't been cowed by her mother, who flew in from Chicago to pressure Georgia into firing her, and Peri had never forgotten that fact. Even when difficulties arose over the shop, Peri reflected on how Georgia had helped her and she stuck it out. Still, the work of two businesses took up all of her days and many of her evenings, and the past five years seemed to have moved quickly. It was as though one day Peri woke up and realized she was almost thirty, still single, and not happy with the situation. It was hard to meet guys in New York, she thought. No, not guys. Men. Men like James Foster. Peri had had a mild crush on the man ever since he'd come back for Georgia, and he remained, for her, the very epitome of the successful, confident partner she longed for.

Of course, James had only ever been interested in the store from the standpoint of keeping an eye on Georgia's legacy to Dakota. And Georgia's old friend Catherine was surrounded by crap up in the Hudson Valley, thought Peri, where she managed her antiques-and-wonderful-things-blah-blah-blah store. Besides, Catherine couldn't even knit. And she and Peri had never really connected; it was more as though they shared several mutual friends but hadn't quite managed, even after all this time, to get to know each other. Peri often felt judged whenever Catherine glided into the shop, soaking in everything with her perfectly made-up smoky eyes, every blond hair in place.

No, over the years the feeling had become more definite that either Peri would keep things going at Walker and Daughter or it would be time to close up the doors to the yarn shop. The desire to keep everything just as it once had been – to freeze time – remained very strong among the group of friends. So even as she advocated change, Peri felt guilty. It was almost overwhelming. Stemming from some natural fantasy they all shared but never discussed: that everything needed to be kept just so for Georgia. For what? To want to come back? To feel at home? Because making changes to Georgia's store, without her presence or consultation, would mean things were really final. Wouldn't it? That all the moments the members of the Friday Night Knitting Club and the family of Georgia Walker had experienced, the good and the bad, *had* truly happened.

That Georgia's yarn shop was the place where an unlikely group of women became friends around the table in the center of the room. Where Anita, the elegant older woman who was Georgia's biggest supporter, learned to accept Catherine, Georgia's old high school friend, and cheered as Catherine rediscovered her own capacity for self-respect and left an empty and unfulfilling marriage. It was at Georgia's that dour and lonely graduate student Darwin found a true friend in director Lucie, who had embarked on first-time motherhood in her forties, and that Darwin realized just how much she wanted to sustain her marriage to her husband, Dan, after a brief night of infidelity. It was at Georgia's store that her employee Peri admitted she didn't want to go to law school, and at Georgia's store that her longtime friend KC confessed that she did. It was here that Georgia's former flame, James, had walked back into her life and the two discovered their love had never lost its spark. And it was at the store that Georgia and James's only child, Dakota, had once done her homework and shared her homemade muffins with her mother's friends and flaked out on the couch in her mother's office, waiting for the workday to be finished so the two of them could eat a simple supper and go on up to bed in the apartment upstairs.

And if that all had happened, then it also meant that Georgia Walker had fallen ill with late-stage ovarian cancer and died unexpectedly from complications, leaving her group to manage on without her.

For just over five years they'd all kept on just as they'd done – still meeting up for regular get-togethers even though KC never picked up a stick and Darwin's mistake-ridden sweater for her husband remained the most complex item she'd ever put together – and Peri had left everything mostly the same in the store. Year after year, she resisted her impulse to change the decor, to redesign the lavender bags with the Walker and Daughter logo, to muck out the back office with its faded couch or to update the old wooden table that anchored the room. She kept everything intact and ran the store with the energy and attention to detail Georgia had demonstrated, had turned a profit every quarter – always doing best in winter, of course – and furiously created her line of knitted and felted handbags with every spare moment. She even found the energy to branch out in new lines, new designs.

Until, finally, she'd had enough working on her handbags late at night and never feeling rested. She put down her needles and jammed out an e-mail in the middle of the night. She required a meeting, she'd written, had broached the remodel. It had been an impossible concept, of course, the idea of changing things. And it took a long while for Anita and Dakota to agree. Still, Peri stood firm, and ultimately the wall came down, some new paint went up, and even the always serviceable chairs around the center table were replaced with cushier, newly upholstered versions. The shop was revitalized: still cozy, but fresher and sleeker. As a surprise – and in an attempt to woo Dakota's emotional approval – Peri had asked Lucie to print an outtake from her documentary about the shop, the first film she had shown in the festival circuit, and had framed a photograph of Dakota and Georgia ringing up sales together, back when Dakota was only twelve and Georgia was robustly healthy. Appropriately, the picture hung behind the register, the Walker and Daughter logo next to it.

'She would have liked that,' Dakota said, nodding. 'But I

don't know about the changes to the store. Maybe we should put the wall back up.'

'Georgia believed in forging ahead,' said Peri. 'She tried new things with the shop. Think of the club, for example.'

'I dunno,' said Dakota. 'What if I forget what it used to be like? What if it all just fades away? Then what?'

Tonight, for the first time, the entire group would see the updated store in its completed form. It was a pleasantly warm April night, and the Friday Night Knitting Club was getting together for its regular meeting. Whereas once the women had gathered in Georgia's store every week, the combination of their busy careers and changing family situations made it more difficult to meet as often as they once did. And yet every meeting began with hugs and kisses and a launch, without preamble, into the serious dramas of their days. There was no pretense with these women anymore, no concern about how they looked or how they acted, just a sense of community that didn't change whether they saw one another once a week or once a year. It had been Georgia's final and most beautiful gift to each of them: the gift of true and unconditional sisterhood.

But if time had not changed their feelings for one another, it had not spared the natural toll on their bodies and their careers and their love lives and their hair. Much had happened in the preceding five years.

KC Silverman had made law review at Columbia, passed the bar with flying colors, and ended up back at Churchill Publishing – the very company that had laid her off from her editorial job five years ago – as part of in-house counsel.

'Finally, I'm invaluable,' she had told the group upon starting the job. 'I know every side of the business.'

Her new salary was transformed, with some guidance

from Peri, into a fabulous collection of suits. And her hair was longer than the pixie cut she'd had in the old days, shaped into a more lawyerly layered style. She'd experimented – for a millisecond – with letting her hair go its natural gray but she decided she was too young for that much seriousness at fifty-two and opted for a light brown.

'If I had your gorgeous silver,' she told Anita, 'it would be a different story.'

Lucie Brennan's documentary circulating on the festival circuit had led to a gig directing a video for a musician who liked to knit at Walker and Daughter. When the song went to the Top Ten in *Billboard*, Lucie quickly transitioned from part-time producer for local cable to directing a steady stream of music videos, her little girl Ginger lip-synching by her side in footie pajamas.

At forty-eight, she was busier and more successful than she ever imagined – and her apartment reflected the change. She no longer rented, but had purchased a high and sunny two-bedroom on the Upper West Side with a gorgeous camel-back sofa that Lucie, still an occasional insomniac, would curl up on in the middle of the night. Only now, instead of knitting herself to sleep, she typically mapped out shots for the next day's shoot.

And the tortoiseshell glasses she'd once worn every day had been joined by an array of frames and contacts for her blue eyes. Her hair, if left to its natural sandy brown, was quite . . . salty. So she colored it just a few shades darker than little Ginger's strawberry blond, aiming for a russet shade.

Darwin Chiu finished her dissertation, published her very first book (on the convergence of craft, the Internet, and the women's movement) based on her research at Walker and Daughter, and secured a teaching job at Hunter College while her husband, Dan Leung, found a spot at a local ER.

They also found a small apartment on the East Side, close to the hospital and college, the living room walls lined with inexpensive bookshelves overflowing with papers and notes. Unlike other women, Darwin had hair free of gray though she'd hit her thirties, and she still wore it long, without bangs, making her look almost as young as her women's studies students.

Peri Gayle, striking with her deep brown eyes, mahogany skin, and meticulous cornrows that fell just past her shoulders, ran the store, of course.

Anita Lowenstein settled into a happy arrangement with her friend Marty, although their decision not to marry came up now and again.

'I'm living my life in reverse,' she told the group. 'Now that my mother can't do a damn thing about it, I'm rebelling against society's expectations.' She'd been joking, of course. Moving in together was a simpler solution, quite frankly, in terms of estate planning and inheritance, and, as the movie stars say, neither she nor Marty needed a piece of paper to demonstrate their commitment.

'We'll just call him my partner,' corrected Anita when yet another of her friends tripped over how to describe her relationship. 'It seems overreaching to call him my boyfriend at this age.'

They had, however, purchased a new apartment together and moved out of the garden apartment in Marty's Upper West Side brownstone, allowing Marty's niece to incorporate that level into her family home. Anita was seventy-eight, though she'd lie about it if anyone ever asked, and certainly appeared younger, with her layered, silvery hair and her well-cared-for hands. Thanks to Anita, Catherine truly appreciated the value of high SPF.

Catherine Anderson's little business flourished north of the city in Cold Spring, though many days she continued to take the train, spending some days in the tidy, expensively furnished cottage she'd recently purchased and others in the San Remo apartment that Anita had shared with her late husband, Stan.

It seemed that five years was about right for all that had happened to settle in, and for the urge to try something different to begin to swell.

'Not much of a surprise if the presents are all out there,' exclaimed KC at the entrance to Walker and Daughter as she wheeled in a red wagon filled with stuffed animals perched inside: a monkey, a giraffe, and two fluffy white teddy bears. Peri stopped trying to rewrap Dakota's gift for a moment to wave hello.

'We should try to hide in the back office and then jump out and surprise her!' said KC, waving back even though she was mere steps away. 'What do you say?'

She and Peri were from different generations – KC was twenty-three years older than Peri – but they were, as the volume-impaired and talkative KC explained to anyone who cared and often to those who didn't, the very epitome of BFFs.

'We help each other get ahead,' KC explained when Dakota asked at one meeting why the two of them spent so much time together when, on the surface, they looked and acted so different from each other. 'We gossip, we go to movies, she picks out my clothes, and I give her legal advice for her pocketbook business.' Their shared devotion to career – and KC's years of experience – also kept up the connection. As proud as she was with her professional reinvention, KC had ultimately traded one workaholic lifestyle for another. Just as she'd put in long days at the office when she was an editor and followed it up with nights reading manuscripts, now she spent her evenings reading contracts on the sofa in the prewar rent-stabilized apartment on the West Side that had been her parents' home.

But while Peri kept up with a steady crowd of pals from the design courses she'd taken, KC's relationship with Peri filled a bit of the gap that had been left by Georgia, who had been a young assistant when KC met her. For a woman who would never describe herself as a nurturer, KC made it a practice to look out for others and to mentor them. And she had a deep fondness for Dakota, who seemed exasperated with her latest concept.

'For one thing, no back office anymore,' muttered Dakota, inclining her head toward KC and motioning her to take a look behind her. 'So it wouldn't work.'

'And for two, we have a no-scaring-pregnant-women policy,' added Anita, who was two steps behind KC and coming through the doorway. As she did every day, Anita wore an elegant pantsuit, and a selection of tasteful jewelry. The oldest and wealthiest member of the club, Anita was also – everyone would agree – the kindest and most thoughtful. In her arms Anita carried a giant hydrangea plant in blue; Marty carried a second one in pink. She nodded solemnly.

'The renovations are excellent, my dear,' she said, though Peri suspected her words were meant mainly to bolster Dakota's uncertainty since Anita had checked on the shop's progress repeatedly.

'I'm here, I'm here,' came a voice from the stairwell. It was Catherine, sweeping into the room with a bit of self-created fanfare and an armful of professionally wrapped presents in brightly colored paper and a large canvas bag filled with several bottles.

'Hello, darlings,' she said, blowing out enough air kisses that everyone in the room got three each.

'Hello, grumpy,' Catherine said to Dakota, lightly wrapping an arm around her shoulders as they surveyed the room.

'I was afraid I was late,' said Catherine. 'Is she here yet?' The store phone rang as Lucie called to say she wasn't able to get away from work and not to wait. Peri looked at her watch and let out a cry of concern. Quickly, KC pulled out a box of cupcakes from the bottom of the red wagon, and Catherine opened a magnum of chilled champagne without a pop.

'When I think of the Friday Night Knitting Club, I always think of plastic glasses,' said Catherine to Dakota. 'It adds a certain *je ne sais quoi*.' She winked at Dakota, managed to charm a shrug out of her young pal. The two had forged a big sister–little sister bond since Georgia had taken her in years ago and let Catherine bunk on Dakota's floor during her divorce; many times in the ensuing years since Georgia died, Catherine's cynicism and over-the-top drama had been the perfect antidote to Dakota's teenage moodiness. Anita remained Dakota's source for unconditional love; Catherine was good at keeping secrets and seemed willing to become her partner in crime, if only they could think up a scheme.

'To Walker and Daughter,' said Catherine, taking one sip and then another. 'To the reno, to my favorite kid, and to the club.' The rest of the women raised their glasses.

Even though the vague unease about the remodel persisted, Peri could tell it was going to be a happy night. Anybody could see that. The gang was all here, together again; the volume was already deafening as everyone spoke at once, trying to cram a month's worth of news into a few minutes. She began to relax as she saw Dakota flop into one of the new chairs, throw her jeans-clad leg over the arm, and bum a sip of champagne off Catherine, the two of them glancing to see if Anita had noticed.

Tonight, the Friday Night Knitting Club would have made Georgia proud. They were holding a special meeting to throw a surprise baby shower for one Darwin Chiu, who was finally, after many long years of trying and hoping, expecting her first children.

Darwin and Dan were having twins.

2

Having children had never been a question when Anita was young; it was simply the expected order of things. Marriage meant babies and babies meant marriage. And everyone wondered when it didn't happen quickly. There'd been no help for a couple like Darwin and Dan, who had waited and hoped for their family. It would have been very difficult to be a single mom as Georgia had been, as Lucie had chosen to be. Though Lucie seemed awfully tired and stressed as of late, and her daughter, Ginger, was not always a sweetie like little Dakota had been. Still, it was nice that things were different. Could be different. Anita believed in having options. On the other hand, sometimes it was hard to know which end was up these days.

Anita had barely breezed into her twenties when she'd married, not that she realized then how young that age would seem to her one day. She'd believed she was the pinnacle of grown-up-ed-ness in her tea-length white dress and lace veil. Stan had seemed so strong and wise – he had an answer for everything, which initially comforted her, then amused her in later years, then grew to be a smidge annoying on occasion. But his confidence in how things should be provided a protection for Anita from the world, and for that she was always grateful.

At twenty-one, she had only seen her life unfolding smoothly, hour after hour, year after year. That was the 1950s – old enough to get married and start a family, naïve enough to willfully edit world wars from day-to-day memory. Buying into a toaster-oven future of domestic bliss, where everything was going to happen simply and easily. On her wedding night it was all possibility and a seemingly endless future: she could barely wait to be alone with Stan and reveal the skills she'd tried to learn from a book. It was a great surprise to discover, later on, that sex didn't solve everything, that it could become routine and sometimes, when she didn't feel like it, irritating. That being in love didn't alleviate petty annoyances and frustrations. And even a good marriage, a wonderful partnership, had its moments.

Anita had lost touch over the years with all seven of the friends who were her bridesmaids, wouldn't know where to begin looking for the flower girl who'd worn a mint-green replica of her own gown and had followed her around the reception luncheon clutching her little basket of rose petals, the little girl reluctant to say good-bye when she left the room with Stan. Her little sister, waving her off.

It was special, really, how the Friday Night Knitting Club had stayed together. They'd done a far better job maintaining their connections than Anita with her attendants. Would the Friday Night girls stand up for her if she married Marty? She knew they would. But it would be so far from a fantasy if she and Marty wed. Theirs was a relationship between equals. Firmly in the real world. Besides, who gets married when you don't know how much longer you'll be around?

'Earth to Anita!'

Anita looked up, startled, a skein of light green yarn in her hand. KC stood in front of her, grinning.

'You were a bit zoned out there, hon,' said KC. 'Why don't you sit down in one of the new chairs and join the group?'

Feeling foolish, Anita let herself be maneuvered over to the center of the room. She hated when the girls treated her as though she was old, needing special care and attention. Ha! Let them get to be close to eighty, work several days a week on their feet – by choice – and deal with three sons who had opinions about everything. Including that they disapproved of her life partner. Those boys should be too busy with their own families to mess about in her affairs, but so they did. Anita clutched at the skein of yarn, so reminiscent of the color of the young flower girl's dress, as she sat down. She forced a tiny smile at KC, who really did think she was being helpful. That Anita was getting somewhat doddering. But Anita wasn't confused. She was preoccupied. With weddings. With the past. With the future. With her middle-aged boys who had temper tantrums whenever there was any whiff of permanence to her romance with Marty. With all the friends of her generation who were starting to disappear with regularity. And not just to Florida anymore.

'Are you working on something?' It was Dakota, reaching out to touch the yarn. Vests had been Anita's garment of choice for such a long time that it still seemed a surprise when she worked on something else. The vests she'd always made for Stan, in patterns and colors she put together herself. An artist – that's what her late husband had called her. She cut back working on them after getting together with Marty because they were so particular to Stan. Of course, she missed the familiarity of the projects, the patterns that she knew by heart, the feeling of the vest taking shape almost as if she was thinking it into being. But it hadn't seemed quite right to still make clothes for her late husband when her new fella sat beside her on their sofa, watching yet another ball game. Oh, she'd made him a sweater jacket with a Yankee logo, which he'd loved, and a seat cushion cover to take to the stadium, but unlike the vests, there wasn't the same room for creative expression. There was only one logo, only one Yankee blue.

Privately, she still had one vest on the go, tucked into the bottom of a basket. Just the very presence of the unfinished piece soothed her, maintained a link to days gone by. Moving forward didn't mean she had to let go of the past, of Stan, of Georgia. It was more about accepting that they weren't around in the day-to-day and living her life accordingly. Grief had its own rhythm. This fact she knew well.

That's how she began making hats for charity and that kind of thing. Something to knit up when the Yankees were on. And how she'd spearheaded the members of the Friday Night Knitting Club to come up with a charity project together. In the beginning – it seemed like eons ago – the club had tried to have rules and activities and even work on the same sweater pattern. Which had been a shared disaster: KC quit after barely trying, Catherine never tried, Darwin tried very hard and made a very ugly sweater, and Lucie finished more than one beautiful sweater and many projects in between. After the funeral, the club met often but found themselves distracted by their emotions, then by their busy lives, and even as they continued to meet, the knitting fell by the wayside.

And that's when Anita had decided, walking up Broadway one bright and sunny morning several months after Georgia's passing, that what she needed to do was rework the pattern for the afghan the club had made for Georgia when she was ill. They'd all done panels individually for that afghan and then put together an extremely large, somewhat wonky blanket that Georgia had loved. In spite of its lack of elegance.

To make her idea succeed, Anita had redone the afghan pattern so it was more of a lap throw – and therefore it was more compact and easier to handle. She also increased the needle size so it would go faster, which was crucial if she had any hope that the barely knitting KC would give it a try, and offered a refresher course during a regular club get-together. In her Anita way, kind but firmly persistent, she encouraged the club to knit a few rows before bed or on the weekend, and she always checked up on their progress. In short order, she'd brought an enthusiasm back to the craft for all of them, as they each worked up as many 'Georgia afghans' as they could and donated them to charity for chemo patients. Their goal, each year, was to finish up a pile of the blankets right before they did their ovarian cancer charity walk together in September. And she even made a prize for whoever made the most afghans: the Friday Night Knitting Club's Golden Needles. It was just a pair of needles glued to a wooden base and spray-painted gold – and Anita won her own prize more often than not – but the awarding of the Golden Needles during the post-walk club meeting became an anticipated ritual.

Their common history and shared goals were part of what kept the group together, even as their lives continued to take them in different directions. But making sure the group stayed together seemed crucial when Dakota was younger, and Anita quietly and efficiently made sure every member felt a responsibility to the group. And a sense of belonging. Doddering old woman? Far from it. Though playing the act was one useful thing about getting older: folks let their guard down around seemingly harmless old people, and sometimes that made it much easier for things to work out as she wanted them to. Anita was not beyond using things to her advantage.

'I hope you're not making something in that color for me,' teased Dakota, running a finger lightly over the minty green.

'No, I just picked it up without thinking,' said Anita. 'The color reminded me of someone. It was quite the popular shade at one time.'

'It's kind of awful, Anita,' said Dakota, raising her eyebrows.

'Very *Miami Vice*,' commented Catherine, coming up to refill glasses and then move on to the next empty. 'But pastels are fine for baby stuff. Did you want to make something else for Darwin?'

Anita put the yarn into Dakota's hands. 'Put it back, dear. I don't want to make so much fuss about nothing.'

Dakota closed her hands over the older woman's, who remained the perfect combination of surrogate grandmother and mentor, who never wavered in being available. Even as she found a new life with Marty. Especially after Dakota's mother had died. Anita managed to both be a constant emotional presence and yet stay in the background to let aside the sudden flood of relatives who all wanted a piece of Georgia's little girl to soothe themselves. Her grandparents Bess and Tom, her uncle Donny: How could they get back all the time they'd wasted being distant with their daughter and sister? And her father's parents, Joe and Lillian, and all her newfound aunties, had their own variation: they'd missed out on so much because her father had kept Dakota's existence a secret for the first twelve years of her life and they needed to make up for lost time. It became exhausting, the endless rotation of weekends in Pennsylvania and Baltimore throughout her high school years.

In another lifetime, Dakota would have found these weekend escapes to be just the thing to get away from an over-involved mother. Once she no longer had a mother, all she wanted to do was stay home – she and James moved quickly into a spacious apartment and she painted and redecorated and did everything she could to re-create the sense that she was still living just above the shop – and try to brainstorm a way to make things turn out differently. If only she could go over every moment, every event, and understand completely what had happened, would she then be ready to live it all over again and get it right this time. Sense her mother's pain and get her to the hospital sooner. Or, better yet, in her favorite revisionist history, she would do a project in elementary school on the importance of going to the gynecologist and convince her mother to get checked out much, much sooner. Crisis averted.

Going through these different retellings provided an unexpected, private solace. All she had to do was be alone and think think think how to save her mother. These imaginings brought with them a sense of control, easing her fears. Her grief, which ebbed and flowed, remained always there. Lurking.

There had been a space of time, in her freshman and sophomore years of high school, when Dakota was so busy with schoolwork and visiting her grandmothers and going to endless grief-counseling sessions at James's insistence – although he never went – that she felt as though everyone was keeping her from spending much time in the store. The one place she wanted to be. And from the club. When she was thirteen, fourteen, fifteen, she had felt a certain relief to be with the women from the group. A link to her mother. And they were funny! Also illuminating as they opened up the adult world in a very non-glamorous way. Without discussing it or making some sort of measure of appropriateness, all of them – from Lucie to Darwin to Catherine to KC to Peri to Anita – had stopped editing their conversations to protect her little ears. And so they treated her as one of the group. Dakota heard about work struggles, relationship challenges, the best place to buy designer shoes half off (thanks, Peri!). She was the only teenager whose best friends were, at a minimum, a decade older. And typically much more. Anita had told her then what she knew to be true: She'd always be wherever Dakota needed her to be.

Eventually, the frantic schedule settled down, and James's mother Lillian didn't cling to her every time she was about to leave and take the train back to the city, reluctant to let her surprise grand-daughter out of her sight. After a while, even Georgia's mother, Bess, began to relax and let go of the fear that Death was going to steal yet another person she loved. That was one of the strange things Dakota had grown to understand in the years since Georgia died: Just because Bess hadn't been the style of mother Georgia wanted didn't mean Bess wasn't heartbroken to lose her daughter. She was. Everyone was. And only a smile from Dakota could make it all better for all of them. They *needed* her to be happy.

It was a tremendous burden.

Anita had talked through all of it with her. Whereas previously she'd never been a fan of long conversations on the phone, Anita had twisted James's arm – not really, she'd just made a pointed suggestion in her elegant and insistent Anita manner – and purchased a set of cell phones so she and Dakota could be in constant touch. Anita was better than a high school confidante: she had no curfew and never got in trouble for receiving text messages during school hours. Seeing as she didn't, of course, actually have classes. Day or night, she never once reprimanded Dakota for contacting her when she was supposed to be doing something else, whether homework or dishes or minding the register at the shop. And if Anita was up in the middle of the night, she was quite likely to text back a reply, gamely attempting her own version of text shorthand.

Now that Dakota was at NYU, Anita often called to say she was in the neighborhood. She seemed to be in the Village often lately, and though Dakota suspected she was making special trips just to see her, she didn't mind one bit.

The two would meet for a coffee over at Dean & DeLuca on Broadway, or just sit in Washington Square Park to the side of the arch and watch passersby. Anita's one rule was that they only say nice things about strangers, ignoring Dakota's smirks, and so they would compliment all the random folk who walked by. Not to mention the older woman seemed to have an endless appetite for discussions about professors and classes and annoying habits of new room-mates. And so the bond between Anita and Dakota had grown even stronger.

'You okay?' Dakota asked now in the shop. 'Is it the reno? Does it bug you that much?'

'No, dear,' said Anita. 'I just got distracted.' She leaned forward to Dakota, who was so tall now that Anita felt tiny as she sat in the chair. The worst thing about babies growing up and getting older was that it invariably meant it was happening to her, as well. She resented the lack of control she had over time. There remained so many things she wanted to do, to say.

'I'm not losing my mind, you know. I was lost in thought.'

'No worries,' said Dakota companionably. 'Besides, I don't think you're going senile. But I'll tell you how to test if someone does: Do something fairly outrageous – rude, even – and see if people still treat you kindly. If they do, you're officially an old bat.'

Anita looked startled, and then laughed, as she always did, at Dakota's frank nature. Sure, there were parts of the young woman that seemed to be lifted directly from her mother – the huge smile, and her willowy frame – and other parts, such as her ability to charm, that were all about James. But so much of Dakota was simply herself: her boldness, her candor, her deadpan sense of humor. The babyish edges of her tween and teen years had been rubbed away and what was left behind was an almost polished, statuesque, eye-catching young woman. She was a bit of a firecracker, that one, with her smart-aleck comments. And the anger that she tried valiantly to suppress. It could be difficult to appreciate what you had – a father, a supportive group, friends – when what you'd lost was so huge. Anita knew this, and she understood.

Dakota was as cute as she'd always been, with her smooth complexion and her bright white teeth shining when she flashed a grin, her long, trim legs that rarely wore anything but jeans. Just like her mother, thought Anita. Always with the jeans. Dakota was the best of Georgia.

Only now she was all grown up and so much harder to protect.

3

Looking after her little girl drove her mental. There. She said it. Not to anyone in particular, mind you, but at least she could admit it to herself. Ginger, darling cutie-pie Ginger, was a royal pain in the butt.

'I've created a monster,' said Lucie to her production assistant, who nodded and smiled and took notes on every utterance she made. 'My daughter is out of control.'

On any given day, Ginger fought against waking up to get to kindergarten, or she suddenly hated her breakfast cereal. She wouldn't wear ankle socks or she'd wear ankle socks only in pink and no other color. Her shrieking scream when she didn't get her way was louder than an ambulance siren and got a lot more attention from passing New Yorkers than an emergency vehicle in the street. During the day, her energy never waned: Ginger kept up a steady banter all day long with her stuffies, her mother, her teachers, her classmates, until she practically keeled over at night, a five-year-old drunk from exhaustion, and had to be carried to bed.

In another lifetime, Lucie had cried herself to sleep because her desire for a baby – a sweet-smelling, cooing, cuddling infant – had pulled at her heart. Now she cried herself to sleep from fatigue and confusion and, in her darker moments, regret.

She'd always imagined that not having children would be a terrible fate. But she'd managed to find something much worse: screwing up as a mother.

It was a never-ending guilt spiral.

Lucie let out a whoosh of air to blow her bangs out of her eyes; she'd dyed her hair brown the week before with a drugstore brand thinking it would somehow fade into the background and be one less thing to think about. But she'd seriously miscalculated the shade and had managed to turn her hair to an ugly facsimile of mud, necessitating that she find time for a trip to the salon to fix things – to go back to the reddish highlights – before she left for Italy in a few weeks. Even though her mother had been born there, Lucie had visited only a few times in her forty-eight years. Her mother's family had emigrated after the war, and Rosie fell for an Irish-American vet, causing a mini-scandal that no one cared about anymore. Times and ideas change, sometimes for the better.

She loved the idea of seeing her cousins if she had any extra time, not that she'd recognize them, and of eating huge plates of pasta, and maybe even sneaking in a little sightseeing. Summer in Italy sounded perfect. On paper. But once the thrill of being a very-much-in-demand music video director – at her age! with her background! – had started to wear off, Lucie was left juggling a lot of egos and tense production schedules. She'd earned a reputation as being a bit of a Ms. Fix-It and was often brought onto sets when the previous director had been fired or quit, or when the costs were running over budget. She was known, quite frankly, as a ballbuster. She micromanaged her sets to the point of driving away anyone not willing to work as hard as she did, and she coaxed and cajoled the talent into wanting to work all day and all night to wrap things up. No one said no to Lucie Brennan.

No one, that is, except for her kindergartner daughter, who never said anything else.

Ask anyone: Ginger Brennan was darling. She named the

furniture at Walker and Daughter – the sofa was called Old Softy – and told stories to the skeins of yarn about what they might be knitted into. 'I think you'll be a jewelry box,' she told some inexpensive cotton, raising its hopes beyond a dishcloth future. She was tremendously attached to Dakota, who'd been her babysitter for years, and the two of them giggled and laughed the afternoon away. And she was a looker with her soft, plump cheeks, her strawberry-blond waves, and those deep green eyes that dared you to defy her heart's desire. Those she must have gotten from her father. About whom she'd begun asking questions just after her fifth birthday last fall.

'Why don't we have a daddy in our house?' she'd asked at Thanksgiving. Previously, Ginger had enjoyed horsing around with Lucie's older brothers, and chasing her cousins in the backyard for endless games of hide-and-seek. But she'd been thoughtful over turkey, sucking on her thumb even though Lucie reminded her several times on the way over that she was too big for such behavior and Lucie's mother, Rosie, clucked her tongue and looked meaningfully at Lucie. When Rosie was on, she was in charge; when she grew tired, she walked out of the bathroom and left the faucet on, forgot what she was talking about in the middle of the story. Grew confused as she watched the TV news.

Ah, yes, thought Lucie as she met her mother's eyes, another speech over dessert about why I'm a bad mother. ('Not bad,' Rosie would say. 'Just not as good as you could be.') But then Ginger had popped out that wet, wrinkly chubby little-girl thumb from her mouth and let her question fly.

For once, the Brennans fell silent. Her very Catholic older brothers, who'd always disapproved of her single-mom-by-choice life decision, flushed with triumph. (Or rather, they'd disapproved of her single-mom-via-sexual-reproduction choice; they'd have cheered her on if she'd adopted an orphan. That would have been A-okay. What they resented was being forced to explain to their children exactly what Ginger had just asked her own mommy.)

'Because we don't need one,' Lucie replied. 'So eat your carrots.'

Inside, Lucie was regretting every moment she'd opted for another story at bedtime instead of anticipating her daughter's questions and answering them before they even became an issue. But it had been too awkward and confusing, even for her. After all, she was the one who set the process in motion. 'Once upon a time, I was in my early forties and freaked out that I'd never find you,' she thought to herself when she imagined how she'd tell Ginger about her conception. 'So I went on a dating rampage and slept with a bunch of guys until somebody knocked me up.' Not exactly the most comforting scenario. Was the most important lesson for Ginger that she was wanted? She'd heard that on TV one time, but it didn't seem to her as though Ginger wanted reassurance. She was refreshingly confident. No, what that one wanted was info. Just the facts, Mommy. Just the facts.

And besides, it's not as though she'd even done a very good job of explaining the basics of reproduction to her daughter, having overheard Ginger explain to her grandmother that babies were born when people rubbed bums together. That nugget also brought a look of consternation from Rosie.

'What? I told her and she got it a little mixed up. So what?' said Lucie to her mother once Ginger had left the room. 'You were the one who told me babies were found under cabbage leaves.'

'Pfft,' said Rosie, pushing air out of her lips to show what she thought of that claim. 'We didn't know any better in those days. Now you have to tell them the facts of life so nobody gives them the funny business. Haven't you seen *Dr. Phil?*'

In all the ways that Lucie was cautious and conscientious and matter-of-fact, she had neglected to consider the one truth of motherhood: she genuinely had no idea what she was doing. And the books, well. Whatever. They didn't work on *her* daughter. She was too smart for psychologists, that was for sure. There was no one-size-fits-all manual for children. She knew. She'd looked for it at the library.

The minute – the second – Ginger could talk she had begun to gain the upper hand. When Lucie shut her eyes at night, finally feeling the knot of anxiety that she carried with her at all times begin to ease as she listened to Ginger's snorty sleeping breaths, she continued to hear in her mind the 'No, Mommy' and 'I will NOT!' and 'No, you do it!' phrases Ginger uttered all day long.

'I'm being manipulated by a two-year-old,' she used to tell Darwin when the two friends met for coffee. Her career was just beginning to heat up back then. Later, as Ginger turned three, four, five, she became only more skilled at getting what she wanted. And Lucie, exhausted from the job that excited and interested her mind, spent from using every spare moment chasing Ginger around and trying to get her to sit still, would give in. She bought peace. It was on sale at the toy store. The doughnut shop. The market, and the movies.

'I love Ginger,' she confessed to the members of the club one tearful Friday night. 'But I *like* her best when she's asleep.'

She thought of explaining to Ginger that she was a donor baby, which she was, in a way. In the sense that the man who fathered her had willingly shared certain parts of himself. Of course, he hadn't been planning on making a baby. That had been all Lucie, from the very beginning. Getting donor sperm the old-fashioned way: she seduced.

Well, not really. She'd liked Will Gustofson a lot. He was a nice guy. Smart. A researcher at Sloan-Kettering when they'd dated. He was attractive. Even fun. But Lucie, who'd been burned in love a few times, had not wanted to work on a relationship. She'd grown tired of waiting, didn't want to gamble with her biological clock. The only relationship she was certain she wanted to commit to was one with a baby. And she got it. But then that baby grew into Ginger. A little person with a lot of opinions. And suddenly Lucie found herself with much, much more than she'd bargained for.

She was still waiting to figure it all out. To know what to do with an aging Rosie and how to discipline Ginger. Her biggest problem before her daughter was born was the sense that her life was in a holding pattern. And yet somehow that sensation had crept back into her days: All she had to do was make it to first grade, to high school, to college. All she had to do was keep it together and try not to be buffeted between a kid going into elementary school and a mother settling into her golden years. When was it going to make sense? When was she going to wake up and not feel tired? When was it going to feel all right?

KC looked at her alarm clock – three a.m. – and felt sick. Not to her stomach in the sense she had the flu, all achy and tired. But sick with disgust. Horror. Embarrassment. It did not matter how open people were to talking about it these days. The damn truth was that it was tremendously unpleasant, waking up in the middle of the night covered in clammy sweat, dripping through her pajamas. She tried cotton nighties. She tried sleeping naked. She tried sleeping in the bathtub. But it was always the same: nights interrupted by sudden soakings. Or a spike in temperature during an important meeting at work in the afternoon. There was no rhyme or reason to any of it. And her periods! Weren't those damn things supposed to vanish? Well, not before they made their last hurrah, heavier and more frequent than ever. She was spending a fortune at the drugstore these days, buying tampons and pads in Super Plus Plus Plus.

You'd think her reproductive organs could just shut down quietly and mind their own business. After all, she'd never used them. Just let them hang out while she lived her life, tried out a couple of husbands who didn't quite fit right, and focused on her career. It's not like she ignored them, either, getting regular checkups to make sure the pipes were working. Especially after Georgia's illness. And what did she get? Nights of misery and a big, bad headache.

Oh, KC, she told herself. *You've become your mother.* Menopausal and grumpy. And it sucked.

At least one night a week, KC came over to keep Peri company as she worked on her pocketbooks. Ostensibly, KC was there to get private lessons to work on her Georgia afghans, of which she completed one – and only one – every year.

Dutifully, she sat on Peri's sofa with knitting needles in her hand, one eye on the television and the other on the newspaper. KC was not the type of personality who could sit still.

'You can put the needles down,' said Peri, who was sorting through her yarn colors, comparing how different shades would stripe together. 'Everyone knows I knit up your Georgia afghan every year. It's too good.'

'Yeah, about that,' said KC. 'Maybe you could throw in a few mistakes this year.'

'Tried that one before,' said Peri. 'I even made those too uniformly.'

'Hmm,' muttered KC, before rushing into the bathroom. She was sweating. Again.

Peri knocked on the door, holding a clean towel. 'You've got to see a doctor, KC,' she said. 'Herbs, hormones, something. Suffering is passé, you know.'

KC poked her head out. 'Sometimes suffering is just suffering,' she said. 'You have to muscle through it to get to the other side.'

'I don't think nirvana is waiting for you beyond menopause,' said Peri.

'Well, we won't know until we find out,' said KC, muttering to herself behind the door. The world, she thought, was lucky she was only smoking.

Typically, Peri's apartment was quiet. A dinner of salad, maybe a little grilled chicken, and then it was on to job number two. Designing, knitting, felting, updating her website, filling small orders for boutiques. She'd changed the feel of the place completely since the days when Georgia and Dakota lived here, buying just-the-right-size furniture for the space – Georgia had always kept a large sofa in the living area – and making the most of the three rooms – each functioned for multiple uses. In Dakota's former bedroom, where she kept her computer desk and her studio, the walls were covered in open shelving to house her personal stash, her needles, her works in progress, her sewing supplies, her ten-year collection of *Vogue*. She'd saved everything that had been Georgia's, tucking it into the large filing cabinet Marty had helped her to move upstairs. Every so often, Dakota came to look through things, after a Saturday shift most likely. Peri never minded, understood that she needed to reassure herself.

'Have you ever seen a binder around?' she asked Peri during one such inspection.

'What, like a school binder?' asked Peri.

'Kinda,' said Dakota. 'I'm looking for something. Sometimes I think it was left behind. I can't seem to find it.'

Together, they checked all the cupboards, and the top closet that had once housed Georgia's memory box, but all that could be found was box after box of Peri's handbag supplies.

'You've kinda turned your home into a workplace, you know that?' said Dakota. 'You may have made the store sleeker but this place is never going to give you any peace. You have no getaway.'

Peri shrugged. She knew Dakota wasn't really looking for anything, of course. Who comes back after five years looking for their notes from middle school? But she just needed to touch, to see, to remind herself what it had been like. To ping that lost, secret part of herself from the past.

4

It was better now than it had been, of course. There were moments when Darwin felt an essential and pure happiness that she had never expected to feel, even though her midsection looked like she had a team's worth of basketballs tucked under her shirt and the stretch marks on her stomach striped her skin like a tiger. A sort of Christmas-morning-smell-of-chocolate-chip-cookies-finally-having-a-baby combination of joy that made her step lighter and her smile come more easily. She indulged her daydreams more often now as the due date approached, falling into fantasy mode and positively lusting after a crib shaped like a tiny fairy-tale carriage that sold in a chichi Madison Avenue boutique for $23,000. It was a million miles beyond her pocketbook's reach and offended every single one of her feminist sensibilities, and yet still she found reasons to stop in front of the store window and gape, the carriage crib glittering and winking as sunlight streamed onto the glass.

There was more: Darwin kept a secret container of talcum powder hidden in her underwear drawer and would take hits of sniff during the day, savoring the old-timey baby scent. Her bedside table was ready to buckle under the weight of the seventeen parenting books she'd read, augmented by a binder's worth of handwritten notes. She programmed a chart on her computer comparing and contrasting differing parenting suggestions and kept a rating scale in order to determine if she wanted a family bed or if she was going for cloth and a diaper service over disposables. Had to factor in all that water use for the washing, you know.

But then she'd catch herself.

'Nothing jinxes life more than getting excited about it,' she'd told her husband each time. 'There's always a smackdown.'

She thought about this danger as she waddled her way across the crosswalk – no more jaywalking for her with two babies on board! – and stared up at the window of Walker and Daughter.

She would have liked to talk about her impending motherhood with Georgia. Of all people, Georgia knew about things being unfair. It was funny how Darwin felt closer to Georgia now, more than she ever had when Georgia was alive. Somehow, over the years, with the disappointments and the keeping up of appearances, Darwin came to believe she finally understood Georgia. She'd have been happy, now, to listen to Georgia's struggles, in a way that she'd never had the patience for when she actually knew her. It was a great irony that suffering could bring the gift of compassion.

Darwin had a feeling Georgia would understand, better than anyone, her mixed-up emotions over the years. That she wouldn't judge her for the ambivalence that crept up sometimes about having a baby. Babies. Plural. Of the sheer dread of all the changes that were coming. Followed swiftly by the guilt over not being in a state of perpetual joy and counting her blessings and instead, harboring deep, deep fears of something going wrong. That's what she felt more than anything. The certain knowledge that things wouldn't turn out well. After all, they never had before.

There had been the miscarriages. Three additional losses after the first miscarriage more than five years ago, back when she was still working on her dissertation. Before she became a lecturer in history at Hunter, teaching an eager crew of younger versions of herself. She remembered that time in her life, when she was bold enough to know everything with certainty and feel powerful because of it. Quite frankly, Darwin could use a little of that moxie back.

Each miscarriage had taken a little bit more of her heart and left her with more questions than answers. The last one came in the middle of the second trimester, after everyone had already sighed with relief and she and Dan had started talking seriously about moving to a bigger house.

'If we hadn't phoned the realtor,' she had told him then, 'this wouldn't have happened.' And her husband had held her and silently cried into her long dark hair, hoping she wouldn't notice even as her scalp grew cool and wet.

The no-reasonness of things was always the hardest to take. She thought of Georgia then, too, how she'd handled her own illness with grace. Darwin thought of her during the many trips to the doctor, then to a different doctor, then on to a fertility clinic. Special care for special problems. She thought of her as medical professional after medical professional stumbled around her insides trying to figure out why she was such a failure. When they discussed testing embryos, implanting only the healthy ones. It was easier, too, thinking about Georgia, because she'd suffered the most. Being dead and all. Darwin liked to imagine her lost babies in a big nursery in some other dimension, where her long-dead grandmother would watch over them and, from time to time, Georgia would pop in and say hello. Tell them she'd just been watching over Dakota and the group at Walker and Daughter and that Darwin was thinking of her kids, even as she struggled to remain sociable.

It's a peculiar grief: the loss of someone no one else has ever known. A private bereavement.

Darwin felt a kinship with Georgia, being separated from her only daughter by death; Darwin had been separated from all of her children by their nonbirth. Darwin had never known how much she desired a baby until she couldn't have one, and then every fiber of her being ached for a child.

How sad Georgia must be, she would think, to miss out on seeing Dakota each and every day. And so, over the last several years, Darwin began to spend many a Saturday afternoon at the shop, especially if Dan had rounds at the hospital, to check up on Dakota. She never hovered: Anita, Catherine, and Peri did that. Instead, Darwin took on a different sort of role, advising Dakota as she prepared for college admissions and introducing her to all sorts of women's studies titles that Catherine and Anita had never heard of. Darwin settled into the role of academic mentor, and in doing so, found a small way to distract herself. To honor Georgia.

She was tremendously jealous of Lucie back then, even as she loved her best friend and adored little Ginger, often babysitting. Still, there was more than one time that Darwin returned from a trip to buy Ginger a teeny pair of mini-sneakers for her chubby toddler feet and ended up crying at her desk in the corner of the bedroom, pretending to work, Dan watching TV in the other room. Knowing her well enough to leave her be.

The worried glances between her parents and her in-laws at holiday dinners, the sympathetic looks when the knitting club got together, the evenings she overheard Dan on his cell out on the balcony, talking with med school friends who'd gone on to specialize in fertility: it had all gone on around her and she held her breath, flipping willy-nilly between despair and hope.

Darwin understood, of course, that it would have been easier on everyone to be optimistic, for her to express the chipper 'It's going to happen for us, it will!' can-do spirit that eases everyone else's discomfort and would leave her to lick her wounds in private. But that had never been her personality, and in the end, it just became too hard.

She'd been grouchy and frustrated for much of the last five years, and she still felt the sting of embarrassment about bursting into tears when Lucie's daughter, Ginger, blew out the candles on her cake at her birthday a few years ago. A sweet girl whose hair she'd brushed, whose lunches she'd made, whom she'd tucked in on countless occasions when Lucie had gone to dinner with potential film producers, and then whammo! Suddenly Darwin let forth with great, hulking sobs as the pigtailed dynamo was clapping along to the Happy Birthday song and accidentally spitting all over the pink frosted cake as she tried to make her wish. Humiliating. It's not that she courted the attention. Or that she wanted to make Lucie, her dearest friend, feel torn between cutting slices of moist chocolate cake for oversugared, ants-in-their-pants little kids or following Darwin into the bathroom to offer a shoulder to cry on. No, Darwin would have preferred to be quite invisible. But it's not as though she could pick the appropriate time for a mini-breakdown. Her heart did that for her, and on Ginger's sweet birthday, the pent-up anger and hurt had simply all flooded out.

She wished she hadn't had to endure the endless banter of 'When are you having kids?' followed up with blame ('You really ought to give Dan some kids') and topped off with prurient curiosity ('Is something wrong?') that she experienced from her colleagues and family.

Don't ask.

Don't tell.

You'd think these unspoken rules would be obvious.

After all the goodie bags had been handed out and Darwin helped Lucie wash dishes, trying to scrub off the thick ring of embarrassment she felt for crying in front of Lucie's mom friends, she had accepted a hug mutely from Lucie's mother.

From their initial meeting at the hospital after Lucie had given birth to Ginger, Rosie and Darwin had forged their own relationship, a curious connection growing out of their close proximity. Rosie had spent a life tending to a boisterous family, cooking and cleaning and wiping noses. Fully aware of Darwin's disapproval of her single-minded housewifery, Rosie 'adopted' her nonetheless, plying Darwin with endless jars of homemade tomato sauce and canned peaches and admiring every professional accomplishment as much as Darwin's own mother back in Seattle. Possibly even more.

Rosie, Lucie, Dakota, the rest of the club, their families: everyone was excited for Darwin and Dan. Everyone felt, too, that their private hopes and energies and even prayers – in the case of Anita and Rosie – had helped in some small way. Darwin's pregnancy was a great cause for celebration.

And yet, with only nine weeks to go, Darwin remained nervous. She had kept a list in her backpack of Things That Could Go Wrong, to which she added new thoughts as they arose.

Item #1: A taxicab could hit me as I cross the street.
Item #2: A taxicab could hit me when I'm in another cab on the way to the hospital.
Item #3: A taxicab carrying Dan could hit me in my cab on the way to the hospital. . . .

Dan caught her writing furiously at three a.m., read the list, discussed each and every item on it as a statistical improbability – taking special care to go over all her medical concerns – and then tore the list up and put it in the wastepaper basket.

The next morning, Darwin fished out the pieces, put them in an envelope, and started a new list. No one, not even her dear husband, was going to jinx things.

Even with all of her furtive crib window-shopping, she had been firm with Dan that they had better not paint the nursery – which was really just a corner cordoned off the living room – or buy any burp cloths or onesies, and definitely not hold any showers. No baby showers! That was her hard-and-fast rule. Only after much negotiation had she consented to attend birthing classes. Darwin had been adamant about wanting to try a natural birth and had researched diligently for a doctor who was willing to let her try.

'We've got to go, Darwin,' Dan told her, even though he'd delivered five babies in med school and a handful of emergency births since then. 'It's important to be prepared and besides, what if I forget?'

Dan never forgot anything. Unless he chose to. Like her one ill-fated night with that friend of Peri's, long, long ago. They'd counseled it out and then it had floated away, just one more piece of their shared history, not necessary to remember. For this, even when she was annoyed with him for tearing up her list, she was eternally grateful.

Though it wasn't like he was going to be doing the actual doctor part anyway. He was supposed to be one-hundred-percent dad in that hospital room – and that meant staying by her side. Because this time was going to be different from all the others. This go-round they were going to come home from the hospital with two babies, of their very own, breathing and sleeping and cuddling. She could feel it rising again, the bubble of hope, and she could see that shiny crib in her mind's eye, could smell that baby powder. Darwin heaved her heavy body up the steep stairs to the yarn shop, heard the excited yelping and *Shh*s coming from her friends as she paused on the landing, hoping to catch her breath before going inside. It took a brief second for the full knowledge to register: The club was throwing her a shower.

Excitement and superstition battled for equal time as KC swung open the door.

'I thought I could hear your huffing out here,' she shouted. 'Get in here, Professor Chiu! You're the one bringing the guests of honor.'

Darwin looked inside cautiously, at her friends rushing toward her with drinks in hand, and Dakota standing at the table and making faces as she pointed animatedly to a large gift suffocated in shiny yellow paper.

It wasn't her overpriced dream crib. But it was close enough. Darwin grinned as the members of the Friday Night Knitting Club swarmed around her, letting Catherine and KC and Anita and Peri feel the two partygoers inside her kicking with glee.

Maybe it was okay to be happy, she thought. Just a little bit.

5

Walker and Daughter was drowning in gift wrap as Darwin tore through her newly acquired baby-stuff booty.

'This is just what I needed,' she exclaimed over every burp cloth, rattle, and tiny pair of socks, tossing the wrapping paper over her shoulder as Peri tutted around her with garbage bags and an electric hand vac.

'Let me just get that,' squeaked Peri. The floor, newly sanded and refinished, had yet to have its first scratch and all that new paint hadn't seen a smudge. It was nerve-wracking, one eye on Catherine's heeled boots grinding into the floor and another worried about the tape ruining the finish. When did she get so uptight? she wondered. She'd been wringing her hands for days over what everyone would say about the remodel – would they criticize the changes? judge her for pushing the timetable? – but she'd never considered that she was more freaked out by the prospect of one of the members of the club scuffing up the wood. Maybe she was losing perspective, she thought to herself, switching off the DustBuster.

'Thank God,' said KC in a stage whisper. 'I thought I was going to have to yell to hear myself think.' She reached over and took the gift wrap from Peri's hands and threw it back on the floor. 'Do it later,' she said. 'I'll even help – for a few minutes. Five, tops. But c'mon, enjoy yourself. Live a little. Watch our Darwin open her toys.'

*   *   *

'What's that smell?' Peri sniffed the air and looked at Dakota. She lowered her voice. 'Have you been smoking?'

'No,' said Dakota. 'Not my scene.' Dakota walked away. Over to stare at the gray wall of purses where once she'd flopped on the shabby old office couch and chatted about the day with her mother. Back in another lifetime.

The smoky scent lingered right around . . . there.

Peri leaned in closely to KC and then put her arm around her friend, casually guiding her to the window but in fact exerting more than a little pressure to propel her forward.

'Are *you* smoking?' she asked.

'Pfft,' said KC. 'See anything in these hands?'

Peri's eyes narrowed. 'What are you thinking? I can't let that smell get into the yarn.' She was not amused as she began pulling open all four windows, the sounds of traffic and honking horns rising from Broadway below.

'Sorry,' said KC. 'I'll put my coat out on the landing.'

'And wash your hair while you're at it. I'll even give you a bottle of water.'

'Oh, come on,' said KC. 'It's not that bad.'

'What's going on? Who takes up smoking at your age?' asked Peri, trying to keep her voice low so as not to disrupt the shower. 'I mean, I know you had a few puffs when you were studying for the bar, but what is this? Some sort of midlife crisis?'

'God, if I have a crisis I hope I do something a bit more dramatic than smoke a pack of cigarettes.'

'A whole pack?'

'No, a few were missing,' said KC. 'Look, I moved offices and there was a pack left behind in the desk.'

'This office didn't come with a waste bin? You thought you ought to recycle by smoking them?'

KC shrugged. 'It was a one-time thing. I was curious – haven't smoked in ages. I'd had a tough day. You know.'

'No,' said Peri. 'I don't know. I've never smoked. You know why? Because it isn't any good for you.'

'Okay, let's stop with the lecture before you get started,' said KC as she took off her blazer. 'I hear what you're saying. But you might want to dial back a bit in general. The store is important, but it's not the only thing. You don't know everybody's everything.'

Darwin was oblivious to Peri and KC. She could not stop grinning. She was enthralled by the balloons, the hydrangeas, the polka-dotted diaper bags from Peri's new line, the two tiny cardigans Anita had knitted with matching booties, the champagne she couldn't actually drink, the cupcakes with all the different sorts of frostings, the stroller she'd been drooling over when she read baby catalogs at night. She had never felt so . . . light. Like she could simply lift off and float away on a joy cloud.

It had always seemed silly, sitting around in a circle and watching someone open presents. Whenever she saw women do that on television programs – she taped *A Baby Story* regularly – she would roll her eyes and make a point to tell Dan that was asinine. How it just glorified conspicuous consumption and therefore set a bad example for the in utero crew. What Darwin had never reflected upon, she saw clearly now, was just how unbelievably fun it was to be the one opening all the gifts. She loved to be the center of attention.

'No one's ever thrown me a party before,' she blurted out, immediately embarrassed. It was the truth – when she and Dan had married they'd popped into city hall and skipped any sort of reception, and they spent her birthdays dining at fancy restaurants that Dan selected after careful research in *Zagat*. He had never suggested or even tried to organize a party, having listened carefully to all the reasons why

Darwin would never want one. Now she felt as though she'd been missing out.

But where was Lucie? The whole club was here and her best friend was nowhere to be seen. If this had happened a year ago, Darwin would have been highly concerned, knowing that Lucie would have been the first one on the scene. But not now. She hadn't even asked Peri when she came, knowing all too well that Lucie was, no doubt, still at work. Unlike when they'd first become friends years ago, when Lucie worked freelance TV production gigs and had a fair amount of flexible time, she was often unavailable these days. And Lucie was becoming well known for being late or calling to say she couldn't come at all, whether it was a club night or meeting Darwin for a quick lunch of tossed chicken Caesar at one of those soup-and-salad places. Now Darwin loved her work, loved to teach, and loved to argue her point until whoever she was talking to was worn into submission. She knew from working hard. From being a workaholic. But it was awfully lonely to be married to a doctor and then have a best friend whose e-mails always began with an explanation of why she hadn't called back yet. Sheesh! Like everyone didn't have too much to do and too little time.

Still, Lucie *had* promised she'd take a few weeks off when the babies came, that she'd be there for Darwin just as Darwin had been there for her when Ginger was born. She was very much looking forward to it all: the birth, Lucie coming over to help, Dan taking a little pat leave, breastfeeding, reading stories, and singing songs. (In fact, Darwin was already reading *Goodnight Moon* to the babies every night, patting her abdomen as she turned every page.) She was so looking forward to the expansion of her little family and to spending time with Lucie that Darwin had even asked her parents and her sister, Maya, to wait a few weeks before coming out for a visit. Instead, they'd be coming closer to the one-month party she was going to throw for the babies. After all, she'd waited a long, long time to see these teeny faces, and whereas she once hadn't wanted very much to do with her family's Chinese traditions, these days Darwin felt a sense of legacy she'd never previously understood. It was a glorious awakening for a woman who'd spent most of her life wondering where she belonged.

The babies kicked.

'Oooh,' said Darwin. 'They love the presents.'

'Can I feel?' asked Catherine, putting out her fingers tentatively.

'My God, you're one of the few people who's ever asked,' said Darwin. 'Mainly strangers just reach out and fondle my tummy if I dare to stop moving. That's why pregnant women are always waddling – we're trying to run away from all your grabby hands.'

Catherine immediately pulled back, but Darwin reached out and placed Catherine's hand on her belly. 'You're okay,' she said. 'Wait for it, wait for it . . .'

'Oh!' squealed Catherine. 'That's like there's an alien in there!'

'Pretty much,' said Darwin. 'Two very smart, perfect aliens. They're going to go to Harvard.'

'I remember when I was pregnant with Nathan,' said Anita. 'I was sick to my stomach the entire time. But it was the fifties, you know, so I was always trying to put on fresh lipstick and comb my hair.'

'And I remember when I was preggers with Ginger,' said Lucie, bustling through the door carrying a computer bag, a handbag, and a canvas tote filled with groceries. 'I had the hugest boobs. They hurt like a bitch but, man, did they look great in a bra. I used to even buy those water bras to boost them up even more.'

'You went to the store before coming here?' asked Darwin, pointing to a head of celery poking out of Lucie's bag.

'Just for a few minutes to get some milk and stuff,' said Lucie, coming over to the table to give Darwin a behind-the-chair hug. 'I didn't have any other spare time. But I'm here now and I see you guys have been partying it up. KC, fill 'er up with whatever you're pouring.' She took the glass of wine, gulped it down, and held it out for another.

'I just had the worst day at work,' Lucie continued after she'd taken a sip from the refill. 'This model was just an absolute disaster. If I said, "Look tough," she looked pouty. If I said, "Look sexy," she looked bored. I was completely pulling my hair out.'

'Your hair looks fine to me,' said Darwin quietly.

Lucie threw her a look. 'You know what I mean!' she said. 'And I have great news – I finally got word that I landed this job directing a music video for the latest European singing sensation: Isabella. I've been dying for it.'

'Congrats,' said KC. 'I think I saw her on that Eurovision contest thing.' She caught Catherine's eye. 'What? So I have satellite. I'm interested in the world around me. Lawyers can afford a lot more channels than editors, that's for sure.'

'Thing is, I barely have time to finish this job, and then I'm going to be in Italy before I know it!'

'What?' Darwin was pushing her black hair behind her ears, as though to hear more clearly. 'Where are you going when?'

She wanted to be genuinely thrilled for Lucie, knew how hard she was working. With effort, she forced a closed-mouth smile.

'I got the Isabella video,' she said to Darwin. 'But it might change things up a bit so we'll talk later, okay? What sort of stuff did you get?' She leaned over to whisper in Darwin's ear. 'I had something sent to the apartment. It'll arrive in a few.'

Lucie stood up again and picked up an organic cotton bunny. 'Too cute! Who picked this out?'

'I did,' said Catherine. 'That's fair-trade cotton. It cost a bundle, but I feel very, very good about myself.'

'I wouldn't have thought you'd have it in you to go all googly for the baby stuff, Cat,' said Lucie. 'You don't strike me as the mommy type.'

'Indeed,' said Catherine. 'I've heard that.'

'Nothing wrong with being child-free, ladies,' said KC. 'Catherine and I aren't kiddie types. The world's over-populated as it is. Besides, I just don't like kids. Present company excepted, of course,' she said, toasting her glass to Darwin's baby bulge and then moving it slightly toward Dakota, then shaking her head.

'Scratch that, kiddo,' KC said to Dakota. 'You're not a kid anymore. Soon enough you'll be running the store and then the world, or vice versa.'

'Running the store?' Peri and Dakota spoke in unison. Was it that time already? There was a brief pause in the conversation, and then Peri was back to compulsively stuffing gift wrap into her garbage bag and Dakota had moved away to stare out the window, watch the yellow cabs roll up and down Broadway, their headlights flashing as the night grew dark. Everyone else kept busy cooing over the double wicker Moses baskets for which Anita had knitted two dishcloth-style blankets in machine washable yarn, laughed as Darwin rubbed them on her cheeks and remarked on their softness.

Running the store? She'd just started college! Why, Dakota wondered to herself, did no one ever stop to ask her if that was what she wanted? All she ever got were assumptions. From her father, that she'd want to go to Princeton as he had. They'd had to make such a jump from just getting to know each other to having *only* each other. He was so unlike her mother in many ways. It had been challenging, the transition from being mostly buddies to James being the decision-maker. Well, she hadn't wanted to go to Princeton. She wanted to go to culinary school to become a pastry chef. But his child wasn't going to go to school for cookie-making, James had said. Making treats for the family or for the club was all well and good, he'd said, but it didn't mean she should throw her life away because she had a hobby.

Going to NYU had been the compromise, sweetened by his reluctant agreement that Dakota could take the occasional baking course on the side. But he wasn't the only one who decided he knew what she was going to do. Even Anita talked an awful lot about how great it would be when she took over the store, tut-tutting Dakota's protestations and launching into yet another version of the time she'd met Georgia in the park. Why walk away from your legacy? they'd wondered. But that wasn't all. Her friends, her dad's mom, her mother's brother, Donny. Everyone had an opinion about Dakota. Was it because her mother was dead or because they were all unbelievably nosy and opinionated? Hard to tell. But the lack of boundaries even happened with strangers. She'd lucked out and gotten a dorm room partway through the semester – it was nearly impossible for city kids to get a place – and her roommate had thought she was joking when she said the picture of Georgia taped to the wall above her dinky twin bed was her mother. Because Georgia was white and Dakota was . . . her own distinctive blend of Georgia and James. White and black. Protestant and Baptist. A little bit Scottish, too. But no one could see that at first glance.

Peri was forthright, telling her she should join the Black Students' Union.

'Everyone is going to see you as black,' she'd said. 'So embrace it. You can spend your entire life saying you're biracial but to white people that's just another word for black, you know.'

Thing was, Dakota didn't want everyone telling her who to be and how to act.

'I don't care about everybody,' she told Peri. 'I just care about me.'

But that didn't make it any easier. And that wasn't even the half of it. Her problems extended way beyond Peri's opinions, her annoying roommate's inability to not leave wet towels on the floor, and the fact that she'd gained ten pounds in less than ten months. No, truth be told, most of her days – and nights – were taken up with thoughts of Andrew Doyle. He was in her American lit lecture and he was one of those curiously attractive guys who didn't quite fit the mold. He wasn't super trim, he wasn't an athlete, he wasn't conventionally attractive. He was at least an inch shorter than Dakota, he had a beak of a nose, he wore the same red-hooded sweatshirt every day and yet he was the funniest, sexiest, most charming guy she'd ever met. His allure – and she'd spent a long time thinking about this matter – was his seemingly endless reserves of confidence. Andrew walked into every room as if he owned the place. God, she loved that about him.

They were totally in the same group. Well, sort of. No, not really. But they did know some of the same people, and had been at the same events fairly often. Like Greg Durant's Christmas party in his Mercer Street studio, and the Earth Day rally at Washington Square Park. Plus, Andrew Doyle *knew* her name. No, he definitely did. Like the time he passed her row in the lecture hall – she was sitting there with her friend Olivia – and he said, 'Hey, Dakota.' Not 'Hey, Dakota and Olivia.' Just her name, as she'd swallowed giggles and almost let out a burp of air as Olivia's elbow dug into her ribs. Not that she knew what would happen if he actually asked her out or anything. Unlike Olivia, who was in a committed long-distance relationship with a boyfriend at

SUNY–Purchase, and Catherine, with her eight million stories of boys at Harrisburg High in the 1980s, and even Anita, who waxed poetic about the day she met Stan, Dakota had a dirty little secret: She'd never been kissed. Not once. Not ever. Oh, she'd had a date for prom, a nice enough guy. A friend. And while she'd debated the pros and cons of laying one on him to get this kiss business out of the way, in the end she'd decided to wait for a kiss that mattered. Or was at least hot. Really, truly, smokin' hot.

She turned back to the group, her mother's boisterous friends; Catherine's cheeks, she could see, were flushed red, her brown eyes dark and hard to reach. For everyone else.

'I really don't hate kids,' she was insisting, a bit too loudly. 'In fact, I'm very good with them.'

'You run whenever you see Ginger,' Peri pointed out. The group laughed.

'I'm not making a joke,' insisted Catherine. The women laughed harder as the expression on her face grew tighter.

Taking a deep breath, she chuckled along with the other members of the club, though inside she felt more and more lost. She glanced at her cell phone to check the time, then began to make noises about having to go and meet someone.

'Recreational sex,' crowed KC. 'You're an Olympic medalist in that sport.'

Catherine gave a small nod. 'Takes one to know one,' she said, gathering up her coat with one hand and briefly squeezing Darwin's with the other. 'Thanks for the pat,' she said softly. 'I appreciate it.'

'Oh, wait, Catherine,' said Lucie, looking up from an intense conversation with Anita. 'You're always going to Italy. I could use some travel tips. It's been years since I went there to see my mom's village. I need to know which hotels and restaurants and . . .'

Catherine nodded and brought her hand up to her face, her pinkie finger at her mouth and her thumb at her ear, mouthing, 'Call me,' before she waltzed out the door. As soon as she was safely out of everyone's sight, she raced down the steep stairs and pushed open the glass door to the street, hoping for some cool night air to chill the stinging on her cheeks. She'd have been a great mom if she'd had the chance, she thought.

A man passing by gave her a quick, appreciative nod, and Catherine automatically sucked in her well-toned gut and tilted her head sideways, revealing her neck to look more vulnerable.

Don't muss the makeup with tears, she hummed to herself. It was the first rule of business: Never muss the goods.

6

The hours of The Phoenix: Furnishings and Fine Wines were impossible to find, or even to predict. There was certainly no such detail on the sign above the front door of Catherine's antique shop, nor were the times of business marked on a poster in the large plate-glass window. Or anywhere else, for that matter. After all, this was Catherine's store, an elegant mix of antiques, collectibles, and pretty much any item or object that struck her fancy. It was just as likely to be opened at seven a.m. (if she couldn't sleep) or at eleven a.m. (if she slept too much). Not in any way a model for how to set up a successful business – it was nothing like the knitting shop her best friend had started long ago in Manhattan – and yet there it was, thriving right on the main street of Cold Spring, in the Hudson Valley, just north of New York City. It was a little jewel box of a shop, with its rich jumble of brocaded chairs and mahogany tables and tinkly crystal lamps.

The Phoenix looked as if a grand salon from another century had been dropped wholesale and wedged into the compact storefront. Entering through the door was like being invited into a regal yet cozy private home of rustling skirts and tea parties, and Catherine's ability to play the welcoming hostess was a strong attraction to her customers. That, and the fact of her former marriage to an old-money investment banker, which intrigued more than a few looky-loos. Was she a downtrodden and cast-aside first wife about whom they could feel superior? Or something far more interesting: a woman trying to begin a real life? Some days even Catherine had her doubts.

The store did a fairly steady business with serious antique hunters – not keeping a regular workday did not indicate anything about the quality of her store's wares – and it remained a popular destination for weekenders, who enjoyed a browse of the furniture and then waltzed through the French doors set in one wall. The side entrance ushered them into a stand-alone cellar and tasting room right next door, filled with wines from vineyards local and far away. That side of the business – for which Catherine had astutely hired a manager – kept prompt hours and did brisk business on weekends, when all the citygoers came up to their 'country' houses and entertained themselves by making gorgeous meals with fresh produce from the farmer's markets and toasted themselves with glass after glass of good wine from Catherine's shelves.

But she hadn't forgotten her inspiration for the store. Set off to one side of the room was a beautiful golden knitted gown on a mannequin, protected and preserved inside a clear display case. In fact, the only sign in the store at all was a tiny cream-colored card with 'Not for Sale' written in calligraphy and set at the foot of the gorgeous handmade dress. A gold plaque on the case revealed the name of the gown's designer.

'Georgia Walker,' it read. 'Designer and founding member of the Friday Night Knitting Club.'

Sometimes, out of admiration or longing or simply in the course of making chitchat, customers would inquire as to the cost of the dress or whether they could have something less ornate made by Georgia Walker for themselves.

'No,' Catherine would say. 'That's simply not possible.' And that was all. She never explained further. Never told them that her best friend was dead. The few times she'd said anything, people screwed up their faces as though tasting something unpleasant. A cup of mortal-i-tea. It's difficult to fake empathy for a stranger. To express concern when none is there.

Unfinished. Adrift. That's how she felt. But who cared? Instead, she'd remember to smile and show them a hundred-year-old teapot with hand-painted birds flying around the spout, distract them with some Art Deco pottery.

On the wall behind the case was a nearly life-size painting of Catherine Anderson wearing the creation, from a time when she was still known to many as socialite Cat Phillips. When she publicly pretended that her marriage was a happy one and her days were filled with shopping. It was a commanding portrait, her brown eyes staring down observers, daring their eyes to dart down the bodice hugging her chest and follow the line of her hips below the generous flowing skirt. Her hair, as sleek and golden as the dress itself, was piled high on her head like a halo. The picture, unlike the outfit, was available. For the right price. To the right buyer.

Catherine was as much part of the entertainment as the wines and furnishings in The Phoenix. There was nothing understated about the blonde, with her large rings and her designer clothes (black on black with touches of black topped off with an unexpected splash of color in the form of a lime bag or red shoes), her honeyed voice and her little flirtations with the handsome husbands of her shoppers. She often wore a diamond D around her neck and loved to explain it stood not for her name, but for 'divorcée.'

Her days were a wonderful challenge, seeing how long she could charm someone into staying at the store. Selling bric-a-brac was quite secondary. Catherine was visibly delighted by every customer who came through the door – especially people she'd never seen previously – and loved to chat them up about every piece on sale. For if Catherine was anything, she was a serious student of art history and antiques: she'd majored in art history at Dartmouth, though she'd also spent a good portion of her college years chasing the man who became her husband. Each table or armoire captured her eye, romanced her a little with its beauty, and then broke her heart by simply selling itself to the highest bidder and moving on to its perfect family. That was how she thought of herself: as a sort of foster mother for items beautiful and tarnished, helping them find a permanent home. It was a skill for which she charged handsomely.

The wine? That was all about the fun.

Catherine needed attention like the average woman needed oxygen, and every detail – from the way her hips swayed slightly as she walked, to the blouses that never seemed tight and yet hugged every curve of her well-endowed frame – was designed to catch eyes.

'Just because a girl moves on from being a trophy wife doesn't mean she leaves her assets behind,' Catherine had said more than once to Georgia's daughter, Dakota. Though Dakota lived with her father, James, the two still enjoyed regular Sunday afternoon hang-out sessions. And, of course, they saw each other whenever the club got together. So life should have been just right. Catherine Anderson was very popular in Cold Spring. And not merely because she ran the most darling little shop this side of New York City.

No, she'd earned her reputation as a colorful character the old-fashioned way: she created fodder for the town gossips. Catherine made repeated relationship snafus soon after starting the business – bedding the hunky cheesemaker down the road, as well as an amusing weekender who'd turned out to have forgotten to mention a wife in the city, and even the fellow who sold her business insurance and who had provided a heady diversion before she discovered she abhorred everything he had to say and that they disagreed on everything from politics to ice cream flavors. She'd even considered trying to heat up a flirtation with a twenty-year-old college student working in the corner bistro. But it struck her as a lot of potential agita for a romp likely to be athletic yet hardly satisfying. Not to mention she'd realized that, as she neared forty-three, she happened to be the same age as the young man's mother.

And all of it was better than her fifteen years married to the insensitive Adam Phillips. Oh, he liked sex well enough: Adam always made sure to have a string of girlfriends in addition to Catherine. And his focus was always about him, him, him. Theirs had been a lonely marriage, and once free of it all, Catherine delighted in discovering that there were many men willing to help her make up for lost time. Men who found her charming. Men who liked her. Men who were . . . generous. And yet nothing quite took.

She wasn't entirely certain what she'd expected by now – wisdom? calm? contentment? – but each day she felt surprised anew that she was unattached. It seemed disloyal, somehow, to her sense of herself as an independent woman to be happy. But she'd always anticipated being married. Becoming a mom. And while she was certainly damn good-looking, and well aware of it, Catherine felt short of breath and panicky whenever she thought about her private life. Her parents had died years before and she'd been distant from her siblings for so long that her sincere overtures about visiting were met with such mild interest that she eventually cut back to random e-mails and the occasional holiday meal.

All she had was an excess of lack. Lack of love. Lack of family. Lack of friends? Catherine wondered about that, too. It was impossible to shake, this nagging sense that she didn't quite belong anywhere. After all this time, Catherine still couldn't let go of the sense she was an impostor. Of being foisted upon the members of the Friday Night Knitting Club by Georgia. That out of respect for Georgia's memory they had let her continue to hang around. After all, if Georgia thought there was something redeeming about her, there had to be, right?

But what if Georgia's confidence was misplaced?

Only in her own shop, when she'd settled into her latest bravura performance of the bon vivant divorcée, did she feel properly hidden and, therefore, safe.

There was something tremendously annoying about a fortysomething woman appearing needy, thought Catherine. Easy to reject somehow because she was old enough to know better. To be better. And so she strived to be great fun when she popped into Georgia's old knitting shop in the city. She still, after all these years, very much wanted to be liked. Just liked.

It was something she'd have found very useful to discuss with Georgia. It remained difficult for her to accept that her old friend had died so soon after they'd reconnected. She preferred, on some days, to pretend that they'd never gotten back in touch, that the twenty years they didn't speak had never been bridged, that way she could fantasize that Georgia was still working in her store and living her life and sometime in the future, a day yet to come, Catherine would contact her and they'd renew their acquaintance. There were moments when she made it all about her, when she felt as though she'd been punished by her mistakes and forced – by God? by the universe? – to experience what it felt like to be left behind and bewildered. To have so many questions and not know who to ask.

Most days, though, she simply gave up trying to understand. She read a book on grief and did the first thing on the list: find a hobby. She took up an interest in wine, sometimes sampled a bit too much. Just every now and again.

The wine side of the business sprung naturally when Catherine decided to try living part of the week in Cold Spring. It was an experiment, of sorts, in commitment.

'You might get to work on time if you didn't have to commute so far,' Anita had suggested, not unkindly. Technically speaking, Anita was also her landlady, because Catherine had moved into Anita's oversized San Remo apartment years ago when the widow moved out to live with Marty. Much to the horror of Anita's three adult sons, who'd been unhappy not only with the appearance of Marty but also with the thought of Catherine in the family apartment.

At first, Catherine assumed that Anita wanted to chase her out of the place.

'You are still going to stay at the San Remo whenever you want, or all the time if it doesn't work out,' said Anita before Catherine had even responded. Just the right thing always seemed to bubble out of her. 'I just worry you are going to spend all your time on the train and not enough time enjoying yourself.'

And so Catherine had found a little bungalow – and, with trepidation, purchased it – which she'd promptly gutted to the studs and combined two tiny bedrooms to make one massive room, adding on a deluxe en suite bath and refurbishing the entire house with cherry floors and white wainscoting. The bright red front door stood out in the short walkway, framed by a path of pansies. The house was, it turned out, the perfect spot for Catherine's various rendezvous. Not to mention she felt at home, decorating with pieces from The Phoenix and selling them when she got bored.

And once she realized the wine selection was so limited

in Cold Spring, she simply spent enough money to convince the store next to her to move across the street and rented out the space for her wine-shop. It was the culmination of turning The Phoenix into what Catherine now described as a 'wonderful things' boutique.

And yet she wondered, often, what Georgia would think of it all. What she'd think of the store. Of Catherine. And of her strong and powerful connection with James.

7

He'd been waiting in the restaurant for a while, Catherine guessed, as she caught sight of James's hunched shoulders through the window. She strode in, bells on the door ringing to announce the arrival of yet another customer on a busy Friday night, and lay a hand lightly on his back as she came up to the table.

'The usual?' asked a tiny Asian waitress, balancing a tray of bright red drinks with tiny paper parasols on her shoulder. Behind her, a loud group of young professionals waited eagerly to get bevved.

'Yes, please,' said Catherine, undoing the knotted tie around the waist of her microfiber camel trench coat as James stood up and pulled out her chair. He was always a gentleman, Mr. Manners, even when he was preoccupied. Another reason why not pursuing the college kid up in Cold Spring was a good idea: that young man had had no sense of etiquette other than the wheres and whys of text messaging. Though she hadn't really been looking to have heart-to-hearts with him, if she was being honest with herself.

Catherine sat down and laid the paper napkin over her dark trousers. The table, she could see clearly, was set for three.

'We've been talking,' he said, motioning across the table-cloth. 'Waiting for you to get here. You're always late, you know that?'

'I know, sweetie,' said Catherine, laying a hand over James's and patting gently. 'It's a lifetime of trying to make an entrance. Hard to shake.' She nodded across the table and took a few sips of water.

'Upset?'

Catherine shrugged.

'Was Dakota having a good time?'

'Not sure,' Catherine admitted. 'She's a little nonplussed about the changes to the shop, not that she wants to fess up. But overall the meeting was good. Darwin was surprised. Really tickled, I think.'

'It's good you all have each other,' said James, noticing Catherine's raised eyebrow. 'It's important for Dakota.'

The waitress glided efficiently up to the table and placed a Scotch above each plate. James and Catherine each took a sip, then another.

'And your guest? Should we wait or order now?' asked the server. Her expression was calm and pleasant and she waited as the duo seemed to consider her question.

'We'll order,' boomed James, a bit too loudly. 'We're never really sure if she shows up, anyway.' He smiled at the waitress, who pulled out a pad of paper from her apron and dutifully wrote as James asked her opinion about the freshness of the asparagus and if they could make General Tso's chicken extra spicy. In all the years they'd been coming, the waitress had only once tried to take away the third place setting. After surviving Catherine's wrath, she let it be, and ever after asked if their friend was coming, never seemed fazed when they ordered enough food for three people. Just in case. In return, the waitress pocketed a handsome tip. What did she care if the two of them were clearly nuts?

Of course it was crazy. Between the two of them, they'd agreed to stop meeting at the little hole-in-the-wall a million times. But it felt better to meet up at the dinky little Asian-fusion joint a few blocks from Walker and Daughter, ordering the sushi rolls and chicken satay that Georgia had loved. It felt like some sort of link to another time, to each food she'd enjoyed, to talk about her without having to be measured and mature.

Sometimes, after a drink or two, they would even address a few sentences to the empty plate. They were long past any sense of embarrassment, had made plain to each other their need to imagine, if only for a few hours, that Georgia was around, somewhere. Somehow.

An hour and many bites later and Catherine was feeling much, much better. She'd needed some food in her stomach, she guessed, something other than the sweet stuff at Darwin's shower. Of course, it wasn't just the food that made her feel better. It was the pretending. The fantasy that they were simply waiting.

'We enable each other, you know,' she said to James as she sipped at her green tea. 'We're off in the head. I mean, who would you tell about this, right?'

It had started, naturally enough, a few months after the funeral. She and James met up for coffee, as they had begun to do a few times when Georgia was seriously ill, on the sly. Away from the shop and from Dakota or anyone else who might see them and get suspicious. Wonder what the svelte blonde and the tall, handsome man were doing, their heads close together, and their conversation furtive. They wondered about it themselves, recognizing in each other a kindred spirit. James and Catherine became each other's confessors, able to reveal the ways they'd hurt Georgia and to offer some sort of absolution.

From one regretful guilty party to another.

Because they really were the only two people on the planet who could truly understand each other, who could say the words they needed someone else to hear without seeming as though they were self-absorbed narcissists.

'I feel like I'm being punished,' he had told Catherine over a steaming mug all those years ago. 'It's divine payback. I get to see her, touch her, win her – and then my karma catches up with me, makes me pay for everything I did wrong by letting me see her and touch her and then it's just all gone.'

'You took responsibility,' Catherine had pointed out. 'You said you did wrong.'

'And this is what I get in return,' he said, crunching his paper napkin in his hand. 'She goes off and dies.'

'Right when it's getting good,' said Catherine. 'Right when it's going to be all right. Right when you need her most.'

'I'm so pissed off.' James had raised his voice loudly enough to attract the attention of the other patrons. Dropping his tone, he continued: 'I wanted a life with Georgia and our daughter and instead I get to live *her* life as a single parent. Alone. Lonely. Confused.'

He hadn't taken one sip of his drink. 'You think I'm a self-pitying jerk?' His eyes met Catherine's in challenge.

'Pretty much,' Catherine had said, meeting his gaze. 'But then I'm no better.'

And that's what made the ritual such a relief. The ground rules were out there from the very beginning: They could say anything. No judgments. And it never left the room. After all, it wasn't . . . typical.

The coffee meetings turned into dinner when Catherine mentioned an article she'd read about setting out a place for the deceased on holidays.

'It's supposed to be cathartic,' she said days before the first anniversary of Georgia's death. 'Wanna try it?'

'That's stupid,' said James, stuffing napkins into untouched coffee. 'Let's go to the Asian place she liked,' he'd mumbled into the cup without looking up.

Sometimes they went to the restaurant often, such as

Octobers when the anniversary of Georgia's death came, and at other times they waited months, hoping to let go and then feeling a need build up and take over and push them, as if on autopilot, to drinking Scotch and crunching egg rolls in the name of Georgia.

'She's my only real friend,' admitted Catherine, who often talked about Georgia in the present tense. 'Everyone else tolerates me because of her. But Georgia likes me, really likes me. She sees the good.'

'Exactly,' James had said. 'She's a people whisperer. Makes you better than you are.'

'She can be bitchy, though,' Catherine reminded him.

'Yeah,' agreed James. 'I kinda like that, too. There's no confusion.'

'She's a good decision-maker,' said Catherine. 'Like the time we both worked at the Dairy Queen and I broke the Blizzard machine and . . .'

On and on they went. For over five years now, a variation of the same conversation, from the 'Remember whens' to the little mishaps they'd had during the week – missing the train, breaking a dish – that seemed so boring in the retelling and yet so necessary to share with someone. It can be very isolating to think there's no one who cares when you get a paper cut.

They left all of the 'should' at the door. You should move on. You should feel better. You should let it go. Instead, they forged a secret partnership, the kind of friendship all the more powerful because it was clandestine. There was their public relationship – always cordial – and then the intensity of their private connection.

This is what they talked about: James's inability to date anyone for more than three months ('Don't want to send the wrong message that I intend to get serious,' he would say). Catherine's choice of paint color in her dining room ('I know everyone says red stimulates the appetite but it just

makes me think of dead animals,' she said, explaining why
she'd opted for deep orange). Her belief after every first date
that every new relationship had love potential ('You were
right,' she would agree following each breakup, whether
dramatic or mundane. 'He was a toad'). James's restlessness
working as a vice president of design for V hotels – it was
a good position yet he felt stifled creatively – and his adamant
opinion that he had to stay put for Dakota's sake. He
appeared to pay close attention when Catherine insisted she'd
developed a phone crush on her Italian wine importer ('Just
the way he asks me how I am,' she trilled. 'And that voice
– va-va-voom. I get weak in the knees when I see the caller
ID'). They kvetched about their shared inability to go more
than two weeks without a dream about Georgia, and the fact
that they both still craved cigarettes even though they hadn't
smoked in over twenty years.

James listened intently when Catherine told him that her
ex-husband, Adam, had remarried and that he and his wife
were having a baby.

'I saw it in the goddamn paper,' she'd said, bitterly. 'I hate
his guts so much. Why should he have any happiness?'

'Who says he's happy?' James tried to cheer her up but
held up a hand when he saw her expression. 'Some people
get it all when they don't deserve it. It's how it goes. And
sometimes people don't.'

Neither one had to explain to the other which category
they'd fallen into.

He hadn't laughed when she very seriously insisted she
was going to write a crime thriller called *Dead Men Don't
ReMarry*, about a serial killer who murders high-profile
men who were cruel to their wives. 'And the killer also
steals their pets and gives them to lonely children who will
love them,' said Catherine, gesturing with her hands to
make the point.

'Sounds good to me,' James had said. 'I am available to read pages anytime.'

In return, she'd given him the ins and outs of winning over Gran in Scotland, had helped him put together a photo album of Georgia and Dakota to take with him as a gift. With James's salary, Dakota had been able to see Gran more often since Georgia had died than ever before, even though Gran was slower to get about now and had a live-in aide to cook her meals and keep the house. Still, she hung on tenaciously to the farm in Scotland, vowed on every phone call with Dakota that they'd be carrying her out with her boots on.

In short, Catherine and James dumped the niceties and chitchat at the door and proceeded to talk about everything and anything, from sex to work to traffic to what they had for dinner the night before: no holds barred. And, most of all, they talked about Georgia.

'None of this moving-on crap for us,' Catherine would choke out as the evening wore on. She said that same thing every time. 'At least we keep it to ourselves. It's not like we take out those "In Memoriam Happy Birthday" messages in the classifieds.'

Their emotions about the friend and lover they'd lost seemed to be there constantly, like a tiny pebble wedged into a shoe and impossible to remove. They could always feel it, pressing, rubbing, hurting. And yet that very annoyance grew to be reassuring in its familiarity. They recognized it in each other and accepted it. This, then, was its own relief.

'Maybe we should sleep together,' Catherine had once suggested. 'You know, crazy over-the-top sex. Lots of huffing and puffing and moaning. That's how we cope with everything anyway.' The fact that she was staring out the window and absentmindedly chewing on an egg roll made it clear she wasn't altogether serious.

'Yeah, okay,' agreed James. 'This time next year.'

'You know,' said Catherine, peeling her eyes from a bickering couple exiting a cab on a rainy New York night and feeling a twinge of envy, even for the togetherness of arguing, 'it's really the only thing I can think of that would be guaranteed to bring her back. She'd come here and kick your ass if you slept with me.'

'Me? What about you? You're the instigator!'

'Ha!' said Catherine. 'Georgia found you irresistible. How could I resist your charm, the way you chew your beef and broccoli and slop it on your shirt every time. You're not so perfect, Mr. James Foster. You're a messy eater.'

'I do? She did? I was irresistible?' And thus they entered the next level of their relationship: spilling all the secret things Georgia ever said about the other. The good and the bad, the surprising and the stuff they already knew. They pored over every conversation remembered, every detail shared, and the results brought a whole new dimension to everything: suddenly, Catherine knew for certain that Georgia thought her old hair color looked overprocessed, and James found out that Georgia had always hated his navy pin-striped suit. And instead of making them feel slighted or angry, the revelations brought new delight. To learn and understand even more about Georgia. It was like finding a hidden cache of treasure, a vault of information they could sift through and in doing so feel as though she was alive. Almost right there. Just inches out of reach.

The dinners became an emotional addiction. An obsession with memory and with grief. But, most of all, it made them feel as though they were able to function the rest of the time, to be available to Dakota, to be professionals in their work life, to have dalliances and sex lives and almost-love relationships. All because they could let their truth out every now and then, could give in to the pain and talk about it, honestly and completely.

No one thought it queer when Anita knit vest after vest for her late husband; they found it an example of devotion.

But Catherine and James knew that world would not make such allowances for them. They were younger. They were supposed to get it together.

'Thank you for not making me feel like a weirdo.' Catherine drained her second Scotch. James well knew she'd cry if he let her have a third drink, what the two of them referred to as a 'G.W.' A Georgia Walker. That extra bit of alcohol to push you over the edge of your inhibitions and guaranteed to bring tears.

Sometimes a good cry was what was needed.

'Right back at you.' He mused, every now and then, what his daughter would have thought of these goings-on. He'd suggested to her one time that they cut a slice of birthday cake for Georgia, only to be met with a look of such disbelief that he claimed it had been a slip of the tongue. And James wondered how Dakota would feel if she knew he and Catherine were as close as they were. On the one hand, she seemed to like that he had built solid relationships with Anita and Marty, with her grandparents, and she always looked forward to hanging out with Catherine. But she seemed to see all of it as hers. Her world, one that she'd shared with her mother, and while he was allowed to visit, he was never able to actually reside there. To fully be a part of it all. Instead, James and Dakota had forged their own relationship, had learned how to be dad and daughter. They were close but there was still a certain stiffness between them, something he worried would always remain. He could never fill the hole in her heart for her mother. And the high school years had been hard. He never quite knew the right thing to do.

'Do you know,' ventured Catherine, clearly toying with the idea of a G.W. as she swished the nearly melted ice cubes in the bottom of her glass, 'that I think you're the only man who's ever been nothing more than a friend to me?'

'I'd have to say the same about you,' replied James, shaking his head a little at the idea. 'If you'd told me that first time I saw you at Georgia's shop, all bee-stung collagen lips and lady-of-the-manor attitude, that you'd become the keeper of my secrets . . .' He paused, then inhaled deeply and let it out slowly.

'Jesus, life sucks.'

'Pretty much,' said Catherine mildly, leaning back in her chair and idly tapping the table with a pack of Sweet'N Low. And then she suggested something she'd never once seriously considered in all the years since Georgia had been gone.

'I'd like you to come with me to something,' she said to James. Her voice was flat as she let out a sigh. It had been a long night, and the Scotches hadn't really helped. KC's comments at the shower had bugged her, no doubt. *I didn't plan to become a divorcée with a dead best friend,* she thought. *But sign me up. Here I am.*

'I think it's time we went to a grief support group, James,' said Catherine, pulling out a sheet of paper from her purse. She'd printed it out months ago, folded it into a square and stuffed it away. 'I think it's time we faced the reality that she's not really coming for dinner.'

8

Things like this happen. That's what people say when they have nothing more useful to provide.

Darwin had been teaching her class on intro women's studies, the same as every other Wednesday of the semester, when the cramping started. Her first thought was that she was going into early labor, and she was excited. Her second realization was also that she might be going into early labor and she was alarmed. Her due date was far off; she was just shy of thirty-two weeks.

'We're going to end early,' she said, grabbing her bag and walking out of the room without a second glance.

A stop in the bathroom, a call to Dan, a cab ride to the OB. Within a few hours, Darwin was officially on bed rest.

Not that she was getting any rest, that is. The bed she had all to herself, Dan sleeping on the sofa in order to give her more room to relax. But who could sleep at a time like this? Besides, she couldn't really ever get comfortable, anyway.

The fear was that she'd launch into preterm labor before the babies' lungs were fully developed. Too much commotion on her part now and her kids would be taking the train to NICU Central. Or worse.

No one had had to explain it to her. She'd had this potential complication on her list of worries, right near the top.

So Darwin didn't resist lying on her side, a pillow between her legs, waiting. And waiting some more. She accepted that the only scenery she was going to see for a while were the two steps through the hall to the bathroom.

Before the spotting, she had had quite a different assumption about bed rest.

Wouldn't it be wonderful, she'd often thought, to be ordered to put her feet up, with Dan offering her glasses of organic milk and unlimited foot rubs. She'd snooze, work on her laptop, maybe even watch an indie film on the DVD.

But the real deal was a hodgepodge of boredom and frustration, combined with a sense of inadequacy and anxiety.

Before the spotting, she'd kept at things full tilt, teaching, schlepping her plump butt up and down the subway stairs, going to stretching classes when she'd rather be snoozing. Forever busy: it was part of the whole new myth of pregnancy, in which women looked pencil thin except for their basketball bellies, and kept up a dizzying pace until delivery. The last thing Darwin ever wanted to admit was that something was putting her at a disadvantage, and she worked diligently throughout her pregnancy. No, she didn't overwork. But she didn't fall behind, either. She wasn't about to let her colleagues use her exhaustion against her, brainstorming brilliant papers while she watched yet another episode of *A Baby Story*.

How stressful to live in a nation where newly delivered moms career back to work after twelve weeks, forced, by a need for a salary, to buy into the convenient assumption that pregnancy, labor, and delivery isn't a major medical experience – natural or not. Darwin held fast to her beliefs about the need for longer maternity leave in America but did so even as she went out of her way to prove to her dean and her colleagues that she was just as competent. Perhaps more so.

There was no space to just let things go and wallow in

the joy and the changes in her body. To nap guilt-free because she felt tired. And it wasn't just about the fact that Darwin had a career: she'd spoken – interviewed, as always, Darwin was still a little abrupt – to the folks at her Bradley Method class, and every woman was in the same boat. Even the stay-at-homes fell prey to the new expectations. It wasn't enough to just cook up a baby in your body anymore. Now an expectant mom had to look great and accomplish everything on her to-do list at the same time.

When she was a teenager, Darwin had wholeheartedly agreed with the common consensus that menstruating was no big deal. But then she experienced the pain, bloating, cramping, back pain, and general grumpiness – in addition to learning how to act like it was just any other day.

'You're only pregnant.' That's what she heard more often than she could count. You're only pregnant.

Yeah, that's what she was: building another human being with her body.

'Surely there has to be some middle ground between not wanting women to be limited in their education, career, and lifestyle,' she had challenged her students as she stood, heavily pregnant, at the front of the room, 'and the cultural pretense that all that is unique about the experience of the human female isn't extraordinary. We coddle or we dismiss. What we need to promote is respect. Think Aretha. R-E-S-P-E-C-T.'

At home, she'd made sure to fit in stretching and reading and even cooking. Darwin, never very good in the kitchen, felt an instinctual desire to stuff their tiny fridge-top freezer with casseroles she made from Internet recipes. Often, though, she'd discover she didn't have quite the right ingredients when she was halfway through, and had to improvise. Substitute a little squash for carrot. Orange food is orange food, right? Dan insisted he ate them when she was sleeping but she suspected – though could never find the garbage to prove it – that he might have been throwing them away.

'That dish was tasty,' he'd say in the morning. 'Want me to pick up some carrots on the way home tonight?'

But there'd be no more cooking in the kitchen now. It was all about taking it easy. Thinking good thoughts. Finding her quiet space.

Waiting for Lucie.

Oh, she'd e-mailed, and she'd returned Darwin's call immediately.

'You okay?' she asked, though the answer should have been obvious.

'Umm, no?'

'Right, no, I mean, seriously,' said Lucie. 'Are the babies okay?'

'They're still on board, if that's what you're asking.'

'Good,' she said, the long pauses between her words indicating that she was most likely not paying close attention. Reading e-mails, perhaps, or editing shots.

'Will you be coming over soon?' It would be nice, she thought, to have Lucie come over. Maybe bring her candied ginger, just as she'd done when Lucie was pregnant. Or maybe Lucie would bring over the layette items that Darwin assumed she must be working up. Surely one of the best lace knitters around didn't just send her best friend a set of rocking horses, did she? Expensive, indeed, and much appreciated. But something more personal seemed called for, she believed.

'Yes,' said Lucie, after a delay. 'Right when I can.'

Darwin had not found the chitchat reassuring.

Look, the truth was that Darwin didn't have a ton of friends. She had Lucie, and then she had the other members of the club, and she had Dan. But building relationships remained difficult for her: she often barreled in with her strong opinions and forgot to listen to others' ideas. It didn't increase her popularity with the other academics at Hunter, and it didn't make her a favorite among Dan's doctor colleagues. So if Lucie seemed to be distancing herself, then what? The prospect seemed bleak.

'She's breaking up with me,' Darwin told Dan softly as he lay on top of the covers, tucking her in before he left to sleep for a few hours on the sofa. She'd never actually had a boyfriend before Dan, so she'd never suffered the humiliation and confusion of being rejected by someone she loved. Well, certainly her mother criticized her. But it wasn't as though she expected her mother to stop taking her calls. Darwin might get an earful, but she always answered.

'I guess I'm just not important enough now that she has all the directing stuff,' she explained. 'Maybe she's meeting exciting people who are funnier and more presentable.'

'Maybe,' said Dan, agreeing not because he thought Darwin was right but because he understood she just wanted his ear. She wanted to let it out and not have to debate or reason as she did every day, just wanted to feel a little bit sad and pore through her emotions without interruption.

I woulda made a great psychiatrist, thought Dan as he looked up at the ceiling, stroking Darwin's forehead, her black hair pulled apart in two pigtails. She was wearing a blue T-shirt that was so large it was roomy even over her ample belly, and she was gesturing emphatically even as she was lying on her side.

'I just wish I knew what I did to upset her,' she whispered. He loved her because she was brilliant, because she was kind, because she was intense and driven just as he was, and because she let down her guard with him and revealed her hidden vulnerabilities.

Dan looked around their room, at the chipped old white melamine dresser they'd had since before they got married, at the wooden desk strewn with papers pushed next to the bed in lieu of a nightstand. It was kind of depressing, he realized, no doubt contributing to Darwin's malaise.

'We need some new furniture,' he said.

'I don't want to pick out anything else,' said Darwin. She didn't want to make things potentially worse by buying items for the babies. She had stopped fantasizing about that extravagant crib except for five minutes every night, when she allowed herself a limited selection of upbeat thoughts. Just enough to keep a flicker of hope, not enough to tempt the Fates.

'No,' said Dan. 'For us. We could use a new bed. A dresser. And what about that living room?'

'I can't go shopping,' said Darwin.

'Sure you can,' said Dan. 'You've got your computer and your credit card. All we need to do is schedule deliveries when I'm here, and we're set.'

'It's not really in our budget,' she reminded him. Not that he needed her to point out the stack of bills on the messy desk, the looming potential medical bills whether things went right or wrong.

'Who cares?' Dan was typically meticulous when it came to staying within their means. His ability to save had helped them squirrel away the down payment on the apartment even as they attempted to pay off their ambitions. It seemed like such a no-brainer, for two smart kids, becoming a doctor and a professor. So good on paper. But when they got more paper – in the form of school loan bills – the cachet of their brainy, white-collar careers faded somewhat.

But what Darwin needed now, Dan thought, was a diversion. From the health of the babies and the lack of attention from Lucie. He'd have called in the entire Friday Night crew but he fretted about introducing too much hubbub. Not to mention that he'd have to clean up to save Darwin from the embarrassment of the dirty-socks-on-the-floor lifestyle they led, and he had no time to clean because he was on call for the entire weekend.

He wished, really, that he had someone else to come in and entertain his wife. But a visit from her mother was not a recipe for relaxation, and his own mother and Darwin had never gotten along.

Truth be told, Dan had been counting on Lucie very much. He hadn't spent quite as much time with Ginger as Darwin had, but he'd done his time in Candyland. And he would have appreciated a little backup when it counted.

'Order as much stuff as you want,' he said, trying to jolly Darwin out of her funk. He wanted to help her find ways to entertain herself and, most of all, to feel useful. She'd never done very well as a couch potato. There was nothing on TV that she ever wanted to watch, she said, explaining that most shows covered the same narrow, antifeminist territory over and over. Egalitarian, functional families do not make compelling entertainment.

'Well,' said Darwin now, thinking of what else she could do and not coming up with much of anything, either, 'I might just take a quick peek at craigslist.'

In the end, it was Dakota who saved her from insanity.

'You're massive!' she'd said upon coming into the bedroom, having arrived for an unscheduled visit.

'What?' said Darwin, raising herself up on her elbows and motioning toward her. 'Bring me the hand mirror that's in the bathroom.' She peered into it as Dakota also looked. 'I am not.'

'You're just looking at your face,' said Dakota. 'Your ankles are like sausages.'

'I can't see that far,' admitted Darwin. 'I assume you brought snacks?'

'Without question,' said Dakota, reaching into her over-stuffed yellow backpack and pulling out some banana loaf. 'I used the kitchen at my dad's.'

'That's it?' Darwin had already broken off a hunk and popped it into her mouth. 'Two bites and I'll be full, so I guess it doesn't matter.'

'Ooh, that's dramatic,' said Dakota, pulling out a binder. 'I was wondering if maybe you wanted to help me with my paper on the world wars and their effect on women.'

'You came over here to ask me to help you with your schoolwork?' Darwin raised her voice.

'Yup,' said Dakota, who often turned to Darwin when it came to matters of education and feminism.

'That's my girl,' said Darwin, raising her arm for a high five. 'Where have you been, lady? I've been sitting on my ass for weeks here!'

'So then I guess things are finally looking up,' said Dakota, leaning in to smack palms with her favorite professor. 'There are times when things go right, you know. And just to prove it, I'm going to teach you how to knit baby socks.'

Easy

It's all about getting the hang of things. Easy does it; take it easy. You'll figure everything out in time. But for right now, just keep trying. Pay attention and avoid the temptation to go further than you're ready. Talk less. And listen more.

9

Keep an eye on the mail.

That was the one and only rule Anita had ever given Catherine about staying in the San Remo apartment.

'I always do,' Catherine had joked, then caught Anita's sharp look. She'd never tolerated Catherine's man-eater humor.

'Do not throw *anything* out,' Anita had said. She wasn't concerned with what Catherine did with her own letters and circulars, of course. She simply explained that she wanted Catherine to put aside every item that arrived addressed to any Lowenstein: Stan, Anita, Nathan, Benjamin, David. No matter that none of them lived in the apartment anymore, that the boys were really middle-aged men who lived with families of their own in Atlanta, Zurich, and Tel Aviv.

Anita had kindly provided Catherine with a wicker picnic basket (not a stitch of gingham in sight) in which to store the envelopes. She placed the basket in the kitchen, off to the side on a long stretch of counter. The kitchen, like every room in the apartment that Anita and Stan had shared, was spacious and perfectly coordinated in every last detail, from the rich polish on the wide-plank wood floors to the deep espresso glaze on the oversized cabinets.

'It seems a bit light this month,' said Anita, peering into the basket and then lifting it up. Coming back to the San Remo was like channeling a past life. A dream she'd had in which she could remember some of the details so clearly while others were hazy and seemed to vanish as she grasped for them in her memory. This spoon: we used it to stir gravy. That cup: it was once my favorite for mint tea.

Anita came over to the apartment every so often, sometimes with Marty and sometimes alone. Catherine would order too much food from the Italian restaurant around the corner and decant a good bottle of wine that she would bring down from The Phoenix.

'It's from Cara Mia, my new favorite Italian vineyard,' said Catherine now, pouring out a glass. 'In Velletri, not far from Rome. The son who handles the exports has this deep, sexy voice – I call sometimes just to ask how the grapes are growing.'

She was quite excited to have Anita over to the house, had been keeping a low profile since Darwin's shower several weeks earlier. She'd been seriously working on that crime thriller she'd casually mentioned to James, for one thing – *Dead Men Don't ReMarry*. But mostly she just felt in a funk.

'I'm one of the few U.S. shops that is importing from them,' continued Catherine. 'It's a family-run outfit, and the younger generation is branching off to try some new grape varietals—'

Anita interrupted her rambling.

'You're skimming the mail,' she said with finality. Anita's tone was even but her pursed lips betrayed her annoyance. 'You're taking my mail and just throwing it away. Dumping it out without a word. And after I expressly asked you never to do so.'

It was true and Catherine felt a rush of guilt. For years, she had dutifully collected every preapproved credit offer and each invitation to refinance the mortgage and cash out the equity, had stacked the cruise brochures atop the ValuPak coupons that arrived weekly. (Really? she'd wondered. Coupons to the San Remo? But direct marketers, it would seem, did not spend a lot of time weeding out their lists. This was why Catherine received her very own set of coupon books to the very same address.)

Rarely, a personal letter might arrive. Or a postcard. Anita had been living with Marty for such a long time that most everyone in her life knew where to contact her. Most likely, the personal items were simply addressed to the San Remo out of long habit or by a friend whose memory wasn't quite what it used to be. She'd always made sure to set those aside.

Lately, though, Catherine had decided to be a little bit more helpful – she was very pleased with her initiative – and had taken it upon herself to recycle the ubiquitous department store catalogs that seemed to reproduce overnight in the mailbox. Apparently every store was in a constant state of Sale Sale Sale!

'Just the junk, Anita,' she said now. Slowly. 'I'm sure you get the same things at home, anyway.'

'That's simply not acceptable, Catherine,' said Anita, her words clipped. 'I do not ask much from you in this regard. I don't care if something seems like a piece of junk, I want it collected and handed over.' She did not look up from the basket. But Catherine could feel the frown on Anita's face and she didn't like it at all.

'Sorry.'

'Did you shake everything out?' asked Anita, still peeved but pretending to be calm to get the maximum information. That old mother's trick. 'Make sure there was nothing stuck to any of those items you threw away?'

'Uh . . . no,' admitted Catherine. 'Were you expecting something?'

'That's not the point, whether I was or not,' said Anita

sharply. 'That's really none of your business, Catherine. Sometimes you are quite presumptuous, you know that?'

Immediately, watching Catherine's shoulders instinctively pull in closer, Anita regretted her harsh tone. It's only a postcard, she told herself silently. Without a word she gave Catherine a hug, followed by a little pat on the cheek.

'I'm sorry, dear,' she said. 'Let's have that glass of wine and get the takeout menu. I'm going to have gnocchi again, I think.'

Catherine forced a smile in return. She always felt that little bit uncertain, even after all these years of living in Anita's apartment, that she was just leftovers. Dakota was the real deal, without question, a genuine piece of Georgia. But she was a remnant from that last summer with Georgia, someone Anita kept around out of pity, even as Catherine felt a strong need to forever be in the older woman's graces. There is no moment we do not want a mother's love.

'No, I'm sorry, Anita,' she said. 'I overstepped, and I'm apologizing.'

Anita waved her off, already seeming to move on, marching into the living room. Typically she enjoyed a good look around the apartment, not so much to check on Catherine's wear and tear on the place as to regale a little story about each piece of furniture. Anita had taken a few antiques, all her photo albums, several paintings, and her wardrobe when she and Marty bought their new apartment. Apart from that, the two had bought pieces together and furnished their home from scratch, leaving Catherine with a beautifully furnished home completely not to her taste. But Catherine had preferred it that way, had enjoyed the sense that she was on a hiatus, vacationing somewhere and not quite ready to make permanent choices. It added to the sense that time – life, even – was on hold. And until recently, she'd found little very comfortable.

'So,' said Anita, sitting down on the sofa she'd picked out with Stan in 1980 and re-covered in rich brocade in 1995. She patted the space beside her. 'I have some news to share with you . . .'

Just like any couple, Anita and Marty had made their compromises. They had to figure out which side of the bed to sleep on, and who would do the dishes, and whether or not it was important to their coupleness to follow the same programs. Not to mention their divergence in hobbies: she liked opera, he liked to go to baseball games. Or, more precisely, Yankee games. She liked to knit; he liked to watch the Yankees on television. She liked to walk in the park; he liked to listen to games on his iPod.

'What do I care?' Anita told Dakota long ago. 'He's a good, sweet man and I'm glad he has an interest. Keeps the mind active.'

And even though Marty had never tried to cast on, Anita accompanied him to watch his team, the players standing around the bases and waiting for someone to pop a fly or whatnot. 'He's tall,' she might say. Or 'If they had a co-ed team, I don't think there'd be as much spitting going on.' Typically she settled into a torrid romance novel, the type she would buy at the drugstore, and only look up when the crowd grew animated. Without fail, she made sure to tell Marty she thought it was a lack of good judgment that Yankee Stadium had a problem with knitting needles.

'Other teams let knitters click-clack away,' she'd say. 'They even invite them to bring their friends. Someone should write a letter to Mr. Steinbrenner and tell him so.' And Marty would solemnly agree, all the while keeping track of the score in his program and carefully filing away the sheet in his Yankee-blue filing cabinet at the deli, with his other important papers.

Now Marty continued to work and went into the deli most days, making perfect sandwiches piled high with pastrami and spicy mustard. It was what he'd done his entire life, taking over the deli business from his father and sharing it with his brother, then buying his brother's share and looking after the whole thing himself. And along the way, he had quietly and meticulously invested in real estate on the Upper West Side, first with the building that housed his first-floor deli and the second-floor Walker and Daughter, then with brownstones and other commercial and residential properties. Indeed, Marty Popper was one of those quiet millionaires who could afford pretty much anything they wanted and yet chose to live simply.

'Who would pour the coffee?' he always said when asked if, at seventy-three, he was getting ready to retire. Though, when pressed, he would admit a certain longing for a tricked-out RV, Anita knitting intently as she rode shotgun and watched the trees go by out the window.

An interest in travel was something they shared. Once he and Anita settled in together, he'd made sure to find a right-hand man to look after things and pick up some of the menial tasks that Marty felt he'd done quite long enough, someone to watch over the deli when he and Anita took the train around the country on yet another second honeymoon.

'We can't have a second honeymoon,' Anita would tease him at night when he clambered in beside her. 'We haven't had a first.'

They were life partners, it was true, but they were not husband and wife.

Marty had never been married and had no children: the very fact that he was a child-free orphan lent a certain ease to their getting together. Anita, on the other hand, brought more than enough troublesome family members for one relationship. She'd caught her children unawares, truth be told, startled them with the idea that she needed companionship and perhaps, not that they dared think too deeply about it, a sex life. It's not that they wanted her dead. Not in the least. They would have just preferred that she act dead . . . in certain ways. That was the thing. Weren't old ladies supposed to just focus on their knitting and their mah-jongg?

Marty and Anita's solution was to chart a neutral course with the children. To always stay in hotels when they went to visit Nathan and his family in Atlanta, for example, so as to avoid the discussion of who was sleeping with whom and in what bedroom. ('It's for the children, Mother,' he insisted, though it was so hard to get her grandkids' attention anyway that Anita doubted they would even notice.)

Anita never felt she saw as much of her grandkids as she wished. At one time, that had been because the kids were young and busy with activities and Anita, afraid to fly, hadn't found it easy to make the trips. But then the grandkids grew older and, lo and behold, they became not less busy but even more so. Even when she was a guest in their parents' home, it truly was a challenge to sit down and chat with her grandchildren, who were always rushing through dinner and running off to games and dance practice and volunteer gigs that would look altruistic on their college applications. She supposed she ran the same sort of household when her boys were young and her hair was brown instead of silver, but now it struck her that the daily lives of children were over-scheduled and overextended.

'All that fun is going to stress them right out,' she told Nathan, who ignored her, as usual.

Still. She hadn't let her sons' reluctance dissuade her from moving in with Marty. They'd discussed marriage many times and Anita had always been clear that she thought it unnecessary and potentially quite complicated. Besides, those types of restraints were for folks under sixty, she told herself, people who lacked the common sense to appreciate the rarity of finding a true companion.

So it was with great surprise, then, that as she stood up at the seventh-inning stretch to let Marty and all the other fans sing away, she noticed Marty wasn't joining in with his usual gusto. Instead, he was sweating.

'Are you ill?' she asked him.

'Nervous,' he said, taking her hand as the last strains of '. . . the old ball game' were being shouted out by people all around them.

'Anita, will you marry me?' asked Marty, fumbling around in his pocket before pulling out a velvet box and opening it to reveal a whopper of a diamond and ruby ring. She blushed as she could feel the eyes of the strangers all around them watching her. But all she wanted to do was giggle. Throw her head back and laugh. At the absurd setting, at this crazy, caring man who thought it the height of connection to share his love of the slowest game ever played with her. And she loved him for it.

Proposing marriage at Yankee Stadium was not something Stan would ever have done. And really, in a way, that was part of the point. Part of Marty's allure. Women don't just like one kind of meal and they don't just like one kind of man.

And that's when she decided. Yes, she was going to marry Marty. And she was going to tell Catherine that she was ready to sell the San Remo apartment.

10

Saying yes was the easy part.

Now her to-do list was out of control – and it had only been a week since the proposal. Anita had saved up the news for a little bit, just to savor it, then shared the details with Catherine and Dakota and James, before sitting down at Walker and Daughter with the members of the club and chirping out her announcement. It was a good night, and she was glad to hear that Darwin was out of the woods and had given birth to her two healthy six-pounders, Cady and Stanton.

Things were coming along nicely for everyone.

'If we're going to get married, we're going to do it right,' she told Peri during one of her mornings at the shop. 'No small affair for us. We are going to have a shindig of epic proportion.'

'Have you set a date, then?'

'No,' said Anita, sighing. 'I'm afraid we haven't made too many strides in any direction.'

Marty agreed to every suggestion she made, even when they contradicted each other. Get married in Central Park? Fabulous. Get married at the synagogue? Fine by him. A reception at the St. Regis? The Plaza? Essex House? Good good good.

'At the rate we're going we'll be ninety before we get anything done,' said Anita. 'We wondered if we should have an engagement party, for one thing, to fly the kids in and have a gathering of family and friends.'

'When's that going to be?'

'We don't have a timetable on that one, either,' she said. 'It's just that there seems to be so much to do: food, location, flowers, dress.'

'Don't do the sensible thing and get a good cream suit,' insisted Peri. 'Wear something smashing. You are the bride, after all.'

'Even if I'm a bit wrinkly,' said Anita. 'Yes, I am a bride. A bride!'

One thing she'd found herself doing every morning after Marty left the apartment was pulling out her old photo albums and studying her old wedding pictures, marveling at everything. Her skin, for one thing; it had been so smooth. Or her hair, all 1950s pin curls and so tight to her head. The red, red lips. The serious way she looked at the photographer, a bravado she'd put on when inside she'd been nervous. The candid shot of her wagging a finger at a person out of range of the camera. She'd forgotten about that until she started flipping through the album again. Remembering again the little flower girl, in her minty-green dress, sneaking chocolates, ruining her white gloves. Anita had been livid, afraid those little dirty fingers would get onto everything. 'Do something,' she'd told her mother. 'Get things under control.'

Marty wouldn't have minded that she wanted to look at the old snaps; he'd have been happy enough to sit there with her at the granite breakfast bar and listen to her talk about her first wedding, her first marriage. She'd never had to pretend that she didn't have a life before him. But somehow it felt better to look at the pictures in private. She didn't have to modulate her tone. She didn't feel as though she had to wipe away her tears, or have to deal with the awkwardness of letting him comfort her under the assumption she was crying for Stan.

If only Catherine hadn't decided to purge the mail!

Anita had looked carefully through every pamphlet and flyer, but there'd been only junk in that darn wicker basket. She'd called Catherine up, quite casually, and said she wanted to come over again. Look around the kitchen; see if anything had fallen behind the fridge.

'The fridge?' said Catherine. 'I've barely opened the fridge in five years, let alone put anything behind it.'

Where was it? Why hadn't it come?

Her sons made clear they thought it odd that she'd left so much behind when she left the San Remo apartment and moved in with Marty, but Anita had taken what she really cared about: the photos, the jewelry from Stan, and the postcards. The pile of blank postcards, mailed from all around the globe, which she'd stored up in a junk drawer in the kitchen. Where no one ever cared to look. She'd actually tried leaving them behind initially, had waited weeks and then returned to collect the postcards surreptitiously, when Catherine hadn't been at the apartment. She felt like a burglar, in a way, stealing her own stuff. And there they were: Big Ben, the Eiffel Tower, and the Colosseum. Bundled together with a worn rubber band and crammed into that drawer. She'd dropped the entire pile in her purse and returned to her new life, the only hint of her attachment to the postcards being her seemingly intense fascination with junk mail. Marty never seemed to notice she didn't look through the random junk that came to their house. She only cared about what came to the San Remo.

'Oh, Sarah,' sighed Anita, looking at the photos of the young flower girl as if they could tell her why she hadn't heard from her baby sister this year. 'What has happened to you?'

★   ★   ★

Leaving Ginger with Rosie was turning out to be more of a problem than a help. Lucie had arrived at her apartment, expecting to find her mother and daughter making dinner as usual. Instead, her mother was snoring slightly on the sofa and her kindergartner was pulling food out of the fridge. The floor dripped in spilled orange juice and cracked eggs congealing on the tile.

'I'm helping,' said Ginger, before putting her finger to her mouth. 'Shhh . . . Nana's tired.'

Lucie sucked in a deep breath. Just what she needed, and only two weeks until she was supposed to leave for Italy. The plan had been to bundle up Ginger with the stuffed bunny she called 'Sweetness,' an Elmo suitcase filled with a week's supply of leggings, cotton dresses, and a healthy complement of Barbie and friends, and pack her off to Rosie's for a few weeks while Lucie took care of business. But if just one day of full-on Ginger stamina resulted in an exhausted mother and an unsupervised daughter . . . who knew what a couple of weeks could bring? Ginger would wind up swinging from the light fixtures at her mother's New Jersey split-level, while Rosie sat in her powder-blue La-Z-Boy with an icepack on her head. It was a recipe for an intervention from Social Services.

She bribed a hungry Ginger with a peanut butter sandwich and an episode of *Sesame Street*, and then covered her sleeping mother with one of the Georgia afghans she'd knitted for charity.

'I just closed my eyes for a second,' sputtered Rosie, drifting off again as Lucie patted her shoulder.

It wasn't fair of her, she realized, to expect her mother to watch after Ginger.

'My mommy's old,' she whispered to herself, feeling the kind of surprise at both the realization and the awareness that it had taken her so long to actually absorb that fact.

Obviously, watching Ginger was too great a burden: she exhausted Lucie, and she was years younger. So what was she going to do about the gig in Italy? Her older brothers and their families didn't have much space for a precocious little girl, even for a few weeks. They'd done their time stuffing chubby legs into leotards and sitting through swim lessons watching little heads proudly blow endless streams of bubbles.

A year ago, she'd have asked Darwin and Dan, of course, who'd have been delighted to take on Ginger and would have treated her like a little princess. But now they were busy with two of their own.

'Busy busy busy,' Lucie muttered in a funny tone of voice, pushing her newly colored russet hair with the back of her hand as she picked up shatterings of eggshell and dumped them into a paper towel. 'Busy with babies.'

She heard her words almost as if someone else was saying them. *Busy with babies.* Was it possible, she thought with a feeling of horror, that she was resentful of Darwin finally becoming a mother? Had she been so used to relying on her support that there was a certain bitterness, a concern that Ginger would no longer be the apple of her honorary auntie's eye?

'Oh my God,' said Lucie, up to her eyeballs in juice and egg and a stomach rolling in guilt, 'I am a rotten person.'

Ginger looked up from the TV screen. 'Oh, Mommy, that's okay,' she said. 'You make very good dinners.'

Just because something is natural doesn't mean it's going to be easy. That's what someone should have said in the delivery room. And then again, later, when they brought the babies in to nurse. Maybe the hospital should put up a sign somewhere. She had looked at Dan, her stalwart, the doctor, but the anxiety in his eyes mirrored her own.

So I have boobs, thought Darwin as her babies began

mewling. *What now?* It's not like anyone ever really needed them before. And that's what the babies were: constant neediness, day and night. Even when they slept they demanded her vigilance, to make sure they were breathing, were warm, were cool, were happy.

There were joyous moments, lots of them. Such as when Cady cried for the first time, followed a few minutes later by her brother. Or when she held them and they just sighed as if to say, 'Finally. Being here with you, Mommy, is the best place in the world.'

She did that a lot, making up little dialogue for the babies, either when she was alone or sometimes when Dan was around. 'I love my little snuggles,' she baby-talked, wanting to hate herself for being ridiculous and not-so-secretly loving it. She found herself spewing an endless stream of nicknames – Bunnykins, Lollipop, Tummyboy, Sillybaby, Dumpling – and pretending to eat their fingers and toes with alarming regularity.

Still. Darwin hadn't washed her hair in days; it was challenging to keep track of the time. She was fascinated and disgusted by her body at the same time. At what it could do, at how much it seeped after all the action. And everything – her body, the twins, the house – was so freaking messy. Gross, even.

Being with the babies was a constant roller coaster – the highs of clean, sweet-smelling, sleeping infants, and the lows of stinky, ill-tempered, wailing balls of rage, growing more red-faced with each passing second she misinterpreted their cues. Trying to change their diapers when they wanted a burp, or swaddle them in an extra blanket when they were already too hot, their tiny little fingers balling into fists and flailing about as if to say, 'Mommy, why are you so *stupid?*'

'I can't do this alone,' she shouted at Dan one night, her breasts leaking, the newborns crying. It was four a.m., and they'd had about a half-hour of sleep between the two of them.

'Let's call your mother,' he suggested. 'Or my mother.'

'No,' said Darwin, starting to cry herself. 'They'll just tell me how to do everything.'

'But we don't know actually what we're doing,' he'd replied, exasperation creeping into his voice. 'Shouldn't we ask for help?'

'I'm smart,' cried Darwin, feeling desperate and over-whelmed. 'I have a Ph.D. Why can't I look after my own babies?'

The books hadn't been clear enough, really. Oh, they alluded to the misery, to the baby blues, to the sense of in-adequacy when the babies couldn't latch on and the pain when her nipples cracked. But those were just theoretical problems. Issues that Darwin had been confident *she* wouldn't have to face.

She really wanted her children. Had dreamed about them for years. So, surely, every moment was going to be a joy, no?

No. Turns out becoming a mother was more than she'd bargained for.

'I'm not ready,' she confessed to Dan as the sun began to come up. 'I'm not able to do this!'

'Well, we're kinda stuck with them now, hon,' he'd pointed out. 'I think it gets better when they're twenty-one.'

But not every feeling was about Cady and Stanton. Becoming a mother was forcing Darwin to think more about herself as a daughter. Imagine, she thought, if Cady didn't call her for a month. A week. A day. How could she stand being apart from her baby so long? And yet she was a hap-hazard communicator with her own mother in Seattle. Rarely called just to say hello.

After three days at home with the twins, meeting yet

another sleepless sunrise, Darwin was ready. Having two babies might have seemed movie-star-esque, but it wasn't so glamorous when you didn't have a staff.

She had her doubts that she'd ever sleep again.

'Call the moms,' she sighed wearily to Dan. 'We need reinforcements.'

Catherine was not afraid of change. She welcomed it. If, that is, she was the person leading the charge. It did not sit well with her at all that Anita had decided to sell the apartment. Not that there was much Catherine had to do. Pack up a few clothes, a toothbrush, a few bottles of wine she'd yet to drink. The little cottage was where she'd unloaded all the items she'd stored for years, the armoire she once had to keep hidden in her large walk-in closet because Adam couldn't stand anything that wasn't sleek and, preferably, made of metal. Like his heart had been.

But it was something altogether different, having to keep step with someone else's timetable, and though she felt babyish about it, Catherine was a little miffed with Anita.

'Is this because I threw out the coupons?' She phoned Anita's cell one afternoon as she sat at The Phoenix, biding time until the wine tasting she was hosting that evening.

'Absolutely not,' said Anita. 'It's just time. And you have your house now.'

'Every girl needs a pad in the city,' insisted Catherine.

'You could well afford to buy one, my dear,' Anita pointed out.

'Well, I like living in yours,' said Catherine, wheedling just a little bit. This never had any effect on Anita, unfortunately.

'We'll talk about it at the next club meeting, dear,' said Anita. 'Right now I'm making a list.'

'Another one?'

'Yes,' said Anita, growing irritated. 'I had three sons, you know. I've never done weddings before. My mother planned mine.'

'Just think of it as a party,' suggested Catherine.

'I am,' said Anita. 'A party for which I need to repaint the apartment, re-upholster the sofa, hire a caterer, find the perfect dress, lose thirteen and a half pounds, and get a face-lift.'

'Let me tell you from face-lifts, Anita,' said Catherine, who'd dabbled in a fair amount of enhancement surgery. 'You look gorgeous, as always. It's not worth the recovery time. I mean, when are you planning to have this thing anyway?'

'For the hundredth time, I don't know! If one more person asks me when it is, I'm going to clock them in the head with this ring.'

Catherine held the telephone out from her ear.

'Are you really comfortable getting married?' she ventured.

'Yes, it's not the marriage part that is causing the problem!' said Anita. She took a deep breath, spoke more quietly. 'There's too much choice.'

'I'd have thought someone of your . . .' Catherine paused, struggling for a word, 'wisdom would be immune from all that bridezilla business.'

'Age has nothing to do with being sensible, dear,' said Anita. 'I thought you'd have figured that out by now.'

'Ouch,' said Catherine. Anita *was* getting crankier. 'Look, the other phone is ringing. Can I call you back later? I've some good ideas and I'd like to help with the planning, if I can. Gotta go, though.'

She sat back on the stool she kept near the register, her eyes surveying all the shiny objects at The Phoenix. Some days Catherine felt powerful and ambitious and she loved the name of her store; other days, she wished she hadn't opened at all. She barely noticed when the grandfather clock chimed, alerting her that it was three p.m. and she might want to actually do a little something before calling it a day. She'd found the clock in France on one of her trips to scour for inventory. Catherine even had a few trinkets – a silver Covenanters cup, and a cherry side table – that she'd brought back from Scotland two years ago, when she had met up with Dakota and James and taken a gargantuan box of Belgian chocolates to Gran. It had been very well received, especially the dark ganache truffles, and yet Catherine had felt uneasy drinking tea in the kitchen with Gran. You feel so a part of things, she thought now, and then you discover it was never really yours. It was always someone else's and you were just a part of the crowd.

'I miss having a person who will pretend to be interested in my laundry list of complaints.' That's what someone had said at the group session, when she and James had sat in a circle with all the other sad sacks. They'd all needed porters for all the emotional baggage they were carrying, the moms and dads and siblings and friends mired in frustrations and confusions. She and James were not quite above their nature, of course, and contented themselves by spending a good part of the time feeling superior, reassuring each other with discreet head nods and raised eyebrows. So it was a bit of a shock to be sniveling with all the rest by the evening's end.

'I miss being significant to somebody,' Catherine had said. She thought of her late parents as much as Georgia in this regard. 'It made me feel important.'

So did attention from a man.

She wasn't so different that way from many women, she realized. Even if they didn't want to admit it. If they spoke about looking for love, or finding a soul mate. It all came down to the same thing: mattering to someone else. Even her ex-husband, Adam, had relied on her, found her useful to trot out in public. She'd had a role, knew what was expected.

She picked up the handset again. The phone hadn't actually been ringing when she was talking to Anita; she'd just felt a moment of envy and frustration.

'There's not a lot of talking going on here,' said Catherine to the shop filled with furniture but devoid of human beings. 'You never ask me how I am,' she told the register. She walked over to a cherry breakfront. 'I'm fine,' cooed Catherine into the glass. 'How are you?'

Catherine strode back to her desk and pulled out a business card, dialing a seemingly endless stream of numbers.

'*Buongiorno*, Marco,' she said. 'I loved the wine – I drank as much as I sold! What a wonderful recommendation. You're going to have to sell me more, no questions about it. So tell me, what's the weather forecast in Rome this summer?'

11

Sooner or later, she'd have to tell the boys, Anita realized as she glared at the glowing letters on the clock radio. Let Nathan rant, David pretend to be interested, and Benjamin sit on the fence. 'On the one hand it's a good idea, Mother, but on the other . . .'

She pulled the covers up to her chin and closed her eyes, pretending to herself that she was falling asleep but really just listening to the soft 'woo-hah, woo-hah' of Marty's deep, steady pattern of inhales and exhales. He was a nice breather, she thought. After twenty minutes she couldn't lie there any longer, eyes squeezed shut, counting breaths.

'Do you think we're doing the right thing?' And then, just for good measure, Anita said it again. Louder this time.

'Do you think we're doing the right thing?'

There was no answer, not that she'd really expected any. Marty was a deep sleeper, and if she wanted his attention between lights-out and dawn, then she had to resort to a well-placed kick in the shins or a pinch of the ear. Denied immediately afterward, of course.

'What!' Marty sat straight up in bed. 'What time is it?'

'Marty,' began Anita, conversationally, as though they were sitting over tea and muffins during the afternoon. 'I'd like to talk.'

A great measure of a man is how he reacts to a midnight awakening when there's no flames or burglar in sight.

Marty switched on the light and swung his legs over the

bed to find his well-worn slippers, the suede toes tucked neatly under his nightstand. 'I'll put the coffee on,' he said, and ambled out of the room.

If they were going to be married, thought Anita, now was finally the time to tell him about Sarah. To tell him *everything*.

'I'm in love.' Dakota was whispering at her over the clothes as they searched for Anita's perfect bridal outfit.

Catherine continued to assess the cream suits in the middle of the boutique. In this shop, unlike the stores she frequented with Dakota, these clothes were spaced miles apart, only two or three outfits to a rack. Love was on everyone's brain, it seemed, from Anita to Darwin to Dakota. Weddings, babies . . . everything came down to sex.

Sex.

Catherine's head jerked up to look at Dakota, who was staring, waiting.

'Love?' Catherine asked, as if she wasn't quite sure what the word meant. And, perhaps, she wasn't. 'What do you mean?'

'I've met a guy,' Dakota said, before pressing her lips together and leaning her head toward Anita, who was just rustling out of the dressing room in a powder-blue taffeta skirt and a cashmere twinset. Dakota's eyes flashed meaningfully: Be quiet!

'Oh, girls, I don't know about this one,' said Anita as she motioned for them to hurry it up into the dressing room. She stood in front of a three-way mirror.

'Are you having a ball or a barbecue?' asked Dakota. 'You seem to be all over the place. One minute you try on a cream suit that looks just like the ones you wear to the shop all the time – "Oh, look, I could ring you up!" Or, "Wait, maybe I'll say, I do" – and the next you seem like you're going to the senior prom. And by senior, I mean . . .'

'Button it, young lady,' huffed Anita. 'Finding your voice does not mean saying any darn thing that comes into your head.'

Anita twisted in front of the mirror. 'Catherine?'

'I think we should go straight to Kleinfeld's,' she asserted. 'You're a bride! Why not go to New York's most famous bridal shop and try on every dress in the store. It will tell you, once and for all, what kind of bride you want to be. Maybe you really want to wear white instead of powder blue. And then we'll take it from there.'

Catherine waited until the door to Anita's dressing room clicked shut, and then she grabbed Dakota's wrist and pulled her close.

'Does your father know?' James hadn't said anything to her when they'd met up for the therapy group, and Catherine was certain he would if he'd been aware of it. His greatest fear was that Dakota would, like her mother, fall for a smooth-talking but immature young man. One who'd hightail it should problems, aka pregnancy, result. This, too, was his legacy to his daughter.

It was no secret among the members of the club that James had found it difficult to accept that Dakota was maturing. She'd regaled them all with details of how much he'd argued against her moving into the dorm. And she'd continued to bring baked goods to meetings now and again, grumbling that her father didn't get it. Of all the things her mother had left behind – a will, life insurance, deeds to the business, guardianship arrangements, the Georgia afghan knitted by the club – she had neglected to come up with some very practical things. Namely, a set of instructions telling James when it might be okay for Dakota to go on a date, for example, or a curfew hour that was in any way normal. He had gone from tiptoeing around in the months after Georgia died to trying to protect Dakota from every possible danger, including a lack of sleep. She had not appreciated having an earlier bedtime in the ninth grade than she'd had in the seventh. Staying out on prom night had been a protracted negotiation worthy of a G8 Summit.

And always, subtly, quietly, Anita or Catherine had stepped in. Suggested other options. Brokered deals. Helped reason prevail.

But sex? Yes, Dakota had heard all about it from her mother, from Anita, from Catherine, from her father. All those perfunctory discussions that had the sizzle of a bad infomercial. Of all people, thought Catherine, she should have been prepared for this one, should be ready to make sure her best friend's daughter had a prescription and be done with it. And yet she felt woozy. Caught off guard. It was easier to forget that Dakota was an adult. And like most adults, she still had a lot of growing up to do.

'Have you gone all the way?' Catherine hissed, becoming increasingly irritated by Dakota's pained expression. Annoyed with herself for channeling a Puritan goodwife.

'No, Catherine,' she said, exaggerating the syllables in her speech. 'Love and sex aren't always the same thing. Haven't you learned that by now?'

God, she was cheeky sometimes! Even more alarming – assuming the tone of voice had been a bit more arch and a little less snarky – was that Catherine could have imagined Georgia saying quite the same thing. 'No, I clearly haven't,' she replied in her mind, as though speaking to Georgia. 'So what do I do with your daughter here?'

'I'm sorry, Dakota,' said Catherine out loud, speaking calmly although her cheeks were flushed pink. 'I really would like to hear about your friend. Name? Rank? Serial number? Where did you meet? It's very exciting when you fall in love. At least I read that in *Oprah*.'

In an instant, Dakota had relaxed. No doubt she'd been

bursting to tell someone, Catherine realized. This was big news for her. For anyone. Love. It always did feel best the first time around, before all the missteps and mix-ups. When everything was fresh.

A seemingly endless stream of chatter burst from Dakota's lips: He was funny, they had a class together, his name was Andrew. And finally, the news she found most reassuring of all: They hadn't gone out on a date yet. He may not even, apparently, know Dakota existed.

Cancel the red alert, thought Catherine, but not for long, she knew. Dakota was a beautiful girl, just like her mother. There'd be more action soon enough.

Anita returned to the main part of the boutique dressed in her street clothes: a beige linen pantsuit that held up well to their stroll about town. It was a pleasantly warm June day, not too humid, and the trio had more shops to visit.

'Anita, when did you know you were in love with Marty?' asked Dakota as they exited to the street.

'Oh, that was the easy part,' said Anita. 'It took a while, however, to realize I wasn't just "in love" but that I simply loved him.'

'Huh?' said Dakota.

'What's the difference?' asked Catherine.

'Someday you will know,' said Anita. Then she caught Catherine's eye. 'And someday you will, too.'

By the late afternoon, the trio was dwindling to a duo. Dakota had promised Peri she'd cover the evening shift as Peri had plans to meet KC for dinner. Supposedly, KC had finally organized her colleagues to finish up work – on time – for once and go have a social evening together. She was also going to bring along the much-discussed potential date for Peri.

The idea of being alone in the store was enticing. Dakota

rarely had that opportunity, to just be in the space of Walker and Daughter. The shop was her home more than any other place in the world. Even if she wasn't sure she wanted it.

She hugged both of the women good-bye, leaving Anita and Catherine to forge on ahead to a milliner in SoHo.

'A hat? Are you sure?' The day was growing longer and longer. Anita was far from a relaxed bride.

'A hat might be just the thing,' said Anita. 'We'll only know after we look.'

Catherine flagged down a cab easily – it was only two o'clock in the afternoon and the rush on cabs by people avoiding the subway in hot summer hadn't yet started – and clambered in, letting Anita get in gracefully. This, she thought, is what the law about only getting in curbside had done: reduced one passenger to an awkward sit-and-slide across the middle, the other still getting a chance to settle in daintily.

'Dakota's been a bit prickly lately,' ventured Catherine, after they'd sat in companionable silence for a while and watched the sights of Fifth Avenue – Tiffany, Versace, Rock Center, the library – stream outside the window. 'She seems unhappy.'

'Of course,' said Anita. 'She's eighteen, don't forget. It's a bumpy time.'

'Yes, but she has all of us around her,' said Catherine.

'Oh, indeed. A hovering group of her dead mother's friends.' Anita laughed. 'We might want to consider that we're not that much of a picnic.'

Yes, Catherine could see that, of course. But that didn't apply to her, obviously. She wasn't like the others. It was one reason why she never really fit in. They were all quite . . . typical. And she, well, she was different.

'Even you,' said Anita, as though reading her thoughts. Catherine sat quietly as Anita discussed the pros and cons of heirloom roses, and was relieved when the cab pulled up to their destination.

Anita was quicker with her bills than Catherine, and paid the cabbie generously.

'Let's get to the hats,' said Anita. 'I'm pretty sure Marty plans to wear a ball cap.'

'Not really!'

'No,' said Anita. 'Not really. I was just curious if you were listening.'

Just off West Broadway, south of Houston, she walked up a set of spiral iron stairs.

'My mother used to wear hats to synagogue,' said Anita. 'She had quite a collection.'

'And you?'

'Oh, I haven't been to a service in quite a while,' said Anita. 'Nathan's wife is religious enough for the entire family.'

'I feel like I'm in a prison of thoughts,' said Catherine.

'Few people are content with just their own company,' said Anita. 'You spend too much time obsessing.'

'It's not something I'd expect you to understand,' explained Catherine, choosing an oversized pink hat and trying it on her own head instead of passing it along to Anita. She looked quite ready for a garden party with her head covered in feathers and lacy ribbon, she decided. Prepared to have serious conversations about the weather and the state of the charity auction. 'Oh, yes, the kids are all getting ready for college,' she'd say, 'but their father and I aren't quite ready to let them go.'

It was a nice fantasy, one of her favorites.

'Why wouldn't I understand?' Anita peered at Catherine under the wide brim.

'Because you have no regrets,' whispered Catherine. 'You are the person who always does the right thing, who knows just what to say, who is kind and fair. You and I are very different.'

'Catherine.' Anita's voice was brisk. 'Striving to be perfect will be your undoing. It is everyone's undoing. Life isn't one-size-fits-all.'

'Name one mistake you've made.'

'Letting Dakota talk me into eating a hamburger at lunch – it's just sitting in my stomach.'

Catherine opened her mouth, then hesitated, thinking again of Dakota and her reaction to Dakota's big revelation. She didn't want to be made to feel as foolish as she'd felt with Dakota.

'Anita, I never know what I'm going to do for Thanksgiving dinner,' she said finally. It wasn't exactly what she meant, but it was close. 'I'm a person without a family.'

'We're your family,' said Anita. 'Me. Dakota.'

'No,' said Catherine. 'That's not what I mean. I want a family family. Each and every day, eating in my dining room with the orange walls.'

'I see,' said Anita. 'That's a bit of a change, coming from you. Is there anyone new on the scene?'

'No, not really,' admitted Catherine. 'Well, I have a phone crush on my wine distributor. He's Italian.'

'Have you met him?'

'That might ruin the magic of the whole thing,' said Catherine. 'It's quite a perfect relationship, in the sense that we only talk. You can get to know quite a lot about a person, you know, when you're not actually looking at them.'

'Looking at each other can be quite fun, too,' said Anita.

'For once, I'm not the person bringing up sex! What is it with everyone?'

'Life!' Anita laughed. 'Relax a little, Catherine. If life isn't over at seventy-eight – and believe me, it isn't – then it's certainly not over in your forties.'

'Easy for you to say,' said Catherine. 'You have it all.'

'The sons I rarely see. Yes, I have *them*, all right.'

'You see them, Anita.'

'Sometimes,' she said, choosing an ivory cloche that fit snugly over her silver waves. 'But somehow they never quite see me.'

12

Dan's apartment was overrun by mothers.

Betty Chiu had arrived, having literally raced from her Pacific Northwest home to catch the red-eye to JFK at the Sea-Tac airport. 'Drive faster, Dad,' she'd told her husband. 'Our daughter has finally come to her senses and called for me.'

Her suitcase had been packed, waiting at the top of the stairs, for weeks.

Her original plan had been to come to New York surreptitiously and set herself up in a hotel, then arrive unannounced at the hospital. After all, they weren't just Darwin's babies. These were her grandchildren.

Maya had talked her out of that plan. No matter what Darwin did or said, Maya defended her. Betty couldn't recall Darwin ever being particularly kind to Maya and yet her younger child was devoted to her older sibling.

'She's asked us to wait, Mother,' she'd said. 'And that's what we're all going to do.'

Maya was always the more reasonable girl. Agreeable. Happy, even. A biologist like her father, she was studious and thoughtful.

Darwin, by contrast, was sullen and sour-faced. Smart, yes. But what good did all those brains do her? Convinced her that she should live all the way across the country, should get married at town hall without inviting her own mother, should write a dissertation on knitting.

And she never told her mother anything. Ten minutes on the phone with that girl and Betty never knew more than what she'd started with. Years of asking when they might have a family and then, finally, they tell her the news, and then spend the next nine months letting her know that her grandmotherly services were only to be required per Darwin's schedule.

Well, no doubt the two little ones changed everyone's mind. They knew when they needed a grandmother around. She'd been right to pack the big suitcase, she told herself now. It was going to be a long summer.

Lucie came to the hospital. Dan had reminded her of that fact umpteen times. But, frankly, that didn't count for much.

'I held Lucie's hand during her labor,' said Darwin, casting half an eye on the sleeping bundles in her arms. They were clean, fed, and asleep. Just the way she liked them. If she didn't jiggle or get too agitated, she might get a good thirty minutes of quiet. Maybe even three-quarters of an hour.

'You should try to take a nap,' suggested Dan, taking the babies one at a time and putting them in their coordinating cribs. The nursery – really an eating area in the living room converted into a bedroom with the addition of some false walls – was a celebration of sage. Light green all over the walls, the blankets, the cribs. Punctuated by the piles of onesies in blue and pink. Baby life, apparently, was very color coded.

The living room, immediately on the other side of the green wall, was already – inexplicably – filled with toys. The children couldn't even hold up their heads and yet they had more playthings than Dan thought he'd ever had in his lifetime. And the size of the apartment was only 850 square feet. Barely enough room for real people, let alone Elmo and friends.

But Dan felt proud all the same. They'd moved from their inexpensive New Jersey apartment when Dan finished his residency in LA and moved back to the city. Eventually, they plunked down everything they had to buy their Junior 4 co-op on the East Side, near the Lenox Hill Hospital where Dan was on call. It was in the back of the building and on a low floor. All very good for getting out in the case of fire, Dan had pointed out, but not so stellar for either a view or a bit of sunlight. And it was quite a tiny Junior 4, which were really just one-bedroom apartments with L-shaped living/dining rooms that lent themselves to being partitioned in exactly the way the Chiu-Leungs had done.

At least their kids weren't going to sleep in the closet, Darwin had said when they closed on the place. Of course, that was long before all the fertility treatments had added to their debt load. What with the cost of in vitro, Dan's bills from medical school and hers from grad school, the monthly maintenance fees and their crushing mortgage liable to reset within two years, Dan and Darwin were in a bit of a cash crunch. More than a bit. They were strapped.

So there were no night nurses, no nannies. It was a very unglamorous business, this becoming parents without money, thought Darwin. Lucie hadn't had any money, either, back when Ginger was born. Before she finished her film about the knitting shop, about the club, about Georgia.

'I made her dinner,' she told Dan, not for the first time, and not for the first time that very day. 'The first night she was home from the hospital. I made spaghetti and meatballs with Rosie. We took turns looking after Ginger and making food while Lucie snoozed on the couch.'

'That was nice of you, hon,' said Dan. He was tired, too, actually. There were good parts about being the dad – great stuff, actually – but the man tended to get lost in the shuffle of the baby process. As a doctor, it made sense: The woman went through the physical stress, the labor pains. But, as a father, he wouldn't have minded a bit more empathy from the world at large. Fewer hearty pats on the back and more offers to mop the floor.

'Are you hungry?' he said to his frowning wife. 'I can do Italian, too, you know. We have jarred sauce in the cupboard.'

'I don't want any food,' said Darwin, following him out of the nursery to the kitchen, which was conveniently attached to the babies' room. Even as she spoke, she opened the fridge and began pulling out leftover containers of rice and veggies. Dan kept his mouth quite shut.

'What I want to know is what the hell is going on with her!' said Darwin. She had that little-girl look that Dan recognized as a lead-up to a crying jag.

'Go take a bath,' he said, nervously watching the door to the nursery. 'I'll bring this in and you can eat in the tub.'

One wail from Mommy and they'd be in business all hours without reprieve, just like the night before and the night before that. Was this what it was always going to be like? Small things were setting off Darwin and when she became upset, Cady and Stanton picked up on her emotions and voiced their shared outrage. He wasn't too impressed with Lucie, either, but he wasn't about to make a big deal out of it. Instead, he had decided to get things under control. Dan had invited Lucie over for lunch the next day. His plan was to get Darwin up and into the shower beforehand, then smash up some tuna and onion with mayo and serve tuna salad sandwiches. He still needed to get something for dessert – fruit salad, maybe? – but he could do that on his way to pick up Betty from the airport. And the whole thing hinged on getting just a few minutes of rest. . . .

The beep of the microwave startled him; he nearly beaned himself on an open cupboard. Dan put out a hand on the counter to steady himself, the crunch of crumbs underneath his fingers reminding him to wipe it down later. Wow. He'd just fallen asleep standing up, he marveled, something he hadn't done since med school. Grabbing the rice and one of the few clean spoons – most of the dishes having piled up in the sink – he headed to the one bathroom in the apartment to make sure Darwin hadn't passed out in the tub.

They were the walking exhausted. And yet he only wished they could have become parents sooner.

'Why are you letting the dirty laundry pile up in the living room?' Betty hadn't even seen the twins yet and she was already critiquing the apartment. When Dan met her at the baggage claim, just in time to pull a very large suitcase off the carousel, she had not looked pleased to see him. Even now she was frowning.

'There is a lot to do,' she said as he carried her bag out to the taxicab line, waiting with all the other passengers to pay for a ride into Manhattan. He'd taken the subway to the airport to save a little cash. Betty had put on her seat belt and then pulled a thick yellow notepad out of her oversized purse, followed up with a gift of an old pen.

'That's for you,' she said. 'So you can write down what I tell you.' And then she launched into a coherent schedule of tasks, a conversation she picked up every time she saw him. 'And one more thing . . .' was Betty's constant refrain.

Now, Dan had always had a friendly relationship with his in-laws, who approved of his medical degree and his obvious devotion to Darwin. (Even if Betty found her daughter to be exasperating most of the time, she certainly still wanted her to be in a healthy marriage.) However, as content as they may have been in their relationship, it was clear to Betty at the airport that her son-in-law was over his head: he hadn't been able to match up the buttons on his shirt to the correct holes, giving him a haphazard appearance. His eyes looked a little puffy underneath his wire-rimmed glasses, and he was constantly yawning.

No, Betty was not about to allow these parenting neophytes to make all sorts of wrong decisions. She had come to the rescue.

'Daniel,' she said now as she surveyed the very small apartment, 'you should hire a service to come and clean up your house. I'll do it for now, but when I'm not here, you won't be so lucky.'

'I can do it,' he said, mentally calculating the annual cost.

'You have no time.' Betty had not flown all this way and slept in an uncomfortable chair between two smelly businessmen to waste her breath in a discussion. She was here to issue orders. 'Children don't need a house cleaned once a month, or even once a week. Children need a clean house each and every day.'

'Do you want to see Darwin?'

Betty shook her head. 'Let her sleep,' she said. 'I'm going to wash my hands, wash the babies, wash the laundry, and then get started on washing the floor. After that I'll make breakfast.'

'The babies are going to want to eat before all that—' started Dan.

'How long do you think it's going to take?' asked Betty incredulously. Clearly, she told herself, it was a very good thing she was on the scene.

In the space of five days, she and Dan had more homemade meals at their tiny dining table than Darwin thought they'd ever had in a row. Her mother always had one pot on the stove simmering for the next meal even as they sat down to eat. Everything in the house was an assembly line: up, feed, wash, feed, clean, feed, scrub – a kid, a floor, a wall. Funny, but she didn't remember her mother being so competent when she was younger. Bossy, yes. Annoyed, yes. But clever? No. Yet suddenly this brisk efficiency made sense, was even admirable.

Having children had somehow made her own mother far more interesting to Darwin. Plus she did the laundry.

'Our clothes have never been so clean,' whispered Dan as he climbed into bed with Darwin for their few minutes of shut-eye before Cady and Stanton started up their hungry chorus. 'Even the dish towels are folded and smell like lemons.'

The change in the household was obvious upon entering the apartment.

'Holy shit,' said Lucie when she came for a visit shortly after Betty's arrival. She'd rescheduled after Dan's invitation, was only now showing up. 'Did you paint? It's like Mr. Clean came to your house and sanitized the place. Even the dingy little corners. You've been de-grunged.'

Betty came bustling out of the bedroom, a laundry basket under her arm.

'More laundry, Mom?' asked Darwin. 'Maybe you should take a break. Come, meet Lucie.' She pointed to her friend standing just inside the doorway.

'Hello, Lucie,' said Betty, who knew that Darwin had a close friend by that name but had never actually met her. Nor had she heard too many details about Lucie and Ginger, seeing as Darwin had resisted opening up to her until she'd arrived with her rubber gloves conveniently tucked away at the bottom of her purse. But no matter: she was more than willing to clean her way to her daughter.

'You should see her suitcase,' said Darwin with enthusiasm. 'It's like Mary Poppins's bag. There's always something to eat, or a gift for the kids, or a special soap that makes my skin feel soft. It's amazing.'

Lucie was taken aback. Over the years, she'd heard one

constant theme from Darwin: She and her mother didn't get along. And yet here they were, acting for all the world like a model family.

'I have no time to talk,' said Betty. 'If I don't secure four washing machines right away, I'll spend all day riding that elevator. And don't make the mistake of thinking you can just put your quarters in and reserve a machine. New Yorkers have no respect for someone else's money.'

'What can I do?' asked Darwin, as Lucie stared.

'Why don't you put together a handful of sandwiches and we'll all have some nice lunch when I get back?' Betty nodded toward Lucie. 'If you're here, you'll get to work. You can set the table.'

Lucie watched Betty march off toward the elevator, then closed the apartment door behind her.

'Shoes off,' said Darwin, pointing to a mat to the right of the door. Lucie obediently took off her loafers and set them next to a row of perfectly aligned sneakers and slippers.

'What gives?' she asked.

'Oh, my mom went out and bought those slippers,' said Darwin casually. 'She thinks we'll be able to keep the floors cleaner, which will be important when the babies start crawling.'

'They're two weeks old,' said Lucie. 'They can't even pick their heads up.'

'I know,' said Darwin. 'But it's always good to be prepared. You know, I never realized before how much my mother and I have in common.' She motioned for Lucie to follow her into the galley kitchen, which, never spacious, was definitely crowded with two people. Darwin began pulling condiments out of the fridge, as well as a tomato and a container of egg salad.

'Who are you?' said Lucie. 'You're so . . . placid.'

Darwin shrugged. 'It's kinda cool to have her around,' she

said. 'Besides, Rosie was all over your place after Ginger was born.'

'I guess,' said Lucie. 'But I don't remember that it turned everything so upside down.'

There was an uncomfortable silence as Darwin meticulously cut thin slices of tomato, moistened the whole grain bread with just a touch of mayo, and spread a medium layer of egg salad.

'Oh, Luce,' she said, suddenly looking up. 'I just remembered that you hate egg salad. Dan made tuna salad before but it's been eaten, of course. By me. I can get you something else.'

It felt peculiar, because they'd spent so much time together for so long, to just forget a preference so easily. Friends knew certain things about the other: favorite TV shows, how much cream to pour into the coffee, and to not be able to remember such things seemed proof positive of their growing distance.

Being a friend was not something that came naturally to Darwin: she hadn't had much opportunity when she was growing up and had cultivated an aloof stance as a defense mechanism. But connecting with Lucie had changed her, opened her up to being a more generous person, quite frankly. All it takes is one good, true friend to not feel so isolated. And the thought of losing that friend was heart-wrenching.

'Lucie,' said Darwin, her heart racing even as she pretended to really, really care about the crusts on her egg salad sandwiches. 'Do you not like me anymore?'

What was going on? Sure, Lucie had had a few theories, but now, in Darwin's Betty-ed kitchen, with the crumbs cleaned out of the cupboards and a stove actually being used, she began to feel something new. Something a little surprising.

'I'm a little jealous,' she said, incredulous. 'It's been hard for me.'

'Rosie does stuff for you,' said Darwin.

'Rosie's getting old,' said Lucie, leaning against the counter and tearing apart a slice of bread, eating it piece by piece. 'I'm more than fifteen years older than you, Dar, and I was Rosie's youngest. She's gotten up there and I guess I haven't noticed.'

'Or made a point not to notice.'

'Yeah, that, too,' said Lucie. 'I've got a kid entering first grade in the fall and a mother who should be thinking about nursing homes. It sucks. And then there's Dan.'

'What about him?'

'He exists,' said Lucie. 'He's here. You have a guy and I don't.'

It had felt fair, somehow. An arrangement. She got to be a mom to Ginger, and Darwin was wife to Dan. They each had a piece of the puzzle and could share, in a way, the other part. Ginger would have a devoted auntie and uncle, always up for endless rounds of horse and Play-Doh projects, and Darwin would have a baby for cuddles and squeezes. Lucie always had a place at the table for whatever meal Darwin was ordering. In return she shared Rosie, with her stories of growing up in Italy and raising her family in New Jersey, and Rosie included Darwin and Dan in endless family barbecues during the long summer weekends. It was a trade. They each had something the other coveted.

So what did it mean now that Darwin had everything?

It meant that Lucie was going to be a third wheel. That was her fear, anyway. Finding out that what she had to offer – time with Ginger, cookies from Rosie – was far less valuable. For another thing, it made it very clear to Lucie that *she* didn't have a partner. That shouldn't exactly have been a startling revelation, seeing as she set out to become a single parent and all. But that was years ago. She'd planned very well. For then. She just hadn't been able to divine her future needs with as much accuracy.

Now Lucie wouldn't have minded someone to run Ginger to ballet class, or to have the secret knowledge to corral Ginger when she was having one of her tantrums and make her stop. Or maybe – just maybe – someone with whom to enjoy lazy, middle-of-the-night, pleasant sex. Humans like to pair up, she thought. And while she hadn't exactly become a nun, juggling a soaring professional life with mommyhood didn't exactly lead to a frequently scintillating private life.

But did it mean she should have told Will she'd gotten pregnant, maybe settled down and done the white picket fence, er, tiny one-bedroom-converted-to-two Manhattan apartment thing? She wasn't sure. Though such a future, which might have become hers had she made different past decisions, seemed newly attractive as she watched Darwin make sandwiches and flutter about. There was something so unusual about Darwin, so starkly different from how she'd ever seen her.

'You're like someone who's just had the most amazing orgasm,' said Lucie. 'You look totally calm and zoned out at the same time.'

'Uh, we're so not having sex,' Darwin reminded her. 'Even when we get the okay, it's going to be years before I'm open for business. I hurt.'

Lucie waved her off as they carried their sandwiches to the table, walking through the door in the kitchen that adjoined the babies' room, glancing at the infants, who were beginning to sleep much more soundly now. After a quick peek, the two exited out to the compact room that comprised both the living and dining area.

'That'll pass,' said Lucie. 'The desire for sex returns. Trust me.'

'No sex talk when my mother gets back with the clothes,' said Darwin. 'I'm not sure she knows how babies are made.' She laughed.

'That's it!'

'My mother doesn't understand sex?'

'You're laughing.'

'I'm more relaxed than I have been in, well, ever,' said Darwin. 'I mean, don't get me wrong. I've started a new series of lists.' She went over to a binder on the living room coffee table about three steps away. 'Medical concerns, saving for college, friend-making skills, miscellaneous. I'd have more categories but I haven't had much time to get going yet.'

'You look exhausted but relaxed,' insisted Lucie.

'I'm sure it's just the hormones,' Darwin replied. 'My mom is in my home twenty-four/seven and it seems pretty good to me. So I've clearly lost my mind, yes, but I've just accepted it as the new normal.'

'Dar, I know I said I'd be here and I totally bailed,' said Lucie. 'So I want you to know that I'm going to try to push back the shoot in Italy and stay here for a bit.'

'When are you supposed to leave?'

'Really soon.'

'What if you lose the assignment?'

Lucie took a deep breath. 'I'd rather lose a work assignment than a friend,' she said.

In a millisecond, Darwin was out of her chair and pacing around the living room.

'It's that sort of attitude,' she began, waving her index finger in the air, 'that keeps women struggling in the professional realm. A man would never do that.'

'Probably,' conceded Lucie.

'You worked hard to get to this level,' said Darwin.

'Yup,' said Lucie.

'So why on earth do you think I'd even consider letting you make such a ridiculous mistake?'

'Because I've been a lousy friend and now I'm ready to step up.'

'Well, bully for that, Luce, because it's about time,' said Darwin. 'But the kids and I aren't going anywhere. You've got a lot of time to grovel and be nicer to me. In the meantime, I think you should set a good example for Ginger and the twins about the global marketplace.'

'So you're saying . . . what, exactly?'

'I accept your kind of lame-ass apology,' said Darwin. 'And I expect you to make one hell of a video.'

Just then Betty fumbled at the door, trying to get her key into the lock and turn the handle at the same time.

'Well, one last thing, because I'm hightailing it out of here before your mom throws me in the laundry,' said Lucie, going over to the front door to unlock it for Darwin's mother and to pick up her handbag at the same time. It was a roomy blue felted computer case more than a purse, part of Peri's new business line, and Lucie found the pleather bottom meant she could load it up and not worry too much about sag. She returned to the table with the blue bag, placed it on the chair she'd just been sitting in, and withdrew two tiny little knitted hats, white with a delicate stripe of green and yellow.

'For you,' she said.

Darwin's eyes watered, just a little. 'It's just the hormones,' she yelled, forgetting – and instantly regretting – that her voice would set off her tiny duo in the thin-walled nursery.

'Okay, okay, I'll just cuddle them for a little bit,' said Lucie. 'But then I'm really going.'

Betty continued to fold towels and socks and underwear without seeming to pay any attention to her daughter and her friend. But she was pleased. A mother never tires of seeing her own child flush with happiness, she knew, as she watched her Darwin proudly show off the twins to her dearest friend.

13

Taking the PATH train to New Jersey was a regular weekend ritual for Lucie and Ginger. Not every weekend – that might have been a bit too much family togetherness – but often enough that Rosie's house was familiar (and fun enough) to be bribe-worthy. How often had her daughter heard that if she only ate one more vegetable, Lucie would take her to Grandma's for homemade spaghetti and meatballs? So it was a familiar anticipation as the two Brennans rushed around to pack up a pair of nighties and some fresh socks and panties for an overnight. They tucked it all into one roomy deep pink-and-orange felted backpack (a Peri design in which Lucie had given some input) and made sure to bring Sweetness, Ginger's stuffed bunny, tied to the outside of the bag by his ears.

Lucie worked even longer days than usual for several days beforehand to make sure she didn't need to put in any editing or production hours over Saturday and Sunday. It was important to her that the entire family be together before she left on her trip, especially since the scope of the project was continually being expanded.

'Looks like I'll be in Italy for most of the summer,' she told Darwin over the phone. The two had resumed their daily chats, though they were, by necessity, brief now that the twins were liable to interrupt at any given moment. The two of them fairly flew through the ins and outs of their days, trying to stuff as much conversation into five minutes as was humanly possible, waiting to see what would be the first to bring the chitchat to a halt: work, babies, or Ginger.

'Cool,' said Darwin, as the rising crescendo of unhappy infants began to drown her out. 'Gotta go.'

But as the Italian project grew larger, so did Lucie's worries over what to do with Ginger. Summer camp was her initial thought, followed by visions of her thumbsucker calling from a pay phone, Sweetness dangling from her arm. 'Mommy, I'm homesick,' she'd cry as Lucie was powerless to rescue her quickly. Besides, Ginger hadn't even graduated to all-day-school yet; she was hardly going to last through sleepaway camp.

Her brothers, whom earlier she'd considered and rejected, grew more appealing. It was part of the reason she had encouraged Rosie to invite everyone over to the house for a big family party: she could ask if someone would be able to add another to their brood for the summer. She'd do it for them, right?

Not so much. Sure, Lucie had watched her nieces and nephews a few times over the years. But she left most of the heavy lifting in that regard to her mother, who seemed to thrive on taking care of everyone. For Lucie, having a baby in her forties meant she was completely out of step with everyone else's family dynamic: her brothers and their wives were tantalizingly close to sending the kids to college and learning the related joys of empty-nestiness. Ginger, on the other hand, needed a bath, two stories, a sip of water, a song, and another sip of water before she settled down for the night. And that was all before nine o'clock in the evening.

The humidity wasn't too bad for a Saturday afternoon in early June and for that Lucie was grateful. She ushered Ginger into Rosie's spacious split-level home – the same place where she and her brothers had grown up – and made a beeline for the kitchen, even as Ginger took off in search of her very glamorous-seeming teenage cousins.

'Andi has the patience of a saint,' Lucie said to her brother Mitch, about his eldest daughter. 'I'm so grateful for the break.'

Rosie was bustling around the breadbasket making sandwiches – her traditional greeting. Hellos were met with mile-highs, lazy afternoons punctuated by fruit and brownies and sometimes entire meals with meat and veg, and evenings were typically multicourse buffet-style adventures.

Lucie reached into the fridge for the fresh-brewed iced tea that was always on the shelf. 'Want a glass?' she asked, her head in among the shelves. When she straightened up, her brother was no longer in the room.

'Mitchell?' she queried, walking out to the backyard, glass in hand. 'Iced tea?'

'You know, you're something else, Lucie,' he said, in the way that made her stomach drop. Oh, no, she told herself. Here it comes again. Lucie does wrong.

'What's up?'

'How can you let Mom cook like that in there?'

'You eat the food, too.'

'Yeah, but my wife helps out,' said Mitchell.

'You could do something yourself,' she said. 'She didn't sign up to be your proxy.'

'I do plenty. I muck out the leaves, clean out the garage, take the car in to get fixed,' he said. 'And what about you? Mom goes into the city several times a week to watch Ginger. She's in her freakin' eighties.'

'I know how old our mother is, Mitch,' said Lucie, taking a sip of the drink she'd initially offered her brother.

'Well, you sure as hell don't act like it,' he huffed. 'You come in here and act like a guest, letting my kids babysit, Mom cook, and you hold court at the dining room table yapping with your anecdotes about film shoots and rock stars. You aren't so special, Luce. It's not that long ago I was sending you extra money just so you could make the rent.'

She bristled. 'I've offered to pay you back many times,' Lucie reminded him. Mitch was significantly taller than she was and she hated how she felt awkward and intimidated to be reamed out by her big brother. Out of the corner of her eye, she could see her nieces and nephews observing them closely.

'I don't need that money,' said Mitch.

No, thought Lucie, *because then you couldn't hold it over me*. Wisely, she kept her mouth shut.

'So what's the real deal here, Mitch? I don't wash enough dishes for you?'

'She's losing her mind, Lucie,' he said. 'And you know what galls me? You're the only single one of us and you do the least. You think it's easy being married and holding down a job and still rushing over to take care of Mom? Where are you in this whole thing?'

'I live in the city,' said Lucie, hearing the harsh tone in her voice. Damn, she hated the way she could feel herself regressing as soon as things began to heat up at Rosie's. Everyone played the same role time and again: Mitch would stir the pot, Charlie would try to smooth things over, Brian would side with Mitch, and Lucie would alternately feel either babied and inadequate or picked on and bullied.

She held up a hand. 'I don't think you're saying quite what you mean to say,' she began.

'What the hell?' Mitch was angry now; before, he'd just been ticked off. 'I know exactly what I want to say. You're a slacker within the family, and it's time for you to make an effort.'

Lucie stood there, dumbfounded. One week it was Darwin pointing out she hadn't been so hot, now it was her brothers.

'Patsy and I have a three-week cruise planned – which you've known about for months,' said Mitch.

'I know,' said Lucie. 'Hope you have a great time. Relax a little.'

'So we're just going to leave Mom, then, is that it?'

'There's Charlie and Brian in all of this,' Lucie pointed out, hazily making out her brothers through the window. The two of them were steadfastly watching a ball game on television, and even though she waved, they didn't make a move in her direction.

'Do you know Charlie saw her drive right through a stop sign last week?' Of all of them, her middle brother had always been her favorite. He had never seemed particularly annoyed with Lucie – he was the one who taught her how to do long division and who used to come into the city to take her out for a good steak dinner when she was struggling – and it angered her that Mitch seemed to believe he had the right to speak for Charlie. He always had to be the man in charge.

'You've never skipped a stop sign?'

'Oh, it gets better.' Mitch wasn't about to take any questions. 'Charlie followed her for an hour as she drove around town. She got lost, parked and reparked her car multiple times at the grocery store, and then nearly hit another old lady backing up.'

What was hard was knowing part of what Mitch said was true. Rosie was getting in over her head. She couldn't keep up with the schedule she did at one time, or do all her chores herself. It's too much. That's what people say. It's too much. But the moment you finally admit it's too much probably comes long, long after it should have.

It also bugged her that Mitch seemed to be taking out his frustrations on her.

'So we should get Rosie to cut back on her driving,' said Lucie. 'Take a taxi to the grocery store.'

'She's not going to just hand over the keys.' Mitch looked at her as though she was an imbecile. 'I told her it was making a noise and that I needed to take it to the shop. I drove it around for a bit, brought it home, ripped out the spark plugs, and told her we'd have to wait for a new part to come in before it'll work again.'

'You lied to her,' said Lucie.

'Damn straight,' said Mitch, rubbing the top of his short hair with his fingers. 'This is what it's coming down to. Mom is not going to march into old age gracefully. No one is happy to become elderly. For a smart kid, you're pretty stupid.'

'So what now?'

'So I think we need to take turns coming out and staying with Mom, running errands, that kind of thing,' said Mitch. 'And frankly, the guys and I have decided it's your turn. You ought to skip your fancy trip to Italy and be here with your family when you're needed.'

'"The guys and I"? Who put you in charge?'

'God. When he decided I was going to be born first.'

'That may apply to getting your driver's license before anyone else, but I'm sorry to tell you, Mitch, that's not going to work here.' Lucie's voice squeaked as she felt her frustrations build. 'So you go off on a vacation, I turn down a career-making opportunity, and Brian and Charlie watch baseball and eat meatballs. What are you thinking?'

'You are not helping.'

'You want to know something?' Lucie was yelling now. Her nieces and nephews would have much to whisper about later, she guessed. 'Sometimes I'm selfish. And sometimes I do what I need to do to put Ginger first. I want to go to Italy. It's good for my career and that is good for my bank account now and my professional reputation in the future.'

'You're her daughter,' he said. 'As a girl, you should be here.'

'We're all her kids, just the same,' said Lucie. 'I'll do my part but I'll be damned if I'm going to buy into this guilt trip you're serving me. There's no rule that a daughter has to do more than a son, and there's sure as hell no rule that single people should give up their lives so married people get a break. I'm sorry, Mitch, but within this family we are equally important. Whether I have a husband or not.'

She walked away, then spun on her heel and shouted even louder, raising her arms above her head for emphasis, 'And don't think for half a second that I'm going to run crying out of here and ruin my last weekend with Mom before my trip,' she said. 'I'm going to be laughing and joking and eating spaghetti and loving every goddamn minute of this weekend, whether you like it or not.'

By the time Monday morning arrived, Lucie was still upset as the beeping of the alarm clock jolted her into consciousness. She didn't move, just listened to the insistent noise of the machine as she ran through her mental checklist: breakfast, wake up Ginger, feed her, wash faces and teeth and hands, get her dressed, take her to day-care, and then go to work. No, wait, scratch that. She was supposed to meet Catherine to talk all things Italy. All she needed was five more minutes, she thought, as she rooted around on the night-stand with one hand, trying to smash the right button that would silence the alarm. Lucie had long suffered from recurrent bouts of insomnia and Mitch's tirade hadn't exactly helped her get a restful weekend.

'You look like crap,' said Catherine, waiting for Lucie inside Marty's deli. Just below Walker and Daughter on street level, it had become a bit of a meeting place when Peri hadn't yet opened the shop. She kept Georgia's opening time – ten a.m. – strictly. Catherine suspected, with a healthy amount of respect, that Peri probably stayed in bed until nine-thirty. Now, hanging out at the deli lacked a certain elegance, and Catherine didn't quite seem to fit in as she sat at a table situated not far from the refrigerated sodas, but it was central and familiar. Besides, the coffee was great.

'Nice,' replied Lucie. Catherine always made her feel as though she hadn't quite mastered being grown up. Putting together a chic outfit. Getting a great haircut. And there was always a certain standoffishness about Catherine, something she couldn't quite put her finger on. Both Anita and Catherine were significantly well off, and yet Anita managed to seem like just one of the gang. Well, the wisest one of the gang – but a member just the same as anyone else. Catherine, however, always seemed to hold herself just that little bit apart. So meeting up with her for coffee was atypical, and Lucie felt a certain reluctance as she entered the air-conditioned deli.

'I'm sorry,' said Catherine. 'You do look tired but that was rude. I have a clinical inability to keep my yap shut.'

'I have a brother like that,' said Lucie, and found herself unburdening her worries. Sometimes when things are on the brain they have a tendency to just spill out and Lucie was on edge.

'All you can do is what you can do,' said Catherine. 'You can't make him feel any differently than he does.'

'I know,' said Lucie. 'But that doesn't make it any easier. I still want my brother's approval, you know?'

Catherine shrugged. 'My family doesn't do close-knit, so no, I can't say I relate personally,' she said. 'However, we all want to be liked and appreciated.'

'I hate seeing my mother get older,' said Lucie. 'She is such a firecracker. It's weird to think my brothers have taken away her car.'

'That kind of thing is uncomfortable for a lot of people,' said Catherine. 'I wouldn't know, though. My parents died a while back. In a way, I kind of envy you, being able to make this transition with your mother. I bet it's tough, but it also makes sense. There's not so much "why why why" going on.'

'Nah,' said Lucie. 'There's still that.'

They sipped at their coffees quietly for a few minutes until Lucie pulled out her questions about restaurants and shopping in Rome. And Catherine, who loved to share her expertise as much as the next person, obliged by revealing her favorite locations.

'There's only one problem with my plan,' admitted Lucie. 'I don't have child care. It's obvious I can't leave Ginger with my mother, and I dare not ask my big brothers to mind her.'

'The downside of having children,' mused Catherine, as though ticking off an item on a mental list. 'They can be inconvenient.'

'I thought of hiring a nanny but I've made a few inquiries and so far I haven't found anyone I feel comfortable having with me all the time.'

'Why not take someone obvious,' said Catherine. 'Someone who is available immediately, works for pretty much peanuts, and has a flexible schedule? And she knows Ginger?'

'I'm not following,' said Lucie, smoothing her hair behind her ear. 'Darwin's got the twins . . .'

'Dakota,' said Catherine triumphantly. 'How perfect would that be? She could use a bit of time away from the city, I think. There's too much temptation.'

'Huh?'

'Is Dakota a good babysitter?'

'Totally great,' said Lucie. 'But it never occurred to me to take her along – I figured she'd have a summer planned out already. The shop and all.'

'Plans are made to be changed,' insisted Catherine. 'You ask her and see if she doesn't jump at the chance to go to Italy. Besides, I'll be there, too.'

'You're going to Italy this summer?' Lucie couldn't quite put her finger on it at first. Could it be that she was actually a tad disappointed? Italy had felt like her special thing – she wanted to see the members of the club crowding around to look at her photos and hear her stories – and the thought of Catherine being there, as well, left her a little . . . deflated.

'I totally need a vacay,' said Catherine now. 'I've spent weeks just researching ideas for Anita's wedding, and frankly, I am exhausted. She's a lovely woman but a complete bridezilla. You never know who it's going to happen to.'

'When's the big day, then?'

'Oh, that's just the thing,' said Catherine. 'No one bloody well knows, least of all Anita. If we're not off trying on hats or shoes, she's over at the apartment searching through all the drawers. I don't know if she lost something or she's just under so much stress she's gotten a bit squirrelly.'

Catherine didn't meet Lucie's gaze as she was talking. In fact, she'd recently come across some junk mail of Anita's in a drawer near the register at The Phoenix. She'd clearly taken it up there by mistake. Among the circulars and real estate updates was a postcard with a stamp postmarked in March. Catherine had been so embarrassed to see it that she immediately stuffed it back in the drawer. In over a week, she hadn't mentioned the postcard to Anita, even as they shopped and lunched and chatted almost daily. It was a weird little thing anyway, with only Anita's San Remo address written on the left. There was no message. It was like a spy note. Maybe if she dipped it in lemon or held it up against the light . . . Catherine looked back at Lucie, who was talking quickly.

'So why not go to . . . Vienna? Or Scotland again?'

'I did both last year,' said Catherine. 'Besides, with you and now Dakota in the picture, we can meet up for cappuccinos and pastries.'

'I haven't even asked Dakota yet,' said Lucie. 'I haven't even thought about it.'

'What's there to think about? Your choices are a stranger here or a stranger there,' said Catherine matter-of-factly. 'Or you take someone you trust and you know Ginger will be looked after by someone who's fond of her.'

'But at eighteen, that's a lot of responsibility for a summer.'

'Lucie, Dakota is nothing if not far too old for her age,' said Catherine. 'It'll be fine. You'll see.'

'And what are you going to be doing in Italy while I'm shooting and Dakota is babyminding?'

'Oh, I'll search for pieces for the shop, taste some wines, that sort of thing. It'll be a good break,' said Catherine. 'I've become a little stuck in some bad patterns and I'd like to try and change things up.'

Using the Internet was a curious business. Efficient, in that she could type in the names of places that Catherine had given her and come up with endless reviews and commentaries on practically anything. She could find pictures of street corners, apartment swaps, blogs about airline meals. It was an extravaganza of the quirky and the unique. But there was always the danger of too much information. Googling people from the past: Was there any greater use of the Web? Wasting time researching, like she was doing right now, when she should have been working. Lucie's goal for the day had been to make significant headway blocking out shots and ideas for the series of interlinked lovey-dovey pop song videos for Isabella's new *Timeless* album. She won the assignment with her idea to do videos for each song on the album that could be put together as a single story – a short musical film, essentially – or each video song could be run individually. It was the idea of mix-and-match separates brought to music video to create one cohesive ensemble. Lucie's story concept was to have Isabella being chased through the streets of Rome in period costume after period costume, conveying the idea that her love was lasting through the ages. A bit hokey, true enough, but sometimes that had its own appeal.

Problem was, she couldn't stop opening new browser windows, the desire to do the one thing she'd never allowed herself to do in over six years. Her fingers floated over the keyboard, tracing the letters W-I-L-L-G-U-S-T-O-F-S-O-N without actually making contact. It's very hard to unmake a decision that's been made. This she knew. And yet all the talk about Rosie getting older and Ginger asking about her father and the sleepless nights ruminating what could happen if there was a tragedy. Like what happened to Georgia. Where was Ginger's biological dad? The casual boyfriend who'd shared his sperm and then found himself dumped by Lucie? Maybe she could pull a James and Georgia, build a happy family for herself now that she was in a different place and could use a little help. She'd looked to Georgia as her role model in so many ways, and now that she had all these questions, Georgia wasn't around to answer them. Sometimes it left the club bereft when they thought of Georgia. At other moments, it was simply inconvenient, such as when they wanted to ask her opinion about a stitch. Or what had she said when Dakota asked about James.

'I dunno,' was what Dakota had said when she'd asked after a night of babysitting, and Lucie warned herself not to push it, suspecting she was tiptoeing into dangerous emotional territory.

'But you were happy to meet James, right?' A bit of

investigation wouldn't do much damage, she told herself. After all, she needed to know.

'Yeah, I guess,' she said. 'He was nice. Funny. A bit weird. We did a lot of stuff together.'

'So it was worth it?' asked Lucie.

'Maybe,' said Dakota. 'Though sometimes I used to wonder if I was only ever allowed to have one parent. Maybe there was some sort of quota. Like if he hadn't come back into the scene then maybe Mom wouldn't have died. Stupid, I know.'

'That's not what happened, Dakota,' said Lucie.

'I know,' said Dakota. 'It's just a thought I have sometimes. I was just saying so. Because it's nice to have a dad. Sometimes. Not always, though. It's just what is. He's what I have.'

'And if you'd never met him?'

'Then, not to point out the obvious, Lucie,' said Dakota, speaking slowly as though Lucie were a little thick. 'But then I'd just never have met him. That would be what is.'

'It's not better, then?'

'I dunno,' said Dakota, who began shaking her head and packing up the books she'd brought to study after Ginger had fallen asleep. 'I haven't perfected my time machine yet to compare my real life against the imaginary alternative.'

Lucie paced through the house now, checking in on Ginger, who had pulled her covers over her head, no doubt in an effort to hide from the monsters who lived under her bed. (Pip and Butter, she'd told Lucie their names were, and they liked to eat Ginger-flavored toes.)

'Do you need your father, little girl?' she'd whispered to her sleeping daughter. Would it be so simple? she wondered. Georgia had loved James: there was that to consider. Lucie had merely enjoyed sleeping with Will. And he was interesting. But what were they going to do? Pick up where they left off? Well, what if they did? Would that be so bad? Sharing a babysitter with Darwin and going out for couple dates? She returned to her keyboard, at the name typed neatly in the Google search window. Waiting for her. All she had to do was press down the keys. Because odds were good that she was going to find what she was looking for, that was for sure.

All she had to do was press.

14

The worst thing about being a college student was that you had to come home again in the summer. Had to move back into your high school bedroom with its blue walls from your ocean phase, submit to your father's high school rules because it wasn't worth the energy to fight them and you weren't likely to be successful anyway, and spend every day walking the twelve blocks to Walker and Daughter to wait for the die-hard knitters to show up and get a fix. The rest of the day was just killing time. Let's face it, thought Dakota, summer is tough on a yarn shop. And it was going to be tough on her.

Sometimes all she wanted was to be at the shop and just sit; other days she fought the urge to walk on by and never stop.

This is what no one seemed to grasp: She was a motherless daughter. And her missing mother was in every inch of Walker and Daughter. It was like confronting her absence all over again. 'Welcome to Walker and Daughter. I'm the daughter, Walker's dead.'

Then again, Peri was so busy trying to take over the store and turn it into a handbag boutique that the knitting shop was apt to get lost in the shuffle. *So let her have it! I don't want my mother's shop,* thought Dakota. *I want my mother.*

The loss had become the essence of who she was. And she grew to live with the little nubbin of emotional ache that was always there, secreted away in a place no one could touch.

She even defined her friends: those who knew, and those who didn't.

Dakota concentrated late at night on remembering the sound of her mother's voice, thinking through her favorite phrases until she was sure she had her mother's cadence and tempo just right. 'Hey, muffingirl. Hey. No thirdsies.'

In this way, she could do something to prevent the forgetting.

Sometimes she felt angry, especially when well-meaning people, like her grandmothers Bess and Lillian, yabbered on and on about how her mother was in a better place. Dakota wanted Georgia to miss her, wanted her to be sad that they had to be separated. To be in some sort of heaven, but a little bit melancholy about the whole thing, you know? Eating supper with God and telling him about her little muffingirl still on earth. Have him commiserate about the circumstances.

'My experience is not yours': that's what she'd yelled at her father when he told her she was acting out, that he wasn't happy she wasn't putting in enough time at the shop. 'You have obligations,' he'd said. 'Responsibilities. It's not what your mother wanted.'

No other college kids she knew were part-owners in thriving retail businesses. They spent their summers doing internships and flying off to Australia to chase dingoes and earn extra credit in the process. But for Dakota it had looked as though it was going to be one long, hot summer, baking on the pavement as she shuffled her way to the shop and then listening to Peri lecture her on this, that, and the other. She remembered when Peri had been the coolest, most glamorous person she could ever imagine. Now, most of the time, she was a nag. Oh, she had her moments, like when she gave Dakota a makeover before NYU, going through her closet with her and helping her look like a more sophisticated version of herself. But mostly things were tense, and one or the other of them grumped through the day.

And then Lucie sent her magic e-mail. Although Dakota mainly communicated with her pals via text message, she did try to check e-mail regularly. It only seemed fair since she had such an unusual complement of maturing older ladies in her life, who still thought e-mail was all that.

'Any interest in being my sitter in Italy?' That was the first line in Lucie's message. Um, yeah. Lucie had sketched out a plan: she'd provide room, board, flight costs, and a very small weekly stipend. In return, Dakota was called upon for full-on Ginger duty. But – and this was what sealed the deal – Lucie would cover the costs for both of them to do whatever cultural things Dakota was willing to do. In short, expose Ginger to anything and everything and have an amazing experience in the process. It was, as they say, a no-brainer. And with the offer, Dakota knew she could rescue herself from a summer sleeping underneath the original Georgia afghan, staring up at the ceiling and wondering what she could do to save herself from the future that had been planned for her. It was going to be perfect.

The only thing that would have made it better was if she'd actually managed to talk with Andrew Doyle before the end of the semester. Then again, imagine how attractive she would seem after a summer in Rome . . .

'You're not going.' There was no one else in the shop – no customers, no Anita – and Peri was not bothering to play nice. The air in the shop was stuffy, due to the humidity, and tense, due to the subject.

'I beg your pardon?' Dakota crossed her arms.

'You are going to show up for work here, just like you are scheduled to do, for the summer,' said Peri.

'I'm sorry,' said Dakota, jabbing a finger in Peri's general direction. 'But the last time I checked, I owned this place.'

'Your mother owned this place,' spat out Peri. 'But you know who also has a piece of the action? That's me. Your boss. And I'm telling you that you can't just waltz in here and announce you're not going to make an appearance this summer.'

'My boss?' Dakota began shaking her head. 'What sort of garbage is this?'

'It's reality,' said Peri. 'You are a spoiled little girl and everyone else dances to your tune while I work my ass off to make sure this business continues to flourish.' Peri began pacing up and down the floor of the shop.

'I have kept my mouth shut for months,' she shouted. 'Your every whim is catered to by a cadre of women who adored your mother. And you, you just spit on her hard work every chance you get. You don't want to show up for work, you don't want the store renovated. And you know who might like going to Italy, Dakota? Me. I've never been. I'd like to sit around drinking cappuccino and reading Italian *Vogue*. But you know what? I have a store to run. And believe me, honey, you are so not *my* boss.'

'And what about Anita? She's been here long before you were!' Dakota was sputtering. 'Since when did you begin to walk on water?'

'Since I put in the time,' said Peri. 'I have paid my dues over and over again.'

'So all along you've hated me, then,' shouted Dakota. 'You were never my friend.'

'I have always been your friend,' said Peri quietly. Calmly. She sat down in an upholstered chair at the table in the center of the shop. 'And I'm your friend now. If I didn't give a damn about you and about this business, I would say "*Arrivederci!*" But I'm not going to let you behave this way. You want to be a grown-up? Behave like one.'

And what did that mean, anyway? Stuff down all of your emotions and suffocate to death in a job you didn't want? Dakota stared at Peri, feeling her hope for the summer evaporate within her.

'You don't know what it's like!' she screamed. 'To you this is just a business. But to me it's all my life.' Dakota walked over to the closest bin of yarn and began grabbing out the pink cashmere, skein by skein, piling it up in her arms. 'This one is building castles with the new shipment of yarn in the back office while my mother tallies receipts. This one is having my father give me my first bicycle,' she shouted, reaching onto the shelves for blue, for gray, for red. 'This one is coming back from Broadway shows with Anita. This one is watching Lucie's film about my mother. This one is sitting down with all of you, meeting after meeting, and having to listen to your feelings. I don't care. Oh, I know, if I want to be a grown-up, I should.'

She flung the entire pile of yarn onto the table. A skein of purple merino rolled onto Peri's lap.

'But I don't! It's me. I win. My pain trumps yours. Everyone's. She was my mother and she's gone. And everyone expects me to give a thumbs-up to running her store. You want to know something? My mother wanted to be a writer. She went into the knitting stuff because she was poor and she was pregnant. This isn't her dream. It's sloppy seconds and I don't want it for her anymore.'

'Dakota, just calm down,' said Peri, her face no longer stern as it had been moments before, but creased with worry. 'You are like a little sister to me. I was just trying to make you pull yourself up by your bootstraps.'

'There is no moment when it gets better. Don't you understand that?' Dakota sunk into another upholstered armchair and began to sob hysterically. 'It's all acting. I just want a break. I just want to get away from it for once. I just want to stop being in the shop for a while. Let me go. All of you! Why can't the club just let me go?'

'Oh, baby,' said Peri, coming over to hold on to Dakota as she cried. She didn't even flinch as Dakota's nose began to run and the whole mess fell onto her brand-new taupe blouse, didn't pull away as Dakota cried harder.

The deal was struck: If Dakota could find a replacement to work in the shop, then Peri would go along.

'I'm surprised your father agreed,' commented Peri, long after the tears had subsided. Dakota was thankful summer was a slow time at the shop, mortified by the thought of a stranger witnessing her meltdown. Or, worse, a stranger looking for mounds of pink cashmere and leaving in fear it was snotty and tear-stained.

'I didn't talk to him yet,' admitted Dakota. 'I figured, I'm eighteen, and therefore . . .'

'Do you pay for college yourself?'

'You know I don't,' said Dakota. 'It's some combo of him and the money from my mother's estate.'

'Do you control that money?'

'Not until I'm twenty-five,' she said, knowing full well that Peri knew all of these details already.

'See where I'm going with this?' said Peri. 'Chronological age does not signify adulthood in this country. It's all about who is paying the bills.'

'So I'm a kid because my dad controls me with his wallet?'

'In a manner of speaking,' said Peri. 'In practical terms, it means you're going to have to get his permission to go to Italy or you may be desperate to work here in the fall because NYU isn't getting its bills paid. Know what I mean?'

* * *

Dakota was a procrastinator. So, if she'd had her druthers, she wouldn't have asked James until she had to catch her flight. But then she realized that (a) he had her passport in his safe and (b) he was planning a vacation for the two of them. In response, she baked up a beautiful chocolate and strawberry pie, in addition to a dinner of takeout Chinese. Dakota was a baker, not a cook.

'We should celebrate your first year of college,' he said, forking up a mouthful of flaky crust covered in dark chocolate and ripe berry. Dakota felt guilty imagining the money he would spend on flights and guidebooks if she didn't say anything.

'Dad,' she said. It was strange to remember that when she'd first met her father, she was twelve, and she initially called him by his first name. What a difference a few years and a shared tragedy make, she thought to herself.

'Dad.'

'This must be serious,' he said. 'You've addressed me twice. Let me guess. You want to fly first-class. Well, I think we can arrange that.'

'No,' said Dakota. 'That's not it.'

'Don't worry,' continued James. 'I know you have to work in the shop for a little bit. We'll go at the end of the summer, after you let Peri have a bit of time off. Then she won't mind giving you a bit of a break.'

'Dad, I'd like to go to Italy.'

'Great idea!' said James. 'They're just opening two new V hotels in Venice and in Rome. The weather will be hot, though.'

'Not what I meant,' said Dakota. 'Lucie has invited me to go with her when she goes overseas to do the film shoot for that Italian pop star. I told you.'

'You told me Lucie got an exciting assignment,' said James, very slowly. 'You didn't tell me this other business.'

'That's because it's new.'

'So you'd be a production assistant? Her helper or something?' James frowned. 'I never knew you were interested in filmmaking, Dakota.'

'No, you've got it all wrong,' she said. 'She's asked me to come over and look after Ginger while she's working.'

'What?' James looked at Dakota as if she'd lost her mind. 'You want to take a job as her daughter's nanny?'

'Yeah,' said Dakota. 'I like Ginger. I want to do something different.'

'I like Ginger, too, though she's always seemed a little hyper,' said James. 'But there's a huge difference between being someone's occasional Saturday night sitter and becoming their nanny, Dakota. And I'm not sure if I'm so comfortable with that. For me. For you, a young black woman.'

'Biracial,' she corrected. 'I'm Afro-Scottish.' James didn't crack a smile, as he usually did in an attempt to humor her. Dakota wasn't so sure she was joking.

'You could do a lot of other things this summer,' James pointed out. 'Not to mention there's the shop.'

'Peri and I talked about it already,' she said.

'Before you even discussed it with me?' James felt increasingly unnecessary in his daughter's life. She had Peri, Anita, and Catherine when she needed to talk. Lucie to take her to Italy, apparently. Darwin to critique her papers. And her father to do . . . what? Pay the bills. That's what it came down to: He was extraneous. Necessary only as a paycheck.

'It just happened,' said Dakota, but her explanation sounded lame, even to her.

'No,' said James. 'No, I have not worked my entire life to have you become someone's nanny just because you think all the rules don't apply to you. You are going to be a businesswoman. Eventually you'll control your interest in the store, and you can be a silent or active partner. It's up to you. Want to do something else? Become a doctor, a lawyer, a statistician. I don't care,' he said. 'As long as you're not baking cookies or wiping the ass of some little white girl.'

And with that he pushed back from the dining table and, taking large strides, marched across the apartment to the master bedroom. He entered, and then quietly but firmly shut the door, leaving Dakota to cry for the second time in one day.

15

Anita sat at the large dining room table that had once been hers – was still hers – and waited for Catherine to bring out coffee. The two of them were going to meet the realtor and walk through the apartment, and Anita was a mix of nervous sadness, even as she was ready to let the apartment go. She didn't hear the buzzing in her compact brown leather purse, the result of several frantic texts from Dakota over the course of the morning. And while she was always prepared to look after her dear young surrogate grandchild, right now she had a few problems of her own that required a little extra attention.

She'd been so distracted when she was getting dressed that she accidentally pulled off a button from her creamy beige suit and had had to reattach it before she set out for the day. Marty had suggested no one would notice; that was not what Anita wanted to hear.

She sighed loudly, as though she had been left to her own devices for far too long.

As if on cue, Catherine came out of the kitchen backward, pushing the door with her butt and balancing a mug of coffee in each hand. She looked very chic in a slim-fitting pair of black slacks and a loose, multicolored silk tunic set off by a chain belt. Her blond hair was held back by a black headband. Inching precariously toward Anita, she handed her a cup. Anita took the drink but didn't put it down, looking at Catherine with meaning.

'Right,' said Catherine, after a pause of several seconds. 'Coaster.' She went over to a large hickory sideboard, a very nice Revolutionary piece, one of the few she really loved here at the San Remo apartment, and took out a set of wild-flower coasters to protect the nice wood. She put them on the table and pulled out a chair next to Anita.

'What do you think?' asked Anita, pointing to a picture of a multi-tiered cake in Wedgwood blue.

'Ah,' said Catherine, looking at the magazine and taking a sip of the too-weak coffee. She never could get it right: either too many beans or too few. This was yet another reason she had developed a liking for Marty's deli. 'You've brought over your stash of wedding porn.'

She laughed. Anita did not.

'I beg your pardon?' said Anita, noticing as she spoke that she'd spilled a drop on her light-colored outfit. Drat.

'Every bride-to-be becomes addicted,' Catherine informed her. 'To the magazines. The reality shows. The thrill of the hunt for the perfect dress. It's happening to you, Anita, I can see it.'

'I just want to get it right,' Anita replied, quickly adding an 'again' lest there was any implication otherwise. Stan was a wonderful man, and if he hadn't died unexpectedly, she knew she would have spent the rest of her life in this very apartment with him. Remembering coasters for the coffee.

She hesitated for a moment, then pulled out an old photo-graph. It was Anita as a young bride, a bouquet of roses cradled in her arms, Stan at her side. This was the only photo in which Catherine had seen Stan as a young man. His thick, dark hair, although neatly trimmed, couldn't seem to hold back the wave at his hairline. He was tall, broad-shouldered, and, even in this decades-old snapshot, projected an aura of self-confidence. His hand was in his suit pocket and he grinned at the camera. A happy man. A happy day.

'He was a hottie,' said Catherine, playfully elbowing Anita. 'No wonder you had three babies.'

Anita gestured with her hand, as though waving Catherine away. 'Well,' she said slowly. 'Yes, maybe. Oh, I've spent too much time with all you girls, and all your talk.'

'Hey, you give us hope for the future,' said Catherine.

'Oh, you, now, you fall in and out of relationships like you're trying on new clothes,' said Anita. 'There's nothing wrong with staying put.'

'Marty's giving you a reason to stay put.'

'He's also a very handsome man, it's true,' said Anita. 'And a lot of fun. I've been lucky. Twice. Some women never even get one chance at real love.' The words were out of her mouth before she could take them back. Damn! She really was distracted. Typically Anita took great care with what she said.

'Too true,' said Catherine. 'I'm the walking example of the woman Cupid forgot.'

'You are happy now,' said Anita, trying to cajole. 'The store, and the darling little house, and you really are looking wonderful. I like this softer blond you've been doing, more golden and less yellowy. So nice.' She reached out a hand and patted Catherine's hair lightly, as Catherine almost involuntarily leaned in to Anita. Her motherliness was like a magnet, drawing people into her orbit of kindness. Made them eager for her approval.

'It is what it is,' said Catherine. 'My life. Not so much to say.'

'I can put these silly things away now,' said Anita, closing up her books and magazines. 'My, what delicious coffee.' She took another substantial but not indelicate sip and nodded toward Catherine.

'I'm going away for the summer,' Catherine said. 'So the apartment will be easy to show, don't worry about that. I'll move my things up to the cottage and then I'm going to fly to Italy, spend a little time on the coast, go up to Rome.'

'But who is going to help me with the wedding?'

'We don't even know when it's going to be – and if we're going to try for any of the big hotels we'll have to submit dates ASAP. I don't even know if we could get something booked in less than a year.'

'All the more reason for us to plan it now.'

'You and Marty could elope,' said Catherine. It was a throwaway comment, with only a dash of a secret hope to get herself out of the potentially endless cake tastings she feared were in her future. 'Why a big wedding anyway? You don't need it.'

'Of course we don't need it,' bristled Anita. 'We *want* it. If we're going to get married, then we're going to shout it from the rooftops. And either you're with us or you're against us!' She raised a finger to make her point.

'Whoa, there, bridezilla,' said Catherine. 'I'm one of your allies.'

Anita sat up a bit straighter in her chair and Catherine felt a sense of alarm that finally, Anita was going to let loose and let her know just how little she did think of her. The moment she'd been waiting for. Fearing. The confirmation that she was just an outsider, a stray.

'Catherine, I apologize,' she said formally. 'It's not you who has upset me. It's my oldest. It's Nathan.'

'Oh, that's okay,' said Catherine quickly, feeling a twinge as she thought of that postcard she hadn't yet told Anita about. She'd have a right to be angry then. 'What has Nathan done now?'

Over the years, the club had heard tell of many of Nathan's antics. He lived with his family and his wife of seventeen years in Atlanta and very much wanted Anita to move south to live in the guesthouse. Which would have been a wonderful thing had Anita not been so adamant about wanting to live her own life. The presence of Marty caused him endless consternation.

'He's flying in,' Anita said now. 'Word has gotten around that I'm selling the apartment.'

'You didn't tell him yourself?'

'Oh, I just did,' she said. 'Last night. He asked me what the hell was I thinking to sell his father's home. So I told him what's been plainly obvious for over fifteen years: His father is dead and he's not coming back. Well, you'd think it was the first time he heard the news.'

'Ouch.'

'Ouch nothing,' said Anita. 'I gave birth to that boy, and two others besides. I'm the mother here. They're not in charge and I don't care how long I have to tell them so.'

'So is the broker still coming by today?'

'Of course the broker is still coming!' Anita frowned. 'Why wouldn't she be coming? Do you think Nathan phoned her up and told her she shouldn't keep her appointment?'

Anita checked the watch with the thin gold band around her tiny wrist. It was eleven o'clock; she'd been so busy look-ing at the magazine feature on wedding cakes she had lost track of time. The broker should have been here forty-five minutes earlier.

'That little so-and-so,' she muttered, her face flushing red. 'He's going to get an earful when I see him tonight.'

The moment he crossed the Triborough Bridge. That's when he felt like he'd returned home. The sight of the city and all the buildings reaching for the clouds felt powerful. Atlanta was a great town, he loved it, but New York had his heart. Once a New Yorker, always a New Yorker.

Nathan Lowenstein reached into his pocket and began counting out bills, getting ready for when the driver made it to their destination. He'd decided to go to his hotel in midtown, drop off his bags, and then walk the nearly thirty blocks to his mother's new apartment. It wasn't really new in the sense that she'd just moved in, but it felt strange and unfamiliar whenever he'd visited.

'You ever been to New York before?' asked the cabbie.

'What's your favorite thing?' said Nathan, not answering the question directly.

'Ah, I can hear it in your voice,' said the cabbie. 'You're from around here. Guess I won't take you the long route, then. Just kidding!' He slapped the seat beside him. 'I like the hot dogs. Drive up to the corner and the guy'll bring it right on over. With mustard. You?'

'I like the San Remo,' said Nathan. 'Most beautiful building in the world. It's where they set *Ghostbusters*.'

'Yeah, that's right,' said the cabbie. 'You know, they make a lot of great movies in this town . . . ' Nathan watched out the window as the driver continued to ramble. They drove briskly through the park, saw a young mother wiping ice cream off her son's messy chin. He smiled, recalling long summer days in the park with Ben and David, Anita laying out a blanket for a picnic of cheese and crackers and apples. His father was a serious man, hardworking, often busy. But his mother had kept things light. And efficient. She picked out their clothes at night until they were well into their teens, signed them up for ballroom dancing classes and etiquette lessons. Made sure they did their homework – but only until ten p.m., as bedtime was strictly enforced. She never ran out of time to hear about the ins and outs of their days, whether it was the trauma of middle school or the anguish of choosing his college thesis topic. His mother was one of the good ones. Funny and pretty and ready to laugh. His childhood friends, he could appreciate from this vantage point, all had crushes on her.

She loved to obsess over the details. His bar mitzvah had been followed by a wonderful party. Mother had spared no expense for music and food and she invited everyone they knew. His aunt Sarah had laughed and joked all night, one of the few times the family had been all together. She had been great fun, his aunt, taking him to Coney Island to ride the roller coaster or to look at the dinosaurs at the Museum of Natural History. She'd been at the dinner table several times a week, cooking in the kitchen with his mother, the two of them working side by side to make delicious meals for the entire family. His grandparents were thoughtful and kind, but his aunt had been more like a friend. And then she'd simply vanished. His mother took the photos out of the living room, and his father instructed him not to ask about Aunt Sarah anymore. It was one of the few instances when he was truly angered and confused by his mother's behavior. Like now.

His father had taken him aside at his bar mitzvah, showed him his gold watch, and told him that he could not believe so much time had gone by since Nathan was just an infant. 'I am so proud of you today,' he had said, 'and one day you will be the head of this family.'

In later years, his father had worried often about Anita. He'd even encouraged her to take up working at that little knitting shop, something to keep her busy. 'Maybe if you boys lived closer,' his father had said, 'your mother would spend all her time chasing grandkids.' Instead, it was declared that Mother was a textile artist, and even as things got stranger and stranger – when she seemed to practically adopt the owner of the shop and her daughter – Nathan held his tongue. Or, rather, his father held it for him. 'If it's not hurting you or your mother, then you keep the peace.' That's what he'd been told. 'One day you'll have to make the decisions around here,' his father had said, 'but your only goal is to make sure your mother is happy.' 'You must protect her,' his father had said, 'because she lives in a bubble. She's never had to face the real world.'

And yet nothing Nathan said or did made any difference to Anita. She ran off and shacked up with some guy who owned a deli, and now she was planning to sell the family apartment. For no reason other than she declared it was time for a change.

Well, it was time for a change, all right. Nathan agreed with her there. But the thing that needed changing was this relationship and his mother's attitude about it. While it seemed inconceivable that Anita and Marty had the sort of full-on sexual relationship most couples had – she was his mother, for God's sake – it was clear this man had tightened his grasp on her. Marriage was simply out of the question.

He'd done a terrible job looking after his mother, he knew. He'd failed Stan, let the family down. Nathan had worked very hard to come up with ideas that would appeal to Anita, that would take some of the strain out of her life. But she was petulant and difficult, refusing to move so he could take better care of her – refusing, essentially, to admit she was getting any older – and over the years she'd kept her visits shorter and shorter. During one dramatic Passover, in which his mother left immediately after dinner to go see her friends in the knitting club, his wife, Rhea, had yelled at him for her rude behavior. And certainly the mother who insisted on manners never taught them to leave guests sitting at the table while you went out to meet your pals.

The entire knitting thing was just the start, however, of the multiplying sense of crazy. Then there was Marty, the selling of the apartment, a wedding, and who knew what else? And through all of it, his mother seemed confused as to why Nathan cared so much about what she did. 'You're my mother,' he told her. It explained everything to him. And nothing, apparently, to her.

How awful it was to know your own mother didn't much like you anymore. There was a time when she had tucked him in at night, wiping the toothpaste that stuck to the corners of his seven-year-old mouth, and told him there was nothing in the world that would ever make her stop loving him. But there was, and it was such a small word, too.

No. He'd said no. 'No, Mother, you shouldn't live alone.' 'No, Mother, you shouldn't work at the knitting shop.' 'No, Mother, you shouldn't date this man Marty.' 'No, Mother, you shouldn't sell our family home.' 'No, Mother, you can't marry someone else.' She hated him for it. He'd lost his mom. And all because he was trying to uphold the promise he made to his father years ago.

His dark brown hair was mussed from the wind on the walk north. Nathan caught sight of himself in the steel around the elevator, his khakis relatively crisp and his blue shirt bright. He pulled a hand through his hair and turned slightly sideways to check out his stomach. Pretty flat, he thought approvingly. It was amazing what endless sit-ups could do. He'd started exercising daily once the problems began with Rhea at home. As much as he didn't want to get into a squabble with his mother, and therefore dreaded seeing her, he was also pretty thrilled. It had been a long, long time since it had just been the two of them, no younger brothers, kids, or wives around. Marty, she had promised, would be out when he arrived. Just so the two of them could have some time to talk.

'Hi, sweetheart,' Anita said as she opened the door to the spacious apartment she shared with Marty. It was a Classic Six, with two bedrooms, ample living and dining rooms, and a maid's room that Anita had the luxury to be able to use merely to store her personal stash of yarn.

'Hello, Mother,' said Nathan, feeling both elated and apprehensive. He leaned in to kiss her soft cheek. She still wore the same perfume as always, Chanel, and her scent was the same today as when he was a seven-year-old boy in 1962. Anita definitely looked older – there were more lines in the face overall, he thought – but she remained so beautiful. So elegant. She smiled warmly, her eyes sparkling. And Nathan felt, as he did every time he saw Anita, a tremendous sense of good fortune that this lovely lady was his very own mom.

'I brought you some chocolates,' he said. 'I just picked them up at Teuscher.' He handed over a large gold box tied with a pink ribbon.

'How lovely,' said Anita.

'Maybe we could eat a few and talk,' said Nathan. 'I brought photos of the kids playing in a soccer tournament last week.'

He stood awkwardly just in the foyer, taking in the stream-lined look of the apartment's decor, with its white-on-white color scheme, only a few colored throw cushions and some paintings around for punch. Even the furniture itself was sleek and modern, unlike the more elaborate rolled-arm sofas and warm wood pieces his parents had favored at the San Remo. It was like she'd become another person entirely, with different tastes. But still, apparently, the same old friends.

The phone began ringing, and his mother strode briskly across the room to retrieve the handset.

'Anita?' Nathan could hear the voice on the other end of the phone clearly.

'It's Dakota,' his mother mouthed at him, covering the receiver with her hand even though she wasn't making any sound.

'What is it, dear?' She waved at Nathan to move into the apartment, make himself at home. At home. Now there was a concept. He'd have to go over a few blocks to the San Remo to do that.

'I've been trying to reach you all day!' Dakota was sniffling and talking at light speed. 'Lucie asked me to go to Italy with her to be Ginger's babysitter, Peri got all mad about it but then we were okay, but Dad said no and now *he's* mad at me. I don't know what to do.'

She took a straggly breath, confirming Anita's suspicions that tears had preceded the call. Over on the sofa, Nathan fiddled with the pieces on the chessboard. Sensing the pause in the conversation, he twisted around in his seat and smiled expectantly at his mother. He wanted to tell her that he'd decided to leave Rhea but he was hesitant. He wanted to tell her he'd had his best financial year ever. He wanted to tell her why he thought getting married was hasty, and why he worried. He wanted her to listen as she used to do when he came home from elementary school and a glass of milk solved all his problems.

'Anita,' said Dakota again, and Nathan watched his mother turn to the phone. 'You've got to talk to me now. What do I do?'

16

Morning, noon, and night: each moment was a question of how to handle the babies' needs. What to do? And, miracle of miracles, her mother had a useful suggestion most of the time. Darwin was amazed at how her mom had suddenly gotten so smart.

Betty had been sleeping on the sofa for weeks now. After all, there was no point in her flying back to Seattle when she'd just have to come out for the one-month celebration. Not only that, but Betty took on all of the party planning, and when Dan looked more than somewhat alarmed at the mounting costs, she had graciously offered to help out.

'Not necessary, Mom,' said Darwin. 'We can afford whatever our children should have.'

'Ha,' said her mother. 'You're still taking painkillers, apparently. If you had so much extra cash you'd probably live in a house with a guest bedroom for your mother.'

'Well, we can cover the party.'

'What? And raid my grandchildren's college fund? I wouldn't hear of it,' said Betty. 'You wouldn't even share your wedding with me but now, now I can do something.'

The party, held in a good Chinatown restaurant, was a nice blend of family – Darwin's father and sister had flown out, as had Dan's parents – and friends. Dan's mother made it very clear she wanted a turn staying at the house to care for Cady and Stanton. All the members of the club were there, as well as Rosie and Dakota's father and Anita's son visiting from out of town, and several of Dan's hospital colleagues. Not to mention the two guests of honor, who put in alternately sleepy and screamy appearances. Still, it was very good, realized Darwin, to get out of the apartment. She'd been cooped up for long enough. And even though she was still wearing her second trimester maternity clothes – her stomach's poochiness had yet to recede – she'd made a special effort, putting up her long black hair and wearing a dark red lipstick she'd bought at the drugstore for just the occasion. (And while she would do anything for the twins, she paused at the idea of getting a 'new mom' do, chopped off at her ears.)

Though after a long period greeting all of the guests, Darwin sneaked over to a corner to catch up with Lucie and snack on the goodies. Breastfeeding may have been a great way to lose weight, according to her multitude of books, but it made her damn hungry *all* the time.

'So everything's all set, then?' she asked, biting into a dumpling and chewing thoughtfully. 'It's all "When in Rome" from here on in?'

'Everything's organized but child care,' said Lucie. 'I've been given a generous allowance to cover that aspect.'

'Wow,' said Darwin, surprised. 'I guess you really are hot.'

Lucie rolled her eyes. 'Thanks for the shock,' she said. 'So now I'm just holding my breath to see if Dakota can make it. I know there's the shop and all that, but Catherine is confident things will work out. She's psyched about the idea of Dakota being in Italy.'

'They're pretty close, those two,' said Darwin, who had heard quite a lot about Lucie's frustration with the fact that her summer adventure seemed to be getting more crowded all the time. 'Catherine could be very useful overseas. I bet she can get all sorts of great tables at restaurants, and there's no question she's a great shopper.'

'This new happy you is very disturbing.'

'It's all chemical,' said Darwin amiably. 'At some point, I'll stop breastfeeding and then I'll revert to fixing the world and being grumpy in the process.' She nibbled on some fruit. 'Besides, I need to save my energies for the big stuff. I've been informed that it would be in my best interests, academically speaking, to make sure my maternity leave is productive.'

'Meaning?'

'When male academics go on pat leave, you can be damn sure they're working on projects. It's equal-opportunity publish or perish, leaking breasts or not.' Darwin put down her plate. 'Speaking of, I've got to go empty out and offer refreshments to the guests of honor.'

'Wait for just a second,' said Lucie, grabbing her arm. 'I pressed "Return."'

'You Googled Will?'

'So far I've found out his phone number, where he lives, his job, and that he has both a Facebook and a MySpace page,' Lucie told Darwin. 'According to them, he's married.'

'Okay, this is a little obsessive,' said Darwin. 'Kids?'

'Yeah, and they're cute,' said Lucie. 'Not as cute as Ginger, but they have the same nose, I think. They're all freckly.'

The two women walked over to a table of Dan's relatives who'd been hogging the babies all night, and after tearing them away from her mother-in-law, they each picked up a child to take to the bathroom, where Darwin could breastfeed mostly in private.

She waved at Dan, who was animatedly telling a story to his colleagues, before she left the room. He smiled back and gave her a thumbs-up.

'So what are you going to do?' asked Darwin once they'd also dragged in a couple of chairs to the restroom. Babies, chairs, burp cloths, leak pads, water to drink, and water to wipe up the spit-up she was invariably going to get on her clothes. Every task took eighteen steps and half an hour: it was no wonder she never slept.

'It's not like you can just call him.'

Lucie shrugged.

'Can you?' Darwin threw a blanket over her front and began unbuttoning her blouse. 'That's the kind of call every family loves to get. Luce, are you sure you know what you're doing?'

'No, I have no idea what I'm doing,' she admitted. 'But doesn't Ginger have a right to know her father?'

'I don't know,' said Darwin. 'Whose rights should triumph here? Whose needs are more important? It's one thing if Will were a deadbeat dad, Lucie, but you and I both know you weren't exactly looking to make things permanent.'

'What if I've changed my mind?'

'Now *your* hormones are going crazy,' said Darwin. 'Look, I'm going to be blunt. You don't even know anything about this man. All I'm saying is that you should think long and hard before you throw a nuclear bomb into his happy family life.'

'Darwin Chiu, you are never predictable, that's for sure,' said Lucie. 'A while ago you would have told me to find this guy and sue him for paternity.'

'Well,' said Darwin, as she jostled her sleeping child awake so she could finish eating, 'people change. Life is just a process to figure out who we are.'

'You're a philosopher.'

'No,' said Darwin. 'Still a feminist historian. But new perspectives can bring us all to greater insight, no?'

Over by the buffet, KC was filling up her plate. Peri and Anita were holding a seat for her at their table, as they chatted with Darwin's mother. She'd been late, of course. KC was late to everything nowadays, caught in a line to catch a slow elevator on her way up from a smoke break, or getting to her intended destination – a dinner with Peri, the party tonight – and having to spend the first ten minutes standing outside, puffing away. The thing was, she couldn't even explain it. Like a lot of women, she'd smoked socially years ago. Back when it still had the vestiges of glamour and sophistication. And then she'd dutifully made a massive effort to give it up and take up Jane Fonda aerobics instead. So what on earth made her try it again? A little stress, a little boredom. The looming specter of menopause.

'Keeping my hands busy,' is what she said whenever a colleague from the legal department saw her doing the chimney act out on the sidewalk. Thing was, her little joke smoke had gotten way out of control. She thought it would make her feel young. It didn't. The little suckers were exceedingly more expensive than in the olden days, too. No one had forced her. There was no peer-pressure smoking gang among the legal beagles at Churchill Publishing. Just an empty pack and a nagging desire to taste a cigarette again. Would it be as good as she'd remembered? And then there was that old saying that smoking can help you lose weight. (Yeah! By killing you!) Still, KC was curious, especially as she'd felt her clothes beginning to get a bit tighter as she went into menopause. That had always been her downfall – her mother always said so: she just had to know when she might have been better off to just leave well enough alone. No doubt that's what led her into marriage number two. And yet it was that same drive that got her to law school and to her new career. Well, that and Peri's LSAT tutoring.

She returned to the table with a plate full of noodles and prawns.

'How can you eat all of that?' asked Peri.

'Easy,' said KC. 'Just watch me.'

'You must be one of those women who can eat anything they want and it never shows,' said a tall, distinguished-looking man in a dark suit. He reached out his hand. 'Nathan Lowenstein. I brought my mother, Anita.'

'KC Silverman. Not easily impressed by fake compliments.' She turned back to her food, though she nodded as Catherine joined them at the table. 'And can't Anita bring herself? And what about Marty?'

'Hi, Catherine,' said Peri, nudging KC under the table so she'd stop being so rude. KC ignored her.

Nathan half rose from the table, no longer paying any attention to KC as he watched the lithe blond woman approach the table. Catherine was wearing a black sleeveless mock turtle in a light stretch fabric over a pencil skirt; her open-toed shoes revealed nails painted a deep orange.

'Nathan,' he said. 'And if you are Catherine, then you must be our house sitter at the San Remo.'

Catherine inclined her head. 'Yes, indeed.'

'Well, thank you,' he said. 'You've been a big help, looking after things.'

'It's a beautiful apartment,' said Catherine. 'The views over Central Park are stunning.'

'I'd love to come by and see the place,' he said.

'Sure thing,' said Catherine. 'Just call. I can make sure to do some errands and let you have some privacy.' The phone in her tiny handbag began beeping: It had to be Dakota. 'Excuse me,' she said, gliding across the room to her young friend.

'You don't have to text me when we're in the same room,' said Catherine.

'Uh, whatever,' said Dakota. 'I thought you were going to talk to my dad.'

'Well, I did want to visit with a few people,' insisted Catherine. But, seeing Dakota's earnest expression, she relented. 'Why don't I peel him away from chatting with Marty?'

'Hey, don't James and Catherine seem to be pretty intense over there?' said KC, wiping her chin as she continued to tuck in vigorously to her food. 'It may not be any of my business, but there sure seems to be something between those two.'

Lucie had come over to sit down at the table, having helped Darwin return to the party and hand off the babies to Dan so he could show them off for a while. She and Peri swiveled their heads at KC's words, seeing immediately how close Catherine was sitting to James, the way she leaned in as though she needed to be closer in order to hear.

'She's kind of a pro,' commented Peri dryly. 'Men just lap her up.'

'Cat and James?' said Lucie. 'It seems farfetched. It's not as though he can only date women who hang out at Walker and Daughter.'

Just then Dakota ambled on over to the table.

'Hi guys,' she said, accustomed to joining in on whatever was the topic du jour. 'What are you talking about?' The women always spoke freely in front of her and she found their candor amusing (as when Peri detailed the really, really bad first dates she'd had) and occasionally gross (such as when KC described her night sweats and hot flashes in great detail).

KC looked up in the middle of a beef rib. She was quiet for just a second too long. 'Nothing,' she croaked. Damn, she thought, listening to her voice. She was even sounding like a smoker, throaty and hard-livin'. 'We can't even remember what we were just saying.'

*   *   *

Across the room, Catherine and James were having an intense discussion, oblivious of the other partygoers around them.

James had filled Catherine in on the background of his disagreement with Dakota, and Catherine – wisely, she thought – pretended that she hadn't heard the entire story already.

Thing was, James seemed to have definitely made up his mind, and he wasn't about to let Dakota go with Lucie.

'Oh, my goodness, James,' said Catherine, after hearing his list of reasons. 'Surely you don't believe for even half a second that Lucie Brennan needed child care and thought, "Oh yes, Dakota's black, she'll do."'

'You're not getting it. It's not about Lucie specifically,' James explained. 'It's about assumption, perception, sense of self. How I want Dakota to see herself.'

'She sees herself as an eighteen-year-old with a difficult father.'

'It's about a lot more than that,' he said.

'Look, you have a cleaning service, don't you?' asked Catherine.

'There's nothing wrong with honest work, whatever it is, and you're not going to twist me into something I don't mean. It's not about being better than somebody who cleans or babysits for a living,' said James. 'I wouldn't disrespect someone in that manner. But the truth is, Dakota is a young black woman, and I don't think she understands how people can judge.'

'So call her something else, then,' said Catherine. 'Lucie's personal assistant. Maybe she can do a little bit more, answer e-mails or something. Make it more intern-y.'

'That might be a start,' said James. 'But then there'd still be the issue of her being in Italy and me not being around if something went wrong. I've never left her side, not once in all these years.'

'You're a good dad,' agreed Catherine. 'Bossy and opinionated. But well-meaning.'

'This whole thing has just created problems all around. Anita even came down to have lunch with me near my office.'

'That's serious.'

'Look, I respect and care about Anita Lowenstein as much as anyone,' said James, pushing away the air in front of him in a gesture of conviction. 'She is devoted to my daughter. But at the end of the day, I am Dakota's father. I'm not co-parenting her with the members of the Friday Night Knitting Club.'

'Yeah, but Anita was there for a long time when you were not, my friend,' said Catherine. Their secret, shared dinners had provided them with a framework to speak to each other plainly and honestly, which served them well.

'No need to remind me what I regret every day,' said James. 'But that doesn't change my point.'

'For the record, James, and I hope you're not going to be angry with me, but I suggested Lucie think of Dakota,' said Catherine, who noticed her friend's frown. 'Let me finish. I know how much she loves to travel. And besides, there's something else. I wanted to get Dakota out of town before she did anything . . . rash. You see, there's a boy.'

'You want Dakota to nanny for Lucie because you're afraid she's going to date?' Even as James asked the question, he was secretly pleased to see he wasn't the only one alarmed by the idea of Dakota's fumbling steps into adulthood.

'I know, I know,' said Catherine. 'What sort of craziness is this coming from me? Well, there's a big difference between a forty-something divorcée enjoying the body God and his surgeons gave her and a college freshman getting in over her head.'

'Are you saying that Dakota is having sex?' James's eyes were huge and he swallowed several times in a row.

'No,' said Catherine, reaching over to pat his hand. 'What I'm saying is that she believes she's in love. And rather than let her live her life, I'm advocating interference. In the least obvious way possible: a trip to Italy.'

'I still don't want her to be a nanny,' said James.

'Well, it's just a summer job,' said Catherine. 'Last I heard she was still plotting how to become a baker.'

'Don't get me started on those damn muffins,' said James. 'But this boy information is good to know. Why have you been holding out on me?'

'Emotional turmoil,' said Catherine. 'I prefer to think of myself as too cool for school. Keeping all of Dakota's secrets. But apparently even I have an inner schoolmarm. Who knew?'

'Ah, Catherine,' said James, leaning over to give her a good-bye kiss on the cheek before he stood up. It was getting late and he had a big meeting in the morning to go over the latest developments with V hotels in Europe. 'You're always too quick to dismiss yourself. There's always been more to you than you'll admit.'

17

Bridesmaids! She needed bridesmaids. Anita called Marty at the deli.

'I don't have any attendants,' she told him, in the middle of the early-morning bagel-and-to-go-coffee rush.

'We have time, dear,' he said. 'As of last night you still hadn't decided whether our wedding was going to even be in this calendar year.' Marty cradled the phone between his neck and shoulder as he spread schmears of cream cheese on warm, crusty sesame bagels and wrapped them up in waxed paper. One after the other, as the businessmen and businesswomen stopped in on their way to the subway and work downtown, he fixed breakfast bagels. Many of his customers were regulars whose faces and orders he knew by heart. His favorite customer of all time, however, was having a panic attack on the phone.

'It's all going to be fine,' he said, and he meant it. Because Marty had a plan. He'd asked Nathan to meet him at the deli that afternoon – and he was going to take care of that kid's shenanigans once and for all. He felt somewhat sorry for the man, so caught up in ordering his mother about that their relationship had truly suffered. Plus, Anita had told Marty, Nathan had revealed to her that he was going through some marital problems. Apparently, he'd moved out of the house.

But Marty had tried to reach out to Nathan and been rebuffed repeatedly. He knew the guy thought he was a rube.

And once he'd sorted Nathan out, then he was going to figure out how to deal with this Sarah business.

Anita wasn't sleeping well, and she wasn't eating very much, either. Initially, he'd been more than happy to blame Nathan, but then it became clear that just telling Marty about Sarah hadn't been enough to relieve Anita's burden.

'We used to knit mittens for the boys together,' she told Marty as she started on a pair. They were heading into a hot summer, he pointed out, with not much call for hand coverings.

'I'll just save it until I see her again,' she'd said, but he found her sitting on the sofa after bedtime, working on the project.

'If only' had become a common refrain he heard from his almost-bride, along with 'I just wish' and 'One thing I'd change.' Age, which typically didn't garner much notice from either of them, was suddenly felt keenly. Anita's. Her sister's. The sense of time running out was pervasive and crushing.

He would do anything for Anita, and if it took moving hell and earth to get her to pick a date and buy a dress, Marty Popper was up to the task. But he worried, very much, that Anita had pinned a lifetime's worth of frustration to the belief that everyone would be all right once she found Sarah. And what would happen if she didn't?

'Who would you like to ask?' He broached the subject gently.

'You know who,' said Anita. 'My sister.' The very word – *sister* – implied a closeness, an unshakable connection. Was that true? Just because you share parents, by blood or by marriage, doesn't mean your personalities will be complementary. That you'll enjoy the same activities. Share the same politics. The easier thing with relatives, Anita understood, was to be familiar strangers. To know one another's moods just by a look, to accept all the tiny peculiarities that make up a person's habits, and yet even with all this secret knowledge to manage never to ask each other about hopes and dreams. To assume the very fact of being siblings negated the need to become true friends. This, Anita knew, had been one of her mistakes. One she wanted to fix.

'Okay,' said Marty. 'We can say her name. It's Sarah. And who else?'

'Dakota,' she said. 'And Catherine. She's stepped in to be my right hand with all the planning, and she's really a very good friend. Yes, I think Catherine.'

'Perfect. So now all you have to do is ask her.'

'Do you think she'll say yes?' asked Anita, giddy again. It had been like this for weeks, as her emotions bobbed up and down. Exhausting Marty. Exhausting herself. 'I think I'll call her right now.'

'It's six forty-five in the morning, sweetie,' Marty pointed out. 'She's more likely to be enthusiastic if you wait until at least nine.'

Catherine was lying in bed wearing her buckwheat-pillow eyeshades, willing the day to turn back time and give her more snoozing minutes. When she was in her twenties, even after she realized that marrying Adam had been a huge mistake, she just had so much stamina. They went to galas and charity auctions and she'd be up with the dawn, ready to exercise and dole out a tiny amount of breakfast. Now, one late night and she was wiped out. Ready to sleep in, although it was technically a workday and she might consider putting in an appearance at The Phoenix. The extra summer help she'd hired could more than handle the two sides of the store, though, and that eased the pressure on Catherine considerably. She peeked out one eye from underneath the mask, looking around the bedroom that had once been Stan and Anita's. With its taupe walls and its pencil-post bed that required tiny steps at the foot in order to climb into the luxurious Frette linens. Another reason to love Italy, she told herself. Buying up all the sheets.

She sat up on an elbow, uncertain. Catherine really wished James would let Dakota go to Italy. It would make it easier for her to tell everyone that's why she wanted to go, as well. Instead of saying that she felt like she was caught in a life that was more of the same, day after day. Instead of saying she wanted to meet her phone crush, Marco, and see his family vineyard. That sounded like fun. Another anecdote in the annals of Catherine Anderson, dilettante and fly-by-night. Honestly, a person running a wineshop did not need to fly off and taste at the source. She was just doing what she always did: punctuating her life with splashes of excitement. Trying to give herself a jolt. The store. The wineshop. Travel. Cute boyfriends. A new house that needed refurbishing. The thriller novel for which she hadn't written a word in weeks. So what next? Because, frankly, Catherine was running out of things to do.

And then Anita showed up at the door.

Catherine was still in her pajamas, her hair flat from sleep, when she heard the buzzer. She padded through the apartment in her bare feet to find an excited Anita, dressed in yet another light-colored linen suit, practically drowning under the weight of a binder.

'Here,' she said, thrusting the green book at Catherine as she marched in the door. Her eyes were shining. 'Get up, sleepyhead.'

'It's like, still . . . morning,' mumbled Catherine.

'I'm going to make us some good coffee this time,' said Anita. 'Because now I have a plan.'

'You've picked a date?'

Anita laughed. 'No,' she said. 'But I've picked a bridesmaid.'

'Good,' said Catherine. 'Dakota will do a great job.'

'Well, yes,' said Anita. 'But I'd also like to ask someone else. Someone who's been very patient with me. You.'

'Me?' repeated Catherine. 'I've never been a bridesmaid before, you know.'

'Who cares?' said Anita. 'This book has a fact sheet, and frankly, you have a lot of responsibilities ahead of you. For one thing, you're supposed to be encouraging me to set a date.'

''Cause I haven't been doing that already?' asked Catherine aloud, though Anita was already banging away in the kitchen. Catherine practically crawled over to the door, she was moving so slowly, and peered at Anita bustling around.

'I'm your Georgia fill-in,' said Catherine matter-of-factly. 'And I'm honored to do it.'

'Georgia what, dear?'

'I'm taking what would have been Georgia's place.'

Anita stopped her whirl of activity to gaze directly at Catherine. 'No one will ever fill in for Georgia,' she said firmly as Catherine's lip began to tremble. *What a loser I am,* Catherine thought to herself, *to still burst into tears after all this time.*

'If we were lucky enough to still have her physically in our lives, then I'd be lucky enough to have three beautiful girls standing up for me,' said Anita, discreetly looking away to pretend she didn't notice Catherine was crying. 'As the situation stands, I'll just be able to have two. But what a pair you and Dakota will be.' She continued to make the coffee – a far better brew than Catherine had ever achieved – humming along to herself. Sometimes just taking one step in a direction – any direction – was enough to make things feel as though life was getting back on track.

There were a lot of changes going on all around, from Peri's renovation of the shop to Darwin's babies to Lucie's career adventures to Dakota's insistence that she was in love from a distance. Not to mention Anita's wedding and Catherine's . . . bridesmaiding. Everyone had something new and finally she did, too. She had her official proof that she was absolutely and forever a core member of the club.

The water was running and she was just about to step into the shower when the doorman buzzed.

'Nathan Lowenstein, ma'am,' he said.

'Uh, five minutes, thanks,' said Catherine, looking down at her naked body and rooting around to find something easy to pull on. Her eyes fell on the workout gear in her top drawer and in an instant, Catherine had jumped into yoga capris and a small T-shirt. She ran a brush through her hair and half jogged the several steps to the front door, realizing as she did so that she forgot to put on a bra. It was one thing when she was trying to flaunt. But Catherine did not appreciate being caught out without makeup or being fully dressed.

'Hello,' she said curtly when she answered the door. 'You just missed your mother – she left about twenty minutes ago.'

'Too bad,' said Nathan. 'But I really came by to see the apartment, like we talked about the other day at that party?'

'Right,' said Catherine. 'Not a problem, but I thought you were going to call first.'

'Well, I was in the neighborhood, meeting up with Marty a bit later,' he said. Nathan leaned in the door frame, giving her a teasing, lopsided grin. 'Aren't you even going to invite me into my own home? Or, I mean, my childhood home.'

Catherine stepped back immediately and let him inside.

'You'll find it's very much the same,' she said. 'Only a few things are mine. Otherwise, it's entirely your mother's taste.'

'I can see that,' said Nathan, easing off a light windbreaker and tossing it over the end of the sofa. He walked to the large windows overlooking the park. 'What a view. Even better than I remember.'

He was wearing a polo shirt, Catherine noticed, and his arms were tanned and well toned. There was no mistaking the fact that Nathan was a look-alike for his father in the photos Anita had shared. He was a good-looking man. With a nice ass, Catherine thought, as she stared at his jeans-clad backside.

Nathan whirled around and clapped his hands together. 'Ready to give me that tour you promised?' he asked.

'I, uh, I'm sure you can find your own way around,' said Catherine. 'There's coffee in the kitchen.'

'Okay, then,' he said. 'I think I'll take a look around. Where's your bedroom?'

The secret to making things work out well, thought Nathan to himself as he made his way to the deli, was to always keep people guessing. That's what he planned to do with Marty next. Catherine, on the other hand, had been easy. In fact, he quite liked her, which was something he hadn't expected at all. Nathan had anticipated the apartment being redecorated, but to his surprise, much of the old style was intact. Even that long hickory dining table his mother had always fretted over. Catherine had simply been living there, as she explained to him, because she hadn't been sure where to go next after her divorce and Anita didn't want the apartment to sit empty.

She looked younger without any makeup on, he'd noticed, and she seemed almost shy without it. Her confidence mask.

He'd clearly interrupted her from her morning routine, which is what he'd intended, but he'd been pleasantly surprised to note – discreetly, of course – the way her clothes fit her body. Her obvious lack of underwear. He could never imagine Rhea coming to the door dressed that way, and it excited him. It hadn't taken much to convince Catherine she should invite him and Anita and even his mother's boyfriend to come over for a meal this week. 'Do takeout,' he suggested, 'it'll be fun. Like old times for us.' He shook her hand when he left, then leaned in for a quick peck on the cheek, one hand on her shoulder. A little pushy, to be sure. But now he knew she definitely wasn't wearing a bra.

18

Marty drummed his fingers on a table in his deli as he waited for Nathan to make an appearance, a newspaper untouched at his side. They'd been scheduled to meet over forty-five minutes ago. So far Anita's fifty-three-year-old son had managed to upset Anita with long discussions – in Marty and Anita's own living room, no less – about why she was making a terrible mistake. He even played his trump card: invoking the name of Stan.

'Dad would be horrified if he knew you were marrying another man,' shouted Nathan. Marty hadn't needed to eavesdrop to hear him, sitting in the bedroom pretending to watch television. He'd excused himself to give mother and son some privacy.

'I don't think so, dear,' Anita had said, though Marty had to strain to hear her voice, which was quiet and thin. She hadn't been sleeping well at all since she'd learned her oldest son was arriving. And he was, Nathan informed her, a proxy for all of his brothers.

'I know what Dad would have expected of you,' he said.

'Nathan,' she said. 'You may not realize this but I knew your father a good deal better than you ever did, or will. We discussed all sorts of things, none of which are any of your business. And my marriage is the same: my business, not yours.'

Marty had half a mind to step into the living room and teach the punk kid a lesson. Who flies all that way just to aggravate their own mother? Marty had always looked after his parents, both of them, and he treated them with respect. It was impossible to believe that such a petulant man could be Anita's son. She'd merely raised them, she had already explained to Marty; she couldn't control them. And especially not now that the boys were middle-aged men.

Though one might expect that a middle-aged man with a successful business knew a thing or two about being punctual. Marty was just about ready to call it a day and head home – leaving one of his employees to manage the store – when a whistling Nathan sauntered in, carrying a windbreaker over his shoulder.

'Coffee, thanks,' he said to the employee behind the counter before turning toward Marty, sitting near the wall that was really a refrigerated glass case. 'Oh, hey, Marty, I didn't see you there,' he said, his tone indicating a complete lack of surprise. 'Sorry to make you wait.'

Ah, so he wanted to play games. Not a problem, thought Marty.

'We had a time to meet,' said Marty. 'And it passed.' He stood up and started to leave the deli, waving a good-bye to his workers.

'Hey, hold up there, buddy,' said Nathan. 'I have a few things I'd like to discuss with you.'

'Could have fooled me.'

'Look, we need to get a few things out there.' Nathan took a deep breath. 'I don't want to start off on the wrong foot. And I was more than happy to meet you here instead of some sort of neutral place. I don't think we have to be adversaries.'

'Adversaries are people who are fighting over something, Nathan,' explained Marty. 'You and I don't have a fight. I have a relationship that makes you angry, but that's not the same thing.'

'Please sit,' requested Nathan. 'And I'll do the same.'

Marty pulled out a chair, and sat back.

'I'm glad we're here,' Nathan began again. 'Because we have some issues, if that word is okay with you.'

'I would agree with that,' said Marty. 'But I think they're more your issues than mine. You are Anita's son, and she loves you and her grandkids very much. All of this commotion is very upsetting.'

'Yes,' said Nathan. 'And she's made it abundantly clear that she plans to marry you whether I approve or not.'

'Yes,' said Marty. 'I know.'

'So I think there's a certain matter, then, a protection we need to discuss.'

'I couldn't agree more.'

'As you know, my mother is a woman of substance,' Nathan said. 'Significant substance.'

'Yes, she's a truly quality person,' said Marty amiably. 'But let's get down to brass tacks, shall we?' He reached underneath the newspaper and brought forth a thick envelope.

'A prenup,' said Marty, tossing the envelope to Nathan across the small table.

'Exactly,' said Nathan. 'Though I wouldn't have expected you to be so accommodating. Our lawyers could have put this together.'

'Not at all,' said Marty. 'I preferred to have my own lawyer do it. A man's got to look after himself. And one never knows what could happen.'

'Right.' Nathan spoke slowly, as though not quite comprehending. He opened the envelope.

'You get your mother to sign that and we'll all be squared away,' continued Marty. 'After all, what with this building and the few brownstones I've picked up when the market's been low, I have a nice little chunk of Manhattan. And I'd hate to see any sort of confusion if something should happen to me.'

'What?' Nathan made a face. 'Are you asking my mother to sign a prenup to protect you? Like she's some sort of gold digger?'

'Who talks about their mother like that?' said Marty, shuddering. 'I never suggested any such thing. I merely said it is appropriate to protect oneself. You'll see, if you check the papers, that your mother doesn't get a penny should we divorce or if I die. And I think you'd agree that's the best all around.'

'You want to marry my mother but not leave her anything if you die?' Nathan was incredulous. 'What sort of man are you?'

'The smart kind,' said Marty calmly. 'I know what's what in this world.'

Nathan sat there, silently leafing through the prenuptial document.

'You're not even leaving her your share of the new apartment you bought?'

'Hell, no,' said Marty. 'I bought that place lock, stock, and barrel. Though, if you'll see the fine print, it says she has the right to live there until she dies. I'm not heartless. She just doesn't get to own.'

'My mother bought and paid for your new digs, Popper,' spat out Nathan. 'I don't care how much fucking pastrami you sell in this dive, it would never be enough to buy that pad the two of you are living in.'

'Like I said, my portfolio is more than sandwiches,' said Marty. 'And you damn well better believe I bought that apartment for your mother and myself. And if you don't believe me, well, I guess I don't care.'

'You're a liar,' said Nathan. What sort of man was this joker? He'd been right to be wary.

'You're a spoiled little boy masquerading as a middle-aged man.'

'My mother is a wonderful person,' said Nathan. 'And I can't stand to see her manipulated by you. How dare you ask her to sign a prenup.'

Marty appraised Nathan. He didn't hate the guy. In fact, he understood him. How difficult it must be when your mother suddenly announces she has a boyfriend after years of seeming to settle into widowhood. For Nathan, his parents were probably still a couple in his mind, and seeing Anita with someone else must be irksome.

'Okay,' said Marty 'You're right. No prenups. But we're still getting married, Nathan, and your presence is expected at the wedding.'

Nathan didn't say anything, though his red face betrayed his anger. Without a word, he quietly walked out of the deli and onto the street.

Marty picked up the envelope and looked at the legally binding agreement he'd paid his attorneys to create. It was real enough, all right, not that he'd ever had any intention of presenting it to Anita. And her name was on the deed to their high-rise apartment, without question, and he'd happily bought the place and all the overpriced furniture she picked out to go into it. They didn't have issues with money. They were blessed with the good fortune to have more than enough of it individually, and the good sense to not let it come between them. They'd sorted out their affairs ages ago. Smiling to himself, Marty tore the prenup in half and opened up his *Daily News* to the sports section.

A breeze would have been nice, just to cool him down. But, like everything in his life these days, he got the opposite of what he wanted: a hot, muggy June in New York City, the sidewalk burning in the sun. Dammit! Marty had set him up. He was a conniving bastard, that man: he'd anticipated what Nathan wanted to discuss and then come out swinging. For God's sake, no one needed a document to protect them from Anita.

He'd been had. What he intended was a serious, man-to-man discussion, to try to suss out what Marty was all about. Nathan had fully planned to demand a prenuptial agreement, certainly, and wait to see how Marty would react: it would have been a perfect test.

If he hadn't lost his temper, they might have been able to talk calmly. But that's all he'd been doing lately. Getting angry. Feeling trapped. Suffocating on good meals and calm discussion. With Anita. With Rhea. It was a lot of pressure, being the dad, the husband, the son. The son his mother wouldn't listen to. The San Remo apartment was a symbol of everything Stan Lowenstein had worked toward, and Anita was content to just let it go and he felt powerless to stop her. Failing his father.

Stan, who always backed Anita unconditionally, would not have understood his problems with Rhea. Frankly, Nathan wasn't sure he understood them himself. He was just so . . . pissed off all the time. And the anxiety was crushing. He often wondered how he'd gotten so old – so old, man – with the kids in their teens, and every day, each and every day, looking like it was going to be exactly like the day before. He'd always been a no-nonsense sort, just getting things done, and he had to admit he hadn't thought too much about his decisions in general. Just followed along as though ticking off a checklist: college, career, marriage, kids, paying for college, looking after mother.

And then, last New Year's, the clock hit midnight and he stood on the stairs of his home in Atlanta, watching all the guests – the women who kept their figures, the ones who'd let themselves go, and the ones who'd been lumps to begin with, and the men with their potbellies and paunches and various stages of hair loss – kissing and hugging and wishing one another the best. This, he had wondered, is the best?

Rhea accused him of growing distant, and she was right. He was pulling away but to where he couldn't figure out. What he wanted was a time machine, another chance to try again. Would he pick Rhea once more? He very well might. She was attractive, but serious. Always so serious. Controlling each and every minute. The woman was married to her day planner more than she was to him. So then maybe he would do something different, too, if he had a new chance.

Anita had listened, finally, after an hour on the phone with that Dakota character.

'Maybe you'd have more time for me if I took up knitting,' he'd joked, but even he could hear that the words sounded mean and not at all funny. 'Help me, help me, Mom,' he'd wanted to say. 'Everything is broken and I don't know what to do.'

But instead, he gave her the facts that he'd moved out, the kids were fine, he and Rhea were considering a divorce and no, he wasn't sure if anything could be repaired. You can't fix when you don't know what part is broke, he thought to himself now, crossing the street to sit in the park and mull over the building that had been his family's home.

Would his kids, he wondered, one day feel this way about the house in Atlanta? Maybe his own father had taken the train to Queens and looked over his past, too, had been the better man and come home to Anita and his boys and left them none the wiser. That image, too, left Nathan bitter. Even in his imagination, his father bested him.

Catherine had ordered a selection of menu items from an Indian restaurant – chicken tikka masala, lamb vindaloo, an assortment of chutneys – and set the dining table nicely.

But, at the last minute, Anita called and explained that she and Marty wouldn't be coming for dinner after all. Something about Marty and Nathan not being able to be in the same room with each other.

'What about Nathan?'

'Oh, you're very gracious to let him come over, dear,' said Anita. 'I think he's a bit mopey is all.'

'I just ordered dinner for four people,' said Catherine aloud as she hung up the phone. She tried calling James and Dakota, but James was working late and Dakota was going to the movies with her pal Olivia. In the end, only Nathan showed up.

'Thanks for having me over,' he said at the doorway, offering her a bouquet of flowers and a bottle of wine.

'Hope you brought an appetite,' she said. 'I got too much.'

Typically, Catherine would have offered a before-dinner drink, but she was not in the mood for entertaining. It was one thing if Anita and Marty had joined them. But Nathan was new and she didn't much want to ask insightful questions and get to know him. Be polite and seem curious. After all, he was just going to be in town for a week or two. And, it didn't help matters that he'd caught her unprepared in the morning. She'd grown more annoyed throughout the day when she reflected on her morning's interruptions.

'This must be kinda annoying,' he said. 'I get it. But I'd be an even bigger jerk if I just excused myself and left you with all this food. So let's sit down, have a bite, and then I'll eat and run and you can resume your life's activities.'

Catherine was relieved. 'That'd be great, thanks,' she said. 'I appreciate it.'

'No worries,' said Nathan, once again putting his windbreaker on the sofa. 'It'll be nice to have a meal on the old table.'

'And I made sure to put down trivets,' said Catherine. 'Have to keep the hot things off the table.'

Nathan laughed. 'You have me to thank for my mother's obsession with that,' he said, ladling out a bit of curry onto some rice and taking a seat. 'I was home alone one Saturday – I must have been about twelve – and I built a molten volcano on the table. And then I blew it up. There was clay and hot liquid everywhere, and my mother had to try three different guys before she found someone who would refinish it.'

Catherine nibbled at a samosa.

'After that, even if you were just doing homework, my mother would come by and say, "Use a coaster!"' said Nathan. 'What about you? Any childhood mishaps?'

'Oh, no,' said Catherine. 'This is your trip down memory lane.'

'No, really, tell me,' he said, looking at her intently.

'Well, I stole my parents' car when I was fifteen,' she said. 'I wanted to go to a rock concert and they said no.'

'So you're a rule-breaker,' said Nathan.

'I'm an independent thinker,' said Catherine. But she smiled, just a little. Nathan grinned back.

By the time they were finished, Catherine had learned that Anita and Stan rarely fought, that Nathan had once tried to learn how to knit – he couldn't get beyond tying a slipknot, he said – and that he was separated from his wife.

'It's just not working,' he said.

'I understand,' said Catherine. 'I packed it in after fifteen unpleasant years myself.'

He showed her photos of his kids on his cell phone, told her he'd never have left New York if his soon-to-be ex-wife hadn't pushed. Nathan remembered vividly the day the family had moved into the apartment.

'The movers were carrying these heavy boxes and they kept saying, "Where to, ma'am?" and my mother was just

standing at the window right there, looking out onto the
park, and crying, "This is our view, Stan, this is our view."'
He stopped talking for a moment, composing himself.
'They'd earned it all, you see, all the money. My dad worked
and my mom just did everything else. It was a big deal, the
day we unpacked our stuff. I really felt a sense that we'd
done it all together, the whole family. That we each had a
role.'

'You don't want to see her let it go, do you?'

'No,' said Nathan. 'I came here to try and talk her out of
it, or to maybe sell it to me and my brothers. But it's complicated and we all have our own financial constraints and so
on. I don't believe in counting on an inheritance. That much
I got from my dad.'

'I hear he was a great man,' she said.

'The best,' said Nathan, feeling the anxiety rise. 'A real
stand-up.'

'And you look just like him,' said Catherine, to which
Nathan only nodded and seemed to get a tad emotional.

She had heard Anita complain about Nathan many times,
and yet this man seemed to be much gentler than she
would have expected. He was sweet, thought Catherine.
Misunderstood, perhaps. And, more than anything, he
seemed to need some time in the family home.

Catherine insisted he let her call Anita to inform her that
Nathan wanted to stay over in his old room.

'It's fine by me,' she told her friend. 'I'm just going to
move up to my house in Cold Spring tonight.'

'Well, if you're sure, dear,' said Anita over the phone. 'It
would be very kind of you. I think Nathan needs to just
wrap his head around the idea of the wedding, and the sale
of the apartment. Get a little closure, as they say.'

So it was all settled. Catherine packed up a few things
she wanted to take with her – the book she was reading,

her cosmetics – and put it all in a weekender bag by the door.

'I feel terrible that I'm kicking you out of your own home,' said Nathan. 'Your home that's our home, but still. You don't have to do this.'

'It's okay,' said Catherine. 'I'll help you clean up from dinner and then I'll go.'

But after they finished cleaning up, they decided to make tea. And, really, it seemed so silly for her to head to the train at that hour.

'We're two adults,' said Catherine. 'I'm sure we can manage to share the same space. I go to my bed and you go to yours.' But she purposely didn't call Anita back to let her know, and she didn't mention it the next day when the two of them went to meet Peri and discuss the idea of a wedding pocketbook, either.

So, for a couple of days, Nathan became her clandestine roommate of sorts, doing whatever business he did during the day and meeting Anita for dinners. He packed up his luggage and brought it over but kept his hotel room. Anita, he said, wouldn't understand if Catherine was there.

And Catherine even went up to The Phoenix several days in a row, and made the choice to come back to the San Remo to sleep each evening. It was fun, she told herself, getting to know Nathan. Having company around. Like having an easygoing, platonic sleepover. He was hot, there was no question, and he clearly took good care of himself. But most of all, he was funny and sweet, telling her stories about his parents and himself. They ate ice cream sundaes on the sofa, watching television side by side, and stayed up late discussing their favorite movies.

He told her about some of the pieces Anita had left behind when she moved. He even gave her a tour of his childhood bedroom.

'What I really want to know,' he said, unscrewing the mirror from the back of the door, 'is if she's still here.'

'Who?'

'My dream girl,' said Nathan, turning the mirror around to reveal a very 1970s poster of Farrah Fawcett, all feathered hair and big teeth and large tits barely contained in a red bathing suit.

Catherine got a kick out of that one. He was very interested in hearing about the store, enjoyed tasting wines with her, and expressed an interest in coming up with her one morning to see The Phoenix.

'I'd love that,' she said, and they took the train together, chatting all the way.

And every night they said their good nights and went their separate ways down the hall.

Until that morning. Catherine was emptying the dishwasher – she rarely cooked and the top rack was filled entirely with coffee mugs – when Nathan strolled into the kitchen wearing gray jersey shorts and a T-shirt, a newspaper in hand. She had barely rolled out of bed and she was wearing a white tank top and a pair of red pajama bottoms that had fallen low on her waist.

'Great day,' he said, coming up behind her and handing her a mug. As she turned and twisted to reach into the cupboard to her left, Nathan moved a little closer, so her back was almost pushed into his front. Catherine stood still; mere inches separated them. With his right hand, he picked up a cup from the top rack and stretched, over her right shoulder and across her front, placing the mug in the cupboard. It would have been much easier for him to put the cups away with his left hand, Catherine realized, in sort of a hazy way. Her skin tingled even though he wasn't actually touching her. Instead, he was completely in her space, moving his well-muscled arm around her repeatedly, almost as though he were coming from behind to give her a hug. It felt special, being together in a kitchen, putting away the dishes. Intimate and real. This was not the type of day-to-day activity she shared with most men, and so it felt unique. And natural. Nathan smelled very good – citrusy and clean – and all she had to do was stand there, at the sink, as he continued to reach around with mugs and speak softly.

'I slept well,' he told her, his voice quiet and soothing. 'You?'

'Um-hm,' said Catherine. She found herself wishing she'd been drinking more coffee so there would be an endless supply of mugs. She wanted to push back, just those few inches, and let her body rub against his.

'No nightmares,' he whispered. 'You?'

Catherine shook her head. Nathan was at least half a foot taller than she was, and solid.

'Oh, look,' he said. 'We're out of coffee cups.' He put his hands on the sink, one on either side of Catherine's body, and brought his mouth very, very close to her ear. 'Can I help you with anything else?' he asked, and Catherine, almost involuntarily, tilted her head and arched her neck.

'Okay,' whispered Nathan, as he began nuzzling her, then taking playful bites.

Catherine gave in to the sensation to press back with her bottom, and Nathan responded by moving closer, pulling himself nearer to her so she was caught between the edge of the sink and his body. She couldn't even turn around but she felt safe. Protected. Excited as Nathan began kissing the lobe of her ear and then, still holding on to the sink with his left hand, used his right to reach up and turn her head just slightly, so that he could kiss her full on the lips. Deeply. Still with his right hand he applied a small amount of pressure, so that Catherine was falling into him, back against his body, no longer steady on her feet. She opened her mouth again, ready for more, and he obliged, his hand on her cheek, her neck, her tank top, and then, suddenly, he was reaching inside her shirt and stroking her stomach, touching her breast.

She opened her mouth wider, teasing him with her tongue, as his left hand let go of the sink and came to her waist, slowly began to move down the length of her body and into the waistband of her pajamas.

'Oh,' moaned Catherine. This is what happiness would be like, she imagined. Doing domestic chores and making love in between. She brought her arms up behind her, around Nathan's neck, so she could kiss him again. Just as her body began to protest the awkwardness of her position, she swiveled around to face Nathan without breaking the kiss. In an instant, he had lifted her onto the edge of the sink and held her there, his hands tight around her bottom, as he sucked on her lips with increasing force.

'Let's,' he said, leaning her over to her right so he could tilt her body and begin tugging off her pajama bottoms.

'Yeah,' said Catherine, looking at her bare thigh and balancing in that direction to allow Nathan to strip her lower half completely. Crossing her two hands in front of her, she grabbed the bottom of her tank top and pulled it over her head so she was completely naked.

Nathan smiled, licking his lips, and held up his arms so Catherine could pull off his shirt for him. 'Good,' he said, 'good.' He ran his hands and mouth all over her body, stroking and caressing, before picking up Catherine and moving her a few feet, pulling down his own shorts a few inches, and frantically grinding into her on the kitchen counter.

It was quick, too quick for Catherine. He grinned. 'If you help me out a little bit, we can do it all again pretty soon,' he told her, breathing into her hair, still inside. 'Let's try the dining table. We won't even have to use coasters.'

She was delighted to oblige.

*   *   *

Over the space of four days, Nathan and Catherine sampled every room in the house. They slept in his childhood room, screwing several times in front of his Farrah Fawcett poster – his teenage self loved her, he told her – and experimented with different positions in the living room and in the bathrooms. Finally, pleasantly sore, they counted up everywhere they had been, proud of their creativity.

'This,' he said late one night, 'is just about perfect.'

Catherine felt wonderful. It was all very domestic-y, snuggling around the house, making out in the hallways, watching television and then enjoying lazy, why-not-now feel-ups during the commercials.

It was so perfect, so special, that it seemed right to keep it to themselves. There'd be time enough to let everyone know. Catherine felt sneaky, just a bit, by not telling Anita. But it was okay – someday it would be a little family joke they'd all share, right? And that would make it all right.

And Nathan was gorgeous. There was no doubt about that. He was clever and amusing and definitely knew how to use his body to please her – and himself.

'The only place we haven't been,' he told her on their fourth morning waking up next to each other, having wowed Farrah yet again with their ingenuity, 'is your bedroom.'

'But Nathan,' said Catherine, whose room was the master bedroom of the apartment. 'Are you sure you want to sleep in that bed?'

'Who said anything about using a bed?' he asked, playfully smacking Catherine's ass a few times and then chasing her, naked and giggling, down the hall.

This, then, could be her future, she thought, sitting on the sofa at the San Remo apartment. Being with Nathan, being a part of Anita's family. She could be Mrs. Lowenstein the Younger. They'd get his kids for part of the year – maybe

the summers and the holidays – and take them to shows
and trips to DC to see the Smithsonian and all the brilliant,
educational things one should do with children. And then
she'd surprise them with tickets to an amusement park and
they'd ride the roller coasters and win prizes at the midway
games. She'd even, Catherine decided, maintain a warm and
loving relationship with Rhea, Nathan's former wife. Almost
former wife. A few papers to draw up. That was all. Oh, that
was maybe a bit contemporary, the wives all getting along,
but it really was what was best for the children.

She'd seen their pictures, Anita's three grandchildren by
Nathan, many times in the shop over the years when Anita
wanted to brag about their latest accomplishment. But now
she studied the photos in Nathan's wallet when he was sleeping off the sex, covering up Rhea's face with her finger and
mentally putting herself into the picture. The photos were
a few years old, he said by way of explaining how the kids
were younger than he'd described and that Rhea was still
there in his wallet.

'It's not like I can just throw away a picture of my kids,'
he said, and Catherine agreed.

It was perfect. Nathan just needed to get his affairs in
order, he'd said. And all she had to do now was show him
how happy she was and bide her time.

19

Anita was using the minutes between the end of the day and the arrival of the girls for the monthly club meeting to tidy up the bins at Walker and Daughter. Without fail, some customer left a few skeins of the reds in with the purples, or some other colorful mix-up, and Anita enjoyed a quick sort-and-tidy to keep herself occupied. She was just finishing up with some washable blue multi when Dakota and James strode into the shop.

'Anita,' he said. 'Would you mind coming down for a quick coffee?'

Dakota was fairly bursting in an effort to stay still. 'What are you going to say, Dad?' she asked. For days, she'd been needling him about his refusal to even consider the Italian trip.

'Delighted,' said Anita, as though he'd just suggested the tasting menu at Le Bernardin instead of coffee in a to-go cup. She took James's arm and the two left the shop to go downstairs.

He didn't say anything until they'd sat down. And then he didn't begin where Anita expected, with a list of reasons why Dakota should not go to Italy and look after Lucie's daughter. Instead, he talked about Georgia. About how hard it was to move on. The way sadness rose to the surface of his thoughts at inopportune times. About his fear that he'd let Georgia down if Dakota made a poor choice. A mistake.

'Finally,' said Anita. 'Finally, you're talking.'

James shrugged. It was hard to say what he wanted, similar to the things he shared with Catherine, but it became easier as he spoke. A better plan might have been to pick a more secluded setting to spill his guts to the older woman who had been Georgia's mentor, but sometimes what matters more is what is said and not where it is said, right? This is what he told himself, brave enough not to care that strangers might see the tears in his eyes.

'If there's one thing I've learned, it's that grief is individual,' said Anita. 'Quit trying to fit into someone else's grieving schedule. No one thought anything of the fact that I didn't find someone else after Stan. Why not? Because I was a dried-up old lady. But you, such a virile man, you should be rushing out and getting married. Well, that's nonsense. Five years is a blink of the eye in the grand scheme of things.'

'I'm just so . . . at a loss,' said James. 'It's not about relationships. I date. It's about love. I can't even conceive of feeling that way again. And when I think of all the time I wasted . . . I just hate myself.'

Anita watched James intently, waiting for long periods of time to see if he was done talking. The last thing she wanted to do was interrupt. This was the chat she'd been waiting for, the one she always promised Georgia she'd be available to have, and there was more than enough time to get to talk of Italy.

'Life is a peculiar set of coincidences, James,' she said eventually. 'If Georgia hadn't been at the park that day, crying because she thought you stood her up, I probably never would have noticed her there. So you did me a great favor.'

'Maybe,' he said. 'That's crazy.'

'And yet it's the truth. That circumstance led to one of the great friendships of my life. Meeting Georgia and then knowing Dakota saved my sanity after Stan's death. You see? It would be comic if it weren't so tragic.'

'On the one hand, I'm glad,' said James. 'And on the other, I wish I'd just tried harder. Showed up instead of writing letters. I'm so selfish, Anita, I'd wish for you to never have met Georgia if it meant I could have had all those years with her instead.'

'Of course,' said Anita, not the least bit upset. 'Things might have been very different. Sometimes, I like to pretend there's a version of me living in some other dimension that has made none of my mistakes and suffered none of my pain. I like to think about her sometimes, Other World Anita.'

'I get that,' said James, pressing his lips together to squeeze in the flood of emotions. 'Who knows what might be?'

'But let's look at what we do know about this world,' said Anita. 'Georgia's life – and even her illness and death – led all of us to new things. Different decisions. They seem less attractive from this vantage point, maybe, less what you wanted. But in the end they're just different.'

'I was an asshole,' he said bluntly. 'And I'm paying with my heart for the rest of my life. It'll never be enough. When do I get over the loss?'

'When you forgive yourself for all the things you can never change,' advised Anita. 'She loved you. You, and Dakota, and Catherine. If Georgia could see your true self, why can't you?'

'I can't ever have anyone in my life like that again,' he said with finality. 'I would never expect someone to just accept that my sadness is never going to go away. They'd always know they were second best.'

'The sadness is just part of who you are now, James,' said Anita. 'You'll find that person. You will. And when you do, you'll finally be ready to let it go.'

'What now? Decide to let Dakota go off to Italy and find myself all alone?'

'She's going to grow up whether you like it or not,' said

Anita. 'And there will be moments when you might not even enjoy her company. Trust me, it happens. But the love never changes. There never comes a moment when you wouldn't throw yourself in front of a bus to save her life. Trouble is, you only hurt her when you hold her back.'

'There were some options I thought of,' he said. 'Ways to maybe make this summer thing work out.'

'And maybe putting a little space between you and Dakota would help you with your own emotions about Georgia,' said Anita. 'You're smothering her because you're afraid to lose her mother all over again. That'll never do.'

'So what now?'

Anita shook her head. 'I can't tell you. Grief has no timetable. Anyone who tells you otherwise is lying to you, and to themselves,' she said. 'We grieve loss. It's not always about death.'

Anita had news of her own, she told James.

'I'm going to let the girls know tonight that we're holding off on the wedding for a little bit,' she said.

'Nathan?' asked James. But Anita shook her head.

'I have a younger sister,' she began. 'And she's out there. Somewhere. I suppose that, technically speaking, she ran away. But not before I told her to get lost. Years ago, when I thought I was far wiser than I am.'

'Anita, I don't buy it,' said James. 'You're too good to do anything like that.'

'Like anyone, I've learned from my mistakes. It's a terrible thing, what we can say to each other,' she said. 'And, to be honest, from this vantage point the details don't much matter anymore. Years flash by in an instant and one day you find an old photo and it's time to stop pretending that a part of your family is missing.'

'So your sister's alive, then?' James looked puzzled.

Anita reached for a napkin from the dispenser to dab at

her nose. 'If you can believe it, I genuinely don't know,' she said. 'I spent forty years grieving the loss of my sister, and all that time I could have done something about finding her. But I expected she should come to me. And why? Being open to a reconciliation is not the same as making an effort. That's why I had you to lunch that day when you returned in Georgia's life. I needed to find out if you were genuine.'

'I don't know what to say,' he said.

'We're more alike than you may know,' said Anita. 'And in many ways, you were much braver than I've ever been. I don't think it's strange you ache for Georgia, James. I still miss Stan and I also love Marty. It's not a tap you can just turn off.'

'And your sister?'

'Sarah.' Anita pulled out another napkin. 'She had wild curly hair. Dark. The day I saw Georgia sitting in the park, crying, I thought, "Maybe there's Sarah." That's what drew me to her, with her knitting. But that was fantasy, of course. Sarah would have been in her late forties by the time I met Georgia. The mind, it can play tricks. And in this case, how lucky for me that it did. So you see? Actions and reactions. Choices.'

'I never knew,' said James.

'Of course you didn't,' she said, using her hands to pat her cheeks and smooth out her face. 'We all typically don't go around revealing our secret shames. But, sometimes, we are graced with enough awareness to learn from them. Marty and I are going to find her, James. And then we're going to bring my sister home and have our wonderful wedding. All of us, together.'

Upstairs, the women were getting down to the serious business of eating Dakota's maple apple muffins, and sampling chocolate-dipped biscotti. Dakota had been up most of the night, baking, trying to ease her stress.

'I almost forgot,' she said. 'I also brought ginger sparklers.' The soft ginger cookies were a favorite of Lucie's daughter, who enjoyed not only the chewy texture of the treat but also the name.

'Speaking of all things Ginger,' said Lucie, 'I went looking for her father.' She swallowed a mouthful of muffin and, without even being aware of it, reached into the Tupperware container to take out a second muffin. Just to save for later.

'That's a little out of left field,' said Peri, nibbling thoughtfully.

'Yeah,' admitted Lucie. 'But he was easy to find. He doesn't work at Sloan-Kettering anymore but at a pharmaceutical company up in Connecticut.'

'Did you find his address?' asked Peri.

'E-mail and home. Right off the bat,' said Lucie. 'And then I looked up the cost of his house.'

'Whoa,' said KC. 'You are serious, lady.'

Lucie stopped knitting her throw to reflect. 'I don't know. Am I? It's been several days and I haven't called.'

'So five years is nothing but three days seems like a long time?' asked Peri.

'And now I know Ginger has a little brother and another on the way,' added Lucie, not answering Peri's question.

'How?'

'People put photos all over the Web. I found their own postings and I even found ones at Flickr from when they went to a friend's wedding.'

'How much of your day are you spending on this stuff?' asked Dakota, who was only half listening to the chatter as she wondered whether Anita could work her magic on James.

'Clearly too much,' interjected Darwin. 'I think you should talk to a therapist before you make any rash decisions based on middle-of-the-night Google searches.'

'Maybe,' said Lucie. 'But I've been wondering if I should

change that. Send him one of those "Dear Sperm Donor" letters.'

'Those are meant for men who were paid for their genetic material, hon,' said KC. 'You're more of an old-fashioned paternity suit waiting to happen.'

'Oh, I wasn't planning on suing him for child support,' said Lucie. 'That doesn't seem quite fair.'

'Did you force him to have unprotected sex?'

Lucie laughed. 'No, he was a willing accomplice.'

'Then, folks, we have a winner,' said KC. 'You can go after him if you want to. You spill it, you pay for it. That's how the system works.'

'That's not my motive, KC,' said Lucie. 'I'm not looking for a paycheck – I can take care of us just fine.'

'So what, then?' asked KC, who'd always been more direct than tactful.

'I don't know,' admitted Lucie, who'd been packing for Italy for days, trying to organize her computers and her papers and squabbling with Ginger about why she couldn't bring more than one suitcase filled with toys. She was tired and confused, and as she packed, she'd spent chunks of time on the phone with Darwin, weighing the pros and cons of reaching out to Will. Even now, she couldn't decide which option made more sense. 'Maybe I'm just weird,' she said now.

'We all have someone we wonder about,' piped up Catherine. 'The person who looms large in our imagination, whether they were ever as great as we remember or not.'

'Like you and Georgia,' said Darwin. 'You came to the store to find her.'

'And you know what? She's still the one I wonder about,' said Catherine. 'Where is she now? What is she thinking? Can she hear my thoughts?'

'I think that kind of stuff, too,' said Dakota.

'Me, too,' said Peri. 'I wonder what she thinks of the new paint job, or what she'd say when I order too much inventory.'

'No doubt she'd have prevented me from smoking,' said KC. 'There. I've come clean. I'm a smoker. A habitual puffer.'

'I don't think she could have stopped you from smoking,' said Dakota, shaking her head.

'I don't think so, either, kiddo,' laughed KC. 'I'm a lost cause. But as great as Georgia was, she would so kick our asses for spending too much of our lives pining. I just call it like I see it.'

'She'd like to be remembered, though,' said Darwin.

'For sure,' agreed KC. 'She had an ego even when she was just answering phones. And she could have just called this store A Whole Bunch of Yarn on Sale Here but instead she put her own name on the door. She was proud, and rightly so.'

'But don't dwell on her, right?'

'Dwell schmell,' said KC. 'Don't you think Georgia has enough going on trying to get James to let Dakota go to Italy? The rest of us could give her a break, let her spend more time going to the spa or whatever it is that goes on in the ether.'

'You really think she wants me to go to Italy, KC?'

'For sure, Little Walker,' said KC. 'Since never has James come to a meeting and asked to speak to Anita. That's gotta be a sure sign something's going on.' She reached across the group to do a multi-grab in one lean, snagging both a maple apple muffin and a biscotto. Taking a bite, KC winked at Dakota, who was frowning in concentration, wishing she could hear the chitchat one floor below.

'Okay, new topic, right?' asked Dakota. 'So, Catherine, what's in the bag?' Dakota pointed to the compact shopping bag Catherine had brought with her to the meeting.

'La Petite Nuit?' said KC. 'Isn't that the racy little lingerie shop around the corner?'

'I don't know how any of you can even think about sex,' said Darwin. 'I'm never going to go there again.'

'Another month or two, hon, and then it all comes back,' reassured Lucie. 'But in the meantime, share some details. Because surely you didn't bring a lingerie purchase into the Friday Night Knitting Club if you didn't intend to be asked about it. Am I right?'

'Oh, you're right,' seconded KC. 'So who are you seeing?'

'Someone,' said Catherine, who couldn't help but smile.

'Someone we know?' KC was persistent.

'Someone some of you know,' said Catherine. 'But all of you have met him.'

'It's James,' said KC, a note of triumph in her voice. 'You and James are in love. Don't ask me how I know. I'm perceptive about these things.'

'What?' Dakota turned to Catherine. 'Is this true?'

'No way,' said Catherine.

'Okay, okay,' said KC, waving her hand as though to quiet down some nonexistent applause. 'I'll tell you how I know. I saw you guys eating dinner together last month and you looked so cute, sitting all crunched up together and totally ignoring your waitress.'

'What?' Dakota turned to Catherine. 'Is *that* true?'

'Uh, yeah, but not like how she's saying,' she said. 'We're just . . . friends.'

'Like you can be just friends with a man as good-looking as James Foster,' said Peri. 'You know, I would like to find a guy. I'm almost thirty here and things are pretty dry. I'd like to find a black man, to be perfectly honest. But apparently all the good ones are chasing women like you.'

'You're like twenty years younger than my dad,' said

Dakota to Peri, 'so that's totally gross. And you're one of my best friends, so that's even worse, Catherine.'

'I didn't do anything,' said Catherine, raising her voice. 'I didn't buy this sexy little number for James, that's for sure, and James and I don't owe any of you explanations for the fact that we sometimes eat a meal together. And by the way, if spying isn't against the law, KC, then it should be.'

Lucie and Darwin were getting ready to referee when Anita returned to the shop, a bit out of breath from racing up the stairs. She was so excited to share her news that she didn't notice the tension in the room.

'Okay, girls, it looks like it's time to start the Friday Night Knitting Club: Italian edition!' She raised her hands in the air to quiet them, though no one else was speaking. 'Dakota, your father has agreed you can go with Lucie, but he has some further details he'd like the three of you to work out. More on that later.'

Dakota began screaming and raced over to hug Anita.

'Gentle, dear, gentle,' said Anita. 'I also want to tell all of you tonight that Marty and I are postponing our wedding planning while we take a trip this summer.'

'Is something wrong, Anita?' asked Peri, who was hard at work on knitting an intricate but tiny pocketbook to match Anita's knitted wedding coat.

'No,' said Anita, hesitating. 'Well, yes, in fact. But it's nothing to do with Marty.'

She came over to the table and sat down. 'I have a sister,' she began, 'and I haven't spoken to her in more years than many of you have been alive.'

'Where is she?' asked Dakota.

'I don't know,' admitted Anita. 'So we'll be sailing to Europe shortly to try and find her.'

'How do you know she's in Europe?' asked Dakota.

'I don't,' admitted Anita. 'But I have a hunch.'

'We're all going on adventures,' said Dakota, looking away when she saw Peri's face. 'Sort of.'

'Well, Catherine, with the wedding planning on hold,' said Anita, 'I think you can head off to that vineyard guilt-free now!'

'Oh, I don't think I'm going anymore,' she said. 'I was considering a trip down South.' She looked meaningfully at Anita but the older woman didn't seem to pay attention, too busy catching her breath so she could keep talking.

'Peri, I promise to make sure you get a very solid two-week vacation in September, after the charity walk. Darwin, keep doing what you're doing. And KC, I have a plan on how to stop smoking.'

She reached in for a piece of biscotti.

'I'm just so relieved and excited how everything is coming together,' said Anita. 'It's been a very stressful several weeks for me. And, Catherine, you'll be pleased to know you can move back to the apartment until we sell. Nathan just called to let me know he's going back to Atlanta. I'm so relieved: I had a long talk with him over lunch today and I guess I made real progress.' Anita beamed. 'He's going to try and work things out with his wife.'

Intermediate

You're getting better – smarter, quicker, faster – and yet you know just enough to realize how much you still have to learn. Now is when you are ready to take chances. To figure out just how far you want to go.

20

Not every mistake needs to be confessed. Nor every detail shared. That is the one thing she'd learned over her lifetime.

Catherine felt humiliated by Nathan even though their romance – if you could even call it that, she thought to herself – was known only to them. Rejection always hurts. There'd been a phone call that she let go to voice mail, and an e-mail she'd deleted. The details didn't matter, did they, now that he'd decided? A conclusion was a conclusion. The end.

Besides, what could he tell her anyway that she didn't already know? He had a family, she was a fling. And it stung.

'Water,' she told the flight attendant, who'd had to ask twice what she wanted to jolt Catherine out of her reverie. 'Sparkling. With lime.'

What a relief it might be to tell Anita, or the members of the club, about yet another maybe-relationship dissolving just as she was pouring her heart into it. But how could she do that now? Sometimes the great relief of unburdening oneself only adds to someone else's burden. What could she expect Anita to do? How uncomfortable it would be for all concerned. And there would be no point in choosing sides because the only side for Anita to choose was Nathan's. As forgiving as Anita was, she might not be very understanding about Catherine sleeping with her married son, in what was once Anita's very own bedroom, no less.

Imagine: If she and Nathan had worked, it would have been glorious. But revealing the failed romance would only result in potential embarrassment and shame for all concerned.

No, Catherine got herself into the mess, and she was a big enough girl to keep her mouth shut about it.

So there were no middle-of-the-night phone calls, no e-mails, no follow-up of any kind to disrupt what she assumed was Nathan's happy reunion in Atlanta. When the laundry came back – she always sent it out on Mondays and Thursdays – and she found a clean pair of his underwear tucked in with her things, she promptly took a pair of scissors and therapeutically cut them up before throwing them away. Then she did a thorough once-over of the apartment, tossing out anything he'd touched: a bar of soap, a barely used tube of toothpaste, the box of cookies he'd been eating. Catherine made sure there were no more traces of their week of playing house and then she arranged to have all her belongings sent up to the house in Cold Spring.

Being with Nathan had brought her years of living in Anita's apartment to a close: she simply couldn't see herself eating Cheerios and watching television on the same sofa where Nathan had made love to her the week before.

And yet it was lonely not to be able to talk about it: she felt positively bloated by swallowing the story.

Catherine twisted in her first-class seat and sighed, just as the flight attendant returned with her drink. 'You're not going to believe this one, guys,' she pretended to herself she might say to the club, 'but I had a fling with Anita's troublesome Nathan. The sex was awesome! Until he skedaddled back to the wife he said he was divorcing.' At least she thought that was what he said. Maybe he hadn't been quite so explicit. But no! She would not give him an 'out.' It made things too complicated, made her equally responsible. Instead, she tried to visualize everyone's face if she revealed the four-night stand. Anita's disappointment, Darwin's judgment. What did these women know of temptation? Only KC, with her two divorces and her New Yorker's seen-it-all-ness was not horrified in her vision.

She wasn't entirely without boundaries: she hadn't just jumped into bed with a married man. Well, she had. But not really. Nathan had said he'd already filed the papers. Or that he'd started papers. Which was it? There were lots of kisses and touching amid all the talking.

C'mon, Catherine, she thought to herself, *you're smarter than what happened here. A deal ain't done until it's done.*

'I should know better,' she said now, watching the clouds out the window. 'Right, James?' She reached over and patted his hand, a little bit forcefully, to get his attention.

'Hmm,' he murmured, a bewildered expression on his face as he looked up from his laptop. 'I'm sorry, what were you saying, Catherine?'

'Just that Venice is going to be the perfect thing for me,' she said. 'An antidote.' She took a gulp of sparkling water and nodded vigorously, waiting for him to ask the question. Ask what was wrong. Why so glum, chum?

It would be easy enough to tell James but somehow KC's seeing them at the restaurant and telling everyone about it had punctured the safe bubble of secrecy that protected their friendship. She had almost told him days ago but felt a twinge of doubt: What if she told James about Nathan and he told Anita?

If he asked, she decided now, she would tell him. That would be okay. If not, she would suffer in silence.

'I needed to get out of the city . . .' she began, willing James to draw her out.

'Good,' said James pleasantly, and turned back to his work. He liked Catherine. He really did. But today he just didn't

have time to listen. There was a lot ahead of him: he was
going to check on a potential new development in the watery
city for a few days, and then go to Rome to spend the
summer. Watching over Dakota.

The head of the company, Charles Vickerson, seemed
pleased that James was taking such an interest in the
European hotels, and even more delighted when James let
him know he was going to have his daughter work one day
a week for him. James Foster had worked his way up from
being part of the architectural team on a Parisian hotel almost
twenty years ago to being an integral part of the V hotel
empire. And Vickerson was always on guard for companies
out to poach his top execs; that James wanted to get his
daughter involved in the company seemed a good sign to
him.

'I wonder how Dakota is going to do on the plane tomorrow,' Catherine said now, trying to draw out James. 'It's her
first trip without a parent.'

'She was quite thrilled about that, I assure you,' said James,
glancing up from his computer only briefly. 'She'd have gone
to Scotland alone when she was younger, but I never wanted
her to be by herself at Heathrow.'

Catherine's trip, which she'd planned to call off when she
thought she was going to live happily ever after with Nathan,
was back on before anyone knew she'd considered not going.
A trip would be just the thing to run away from yet another
calamity in her love life, she believed.

Though touching base with Dakota to make arrangements
had exhausted her.

'I plan to eat everything,' she told Catherine, and then
spent ten minutes listing all the meals she hoped to consume,
before moving on to all the sights she intended to see. 'And
I'm also going to ride a Vespa, at least once . . .'

I used to be like that, Catherine had thought, feeling used up when she realized it was twenty-five years since she was Dakota's age. *This is not how I meant my life to be,* she told herself. Dakota's nonstop enthusiasm was like pulling up the blinds while recovering from a hangover: her sunniness hurt. Everywhere.

As a ruse, Catherine declared she needed to find some good glasswork for The Phoenix and bowed out of the flight to Rome with Dakota and company, promising to catch up with them later. She rescheduled instead to Venice and made her departure coincide a few days earlier with James's trip. Just because she couldn't talk about how she was feeling didn't mean she actually wanted to be left alone. Though James was hardly distracting company, his nose stuck in his work.

The details of Dakota's summer adventure had been well negotiated with James by Anita, who had planned some serious travel of her own. Dakota would look after Ginger based on Lucie's shooting schedule, but would work at least eight hours each week in her father's office. Filing, researching, typing letters. She was to get no special treatment, James had announced, but he wanted her to learn more about working in a corporate environment. Get some exposure beyond the world of retail and of school. Plus, Lucie and Dakota and Ginger were to stay at the V, down the hall from James. So Dakota was almost on her own, but not really: on the nights when she wasn't looking after Ginger, Dakota had to check in with her father by one a.m. Earlier, he told her, was also quite all right by him.

It wasn't Dakota's idea of a perfect summer, a five-year-old to look after and her father down the hall, but it was better than staying home and working in the shop. So what if she had to play administrative assistant for a few hours a week? She could handle it.

And as for Anita, she and Marty had booked passage on

the *Queen Mary 2*, and Catherine had gone to the boat to see them off shortly before her flight. The two of them were going to head to the UK – they'd already hired a private investigator to meet them when they arrived – and then they were going to systematically glean any clues they could from the nearly forty postcards she'd been saving all these years. Catherine didn't say she had that last postcard: she didn't want to give Anita any reason to feel let down. She'd already let her down enough.

The travel, Catherine knew, was a huge effort for Anita. But her fear of flying meant ground and sea journeys were their only option.

'I've been a wimp,' she'd said to Catherine on the pier. 'Reluctant to confront my fears and regrets with my sister. Now I have to sail across the world to find her.'

Catherine had nodded sympathetically.

'We used to have such fun – she was like my practice baby,' Anita told her. 'I would take her out to the park and we'd eat ice cream cones. Give my mother a break, you know. Sarah was so much younger than I was.'

'How old would she be?'

'Sixty-three,' said Anita, before returning to her memories. 'Sarah was an excellent knitter. I taught her myself. Bubbe taught me, and I showed her. She had perfect gauge. Spot on.'

'Better than you?' asked Catherine.

'Yes,' said Anita. 'Though I'd never admit it. I think of her when I'm knitting up the the wedding coat, you know. Imagine if we could make it together. How fast it would go. How fun. We used to make sweaters together, each take a sleeve, she the front and I the back. Make them for our father for his birthday, that kind of thing.'

Catherine looked out to the Hudson as Anita went on, explaining how Nathan had adored his young aunt – his first and favorite babysitter – and how she spent most of her weekends playing with her young nephews.

'She helped me out just as I helped my mother with her,' said Anita. 'And she was a laugher, always trying out jokes. In another generation, I think she would have been a comedian.'

'What did she do?' Catherine asked, but Anita's face had darkened. She tried to press for details, to find out what had gone wrong, but Anita merely shook her head.

'I'm not ready,' she said. 'I worry that by talking about her I'm just confirming that she's already gone. Don't let people slip through your fingers, Catherine. It can be easy to do and hard, so hard, to take back.'

As for the gang holding down the fort in the city, Catherine had popped by Walker and Daughter before she abandoned the San Remo to pick up a new summery felted tote bag from the Peri Pocketbook line. Her need to see everyone was powerful, almost as though she wanted to continually test her own resolve not to discuss Nathan.

'Seeing anyone these days, Peri?' she'd asked at the shop less than a day before her flight. Typically Catherine was a very organized flyer, but the situation had left her distracted.

'Ha!' said Peri. 'I am the quintessential almost-thirty busy professional female in New York who is shocked and alarmed to discover she lacks a life partner.'

Or forty-something, thought Catherine.

'I thought KC had the perfect guy for you?'

'Oh, you know the type,' said Peri. 'Spent all evening talking about himself.'

Nathan had seemed interesting when he told her about his life, growing up in New York, what Anita was like as a mother. Now Catherine wished he'd just kept his yap shut. She hated knowing him as well as she did. Or, at least, knowing his body as well as she did.

The phone rang, and it was Darwin, asking Peri to messenger over more yarn. Ever since Dakota had shown her how to make tiny socks, she'd become a woman obsessed, enchanted by the idea of Cady and Stanton's little toes clad in Mommy-created footwear. Even when she knew she'd be better off taking a nap, she still tried to knit a few stitches before dozing off.

'So I'm going to focus this summer on giving private lessons to Darwin at her place,' said Peri. 'When she doesn't have Rosie in for a visit. As she said, the more mothers, the merrier.'

'I wouldn't know,' said Catherine, trying very hard to act the role of the interested, engaged friend. But Catherine felt like the walking wounded, shell-shocked in a way she hadn't been for a long time.

'I wouldn't know, either,' said Peri. 'Seeing as I just keep things rolling on here, and trying to get my bags in the hands of D-list celebrities. No trips to Italy for someone here.'

Peri had made it well known she wasn't entirely keen on Dakota's travel, but she'd backed down and accepted a summer replacement in the form of Dakota's college pal Olivia. Unfortunately, Olivia was having difficulty ringing up the gorgeous cobalt blue laptop case Catherine was purchasing. She'd insisted on paying full price and not even using the Friday Night Knitting Club discount that Peri generously offered to her friends.

'I can barely work the register in my own store,' said Catherine sympathetically, before catching the daggers coming from Peri's eyes. In response, she bought a gray knitted backpack and a black beaded evening bag.

Peri, mollified, began wrapping up her purchases with great care, folding them in layers of tissue.

'Going to some great parties in Italy?' she asked.

'Don't know,' said Catherine, who most certainly wasn't

planning on having fun ever again. 'I don't really have an itinerary for the trip.'

'Dakota said you had a lot of work to do, finding one-of-a-kind things.'

'Right, yes, of course there's that schedule,' lied Catherine. She really didn't know what she was going to do with herself, however. She'd already canceled her previously arranged trip to the Cara Mia Vineyard and had let go of the apartment she booked. She just wanted to be on her own and think. And stew. And punish herself for falling into a fantasy future.

'You're so lucky,' said Peri, carefully placing Catherine's purchases in a large lavender Walker and Daughter shopping bag. 'I envy how you have it all together, Catherine.'

'Oh, you know what they say,' said Catherine. 'Appearances can be deceiving.'

Staring at the waves was a profound and unexpected pleasure. Anita spent hours watching the rolls of blue water and foamy white bubbles over and over.

'All is forgiveness out here,' she told Marty, leaning in for a hug as he kissed the top of her head. 'Constant renewal.'

With her acupressure bracelets on her wrists to prevent seasickness, Anita was thoroughly enjoying her days on the boat. She nibbled on tea sandwiches in the afternoon, joined the sixty-year-old brothers who were sitting at their dinner table for a regular game of trivia in the mornings, and indulged her sweet tooth with three scoops of French vanilla ice cream (and an extra wafer cookie) every night. Marty took her to the casino, where she won forty-seven dollars that she promptly stashed in her pocketbook, and they attended several wonderful history lectures. Not to mention she'd brought over a great deal of beautiful yarn – all in cream, her signature color no matter what Dakota had to say about it – so she could work on her wedding coat. Because she'd finally decided what she was going to wear when she married Marty: a long sleeveless gown topped with a delicate and light knitted coat that would fall in puddles and trail behind her as she walked down the aisle. So you see, she told herself as she knit yet another row on tiny size 3 circs, it truly is a good thing there's some time before the big event.

But filling her days was all just a holding pattern until they could get to Southampton and meet with the private eye Marty had selected. She'd brought all sorts of things with her: old photographs, family papers, the stack of postcards – the one of Big Ben had arrived in April 1968 – and contemporary pictures of her own children and grandchildren. She'd even tucked in some photos of the club, and of her working in the shop with Georgia and a young Dakota. No matter where or how she found Sarah, she was determined to catch her up on the details.

'It's possible she's passed on,' said Marty, once again finding Anita at the railing, staring out at the ocean. 'There's been no postcard. Let's be prepared for the disappointment.'

'Nonsense,' said Anita, not lifting her eyes from the water. 'She's a good fifteen years younger than I am. She's only sixty-three.' But even as she said it, she realized again how much time had passed and she frowned.

Anita had anticipated all sorts of scenarios. That she might not recognize Sarah, or that Sarah would look very tired from years of struggle and hard work, or that she and Sarah would meet again and discover they had nothing whatsoever to say to each other, even after all this longing. The gap had grown too wide and the distance could not be bridged.

She alternated different worries for different days so that she could properly wear herself out with every concern.

Anita tried to remember Sarah's favorite songs, favorite colors, and favorite foods. Chicken soup, she thought. Or maybe that was Nathan? What if she'd simply mixed it all up over the years and the crumbs of Sarah she had held on to were really parts of someone else's story? Wasn't that, in its way, worse than losing her outright?

'Did you and your brother Sam ever have a big fight?' she asked suddenly.

'Oh, yeah, we were squabblers,' said Marty. 'But when it came down to things, we've always made it work.'

'Sarah was more like my daughter, sort of, than a sister,' said Anita. 'We couldn't giggle and whisper late at night because I was practically out of the house by the time she came along. But she always felt like a gift.'

Marty nodded, paying close attention even though they'd talked of little else but Sarah for days, weeks, now.

'How easy it is to forget how things used to be,' Anita said finally. 'So few things cause scandal anymore.'

Alone in Venice – James had moved on quickly to Rome – Catherine did her best to play tourist: she drank a glass of wine and listened to a violinist in Saint Mark's Square, and she went to the studio of one of her favorite glassblowers and spent an astronomical sum of money until he nodded his approval at her and she felt, for a brief moment, worthy.

Then she felt disgusted with herself.

You're lost again, Catherine, she told herself as she took a water taxi back to her hotel for a quiet lunch alone. She was doing so well and then . . . what? Lonely is lonely but was she really going to let herself wander through life as one half of a mysterious whole?

It'd be no good to trudge her way through a city as glorious as Venice, she told herself, as she put on a large hat to shield her fair skin from the sun and made her way to the Museum of Archaeology. She investigated the ivory carvings and mummies, and admired bust after bust of handsome Roman generals and emperors. After a while, in spite of the craftsmanship, in spite of the presentation, she began to giggle.

They were all the same. Over and over again. The heads, the pose. Oh, maybe a nose here or there was different. But the busts were simply repetitive.

'Someone should have broken the mold,' she said to a madras-shorts-clad tourist beside her, who frowned to demonstrate he was a solemn art connoisseur who took museum visiting very, very seriously.

Each figure looked confident and handsome. Self-assured even after two thousand years. Surely they must have been frightened some days, thought Catherine, facing dangerous battles or watching their friends die. Certainly, too, they anguished over wayward lovers, though they likely had the luxury of strangling more than a few.

How peculiar, she realized, that as an art history major she'd spent years admiring form – the beauty and the perfection – and not wondering very much about the men behind the great statues. The subjects, putting forth their best impressions, keeping their privacies to themselves. The artists, choosing to reflect only what was ideal, and ignoring, for example, double chins and scars and wrinkles. And in doing so, their monumental talents had all but wiped clean that which made each of these men unique. All that had been left behind was the impression of their power.

It was an approach that once made perfect sense to Catherine. But not anymore.

'I am my own artist,' she said aloud. And with her focus on being perfect, perfect, perfect, she was always trying to obscure Catherine the woman. Over and over: she did the same thing. And, unlike these great faces, in doing so she gave away all her power and esteem.

'Time to try a new pattern,' she said, to herself this time. She hadn't been in love with Nathan, she knew; she'd been in love with the idea of living Anita's charmed life. Of getting a ready-made family, tied up with a bow. Of knowing with absolute certainty that she had a place.

But she'd always had a place. With herself. She'd just forgotten.

'Thank you, Julius. You've been a great help,' she told the statue, barely registering the museumgoers who stepped cautiously around the woman talking to the artwork. 'I'll buy you a drink when I see you in Rome.'

21

The flight to Rome had been a miracle. Ginger wanted to do anything and everything Dakota did, and that included sitting quietly, speaking in a low voice, and sipping at her juice slowly.

'Let's have a conversation,' the five-and-a-half-year-old strawberry blonde said to Dakota, who was sitting on her right. Ginger had the middle seat, tucked in between her mother and her new best friend.

'Excellent idea,' agreed Dakota, who reached down to her backpack and pulled out an American Girl catalog. 'Let's discuss which dolls we like and why,' she said, as Ginger nodded vigorously and Lucie, so pleased she'd persevered with James, whipped out a cushy neck pillow and dropped off into an exhausted sleep, not even minding being stirred by Ginger's and Dakota's giggles as they laughed at her snoring.

Their arrival at the Rome airport was less sanguine, however, when they discovered that their luggage had inexplicably been sent to Chicago.

'It will arrive soon,' said a man with a clipboard in heavily accented English.

'When?' asked Lucie forcefully.

'Maybe tomorrow,' said the man, before adding, 'Or the next day.'

'You said Polly would be safe,' accused Ginger, pointing a chubby finger at her mother.

'Toys,' said Lucie by way of explanation to Dakota, before insisting to her daughter that Polly and friends were simply on a longer flight.

'It'll be okay,' said Dakota, 'I have an extra T-shirt in my backpack that you can wear.'

Instantly, all worries about the toy bag were forgotten.

Clutching carry-ons and Sweetness, Ginger's stuffie who had been the sole member of the toy community to sit with the people, they made their way through customs and to the waiting car, ready to take them into the newly refurbished V hotel in Rome. Staying there had been one of James's many conditions, but Lucie was more than happy to stay there. Dakota had been less impressed, frustrated by her father maneuvering his way into her adventure. She imagined he'd still be following her around when she was thirty.

'Beggars can't be choosers,' had been Catherine's response to Dakota's entreaty that she prevent James from tagging along. 'I've heard of far worse things than working in the international development office of V in Italy. Your father's a talented man and, against your best efforts, you just may end up learning something.'

Catherine had also been a pain lately, hard to get hold of for a chat and so on.

But her first sight of the Italian countryside as the small auto careened up the freeway toward Rome thrilled her.

'I love seeing new places,' cried Dakota, staring out the car window.

'Me, too,' said Ginger, reaching over to Lucie and holding her hand absentmindedly.

In short order, they were in the city, watching the shops and homes fly past outside the window, people strolling on the sidewalks, choosing fruit, talking into their cell phones. It was just like New York except it was completely different.

'Even the old ladies look fashionable,' exclaimed Dakota, twisting her head to catch peeks out both windows.

'Yeah,' enthused Ginger. 'Nice ladies!'

The taxi sped through the fortifications of the ancient city, the brown stone and brick remarkably intact.

'Can't you just feel the marching footsteps of the centurions?' asked Dakota.

'That's just a scooter in the distance,' laughed the taxi driver. 'The energy of Rome will win your heart. You will love it!'

'Oh my God,' said Dakota in reply. There, more impressive than seeing the building on any television program, were the wide arches of the Colosseum.

'It's just right there, on the side of the road.'

'Yeah,' seconded Ginger. 'Look, Mommy.'

The car continued moving with the traffic – there was no time, no place to stop – but the honking and noise of the city faded away as Dakota gaped. On either side of the street were columns that once held up buildings and now stood, majestic and alone, a reminder of days gone by.

'It's really . . . real,' said Dakota. 'The past is present. Right here. This is people. It's like feeling ghosts.'

In a way that her trips to Scotland and even seeing its castles had not quite made clear, Dakota felt awe like she'd never previously experienced. The modern-day Roman actors dressed as gladiators and taking photos with the tourists notwithstanding, Dakota felt a deep joy at seeing the proof of this ancient civilization. A world that had left its remnants behind. 'Look at us,' the ruination seemed to say. 'We were here. This was ours. And now we're gone. Everything disappears. Everything stays.'

Finally, then, this was a city that understood her soul.

'Dakota's crying,' said Ginger confidently to Lucie. 'She doesn't like Rome.'

'Are you kidding?' Dakota reached over and rubbed the top of Ginger's head. 'I love it!'

'Me, too!' shouted Ginger, earning them a sharp glance from the driver as they made their way to the V.

This summer, Dakota knew, would be a time of discovery. Each passing second revealed something new and glorious – and she wasn't even out of the car yet!

She didn't have any idea what she was looking for. But here in Rome, she was going to find it. She just knew it.

Getting to the V, checking in, riding up the elevator to their suite – a room for Lucie and Ginger and a room for Dakota – and ordering up a platter of breakfast was more than enough for one day, Lucie declared. Ginger was practically comatose on the sofa, lolling about and trying to stay awake to keep listening to Dakota, who was still going on about the Colosseum.

'And you haven't even been inside yet,' pointed out Lucie.

'I know,' shouted Dakota, before lowering her volume. 'If it's this cool from the street, imagine what it's going to be like when I get through the entrance!'

'We'll see it all, I promise,' said Lucie. 'Together and when you're exploring on your own. But for now, let's have a nap.'

'No,' muttered Ginger, out of force of habit. She could barely keep her eyes open. Lucie covered her with a blanket and, making sure the door was locked, went to her bedroom and took a long, hot shower – flights always left her feeling grimy – before flopping down onto her pillows and sleeping.

When she opened her eyes, it was dark in the room. And, when she opened the blinds, dark outside. Dressing quickly, she ventured out into the living area. Ginger, clutching Sweetness, didn't stir. And a few knocks on Dakota's door produced no reply. She went to her handbag and picked up her global cell phone and checked the time: one forty-five a.m. Had they really managed to sleep for ten hours? Wow. They must have been more exhausted than she realized. Picking up Ginger, she carried her to the bedroom and undressed her, slipping her sweet baby and Sweetness together under the covers. 'I should have brought shin guards,' she said to herself, remembering how much Ginger could kick in her sleep. And then she crawled into bed next to her daughter and nodded off quickly.

When she awoke again it was still dark. No. It was even darker. There was no light at all, in fact: the blinds were very effective at their chosen profession. Something was missing. There was no clock radio with red numbers blinking at her. That was it. Feeling disoriented and thirsty – hungry, too – Lucie stumbled her way to the living area of the suite, just as Dakota was coming out of her bedroom in a long T-shirt.

'What time is it?' she asked, rubbing her eyes and yawning.

'I honestly don't know,' said Lucie, who picked up a phone to call the lobby. Dakota waited as she asked for the hour and then hung up.

'It's a quarter to two in the morning,' she told Dakota. 'Only I swear I was up at this time hours ago.'

'We slept until the middle of the night?'

'Yeah,' said Lucie, reaching into her purse and checking the time on her phone, which seemed to think it was nine forty-five a.m. 'Oh, man,' she said. 'I could have awakened us all at a normal hour, but my phone's time was off. We have now officially slept through our first day in Rome.'

'I am so starved,' said Dakota. 'Any limits on the minibar?'

'Not tonight,' said Lucie. 'Let's raid that sucker and eat all the ovepriced chocolate and snacks we can find.'

'Should we wake up Ginger?' asked Dakota.

'Oh, Dakota. Definitely not,' said Lucie. 'I can see you still have so much to learn.'

Three first-class tickets. That's what Catherine bought on Monday morning, one for herself, and two more for the young couple with the giant backpacks waiting in the station.

'Why?' they asked, clearly confused, when she presented them with the tickets.

'Because I've never done anything like this before,' she said, feeling quite satisfied with herself. She hadn't brought a book or a magazine with her for the train journey to Rome. Instead, she was going to sit by herself for a little while and stare out the window. And then she was going to use her very expensive phone minutes and call someone she'd never taken the time to get to know: KC. The only person she imagined wouldn't be horrified at the Nathan debacle. Catherine suspected they might, in fact, have a great deal in common.

Plus she was going to eat a very delicious panini-style sandwich with sun-dried tomatoes and chicken, and not worry about getting crumbs on her pink silk blouse and cream skirt, and she wasn't going to limit herself to just half a sandwich lest it all go to her hips.

Catherine settled into her seat and put on her sunglasses, ready to be dazzled by the green Italian countryside.

After an hour of soaking in all the charming homes she could see, Catherine dialed KC at her office. It was near the end of the workday.

'KC Silverman,' boomed a voice with a strong flavor of New York.

'KC, it's Catherine,' she said. 'Catherine Anderson.'

'Uh, this is unusual,' said KC, never one to hold back. 'Is something wrong? Did you get thrown in jail? Because I'm not that kind of lawyer, you know. I do contracts.'

'No, I just wanted to say hello,' said Catherine.

'Well, that's lovely,' KC said evenly. 'What's the occasion?'

'I don't have one,' said Catherine.

'Well, you've never once in five years ever talked to me outside of our club meetings,' said KC. 'You see Lucie, you go by the shop, obviously you connect up with Dakota and Anita. I bet you even see Darwin. But you've never ever phoned me before.'

Catherine paused for a moment, thinking how to play it. She could blame KC, convince her she'd been sending unfriendly signals. Or she could pretend the connection dropped and she lost the call. That would be easiest. But, ultimately, she decided to embrace her inner Catherine and be upfront.

'You're right,' she admitted. 'It's funny how you can run in a circle of friends and yet still not be close to some people. I didn't really know you and I haven't done much to remedy that.'

'Well, it's not all on you,' said KC, mollified. Her bark was worse than her bite. 'I figure you're kind of a prissy pants anyway.'

'Oh.' Catherine's hurt tone carried across the ocean, with a slight ten-second delay.

'Now don't get all bent out of shape,' said KC. 'You also have a good sense of fun.'

'Yes, I do, don't I?' agreed Catherine enthusiastically.

'Catherine, has something happened? To you, I mean, and I'm serious now,' said KC. 'This call is so out of the blue. And I just want you to know that you can talk to me, you know.'

'That's why I'm calling,' said Catherine. 'Bad breakup blues. But I wanted to talk as one triumphant single woman to another.'

'Am I triumphant?' asked KC. 'I don't know about that. But I'm mostly content in my own skin. I think that might be even better.'

'I spend a lot of time pretending,' said Catherine. 'Do people take me seriously? I wonder.'

'You can be a bit . . . hard to know.'

'KC, you suggested at Darwin's shower that you and I are alike because we don't want children,' said Catherine, feeling a bit awkward. But if she was going to share, she might as well embrace it. 'But the truth is that I simply don't have any. Not that I didn't want any.'

'Well, I'm learning something new,' said KC. 'But why are you telling me?'

'I'm telling myself,' said Catherine. 'But the last time I talked out loud I got a few strange looks.' She laughed.

'I guess I figured you'd understand,' she added.

'Because it's past my time and you're wondering if I have regrets?' asked KC.

'Maybe somewhat,' said Catherine. And then: 'Yes.'

'There's a lot I would change but some people aren't meant to be mothers and other people don't need to be mothers,' said KC. 'I'm one of those. I don't feel an absence of children.'

'So everything's hunky-dory, then?'

'Hardly,' said KC. 'I've made my mistakes.'

'Like what?'

'What is this? Long-distance *Oprah*?' KC sighed, then relented. 'I poured my whole life into my career when I was an editor. And when I was laid off back in the day, I was completely undone.'

'Like when I left my husband,' said Catherine.

'Similar but different,' said KC. 'You made a choice. I had a choice made for me. But in the end, we both had to reinvent. Now I pour most of my energy into *myself*. My law career is intellectually stimulating but it doesn't define me.'

'I'm still trying to define myself,' said Catherine. 'I embraced my independence but somehow everything is just all about me. I am totally self-focused.'

'We've all noticed.'

'Well, I'm tired of it.'

'Necessity is the mother of reinvention. So you see? We're mothers after all.'

'I'm looking out the window and there's this stout woman putting wet laundry on a line,' said Catherine. 'That seems so wonderful. Sometimes I wish I knew what every day would bring.'

'You do,' said KC. 'It brings more questions. And by the way, I hope you're not going to go all "back to the land, fruit of the earth" on us, are you?'

'No, it's just that . . . ' Catherine paused.

'Grass-is-always-greener syndrome knows no international boundaries, apparently,' said KC. 'Don't flatter yourself by assuming yours are the more complex challenges than that woman doing her laundry. You don't know her story. She doesn't know yours.'

'You seem different out of context,' said Catherine. 'More clever. I'm glad I called.'

'Oh, no you don't,' said KC.

'Don't what?'

'Call and pick my brain for good advice and then not offer anything in return,' said KC. 'You were heading toward hanging up on me and just said you're trying not to make everything all about you.'

'Oh,' said Catherine. 'Right. Sorry.'

'So I'm fine, thanks for asking,' said KC, before bursting into a series of hacking coughs.

'You don't sound fine,' said Catherine tentatively.

'I'm not! I can't seem to stop it with these cigarettes,' said KC. 'It seems ridiculous but I started as a lark, something to make me feel young, and now I get edgy if there's not something in my hands. Anita's book suggestion didn't do much to kick my cravings.'

'I have an idea what you could do,' said Catherine.

'I know – so did Anita,' said KC. 'I'm on my eighth dishcloth.'

'What? I was going to suggest you get a dog,' said Catherine. 'You got a job as a dishwasher?'

'No, I'm knitting, you wingnut,' said KC. 'I went to a shop in SoHo to get supplies.'

'You didn't even go to Walker and Daughter?' Catherine couldn't help but smile.

'And have Peri know?' KC was gruff. 'I've spent years cultivating a non-knitting attitude.' She paused.

'Also, she won't let me in the store without making me go upstairs to her apartment and drop off my coat and my bag and, sometimes, even change into a pair of sweats. She turned into a menace the minute Anita was on that boat,' said KC.

'Peri is only trying to get you to stop smoking,' said Catherine. 'And protect her bags.'

'Oh, I know,' said KC. 'The problem is that it's just not working. Any suggestions?'

'Apart from the dog? Knitting? Quitting cold turkey?' asked Catherine. 'Yes. Chew that nicotine gum. Take up yoga. Go to Peri and tell her you need her support and not just her list of restrictions.'

'I'll take it under advisement,' grumbled KC.

'Other than that, I guess all either of us can do is work at it,' said Catherine, before saying her good-byes and tucking into that delicious sandwich. 'And then work some more.'

22

Dakota packed a suit at her father's request, a linen-blend skirt and jacket, and wore it to her first half-day at the office.

'Hello, Dad,' she said when he came to the suite door. 'Or should I call you Mr. Foster?'

'Dad will do just fine,' said James. 'As long as you knock off that tone of sarcasm.'

Together they made their way down the hall and to the elevator, riding in silence with a group of travelers who were nattering over their maps of the city. Dakota envied them their work-free schedule.

'I wish I was going sightseeing,' she said.

'Not my fault you slept through an entire day,' said James, playfully putting his arm around her shoulder. 'There will be lots of opportunities to noodle around. But for now, I want you to come around and meet the staff of the hotel.'

'So I can ask them how they like their coffee?' Dakota was joking; James had already explained that her days would be spent taking notes at his meetings and other, even more boring, tasks.

'It's a good way to give you an idea of how the business runs,' he said. 'Also how people work together in different environments.' To top it all off, she'd have some thrilling filing to do, and, later on, a report that had yet to be decided.

'You'll have a project, don't worry,' said James. 'But let's dive into our work before we get to that point.'

A good enough plan, really. Besides, she only had to work in the office when she wasn't scheduled to be on Ginger duty. Lucie had this morning free, and when Dakota left the suite, she was doing her best to convince Ginger she'd be able to survive the few hours away from her favorite babysitter. And although not so keen to work with her dad, Dakota was kind of looking forward to a break from the five-year-old. Though there was something strangely neat about the way her father seemed so excited to march her around.

'. . . and this is my daughter, Dakota,' he said, for the zillionth time, as they made their way through various departments and finally to a low floor in the hotel that seemed to be made up of many offices.

'We'll be working here,' said James, showing her to a spacious office with two desks.

'In the same room?' asked Dakota. Then, practicing a more professional tone: 'How nice.'

James lit up at her comment. 'It is great, isn't it?' he said. 'We haven't spent time together like this since before you moved into the dorm. Some days we could even meet for breakfast beforehand.' He seemed so pleased that Dakota didn't want to remind him that she was only going to be working with him once or twice a week at most.

'Breakfast sounds good, Dad,' she said now.

James snapped his fingers. 'I know just the thing,' he said. 'The greatest perk of having a hotel at your disposal. Let's go grab some cappuccino and biscotti directly from the chef.'

Of all the fun places Dakota had now seen – the outside of the Colosseum, Edinburgh Castle, her Gran's cottage in Thornhill, her grandmother Lillian's house in Baltimore, her grandparents' farm in Pennsylvania – nothing compared at all with her desire to go inside an honest-to-goodness working restaurant kitchen. To, maybe, even meet a genuine pastry chef, mixing batters and folding cream. Asking them to stay and observe, or maybe even to fetch a spoon and taste!

'Do I look all right?' she asked as her father looked at her quizzically.

'Same as you did five minutes ago,' he said. 'And I told you that you looked very nice then.'

'Right,' said Dakota. 'Thanks, Dad.'

They were just about out the door and on their way, too, when a staffer knocked on the open door and asked her father to look at some papers. She could see the way the employee fidgeted, clearly nervous around James. Maybe what Catherine said was right: Her father was a big deal around here.

'We'll go later, Dakota,' he said, sitting at his desk, papers in hand. 'Why don't you sit down and play around with the computer, get yourself acclimated, and then you can come with me to the planning meeting at eleven?'

'Okay, Dad,' she said, watching her tone for any sign of disappointment or attitude. It was easy to be annoyed by him, that was true, but it was difficult when he seemed so excited to have her around. You could always say one thing about her dad: He was genuinely thrilled to spend time with her. Too bad she couldn't bottle up a little of that enthusiasm about herself and sneak-feed it to Andrew Doyle back at NYU.

The train arrived in Rome by early afternoon, though Catherine had snoozed for the last hour, lulled into unconsciousness by the constant and steady motion. She had only a few small pieces of luggage with her, having sent some of her belongings directly to Rome, and the laptop bag she'd purchased from Peri. She'd found enough energy, on the train, to eke out another few pages of *Dead Men Don't ReMarry*, adding in a new character named Nathan, who also met an untimely end. Much better, she thought, growing alert as the train came to a stop. She closed her laptop, tucked it away, and gathered her bags, strolling away from the platform and into the high-ceilinged Termini Station. A sea of taxicabs waited just outside the glass-fronted building, and Catherine marched out toward them confidently.

'No go,' said a driver as she approached.

'I'm sorry?'

'No work,' he said. 'Off.'

Confused, she tried the taxi next to him; maybe she'd have better luck, she reasoned.

This man held up his arms. '*Sciopero*,' he said.

'Could you repeat that?' asked Catherine, when the young backpackers whose tickets she'd bought sauntered by.

'Strike,' said the guy. 'The cabbies aren't driving today.'

'Oh,' said Catherine, uncertain as to how she was going to make her way to the V. She could call James, she supposed, and get the hotel to send a car. Or she could hoof it, toting her luggage with her. She took a few preliminary steps, trying to visualize what it would feel like to cover a distance of some number of miles in her sling heels. Not so good, she guessed.

She scanned the area around the station until her eyes fell on the row of scooters, some with riders getting on and off, others sitting alone and awaiting the return of their owners. Dakota's comment about riding a Vespa, even just once, rang in her memory.

'*Scusi*,' she said to one helmeted driver standing at a red Vespa, clearly getting ready to take off. She waved a fifty-euro bill and mimed herself climbing aboard.

She was met with a shrug. 'Okay,' said the driver. It was a woman. Catherine smiled. See? She didn't need some man to rescue her, she thought, as she put her bag on the luggage rack. She was going to clamber aboard, laptop in hand, and ride girl power all the way to her destination.

The V hotel was large, but not out of place in its surroundings, with a lot of glass and many floors rising into the sky. Catherine popped off the scooter, paid the ersatz chauffeur, and strolled into the lobby feeling better than she had in a very long while. But then a quick blip through the streets of Rome – a smidge grubby, it was true, but then people had been making their homes here for eons – and Catherine was absorbing the energy and vitality of the city. She'd been before, of course, but it had never felt quite so rich with possibility. She felt as though the city itself was nourishing her as she scooted past Trajan's Column and the domed Santa Maria di Loreto, a compact little church that was one of those places where she enjoyed sitting and thinking after a long afternoon of walking. For some reason, it seemed far easier to make her way around Rome in heels, like all the women here in their stilettos, than it was to do the same at home. And now she was here. Repaired. Rested. Ready to see her friends.

Her room was set, just as she anticipated, and there was a huge gift basket filled with fruit and chocolates and what looked to be several bottles of wine waiting on a marble table just inside the doorway. The space was large, done in creams and golds, with a nice seating area and a bedroom off to her right. She could see there was a large bouquet of flowers on the nightstand. And, for a city known for its tiny hotel bathrooms, a quick peek let her know that she wouldn't be missing her typical American comforts, with a large tub and even a separate shower. Clearly, V hotels – with thoughtful design by James Foster – made the living easy. As soon as she could peel free of her skirt and blouse, Catherine was standing under the hot streaming water, sampling the complimentary shampoo because she hadn't even bothered to look

into her bag before stepping in. The urge to sing was powerful, but she restrained herself until she had a better idea if
the hotel walls were thin. No use in tormenting her neighbors,
she thought as she unwrapped a bar of soap.

She wasn't entirely cured, she knew. The sense that she
had to keep going, to stay up lest she become morose and
fall into a vat of Nathan-induced self-pity, was palpable.
Catherine could feel her emotions gnawing at her elbow. But
she just wasn't going to give in. She was tougher than that.
She knew it.

Ninety minutes later, dressed in a crumple-resistant
black sleeveless dress she always brought in her carry-on,
her hair dry and her makeup reapplied, although very
lightly, and Catherine was ready for a glass of wine and a
reunion with her friends. Maybe this, too, was a sign, she
thought, realizing she had only been away from Dakota
for a short period, and already she was missing her
presence. No one had sent her a text message in days. She
was even looking forward to seeing little Ginger. Perhaps
the external reading she'd always been searching for to let
her know if she fit in was actually something quite internal:
not so much how her friends felt about her as how she
felt about them.

Catherine snuck a peek into her gift basket, unwrapping
a single chocolate and letting it melt in her mouth as she
searched for the card. The flowers in her bedroom were from
James and Dakota, along with a note about drinks in Lucie's
suite at eight p.m. So who could have sent her this bounty?
she wondered.

*Welcome to Roma! Compliments of Cara Mia Vineyard.
Marco Toscano.*

Marco! Of course. Her favorite wine exporter: he of the
smooth voice and playful phone chitchats. Although
Catherine had initially intended to make a trip out to see

the vineyard, the fact of the matter was that she was already committed to selling the wine. There was no need to make the journey. Clearly, though, Marco was worried that her lack of desire to see his family's operations signified something else. A crisis of confidence, perhaps. Well, on that scale he'd been right, thought Catherine, but it wasn't related to work. Scooping up a handful of chocolates and tucking two bottles of wine under her arm, she headed out to the elevator to make her way to Lucie's suite.

'Oh my God,' mouthed Dakota when she answered the door and saw Catherine, before slipping out to the hallway. 'Isabella is here! You know, the singer?' She kept her voice low and looked this way and that, as though conducting a spy mission.

'Hi to you, too,' said Catherine, handing her the bottles of wine.

'Yes, yes, kiss kiss, hug hug,' said Dakota, rolling her eyes.

'Since when do you follow Italian pop stars?'

'Since she's sitting in our living room,' said Dakota, babbling excitedly. 'Besides, she has an English album. She was at the Grammys last year? Broke up that movie star's marriage?' Dakota waited for the lightbulb of understanding to go off in Catherine. It didn't.

Dakota sighed, tried to re-explain just why Isabella was so interesting to a college kid from New York. After a while, she frowned. 'You seem different. Your skin is smoother or something. Did you change up your hair? It looks less done. But no time for beauty secrets now, Catherine!' Catherine hadn't said a word in the midst of Dakota's ramble about movie stars and singers and *People* magazine. It was as though Dakota hadn't spoken with her in months, she seemed to have so much to say.

'And so now Isabella is in the next room – along with,

like, eight million members of her entourage – and she just complimented my outfit.'

Catherine paused to really take in what Dakota was wearing: a red knitted tunic in a lightweight cashmere blend that had a series of interlocking cables across the front. The band at the bottom fell just below her butt to skim the top of her thigh.

'You're wearing legs tonight, I see,' said Catherine. 'Isn't that the sweater you made in your senior year?'

'Totally,' said Dakota. 'I reinvented it as a dress. Cool, yeah? Isabella wants one just like it. And she's a size zero. She'd make anyone – even you – look fat.'

'Pouring on the charm today, aren't we?' asked Catherine. 'Do I get to go inside this extravaganza? I didn't realize it was a party.'

'The party's not supposed to be until later, up on the roof deck,' said Dakota. 'But Isabella and her manager came by to hammer out a few details with Lucie. Shooting begins tomorrow.'

'Is James here?'

'I thought you just saw my outfit,' said Dakota. 'I wouldn't be wearing that if he was coming. He's working late. Some sort of problem in Singapore or something.'

'Shouldn't you know what's going on?'

'Interns don't run the show, Catherine,' said Dakota. 'All I do is take notes and file.'

'How many days have you even worked?'

'Most of today,' moaned Dakota. 'So I've only seen the city from the car.'

Spontaneously, Catherine reached around Dakota, chocolates still in hand, and gave her a big squeeze, careful of the wine bottles she'd handed to Dakota.

'Oh, it's so hard to be eighteen and trapped with a summer job in the most glorious city in the world,' Catherine said, mocking her.

'Well, it's not completely bad,' said Dakota breathlessly, looking over her shoulder this way and that before lowering her voice. 'I met the chef.'

She waited for the awe to hit Catherine.

'That's nice,' said Catherine. 'You know, I've really missed you. But if your father sees you in this dress – not that it doesn't look good – I'm not going to take the blame if you try to fob it off as my suggestion. *Capice?*'

'Got it,' said Dakota. 'Though who cares about a dress when I can hang out in the kitchen.'

'Hang out?'

'Didn't you hear me?' asked Dakota. 'I met Andreas. In the kitchen. The kitchen!' She jumped up, exposing every inch of her long legs. Now Catherine looked around, making sure no one – especially James – was coming down the hall.

'He was making a chocolate torte and he let me watch him and then he said, "Would you like to get the cream out of the case?" – and it was completely huge and filled with all sorts of fruit and milk and everything you could think of – and I said, "Sure, chef." I just called him "chef," like I worked for him! And then I watched him put the torte in the oven.'

'Sounds . . . cool,' said Catherine, who rarely cooked, and baked even less often.

'Cool?' snorted Dakota. 'It was a revelation. My dad didn't even notice that I was gone for two hours. Andreas made pastry, and teeny cookies to go with espresso, and then he made a raspberry-lime granita. And he let me try it!'

'Was it good?' asked Catherine, feeling her stomach rumble.

'Good does not begin to capture the magic that is Andreas,' said Dakota, as though she were marketing his career. 'It was ethereal. As all food should be.'

'Ask this Andreas if you can make me some muffins,' said Catherine. 'I need a Dakota treat.'

'Do you think he would?' Dakota was wide-eyed.

'I doubt it,' admitted Catherine, regretful that she'd gotten Dakota's hopes up.

'Well, that's okay,' said Dakota. 'He said I could come by after the lunch rush anytime. Nice, right?'

'Fabulous,' said Catherine. 'Now can we please get out of this hallway?'

'Of course,' said Dakota, opening the door to reveal Lucie in an intense conversation with a man to one side of the room. Sitting on the sofa, fronted by several bottles of red wine on the table, sat a very slight girl – she must have been in her early twenties – with an enormous crown of curly ringlets. She was dressed in what seemed to be several layers of handkerchiefs, thought Catherine, who typically appreciated the art of skimpy dressing.

'*Vino!*' shouted Isabella, nodding to Dakota as though she'd gone out with the sole purpose of finding Catherine to bring more wine.

'Catherine!' said Lucie, standing up and coming over to greet her. The relief on her face when she saw the bottles of wine in Dakota's arms was noticeable. 'Do you mind if we serve this? I have more coming up but the guests are very . . . thirsty.'

In a few moments, the bottles were opened, and introductions made. Isabella drank one glass, then two.

'I love this wine,' she said, her English close to perfect. 'Gorgeous and light.'

'It's from the Cara Mia Vineyard,' said Catherine. 'I sell it in my store in New York.'

'In New York? How can they let this good Italian wine even leave the country?' said Isabella.

'The same way they export you, I'd guess,' said Catherine, instantly interrupted by Lucie.

'If you like it so much, we can get more for you,' said Lucie, nodding toward her famous rock star.

'Yes, please,' said Isabella. 'And not just a few bottles. I want several cases.'

Dakota's eyes widened.

'Oh, not to drink up in one day or something,' she said. 'But I know enough to commit when I see something I like. Get me more wine, and make sure some of it is on set.'

Isabella came over to Lucie and solemnly took her hand. 'I know you'll make me look gorgeous on camera,' she said. 'And I wasn't joking about this Dakota's dress. Let's get the stylist to make me something like that.'

'It's hand-knit,' said Lucie. 'Dakota knitted it.'

Like a floodlight, Isabella turned all her charm and attention on Dakota. 'Wouldn't you like to make something like that for me?' she asked.

'Yes,' said Dakota, entranced by her brush with a famous person. Wouldn't this make quite the story to tell Andrew Doyle?

'So then it's all settled,' said Isabella. 'Shooting begins Thursday, you will get me my wine, and you will make me a dress. Like yours. Shorty-short. And maybe tighter.'

'I can't do that in two days,' said Dakota. 'It'd be quicker if I left off the sleeves.'

'Good,' said Isabella, taking the unopened bottle of Cara Mia Vineyard wine from the table and tucking it under her arm.

'And shooting begins tomorrow,' reminded Lucie.

Isabella grinned, her eyes sparkling. 'Okay,' she said easily. 'But you won't see me until Thursday.'

And with that, she glided out of the room, taking her manager and her friends with her, and leaving Lucie, Catherine, and Dakota wondering just what they'd gotten themselves into.

23

Finally. After a day of watching Ginger, spent mainly watching a clown at Piazza Navona and haunting a variety of toy stores, and another afternoon typing up notes for her father, Dakota had been granted a beautiful day all to herself. Lucie was going to need her that evening because the shoot was starting at night – Isabella was confirmed to show up – but for seven hours she was free to do whatever she wanted.

She followed her eyes, lured by domes this way and that, and her nose, smelling delicious food being cooked in some building nearby. In every direction, there was something to pique her curiosity, and she practically ran from one spot to the next, fascinated by everything from young men having earnest discussions over cappuccino to the bizarre display of tiny Mussolinis and Nazis in the toy store window.

'Now there's something you don't see every day,' she said aloud, to no one in particular.

She folded up her map into the pocket of her jeans jacket and simply let herself wander, experiencing the joy of discovering a fountain with turtles in the middle of a neighborhood, not seeing any sign of explanation or anything other than apartments and cars nearby. This, then, was Rome, a city built upon a city built upon a city. She rang a bell to be let into a fancy china shop, the sole clerk sitting at an elegant desk, seemingly oblivious to the gorgeous array of plates along the wall and up to the twelve-foot coffered ceilings. A china plate fantasy. The building itself stood just behind a huge set of columns, Latin letters etched on their front. A few steps away, an apartment building had been finished inside the ruins of what looked like an ancient theater, with modern brick and glass windows above rows of arches, the 'lawn' a series of pieces of fallen marble and stone, some of it intricately carved, just lying around like so. A small sign in multiple languages warned passersby about taking a souvenir ruin or two. How much history must be here, thought Dakota, to be able to just let it sit here, waiting until there was enough time and money to come and collect it.

She took photos of churches and cafés, of cobbler shops and drugstore windows. Of Vespas parked and on the move. She bought herself too many pastries to even eat by herself, eager to taste all the flavors and enthralled by the painstaking tissue paper wrapping and thin string placed around each treat. A Danish stuffed into a white bag as was done back home never seemed more amateur when compared with the love the baker and his wife showered on each and every pastry. His gift to the world.

Dakota put her fingers in the Mouth of Truth at Santa Maria in Cosmedin, and she stared across the street at the Temple of Portunus, amazed at how the old and the older collided with the new, as buses and cars honked their way up the busy road to head to what Catherine told her was called 'the wedding cake' – the monument to Victor Emmanuel – and the ruins of the Roman Forum.

But she felt drawn to go in the opposite direction, her wish to get to the Colosseum notwithstanding. Dakota crossed a wide bridge – the Ponte Fabricio – over the Tiber to poke her head into the church on the Isola Tiberina, and then she wandered the streets of the Trastevere neighborhood, snacking and sampling from all manner of bakeries and gelato shops.

The trick to finding the freshest, most natural gelato, Catherine had told her, was to check the color of the banana gelato. If it was yellow, it was artificial. But if it was a creamy color, even a fair bit gray, then it was the real deal.

Dakota walked around the long stretch of walls of a cloistered convent, wondering about the women inside, and then she joined an impromptu soccer game in a random square, trying desperately to keep up with the ten-year-old dynamos who kept laughing at her inability to kick the ball very far.

That was when her feet finally registered their protest: Dakota had been on the go all day long and her body ached for rest. And Rome, unlike any other city she'd ever seen, had a church on every corner. Good cover for a chance to get off her feet – she could often even put her shoes up on the kneeler – and seem very pious at the same time. Dakota was not religious by nature; her mother had been Presbyterian but never attended services, and her father, who was Baptist, tended to go to church only when his mother, Lillian, was in town or when he and Dakota went to visit. Not going to church was fine by Dakota, who liked having her Sunday mornings free to bake. But still she found her quick dashes into the churches and basilicas to be soothing, some combination of the quiet and of the cool inside the buildings providing a reprieve from her exhausting – and exhilarating – explorations of the city.

'*Sì, sì,*' yelled the boys, trying to get her to stay and play with them. '*Viva il football.*'

Dakota waved them off and headed through an arch toward an ancient fountain in the square in front of the Church of Santa Cecilia, hoping a mist from the fountain might blow her way. The large fountain was centered on a small grass lawn, and all of it was ringed by a raised edge of stone and tile. She walked through the square and into the church, admiring the beautiful sculpture of the prone figure of the martyred Saint Cecilia, the delicate way she turned her face in her suffering and yet projected eternal strength. Lazily, Dakota wandered down into the crypt, paying a white-habited nun a couple of euros to see the excavations below. The remains of a house, an altar to a temple, an early church. All together. Worlds colliding.

Dakota made her way out of the building, stopping to admire the mosaic friezes on the façade. All in all, it was a day well spent. And that's when she saw her: a woman, with curly brown hair, sitting on the edge of the fountain area, her back to Dakota. The woman's elbows were sticking out a bit from her sides and her shoulders had that hunch Dakota knew all too well.

She was knitting.

Not being able to see her face, it was easy to think, for just a split second, that it was her mother there. Waiting for her all afternoon, just to come and have a chat in the church. How long had she been inside? she wondered. The woman hadn't been there when she entered the church and now here she was.

That kind of thing hasn't happened to me in a long time, thought Dakota, as she remembered the period shortly after Georgia died when she would have that strange sensation that somehow, around any given corner, she might just run into her mother on the street. Or she would see a tall, curly-haired figure in the subway and run to catch her, hoping for some sort of miracle or time warp – she didn't care which – to have occurred.

Of course this woman couldn't be her mother. And yet she felt a lump in her throat as she watched this stranger intently work her rows, enjoying the sunny afternoon, oblivious to all.

In her mad tear to see everything there was to see in Rome in one day, Dakota hadn't expected to be confronted by something – knitting – that was essentially hers. So personal. It seemed out of place to see an everyday Roman woman knitting and yet it was perfect. One more great discovery in this beautiful city.

Slowly, Dakota crept up to the woman, drawing out the moment when she'd really see her face and know, without a doubt, that it wasn't Georgia.

She sat down just slightly behind and to the right of the knitter, taking furtive peeks. Her hair was a bit wild, obscuring her face. And she wasn't wearing jeans like Georgia had typically done. But her stitches were good, Dakota could see that, as she worked up what looked to be a crimson sleeve. A sweater for someone. A daughter, maybe.

Dakota closed her eyes, feeling only the warmth on her face as she listened to the faint burble of the fountain water and the steady click-clack of the needles. This, then, was also Georgia's trip to Rome. Tagging along in her memory. Dakota loved knitting, enjoyed the feel of the yarn in her fingers. But she just didn't want to run a yarn shop. She wanted the freedom and flexibility to do her own thing.

The woman pulled more yarn from a skein in her bag, one fluid motion without even breaking rhythm. Georgia had knitted like that. Effortlessly and quickly.

How nice it would be just to have a conversation, Dakota thought, running through all the places and people she'd seen in just this one day. In the end, though, she settled on just one thought.

'I miss you, Mom,' said Dakota aloud.

She stood up reluctantly but she had just enough time to

return to the V to watch confusing Italian television with Ginger and Sweetness before bath and bed.

'*Sì, sì,*' said the knitter, smiling in her direction and raising her knitting just slightly in greeting as Dakota continued to make her way.

24

As wonderful as it was to be in Rome, Catherine remained a late riser, even though she'd been in Italy for weeks. She just stayed on her magical Catherine schedule: no sunrise could get her to open an eyelid before at least nine a.m. And, to ward off any possibility of interrupted slumber, she'd made sure to pack a selection of silk eye masks that matched her silk nighties. All that meant she wasn't very receptive to the loud banging on her door at seven a.m. Not at all.

'Catherine!' She could hear the shout-whispers but tried to ignore them, hoping they would go away. An early house-keeper, perhaps? Unlikely that they'd call her by name.

'Catherine!' And it didn't sound like Dakota. Soon the other patrons of the hotel were going to open their doors and *ssshhh* this maniac into silence. Catherine dove under a pillow, waiting out the noise.

'Catherine, it's Lucie!'

Thwarted. It wasn't like she could simply ignore Lucie. Also, Lucie was smart enough to realize she could just go pick up her phone and call the room. With a heave and a moan, Catherine got up and looked through the peephole in the door.

'Open up!' Yep, it was Lucie all right.

'I'm not awake and I don't believe in unannounced appointments,' said Catherine, opening the door about one inch.

'This is an emergency,' said Lucie. 'A real crisis!'

Catherine let her inside. 'Really?' she said, worried. 'Is Dakota okay? Ginger?'

'Oh, not a real *real* crisis,' said Lucie, making a face. 'An I'm-about-to-lose-my-job kind of crisis.'

'Well then,' said Catherine. 'I'm sure I'll be of great help. Need an extra camera person?'

'No,' said Lucie. 'It's Isabella. She's become besotted with this damn wine you had to bring over.'

'I thought you arranged to get the stock from several of the local stores to put together a case for her?'

'I did,' said Lucie. 'It wasn't enough. She doesn't need to drink it now, she says. She just needs to know she'll be able to drink it at her leisure.'

'So she's demanding more wine because theoretically she might want to enjoy it at some unknown point in the future?' asked Catherine. 'Remind me again why I've been awakened for this so-not-an-emergency-I'm-going-to-get-wrinkles-from-lack-of-good-sleep?'

'Because she's a rock star,' said Lucie. 'And she wants to be comped.'

'Comped?'

'Celebs don't pay for half the stuff they have,' explained Lucie. 'It's given to them. Thank you so much for wearing the sunglasses my company produces: May we please give you the best of our line?'

'Nice,' said Catherine. 'Those who can afford it most get it for free.'

'It's a publicity thing,' said Lucie. 'A celeb uses a product, we the minions run out to buy it.'

'I've never purchased anything I read about in *People* magazine,' said Catherine. 'Except for Crème de la Mer. But that's it!'

She ambled over to the sofa and sat down, curling her bare feet under her and grabbing a pillow to her stomach.

Involuntarily, Catherine's eyes began to close, even as she sat up.

'No,' cried Lucie. 'You have to help me. She wants Cara Mia Vineyard to send her a selection of wines, for free.'

'A few bottles?'

'Several cases,' said Lucie glumly.

'Look, doesn't she have a personal assistant who can call them?' Catherine decided to come clean. 'I practically stood them up. I'd gone on and on about going out to see the vineyard and how it was so important to me and then I just blew it off. I canceled. My contact, Marco, has sent me three or four e-mails suggesting different days, and I've answered none of them. I feel awkward coming in now and saying, "I'd like several cases of free wine for Isabella, please." I don't know her. I don't even know them.'

Lucie paced the length of the suite. 'I have to get to the set in a half-hour,' she said. 'Here's the thing: Isabella fixates. That's how I got hired – she was obsessed with a video I did for a boy band back in the U.S. So she wouldn't settle for anyone else.'

'Compulsion as a path to success?' asked Catherine. 'Instead of just a route to drive everyone else crazy.'

'Her focus is what makes her the top of the charts around here – she practices and practices until she's perfectly amazing. But she's decided she wants this wine. Nothing else will do. In truth, I think she just likes the label.'

Catherine flopped back on the sofa. 'No promises,' she said.

'You're good people, Catherine,' said Lucie, smiling broadly. 'Even when you spend so much time pretending otherwise.'

'And now you'll go and I can sleep?'

'And now I'll go, and you can stay up for an hour and call that Marco guy,' said Lucie. 'The word is that Isabella doesn't want to come out of her trailer until she's certain she's getting the wine.'

'Ever think she's just yanking your chain?' asked Catherine.

'At the rates they're paying, it's not in my interest to question,' said Lucie. 'Ginger's going to head to first grade in Prada loafers.'

'How cute!'

'Uh, I was actually just joking,' said Lucie. 'We could afford them once the summer's over, but I'll be tucking that money into her college fund and sending her to school in Crocs instead.'

She headed for the door. 'Don't sleep!' commanded Lucie. 'I'll be calling you in a few hours to check on your progress.'

'Hi, Marco,' said Catherine in her mind, imagining what she'd say to her phone crush. 'I was wondering if you could send me a truckload of *vino* for this spoiled rock star I don't really know. No, no, I doubt she'll endorse your wine. And I don't think she's going to be able to be photographed carrying it in her handbag. So what are you getting for your generous gift? Not a whole hell of a lot that I can see.'

That approach, she concluded, was unlikely to work.

The cell phone rang and it was Lucie, checking in as threatened. Catherine let it go through to voice mail. And then she took a deep breath and, rather embarrassed, called Marco. She thought of trying to affect a seductive phone persona, but that felt like the old her. Before she and Julius Caesar had had their meeting of the minds.

'Catherine!' cried Marco upon hearing her voice. 'I have been worried about you. One moment I expect you to be coming, and then the next I do not hear from you anymore. I thought you might have gotten ill, or had an accident.'

'No, no, Marco,' said Catherine. 'I've just been very . . .

busy with things in Venice and Rome. My schedule changed.'
She stopped speaking.

'No, Marco,' she said now. 'The truth is that I had some
personal matters to attend to. I've been inconsiderate and
I'm sorry.'

'Is there anything I can do? Are you in trouble?'

'Thank you, no,' said Catherine. 'But I do need to ask
you a favor. For a friend. I don't even know where to begin
because it's not really my place to ask this of you, and . . .'

'Just ask me,' said Marco. 'Anything for you.'

'Marco, you don't even know me,' said Catherine. 'You
have no idea what I'm about to say. We've never even met.'

'I don't care,' he said. 'I already like you. You are one of
my favorite Americans.'

'Have you met any others?'

'Yes,' he said. 'And I like you very much.'

Catherine quickly outlined the situation, then waited for
Marco to offer to either say no or send one case. Instead, he
quickly agreed to send a substantial quantity of wine to Isabella.

'This is really not necessary,' said Catherine.

'But it is,' said Marco. 'Because you've asked it of me.'

'What can I do to repay you?'

'Oh, now you offend me,' said Marco. 'I do not send this
wine with any expectation of any kind. I do it because you
are my friend.'

How nice, thought Catherine. She didn't think a man had
ever done something for her without expecting something
in return. Without even seeing her, or having to flash him a
little bust or thigh. It was altogether refreshing. She passed
along the specifics that Lucie had given her about address
and location, and then she went back to bed, quite pleased
with herself, her good deed done for the day. And, as she
thought about it, probably for the entire summer.

★   ★   ★

The best thing about being self-employed, Catherine had often explained to Dakota, was being able to set your own schedule.

'Sometimes you have to work in the middle of the night,' she told her. 'And other days you can sleep in and eat breakfast at noon.'

Currently, Dakota had eaten early, because Ginger woke up when Lucie was leaving and could not be persuaded to go back to bed.

'C'mon,' she told her now. 'Let's go outside and get some fresh air.' Her goal was not particularly honorable: she planned to march Ginger around until she begged to go home and take a nap.

They saw James at the elevator on their way out.

'Hi, Dad,' said Dakota.

'Hi, Mr. Foster,' said Ginger. 'Want to take Sweetness to work with you?'

'That's very generous of you,' said James with utter seriousness. 'But I'm afraid I just wouldn't know what to do if Sweetness got lonely. She might prefer to go with the two of you.'

Ginger considered James's point. 'You're right, I think,' she said to him. 'But you can come over and visit all of us later.'

'I'd like that very much,' he said, patting Dakota on the shoulder as they entered the elevator.

The weather was overcast as they exited the hotel lobby; the first dreary day in a beautifully sunny – and very busy – two weeks.

'Ginger,' said Dakota. 'Have you ever been to a museum?'

'Yeah,' said Ginger sullenly, looking up through her strawberry blond bangs. 'Look here. Don't run. Don't touch. There's no ice cream. And no fun.'

'Okay,' said Dakota, thinking on her feet. 'Let's try something different. Can you count to ten?'

'Yeah,' said Ginger, insulted. 'One–two-three-four-five-six-seven-eight-nine-ten!' She shouted to bring home her point.

'What if I told you that we were going to go to a beautiful building, and we'll count out ten things,' said Dakota. 'Ten things that you pick out – and you have to tell me a story about each one.'

'No,' said Ginger. 'We trade stories.'

'Done deal,' said Dakota, shaking hands with her charge. 'And if you don't whine at all, we will definitely have ice cream.'

Dakota steered Ginger down and across the street, occasionally checking her map to make sure they were moving in the right direction. Several times along the way, Ginger ran ahead.

'Don't leave me behind, Ginger,' said Dakota. 'I might get lost if you do that.'

'Oh, okay,' said Ginger, falling back to hold Dakota's hand.

In a few minutes, she let go and started to dart forward, entranced by the colorful display in a store window.

'Slow down, cowgirl,' said Dakota.

'But I wanna see,' said Ginger.

'No,' said Dakota. 'You have to walk with me.'

Ginger stuck her hands in the pockets of her capri pants and stopped moving. She was only a few steps away. 'So you come here,' she said.

'No,' said Dakota, who also stood still. Apparently, she'd just entered a standoff with a kindergartner.

'No,' said Ginger.

Dakota leaned on the building and waited, calmly. Unlike Lucie, she had no place she needed to go. She and Ginger could play at this game all day.

'I could run away,' said Ginger.

'I could catch you,' said Dakota.

Ginger thought about this for several moments, then took a few steps toward Dakota.

'You're funny,' she told Dakota.

'You're fun,' said Dakota, who wasn't feeling exactly that. Ginger's favorite word, she was starting to realize, was 'no.' Not just saying it – though she did an awful lot of that, too – but hearing it. She liked to have Dakota stand up to her.

If it was stressful to figure out her life now, thought Dakota, imagine how hard it must be to be five years old and in a position to make all the decisions.

'Let's go get a gelato,' she said, even though it was before lunch.

'Can I have any flavor I want?' asked Ginger.

'No,' said Dakota. 'You can have either chocolate or vanilla. And next time we go, you can pick between two different flavors. But just two choices.'

To her surprise, Ginger didn't put up a fuss at all. Instead, hand on her chin, she thought about Dakota's offer. 'Can I get two scoops?' she asked.

'No,' said Dakota. 'You just get one.'

'Okay,' said Ginger amiably. 'I'll take it.'

The evening promised to be quite an adventure: Lucie called to let Dakota know she could bring Ginger down to the shoot. And Dakota, who had never been around a real set, could barely sleep even though she'd hoped to take a nap alongside Ginger.

She dressed with care, once again putting on her red tunic-style cabled sweater, but this time she wore it over jeans and boots. Catherine came by, wearing black slacks and a camel cape that fell to her hips, wearing seriously high heels. She looked like a giant. Ginger also selected her own outfit: a pink long-sleeve tee over which she layered a SpongeBob shirt.

'And jeans, like Dakota,' she explained to Catherine.

'Very nice,' said Catherine, who was trying to brush the tangles out of Ginger's hair, captivated by the softness of her babyish waves and the sweet smell of her shampoo. She had just enough baby left in her, with her slight chubbiness and round cheeks, thought Catherine, to make you want to smush her little tummy with raspberry kisses. Moments like these, as Dakota put shoes on small feet and tied laces, while Ginger chattered on about whether or not Sweetness would like to be in a music video, made her believe Lucie was a very smart woman indeed. She hadn't waited for some theoretical Mr. Right to come along, but had been brave enough to decide to parent alone.

Of course, when Ginger was putting up a fuss, Catherine told herself that Lucie was nuts. So it was all a matter of timing, really.

But good Ginger was in full force, and the trio took a cab to meet Lucie on the set.

Catherine expected to find a harried Lucie, rushing around, muttering to herself. She often seemed overwhelmed when she came to club meetings, frustrated and on edge. So it was a revelation to arrive at the shoot, get past the security guards, and enter a military-style operation: Lucie was in complete command of the scene. Everyone – the camera operators, the gaffers, the stylist, even Isabella herself – was following each and every direction Lucie gave.

'And cut!' shouted Lucie, before turning to catch a running Ginger in her arms.

'You're so smart, Mommy,' said Ginger. For the second time in an evening, Catherine envied her.

'Catherine,' said Lucie, tamping down Ginger's hair to see. 'Thank you so much. The personal touch went a huge way.'

'All I made was a phone call,' said Catherine, though she was quite pleased with herself.

'I know, but for them to come all this way,' said Lucie. 'I'm eternally grateful.'

'For who to come all this way?'

'Those gentlemen,' said Lucie, pointing to a dark-haired man and a much taller boy, about twenty, waving delightedly and starting to come over.

'Who's that?' said Dakota. 'Because he is cute.'

'That's Roberto Toscano,' said Lucie. 'And his father, Marco.'

Catherine didn't move a muscle. She hadn't expected him to show up personally. And it was one thing to have a nice phone crush on a man, and quite another to have to meet him in person. He looked different from how she envisioned. Not as tall as he sounded, for one thing, and while he was nice-looking, he wasn't quite as movie star–like as she figured he must be. He was, in fact, quite an ordinary man. But then he opened his mouth and she heard that gorgeous baritone.

'It's so wonderful to meet you, Catherine,' said Marco, offering her a handshake.

'I thought for sure you'd kiss her hand,' said Dakota. 'Isn't that what all Italians do when they meet a lady?'

Marco inclined his head and smiled, then took Dakota's hand and kissed it. 'A very beautiful young lady,' he said. 'Your daughter?' he asked Catherine. And for the third time that night, Catherine felt again a sense of something she'd missed.

'I could only be so lucky,' she said. 'But Dakota is the daughter of a dear friend of mine.'

'Well, then we must take all of you out for a wonderful dinner tonight to celebrate our meeting new friends,' said Marco.

'Sure,' said Dakota, whose eyes were firmly planted on Roberto, who was every bit as chiseled as his father was not.

The kid could be a model, thought Catherine, not blaming Dakota for her attentions.

'We couldn't,' said Catherine. 'You've done too much.'

'I insist,' said Marco.

'I don't know about you all,' said Lucie. 'But I'm freakin' starved. It's been a long, long day. Mr. Toscano, you do too much. But I, for one, am gracious enough to accept.'

'Then it's decided,' said Marco. 'Tonight you are all going to savor the flavors of Italy.'

25

There was another half-hour of shooting before they could all leave for dinner, and Catherine pretended to be fascinated by the comings and goings on the set. Marco tried, more than once, to start a conversation: he commented on the weather. Asked about her flight. Told her how pleased he was that her shop carried his family's wines. But none of it made a dent in Catherine's resolve. She was downright cold.

Her natural impulse was to flirt and try to get attention. That had its place, but now that she was trying to recover, she wasn't about to let herself get distracted. Marco's presence was a test. A deep-voiced, wine-delivering, nice-guy test.

At the restaurant, she insisted on sitting between Ginger and Dakota, letting Lucie have the place beside Marco on the banquette. Dakota, on the other hand, was only too delighted to sit next to Roberto, who seemed equally enthralled. As Marco struggled to make conversation with Catherine, Dakota and Roberto chattered away about Isabella.

'She said again how much she likes my tunic,' Dakota told the table. 'She said again she'd like me to make one for her.'

'Oh, no,' said Lucie. 'Here I go again. No sooner does Marco bring the wine than she's on to something else.'

'I told her she could just have it,' said Dakota, sipping a spoonful of chilled carrot soup.

'You didn't have to do that,' said Catherine. 'She just doesn't have to get everything she wants.'

Lucie and Dakota exchanged a look, which Catherine knew immediately was about her.

'We all need a chance to learn,' she said now.

'And to hear the word "no,"' said Dakota. 'Ginger and I have had a meeting of the minds, haven't we, Ginger?'

'Uh-huh,' said Ginger, her eyelids fluttering at the table. 'Mommy's the big boss, Dakota's the next boss, and I'm the littlest boss of Sweetness.'

'Looks like we're going to have to go,' said Lucie, as Ginger laid her head on her shoulder. 'I was so excited to join you that I guess I didn't think.'

'Let's just let her stretch out,' said Marco, moving over a couple of feet and motioning Lucie to move down the banquette, as well. She did so, then adjusted Ginger so she was lying down, her head in Lucie's lap. Ginger fell asleep instantly.

'Thank you,' said Lucie. 'I'm glad I get to stay.'

'I am happy you are here, as well,' said Marco. 'The little girl reminds me of my own when she was younger. Allegra.'

'That's my sister,' explained Roberto helpfully as Dakota nodded at this most illuminating piece of information. 'She's ten.'

'So you're married, then?' asked Catherine, before reminding herself she was very much not interested.

'Yes, at one time,' said Marco. 'My wife was a beautiful lady. Clever. But she passed away a few years ago in a car accident.'

'Let's talk about something else, Papà,' implored Roberto.

'Of course, it's a happy night,' said Marco. 'We had a nice drive from the countryside, and then we get to meet all of you. Especially Miss Dakota, who let me kiss her hand.' He raised a glass and drank, having selected his own wine off the menu, of course.

'So where is your daughter now?' asked Lucie. 'Is she in Rome with you?'

'No,' said Roberto. 'She's at the sea, with our grandmother.'

'That must be nice. Do you like the sea?' asked Dakota, with visions of Roberto in swimming trunks dancing in her head.

'I like all sorts of things,' he said. 'Especially meeting new people and practicing my English.'

'You speak very well,' said Lucie. 'I know only a few words of Italian from my mother.'

'Your mother was Italian?' asked Marco. 'How fabulous. She must know how to cook, I believe.'

'Oh, yes,' said Lucie, regaling him with tales of her mother's baked ziti and chicken parmigiana. 'You know, a lot of Italian-American dishes, that kind of thing. My brothers and I liked it.'

'Of course,' said Marco. 'Now, tell me about your brothers.'

'They're all fairly mad at me,' said Lucie. 'They think I should stay home and look after my mom. She's getting . . . forgetful.'

'But you have important work to do,' said Marco.

For a moment, Lucie thought he might be mocking her. But then she could see that he was really, truly paying attention. Not something she ever anticipated happening when Catherine Anderson was in the room. But Catherine was practically morose, eating only a few bites of the food put in front of her, and hardly saying a word. It was nice, Lucie thought now, to have someone who was interested. She took a big sip of wine.

'This is delicious,' she said to Marco, which clearly pleased him. 'Your family has great talent.'

'Yes,' said Marco, though it didn't feel immodest when

he said so. 'Though this one here wants to be an airline pilot. No grapes for him, he says.'

Roberto shrugged and tilted his head shyly.

'How can you not want to work the land of your family?' asked Lucie. 'I wish I had some sort of legacy.'

'Because maybe he wants to do his own stuff,' interjected Dakota. 'There's no obligation to do what your parents did.'

'What do you say, Catherine?' asked Marco. 'You should join our debate. It's a healthy discussion.'

'It's not my place to have an opinion,' she said. 'So I don't. But don't forget you've always got your Allegra. She just might take over Cara Mia if you give her the chance.'

The hour was late when they all returned to the V. But a pleasant message awaited them in their rooms: Anita and Marty had arrived! They hadn't sent word that they'd even be coming to Rome, and Dakota was ecstatic.

'Let's go see them now,' said Dakota, expecting Catherine to be the cooler head who would prevail.

'Totally,' said Catherine. She was very eager to see Anita, to put the awkwardness of the evening behind her, and to tell Anita about all the wedding shoes she'd been scouting out. Catherine had taken her bridesmaid duties even more seriously since the Nathan affair. She wanted very much to keep Anita's favor.

Like two kids up too late, they got off the elevator and crept up toward Anita and Marty's room, *shhhh*ing each other all along the way. Instead of knocking, they scratched at the door, not wanting to awaken Anita if she was already sleeping.

'About time!' boomed Marty as he let them in. 'Anita's been microwaving the hot chocolate she got sent up from room service for the past half-hour. I was beginning to think I'd never get a chance to drink it.'

'Hi, Marty,' said Dakota, before going straight to Anita's waiting arms for a big hug. Catherine wished she could do the same, but instead kissed Anita delicately on the cheek.

'So you want to hear all about what I've been doing?' said Dakota. 'For one thing, my dad has been trying to turn me into an architect. Lots of information about drawing and stuff like that. But that's okay, because I've also made friends with the chef in the kitchen. I go down there whenever I can. For another, we just had the most amazing dinner, and there was this guy named Roberto? And he's staying in the city for a while because his grandmother's got an apartment and his father said he could stand to practice his English and I said, "Okay," because he's very, very cute.'

'You should breathe, dear,' said Anita, handing the cups of hot chocolate around as there was another knock at the door.

'This is exciting,' said Marty, running his fingers through his thick, white hair. 'A real party.'

'Anyway, so this guy, Roberto . . .' began Dakota, trailing off as she saw her father at the door. 'Later. Don't say *anything*.'

James greeted Marty and Anita, then sat down on the sofa.

'Dakota, I've decided we should go on a field trip tomorrow,' he said now. 'You and I will go to the Colosseum – I've arranged a great tour – and I can show you a bit about how it's built. How does that sound?'

'I might have to look after Ginger,' she said dully. She'd had high hopes for spending the day with Roberto, who told her about the flower market in the Campo de' Fiori and how he loved to wander through. And, even though he hadn't come right out and said so, his words seemed to indicate to Dakota that he might just enjoy her company.

'No, I sent Lucie an e-mail earlier today and she

BlackBerryed back that she doesn't need you in the morning,' said James. 'So we're free and clear. And you've been really eager to go and you've been working so hard. I thought some father-daughter bonding was in order.' He laughed, obviously pleased with himself.

'Great idea!' said Anita, and Dakota knew she was sunk. She pretended to care about the nighttime view – which ordinarily she could watch for hours, the lights of Rome twinkling – in order to get away from everyone exclaiming about how wonderful the next day would be for her.

Besides being smart, funny, good-looking, and into the same music as she was, Roberto had another good quality, Dakota had noticed. He actually talked to her. And now she was going to have to miss the first day of the rest of her life simply because her dad felt lonely. Sometimes life just sucked.

At the very least, she'd expected Catherine to come to her rescue. But she was clearly preoccupied with catching up with Anita and hearing all the details of her travels.

'The trip across the Atlantic was fine,' Anita was saying. 'Very pleasant.'

'The problem began when we arrived in the UK,' said Marty. 'The investigator couldn't have been nicer.'

'And he did so much research,' said Anita. 'Took everything we gave him – her name, passport info, her profession as a bookkeeper – and he pieced together a pretty fair representation of my sister's whereabouts in the late sixties.'

'We found a former coworker of hers,' said Marty. 'Retired now, of course. But she remembered Sarah right as rain.'

'That was a very good day,' said Anita. 'But there were a lot of leads that didn't amount to anything.'

'And let's not forget the private eye had the postcards,' said Marty. 'And they seem to track her movements, we think. They start out in England . . .'

'And go to Paris. Lots of Big Ben and the Eiffel Tower.

But then there were multiple ones from southern Austria, from southern France, from Yugoslavia, and from Greece. And finally the PI looks through the entire pile and starts separating them out and looks up at us and says he thinks it is odd that he sees so many repeats and yet only one from Italy: the Colosseum. Years ago.'

James gave Dakota a meaningful jab hearing that, and she tried to force a pleasant expression on her face.

'I don't get it,' said Catherine.

'What do all those other countries have in common?' said Anita.

'They border Italy,' mumbled Dakota, hoping to wrap things up so she could fire off a text to Roberto before it was too late.

'Exactly,' said Marty. 'There's only the one postcard from Rome. But all the other ones are sent from places you could get to by a train's journey.'

'Just outside the Italian border,' added Anita.

'She gave away her location,' said Marty. 'And maybe she got nervous. She wasn't ready. But still, she kept it up with the postcards. Reaching out to her big sister. That's a message unto itself.'

'Except for this year,' said Anita, her smile a little tight.

Catherine felt a growing unease in her stomach.

'The good news is that we're confident about this theory,' said Anita. 'I think she's here. In Rome. And starting tomorrow, I am going to find Sarah. Finally. I am going to bring my baby sister home.'

26

Standing inside the Colosseum, listening to the tour guide explain the system of sails that provided roof cover for the Romans as they watched the gladiators battle animals and one another, was more fascinating than Dakota had expected. But even more surprising – and more than a wee bit disconcerting – was seeing just how excited her father was to be standing in an architectural marvel. She'd figured he'd be excited, but he was completely over the top, engaging the tour guide in a long and detailed discussion of the fact that the stadium could be filled or emptied of people in a matter of minutes, thanks to the numbering system of the doorways. And the arches. He could not stop talking about the math behind the arches.

Yep, he was that guy. The one on tour who puts up his hand every thirty seconds to either show off the guidebook he memorized and make his own point, or keep asking questions until long after you really needed a bathroom break.

Dakota didn't mind as much as she might have, however, because she'd made contact with Roberto. And no, his interest wasn't all in her imagination: he'd invited himself along when she told him that she was going to take Ginger to enjoy a picnic that afternoon. Every day she spent with Ginger, Dakota slathered her in sunscreen and a ball cap and together the two of them were tourist adventurers. They'd tossed coins over their shoulder at the Trevi Fountain, climbed down into the ruins of an ancient Mithraic temple under the Church of San Clemente, wandered around the Baths of Caracalla – Ginger was quite certain she preferred having a tub all to herself, she declared – and ate plates of pasta at tiny hole-in-the-wall cafés whenever the mood struck them. A week earlier, they'd spent twenty minutes watching a fascinating parade that shut down the street – there were flags, and lots of children tromping along in the road, and a marching group of police leading the way. They waved at folks, who waved back.

'When are the floats coming, Dakota?' Ginger had asked.

Uncertain, Dakota stopped an Italian passerby and inquired.

'That's not a parade,' he said, in halting English. 'It's the Communists. A rally.'

'Oh,' said Dakota, before explaining to Ginger that there would be no clowns that afternoon.

But even the rally felt new and different – maybe even dangerous! – and therefore thrilling. The sounds, the smells, the lifestyle: Rome was such a change from New York. Dakota felt older and more sophisticated just by being here. But she also savored the freedom of not knowing what each day would bring: there was no shop to go to, no discussions to have with Peri, no focus on yarn. Funny thing was, she was doing more knitting now than she had in ages. She'd even found a tiny shop not too far from the hotel, and bought all the supplies she needed: if she didn't have her own kitchen to bake in, she was going to knit herself a cupcake. And a muffin. And maybe even a loaf of pound cake. What was she going to do with all of these items? She didn't know. Maybe give them to Ginger to play with. But ever since she saw that Roman woman knitting earlier in the summer, she felt a renewed sense of enjoyment when she sat down to it. Because she didn't *have* to do it. She wanted to. Everything in Rome was better.

And now there was Roberto.

'Dakota?' James was peering at her and Dakota could see that she was standing alone, the tour guide and the rest of the people scurrying far ahead. 'Are you feeling okay?'

'Just imagining mock navy battles in the amphitheater, Dad,' she said, feeling embarrassed. The last thing she wanted to do was tell her father she was going to spend time with Roberto. Without question, he'd come up with a reason why she needed to bring Ginger to the office and make her draw pictures while Dakota did some sort of computer research. And with Ginger around, it would be all but impossible to slip down to the kitchen and visit Andreas, the pastry chef, who often let her sample a new creation.

James never seemed to notice if she'd been gone awhile.

But even the thought of a fresh pastry – she could practically smell the raw dough! – was not as appealing as an afternoon walking through the park with Roberto. And Ginger, too, of course. She'd have to be careful not to get distracted and lose her, wondering, for a brief moment, about asking Lucie to buy one of those child leashes.

James put his arm around his daughter and looked down at her, though she wasn't that much shorter anymore.

'What a great morning together, right?' he asked. James remembered well the early days of getting to know Dakota, when she was just entering her teens and a bundle of energy. She was a happy, happy kid, he thought now, one who'd grown progressively quieter and more inward as the years went on. Everyone missed Georgia. But he thought of himself when he was in college, eager to figure out who he was and who he wanted to be, away from the opinions and habits of his parents. There were girls, too. Girls he liked, girls who liked him, girls who he wished liked him more. Those had been exciting days, when everything new stretched before him. This was likely the beginning of it, then, the long period of not really knowing Dakota until, hopefully, she came back to him when she was older. She had already started keeping secrets. At least that's what it felt like. But he supposed it was just part of her life that didn't involve him. It didn't seem fair, really: he wanted to know everything there was to know about Dakota, now and always. She was part of him. Not being able to connect with her felt like losing a part of his soul. It surprised him when she didn't want what he desired for her. Couldn't she see that he wanted to make *his* mistakes count for something and the only way to do that was to protect her from making any of her own? Stupid choices change the course of lives.

'Let's grab a bite,' said James, leading Dakota across the street from the Colosseum to a small sidewalk café. 'We can catch up.'

And then she knew: Her father wanted to 'have a talk.'

They took their seats, ordered Cokes, and watched the traffic go by.

'So, Dad,' said Dakota. 'What's on your mind?'

'I thought I'd see how you were feeling about the work you've been doing this summer,' he began. 'Like it?'

'It's fine,' said Dakota. 'But not really what I want to do with the rest of my life.'

'Well, no one is expecting you to take meeting notes for the rest of your life,' said James.

At the table next to them, two older women were arguing over a map. Dakota could not understand what they were saying – maybe it was German? – but she recognized the battle. One wanted to go in one direction, the other wanted to do something different. How easy it would be to tell her dad that she'd seen the light and she wanted to be an architect. Or a lawyer. Or that she was grateful for the knitting shop. His approval was right there, the smiles and hugs and happy daddness of it all, if only she gave the right answers to his unasked questions. Who are you going to be? What will you do?

Neither one of the tourist women was going to back down from her plan, that much was obvious. So why, thought Dakota, didn't one of them just walk away? Do what she wanted anyway? What rule said she had to sit there and argue?

'It's the office thing, Dad,' said Dakota finally, as James looked pained. 'That's not what I want.'

'You're eighteen,' said James. 'You don't know what you want.'

'When does it all begin, then?' she asked. 'The moment when I'm allowed to make my own decisions. Twenty-one? Twenty-five? When I get married? What if I never get married?'

'What are you on about?' asked James, leaning back so the waitress could bring him a plate of bruschetta that he'd ordered.

'I'm waiting,' said Dakota. 'Holding on until the moment when I reveal my dreams. But I'm not so much a kid anymore.'

'You're still very young,' said James. 'You don't know everything you think you do.'

'No, that's just the thing,' said Dakota. 'I'm starting to realize how much I don't know. Every day in Rome is like a gift, waiting to be opened. New people, new ideas. New tastes.'

'Tastes?'

She thought about stopping, not saying it all. But then what was the point?

'I sneak down to the kitchen when I'm supposed to be filing,' Dakota said now. 'Not all the time. But often enough that Andreas is pleased to see me. I even go there when Lucie's home and I don't have to watch Ginger.'

'What are you saying?' James was genuinely perplexed.

'I'm saying I like to eat pastry,' said Dakota. 'I like to think about it, I like to improvise, I like to create it. I'm saying that the one place I feel truly centered is when I'm baking. Even watching someone else – someone way beyond what I can do – is like listening to the most amazing concert. Everything just flows. So beautiful.'

The initial secret visits to Andreas had expanded from just watching to being put to work. 'If you're going to be here so often,' he'd said, 'you might as well grate. Or wash up.' The industrial mixer, all gleaming stainless steel. That had felt like an honor. One time, a late lunch customer had straggled in and Andreas, feeling generous, had shown her how to sprinkle sauce over a ricotta cheesecake that had been ordered for dessert. The rest of the kitchen eyed her suspiciously, but that was as it should be, thought Dakota. After all, she was part of the next wave. She was going to steal all their jobs. She *was* going to run her own kitchen someday.

The challenge was making her father understand – and so far it wasn't working.

'We've talked about this before,' said James. 'Baking is not the career for you.'

'I'm so sorry, Dad,' said Dakota. 'But I have to have enough faith in myself to pursue my own dream. Not yours.'

The tourists had settled into a grumpy silence, nursing their drinks and not even looking each other in the eye. Their competing maps lay on the table but the two of them had not moved. Dakota looked at her father, a knot of fear squeezing at her chest.

'I know,' she said. 'I know you and the trust from Mom's estate have paid for college so far. I know you can tighten the purse strings and that's that. But you know what? If I have this dream, then I owe it to myself to figure out how to make it happen. I need to look into other sources of funding, I think. Loans or something.'

'The choice isn't NYU or you're homeless, Dakota,' said James. 'You needn't be so dramatic.'

'But I have to be,' she said, raising her voice. 'Don't you see, Dad? Everyone is telling me where to go and who to be. Georgia's daughter, James's girl. The thing is: I am not either one of you. I'm me. And I don't want the shop.'

'So what, then?'

'Sell it to Peri, maybe. I don't know!' She took a large mouthful of Coke and crunched the ice cubes. 'I don't know,' she said again, more calmly. 'But I want to go to pastry school. I want to have that opportunity.'

'You're wasting your time,' said James. 'It's not the career you need. On your feet all day, in a hot kitchen. What kind of life is that?'

'A delicious life,' said Dakota. 'The life I want. Even if you don't understand or approve. That can't be why I make my decisions. Because I'm living for you, and I'll never be satisfied. And if I keep the shop because that's what Mom did, then I'm throwing my life away for her.'

'I've already told you,' said James. 'The shop can be something you do on the side.'

'That's not what I want, either. Walker and Daughter deserves someone who loves it all the time. To the right person it would be a bonanza,' said Dakota. 'But to me it feels like an albatross.'

'Never knew you felt so strongly,' said James stiffly. 'Your mother was so proud of that place she put your name right on the sign.'

'Is that reason enough for me to stay?' said Dakota. 'I was a child. I didn't ask for it.'

'I guess that's something you'll have to decide,' said James. 'You're so grown up now, you can figure out things for yourself.'

'No adult I've ever seen is capable of knowing everything

all the time,' said Dakota. 'Dad, I've spent the majority of my Friday nights sitting around with a bunch of older women. And they don't seem to have a whole hell of a lot figured out most of the time. It's all trial and error. And that's all I'm saying. It's time I went out there and made some big-ass mistakes.'

'The world . . .' started James. 'Forging ahead seems much more glamorous in the talking about than the living of it, Dakota. Do you think every day is going to be a joy just because you're making cookies – literally? It won't be.'

'I know that, Dad,' said Dakota, before holding up her hand. 'No, wait. Let me try that again. I have no idea, Dad. But I better start learning.'

So much for a nice outing with his daughter, thought James. He recalled when a new bike was all that Dakota wanted. Now she insisted on taking on the world.

Roberto's few extra days in Rome turned into weeks, with the tacit approval of his father.

'I suspect he wants a reason to keep returning to the city,' Roberto told Dakota as they strolled the gardens at the Villa Borghese, with its wide lawns like Central Park back home. 'He talks often of your friend Catherine.'

'Do they see each other a lot?' asked Dakota, and Roberto shrugged.

She had noticed, in a vague way, that Catherine was keeping a low profile recently, but she'd had more than enough going on in her own life to keep herself preoccupied. Her father had tried several times to discuss, yet again, his position about her college career. All the while, Dakota had been diligently doing her research, coming up with schools and financial plans and just opportunities in general.

The wind came up, just slightly, shaking the tall trees and adding a bit of resistance to Ginger as she scurried about on the grass nearby, having running contests with Sweetness, who bounced alternately in Ginger's hand or up on her shoulder.

'I won again,' she shouted triumphantly after yet another victory against the stuffie she took everywhere.

'That creature is lucky you're looking after it,' said Roberto. Dakota grinned. In addition to the cupcakes she was creating, she'd also knitted a teeny cardigan for Sweetness, and a cap with holes for her ears. She'd done it for Ginger, of course, but she was very glad to see that Roberto had noticed. One part of her wanted to make something for Roberto, too, but that seemed so 1950s. She'd stick to making clothes for the toy.

They'd had quite an afternoon, their trio, renting bikes to ride through the park, and relaxing on the grass afterward with squat bottles of Orangina.

'Hey, hey,' said Ginger, racing up to them. 'Can I jump out of a tree, Dakota?'

'No,' said Dakota. It was their game now: Ginger thought up the craziest suggestion she could and then waited for Dakota to tell her she couldn't do it.

'Can I fly on the wings of a bird?'

'No.'

'Can I watch you kiss Roberto?'

Dakota blushed, looked at Roberto, and then hastily looked away. Truth was, they hadn't kissed. They had sometimes held hands, but mostly they just hung out with Ginger as their chaperone and flirted via text message afterward.

'No,' she said pointedly.

'Is Roberto your boyfriend?' asked Ginger.

'No,' said Dakota.

'Yes,' said Roberto.

Dakota grinned, but only on the inside. 'Okay,' she said casually. It was quite a summer, indeed.

★   ★   ★

Marco went back and forth between the vineyard and the city several times, always encouraging Catherine to join him on one of his drives to the country.

Mostly she demurred. But, just one time, as an experiment, she relented, tying a blue scarf around her blond hair to prevent the wind from mussing her all about. She didn't plan to have any fun, told herself that she was only going to stop Marco from being such a pest, but, in fact, she fell easily into conversation with him. Which, of course, made her annoyed for even going.

'Allegra loves to take drives,' he said, talking about his young daughter as he swerved very, very quickly around the curving road. 'She sits in the back and tells me where to turn.'

'I helped teach Dakota how to drive,' Catherine told him, soaking in the green trees, the tiled houses. 'James brought her up to Cold Spring and we practiced parallel parking on some quiet roads. It's quite difficult to drive in New York. The cabs change multiple lanes at the same time.'

'Thank God, Allegra won't be driving for years,' Marco replied. 'It's hard enough seeing how tall she's growing. And Roberto! Well, he's practically a man already. Bigger than I am, and he's smarter, too.'

It was refreshing, truly, to spend time with a man who couldn't seem to stop himself from talking about his children. Catherine made sure to store up tidbits on Roberto – how he liked to quote his favorite American movie when he was in high school, the afternoon he fell out of a tree at the vineyard as a young boy and broke his arm – that she could later share with Dakota. Because she enjoyed chatting with her young friend and she knew Dakota hadn't much else but Roberto on the brain. And baking. There was always that. But Catherine had even less to add to a discussion in that category. So Roberto details it was.

Marco made a point to call Catherine dutifully every time he returned to Rome to check on Roberto, and several times went to dinner with Lucie, Ginger, Dakota, and his son. Catherine, although invited every time, went only once, when James had also accompanied them. They spent the better part of an evening eating salads and tasting wines and discussing the benefits of working on one's own or for some-one else. James was circumspect but seemed very intrigued by what the winemaker had to say.

'That Marco is one cool guy,' he told her later as they sat at the V hotel bar and had a nightcap. 'Not like those chuckleheads you usually hang around with.'

'I barely know him,' said Catherine. 'I just sell his wine at The Phoenix.'

'Speaking of, how's business?' said James. He found it rather amusing that Catherine would assume it perfectly natural to leave her shop in someone else's hands while she jaunted off to Europe. Peri, at the very least, owned a part of Walker and Daughter and was heavily invested in its success.

'I hear it's going not too bad,' she said, knowing full well he thought she ran a vanity business. She preferred to think of it as a lifestyle occupation.

'Dakota wants to sell the shop,' he told her, sipping at a Scotch. 'It breaks my heart.'

'Georgia isn't in the store, you know,' said Catherine. She was also drinking Scotch, but just one. She hadn't had a G.W. with James in a long time, nor had they felt the need to sneak out to a restaurant and pretend to dine with Georgia. Dakota kept telling her that Rome was going to renew her soul. Perhaps she really did know what she was talking about.

'Right,' said James, raising an eyebrow. 'She's in your store's namesake dress.'

'I was thinking more broadly here,' said Catherine. 'You know, she's in our hearts and all that jazz.'

'Yeah,' said James ruefully. 'But doesn't the store make it feel less like she's gone?'

'Maybe that's it,' said Catherine softly as an idea came to her. 'Maybe the store itself is a stumbling block for Dakota. Emotionally, I mean.'

'Don't know. I can't get her to really open up to me,' said James. 'She thinks I'm the enemy, crushing her cookie dreams.'

'No,' said Catherine. 'She believes you don't understand her. But she doesn't hate you.'

'I feel like an ogre,' said James. 'I just know what's best.'

Catherine began to laugh, heartily. 'Oh, James Foster,' she said. 'That is the funniest thing I've ever heard. No, you don't. You just want her to do what's safest, not what's best. It isn't the same thing.'

James had to admit: She had him there.

'So,' he said. 'Let's talk about playing it safe. I'll start with just one word.'

'Bring it on,' said Catherine.

James drained his Scotch glass before dabbing his lips with a napkin, then standing up from his bar stool. He kissed Catherine on the top of her head and leaned in close to whisper his one word: 'Marco?'

27

The raspberry-lime granita was melting faster than Catherine could spoon it into her mouth, making a delicious fruit slushy, as she idled away the afternoon on the roof deck of the V hotel. She was hiding, yet again, in broad daylight. Everyone assumed she was going on grand adventures and avoiding them all. In truth, she simply took the elevator up several flights and watched the city go about its business, admiring the architectural feats in every direction, the shape of Saint Peter's Basilica in the distance. Oh, some days she wandered around the city – with all the great art everywhere, even a quick half-hour dash into a church could satiate her desire to see the work of masters – but now that Marco continued to pop up unexpectedly, she pretty much stayed put at the hotel.

On the few occasions when they'd been without the gaggle – such as when Marco hounded Catherine to help him choose a new label for Cara Mia's export wines – she had been merciless in her questioning of Marco.

Why did he never remarry? He almost did, he told her, but he ended it when he realized he was just trying to fill his loneliness and he wasn't the right man for the girl. He'd never give her what she truly deserved.

She hated that answer: he was a gentleman even when he was crushing someone's dream.

Was it hard to be a single parent who was a man? Yes, he

said, but it didn't matter. His children needed a constant love, not a carousel of women playing mommy.

She hated that answer, too.

Had he ever had customers at Cara Mia who couldn't pay? Yes, he said, and eventually they always settled up. So he rode through their bad times with them. Loyalty, he told her, is its own reward.

Marco was, without question, a problem. And the problem was that Catherine liked him. She didn't appreciate James pointing it out, either.

Well, we know how that always turns out, she said to herself, her nose practically in her chilled glass to scrape out every last bit of lusciousness.

It was a well-earned treat for rising early. She'd made one trip outside the hotel that day, getting up at the crack of dawn to pay her respects to her new imaginary best friend: good old Julius Caesar, resting in the Roman Forum. She took flowers, as she'd heard many do, and spent a few moments reflecting not on Caesar but on herself. About how she'd want people to think of her once she was gone. The legacy of her humanity, such as it was. And she focused on the new resolution she'd made.

This was the thing of it: Catherine had yet to manage having a relationship and having a life. The casual dating hadn't been more than a pleasant distraction. But the serious ones, the guys she cared about, always led to trouble. She always tried to duck down and merge into someone else's identity instead of maintaining her own. It wasn't falling in love so much as tossing herself aside. She did it with her ex-husband, philandering, cruel bastard that he was, and she did it with Nathan in the space of about a week. 'Julius,' she said, 'I promise to stop playing it that way, and I will.' So there could be no Marco, no man at all, until she'd figured out how not to fall into the trap. Though it was too late to lobby for a spot as a vestal virgin.

Strange how after ages wondering if everyone had time for her, she was making herself scarce just when they all wanted to hang out together. She and KC were e-mailing, something they'd never done before, just sharing news. She told her about Marco, that it wasn't going to be serious. *If you say so,* KC had written in reply. And Lucie seemed to call her with a thought or idea every few days. Dakota came by every so often bursting with a Roberto update, or a James complaint, and sometimes Catherine entertained both Roberto and Dakota when they came back to the hotel after a date and didn't want to spend any more time with Ginger. She listened to Roberto talk about his dreams of being an airline pilot and Dakota of being a pastry chef. She liked those evenings best, when the kids would come on over and drink espresso even though it was late, and talk about anything and everything: the crazy woman stalking tour groups at Palatine Hill, the pros and cons of American versus European Idol, the way they both felt sad often because their mothers were gone. Catherine nodded at all of it: she could empathize with much of what they had to say – whether it was remembering Georgia or her own mother – or at least recall moments when she'd felt many of the same emotions they were going through. Maybe, she told herself, it was better she wasn't a mother. This way she could always just be the friend who cared.

And even if Dakota didn't come by, there was always Anita. Even though she was thoroughly harried by her quest to find Sarah, she and Marty checked in on Catherine every day. She couldn't let her bridesmaid get all mopey, she said.

But Catherine wasn't moping around. She was hiding, yes. Not the same thing. She was calmer than she could ever remember being. Sometimes she pecked away at writing her book, which she enjoyed more and more. 'Long ago,' she told Dakota, 'I was the best columnist at the *Harrisburg High Gazette*, and Georgia was my editor.' Other times, she read classics she borrowed from the reading nook in the hotel café. Reconnecting with who she was: that's what she was doing. Creating a better model for how to be comfortable in her own skin. With her life as it was.

Her cell phone buzzed on the table. Lucie. She'd been calling all day. Another Isabella emergency, no doubt. There'd been several over the course of the summer. Well, Catherine would call her back. Later. After she'd enjoyed a second granita.

Working with Isabella was a headache: new demands night and day, constant suggestions for how Lucie should set up a shot, and an ever-changing entourage. The latest compulsive quest, however, was going to push her right over the edge.

Lucie's phone rang and she whipped it out of her jeans.

'Catherine?' she asked. 'I have to ask another huge favor.'

'Mom got lost,' said a voice. No hello. No how are you. Just the facts. And a lot of edge to the tone. 'I thought you might actually care to know.'

'Hi, Mitch,' said Lucie evenly. If Rosie was really in danger, he would have led with that news, she told herself. Better to play it calm. 'Where is she now?'

'She's at home and I'm here with her now,' said Mitch. 'No thanks to you.'

'Five-minute break, everyone,' shouted Lucie. Then she lowered her voice. 'Is she okay?'

'For now,' said Mitch. 'But who knows what we'll be dealing with tomorrow or even the next day?'

'Did you come home early from your vacation?'

'We would have had to,' said Mitch sharply. 'If we hadn't already gotten home on the weekend.'

'Mitch, I'm on set, and time is money – and not my money, either,' said Lucie. 'Can you give me the condensed version?'

Apparently Rosie had decided she needed some groceries and she couldn't wait until her middle son, Brian, came over after work to take her to the store. So she walked. And when Brian arrived at six o'clock, she was nowhere to be found. Not at the store, not on the street, not at the neighbors'.

'She just waltzed in the door about fifteen minutes ago,' said Mitch. 'I just called Brian back from the police station, where he was going to file a missing persons report.'

'How long was she gone?'

'Long enough, Luce, for Brian to sit here until nine p.m. and no sign of Mom,' barked Mitch. 'It was getting dark and she was still out there.'

Lucie could hear the sound of a receiver being lifted, and puffs of breath hitting the handset.

'Hi, Mom,' she said.

'Oh, such fuss we're having here,' said Rosie. 'I go on a walk in my own town and the boys are calling the police on me. They won't fix my car, and now they're sending me to jail for wanting to have a loaf of bread. Soon you'll all be starving me to death. Stealing my food!'

'No one is stealing your food, Mom,' said Lucie. 'You could have maybe left a note.'

'For who? For myself? "Good-bye, Rosie, see you when you get home. Love, Rosie."' She made a tsking sound with her tongue. 'I was in charge of myself long before the four of you came along, and I'll be in charge for a long time still.'

'It's just that we were worried, Ma,' said Mitch.

'My own children treat me like a prisoner of war,' said

Rosie. 'You know who's good to me? That Darwin. She and her husband brought their babies to meet me.'

'I don't know what she's talking about,' said Mitch to Lucie. 'Ma, Lucie's friend didn't come out here. Now can you please hang up the phone while I talk to Lucie?'

'It's not right that you call Lucie in Italy to tattle on me,' said Rosie. 'I've done nothing wrong but live my life the same as I've always done. So sue me, I wanted a steak sandwich.'

'The ice cream was completely melted,' said Mitch. 'You must have bought it five hours ago. Where have you been since then?'

'I told you,' said Rosie, striking the same tone she used long ago when Brian and Mitch would wrestle too close to her Hummel figurine collection in the living room. 'I was walking around.'

'Ma, just a few minutes with Lucie, please?'

'Fine,' said Rosie, drawing out the word until it seemed at least three syllables long. 'And Darwin and Dan were here on Friday, before you came home. It's not my imagination. You phone them and ask if you don't believe me. A boy who doesn't believe his mother . . .'

Lucie could hear Rosie making a great deal of noise. She knew that old trick: her mother was pretending to hang up so she could listen in. Oh, she may have been losing her memory, but she was still a sly one, that Rosie.

'This situation is getting out of hand,' said Mitch, assuming he was alone on the line with Lucie. 'I think you need to come home.'

'Mitch, you want me to make it go away and I can't,' said Lucie, trying to keep her voice low so she didn't attract attention from the crew or Isabella. 'Mom is getting older. She had some bad days.'

'Or maybe everybody just got a little too nosy for their

own good,' said Rosie quickly, before realizing she'd just given away her eavesdropping status to her son.

'Ma, please,' shouted Mitch, as Rosie harrumphed and slammed down the phone. 'I'm going to have a goddamn heart attack, here, Lucie.' His voice cracked. 'This is really taking a toll. You don't see what I'm talking about because you're not here often enough.'

There was no doubt that Mitch was annoying. Argumentative. Dismissive. Bossy. But he was also her older brother. And, Lucie hated to admit, there might be a kernel of truth in what he was saying. That's what she hated the most.

Hours later, Lucie wearily returned to her suite at the hotel. Ginger was fast asleep in her bed, and Dakota was dozing on the sofa, yet another incomprehensible Italian drama on the television. They really ought to provide closed captioning, she thought. She took her phone into Dakota's bedroom, so as not to disturb her daughter, and dialed Darwin.

'*Ciao*,' said Darwin. 'I recognized the number.'

'Save me,' moaned Lucie into the phone. 'I've just been force-fed a huge helping of guilt.'

'Rosie,' said Darwin immediately.

'Oh my God,' said Lucie. 'If you know that already . . . Did you go out and see my mom last weekend?'

'I told you I was going to,' said Darwin. 'Last time we talked.'

'I know, I know,' said Lucie. 'It just seemed out of context to hear Mitch say your name.'

'He wasn't there,' said Darwin. 'Brian had just left before we got there; he cleaned out the storm drains.'

'You didn't have to do the whole schlep to Jersey, Dar,' said Lucie, rubbing her eyes. Oh, she was tired.

'Of course we did,' said Darwin. 'Your mother knitted us an entire layette for each of the kids. I mean, it was gorgeous.'

''Cause you know from knitting?' Lucie laughed. Even though Darwin was on her sock jaunt, she was rather infamous in the group for never repairing her mistakes or checking her gauge. In short, she was a sloppy knitter.

'Oh, you wait until you get home,' said Darwin now. 'I have moved on from socks, my friend. The kids only have so many feet. Now I am pumping through the Georgia afghans like nobody's business. I am going to so be the top this year.'

'What about Anita?' said Lucie. 'She always makes the most.'

'Well, word on the street, from Catherine via KC to Peri, is that she is making a wedding coat.'

'I see her all the time and I don't even know this?'

'I guess because you're always hanging out with that wine guy,' said Darwin. 'So any details worth sharing?'

Lucie peeled off her jeans and slid under the covers of Dakota's bed, hoping she wouldn't mind.

'No,' she admitted. 'He's very nice. Everybody's friend. It makes me wonder if I've missed too much. Though we're always surrounded by a ton of other people. It's like those group movie dates when you're in middle school. Know what I mean?'

'Not really,' said Darwin. 'I never had a boyfriend before Dan in college. But I saw something like that in *Saved by the Bell*.'

'Well, he seems very interested in Catherine, mainly,' said Lucie. 'Which kind of burns me because she always gets what she wants, you know? First she comes to Italy, then a little bit of loving . . .'

'So Catherine *is* dating him, then?' asked Darwin.

'It's all a bit odd, actually,' said Lucie. 'She broods and he stares.'

'Very dramatic,' enthused Darwin.

'Annoying,' corrected Lucie. 'It's not that I like Marco Toscano. I'm too damn busy for all that jazz. But I like the idea of being pursued.'

'Well,' said Darwin, 'it's not like there's just one man in Italy. Is there?'

'No,' said Lucie. 'He's just the only one I've met.'

'Didn't you go to Italy because it was going to be great for your career?'

'Yes, Professor,' said Lucie.

'So what's all this getting sidetracked, "Maybe I oughta have a romance" stuff?' said Darwin. 'I get that we all have to eat dinner, but don't try to twist it into something it isn't.'

'I might like to have a partner, too, you know,' said Lucie. She wasn't in the mood for more than one lecture in an evening.

'I thought you said he was a widower with kids,' said Darwin.

'He is,' said Lucie. 'He really seems to be a caring father.'

'So you're looking for a dad for Ginger, then,' said Darwin. 'Is this about Will?'

'No,' said Lucie. 'I like him. I'm interested.'

'Interested in being a mother to his children?'

The line was silent.

'Are you asleep?'

'No,' said Lucie, though in fact her eyes were closed. 'You know I'm not looking for more kids. Ginger is enough. But you never know. We could work our way around it. Or maybe just have a fling in Rome.'

'Oh, don't give me the old *Sound of Music* "There's always boarding school" routine,' said Darwin. 'If you'll remember, that guy ends up marrying the nun with the bad haircut. The one who loves his children. Not the ambitious blondie who lurks about making eyes at him.'

'I'm not blond,' said Lucie, before laughing uncontrollably from nervousness and exhaustion. 'That's Catherine.'

'Luce, any minute now Stanton is going to scream for no apparent reason,' said Darwin. 'Are you into Marco the wine guy or not?'

Lucie groaned and rolled over in bed.

'No,' she admitted. 'I just like the idea.'

'Is this about Will?' Darwin asked again.

'Yes,' she moaned. 'What are you, a psychologist now?' Lucie pulled the covers over her head.

'It was seeing Marco be sweet to Ginger,' she said now. 'Got me wondering if I ought to just call up this Will and let him know. Do everyone a favor.'

'If that's what you want, I'll be supportive,' said Darwin. 'But have you considered he might demand visitation? Are you willing to share Ginger on someone else's terms?'

Lucie's eyes flew open.

'I hadn't quite considered *that*,' she admitted. 'Maybe I'm in over my head. I have too much going on!'

'I know,' said Darwin. 'Your mother.'

'Darwin, give it to me straight: What's the situation with Rosie?'

'She's good: bubbly, friendly, fussed over the babies,' said Darwin. 'But she made a few mistakes. Left the oven on for a while after she took out the cookies, for example. Stuff you and I might do and it's no big. But then she seemed a bit foggy at times. Dan told me to suggest you or your brothers should visit her doctor, and maybe take her to a neurologist.'

'So Mitch might actually be onto something?'

'I don't know,' said Darwin. 'I'm only the real doctor around here. Dan's just the M.D. But he can call you when he gets back from the hospital.'

'Not tonight,' said Lucie. 'I'm fried. Isabella has decided

she needs to wear a piece of hand-knit couture in the video, and in the accompanying Italian *Vogue* fashion spread.'

'What about the minidress Dakota was making?'

'It's fabulous,' said Lucie. 'Isabella wears it all the time now that hand knits are her flavor of the week. Or month. It's hard to tell how long her mini-obsessions last. But she's very insistent. She wants me to find her a hand-knit gown.'

'I hope you didn't,' said Darwin. 'Just because you're frustrated with Catherine over this Marco maybe-not-even-a-fling-thing, she's helped you out more than once. Like with the wine? And getting Dakota to come over?'

'What can I do?' said Lucie, her voice tinny from lack of sleep. 'Isabella's the flightiest, most difficult person I've ever worked with. But this job is lucrative, and it could have a great impact on the type of stuff to come later.'

'So you told her . . .'

'That I know of a gorgeous gown in New York that is so amazing it has its own name,' said Lucie. 'I promised I could get her the Phoenix.'

28

Anita chose her outfit with care, being sure to wear a pair of earrings that had been her mother's. Something Sarah would recognize. Something she would have seen often. And for that there was only one option, a pair of mother-of-pearl discs in sterling silver that their mother wore for all dress-up occasions. The Schwartz family had been just fine, but they were not wealthy by any stretch. Luxuries were just that. Besides, most of the extravagances they had in later life came from Anita and Stan; most of her mother's remaining jewelry were items Anita had given her.

'It's today,' she reminded Marty, sitting, dressed, on the side of the bed and gently shaking him awake. 'We should be sure to get ready with enough time.'

It was five a.m.

There'd been no sleep for Anita the night before, as she tossed and turned yet again, imagining what her sister would look like. Silvery hair, like her own, or would she dye it? What if she was unhappy to see them? What if, what if, what if: Anita had thought of everything.

After the weeks of searching, it had all come down to paying a private investigator and a young student to research government documents – including marriage certificates – and find all the Sarah Schwartzes who were in the city. And then they broadened it to the entire country. They'd looked for women with that name, with Schwartzman and Schwartzmann and any variation on it they could think of, who'd shown up in records between 1968 and now. It was Italy: there weren't so many. It's not like they were looking for a John Smith in New York City.

So that was an advantage. They'd gone to the synagogue, of course, a majestic building in the area that had been the Jewish Ghetto since ancient times, many of the shops still specialized even though the neighborhood's name belonged to another time and place.

And Anita had joined her hired team at the computer, often scrolling through files that had been uploaded over the years. She also pulled on latex gloves – to protect her well-cared-for hands – and dug through the paper files that languished in boxes. They looked for Sarahs who were Schwartzes (and all its variations) in the present and Sarahs who had said surname in the past, before weddings or name changes, for example. And then they'd systematically worked their way through the list, traveling outside of Rome several times over the summer with their hired PI to meet Sarah. Only each and every time, as they knocked on a door and Anita held her breath waiting for the moment when she'd finally see the woman who'd once been her flower girl in a minty-green dress, the woman wasn't Sarah. Oh, she was a Sarah, of course. Just not *the* Sarah they were looking for.

But now there was only one name left. And, by process of elimination, she clearly had to be the right person.

Later in the morning, they folded themselves up and into their researcher's Smart car for the short drive to the suburb of Saxa Rubra, not too far from the city. Anita, although nervous – she'd been clutching a handkerchief so tightly her knuckles were white – was laughing and joking in a way she hadn't done so far in all of their searching.

'I know it,' she told Marty. 'I feel in my bones that I will see Sarah again.'

At a cozy café, the group fortified themselves with cups

of espresso before climbing the steps of a tidy suburban home in Saxa Rubra, a row of white flowers set underneath the windows.

'Very clean windows,' said Anita, pointing them out to Marty. 'Sarah was always a neatnik.'

They knocked and waited. Then knocked again.

'*Buongiorno,*' said the woman, who appeared to be in her sixties, looking at them curiously. 'Can I help you?' she said in accented English, something about their clothes or mannerisms pegging them as non-Italian. 'Are you lost?'

Anita couldn't help it: the tears flooded out of her eyes and down her cheeks and she felt wetness on her face before she was even aware she was bawling.

The woman frowned, a kindly look of concern.

'Do you need me to call a doctor?' she asked Marty. 'Is she okay?'

She turned to their research assistant. 'There is a hospital about ten minutes away,' she said. 'Your grandmother might need someone to help her.'

Anita, who'd maintained such composure when Stan had died, when she'd lost Georgia, when Nathan bellowed, when Dakota sulked, had finally lost it. All the bitterness and fear and regret and anger that she'd swallowed seemed to bubble to the surface all at once, and she was incapable of holding it back any longer.

Anita knew, and then she didn't know. How it would feel.

'It's your sister,' boomed Marty. 'From New York!'

The woman shook her head, closed the door a few inches, as though reminding herself to be wary of the trio of strangers on her doorstep. Who knew what could happen in this day and age? Even benign-looking American tourists from her own generation could be scam artists – or worse.

'I don't have a sister,' she said as she tried to shut the door. Marty put up a hand as though to hold back the door and stop this woman from closing off their last chance, his heart breaking as he guessed what Anita was about to say.

'It's not her,' was all Anita could get out before losing all composure and sitting down on the step. Marty sat next to his love, his arm around her, as she cried it out and poor, confused Sarah Schwartz – same name, but from a different family altogether – watched the odd American strangers from the safety of her living room window.

There was no need to be late, Anita told herself. She had cried in the car, she'd cried in the bathtub, she had cried in bed, she'd cried over dinner and again at breakfast. Marty was alarmed, she could see that. Well, there was disappoint-ment, she told him. And then there was devastation.

She hadn't realized quite how much her confidence had tricked her into thinking all she had to do was the right set of steps – like solving a math problem – and that once she'd done the hard work, then the gift of finding Sarah would follow.

But Catherine was coming by to take a look at the progress she'd made on the wedding coat she was knitting – not enough, Anita had to admit – and then the two of them were going shopping on Via Veneto. She put on extra layers of blush and powder, trying to cover the puffiness in her face, but only succeeded in making herself look, well, old.

Everyone else was having the summer of their lives and Anita felt as though she was falling apart.

'Look who's here,' said Marty, poking his head into the bedroom. He very much wanted to see Anita perk up again. 'It's Catherine.'

Their plan was to go to as many dress shops as necessary, one after the other, looking for the creamy, two-piece gown Anita envisioned underneath her knitted wedding coat. The garment, which she showed to Catherine, was still in its beginning stages, and Catherine didn't quite know enough about patterns to understand what she was looking at. Still, the piece of the front that Anita had done looked intricate, with an almost rope-like raised design on the smooth background. The stitches were so tiny and uniform that the section looked like something made on a machine.

'You're amazing,' said Catherine, before taking Anita by the hand and leading her out of the hotel and into the sunshine. They strolled awhile in comfortable silence before Catherine tried to broach the subject of the past few days; Marty had filled her in on the specifics.

'You look exhausted,' she said. 'Why don't we stop for an espresso?'

'I don't need to be coddled, that's for sure,' Anita replied. 'I had a setback. A big one. These things happen, even to me.'

'I'm sorry,' said Catherine, slipping her arm through Anita's. 'We don't have to talk about it.'

'Well, if not with you, then who?' said Anita. 'Marty has listened long enough.'

Catherine couldn't help feeling a bit of pride that Anita would consider her a confidante, like being picked first in gym class. She liked it, being someone's go-to girl.

'My sister was a thief,' said Anita. 'There. I caught her, my father had a heart attack when I told him, and she ran away. That's the story. Cue to us walking down the street forty years later and the only thing I've heard from her is one blank postcard that arrives around the day she took off.'

'Your sister was a burglar?'

'No, a thief,' said Anita. 'She stole, she didn't break into people's houses. She wasn't a criminal, exactly. Just dishonest.'

Catherine was stumped. What should she ask next? Was the conversation done? Or did Anita want her to press?

'What did she steal?' she asked. In truth, she'd been looking forward to the day so she could run some of her own issues through the Anita-mometer, getting a reading on what she ought to do. Being the listener – and potential adviser – for a woman she'd always looked up to felt quite unusual.

She could see the tears building up in Anita's eyes.

'Dignity,' said Anita. 'Self-respect. Honor. Trust. She stole a lot of trust.'

'So she slept with Stan?' concluded Catherine, nodding her head in understanding.

'Why does it always come to men with you?' said Anita, looking at her with disapproval. 'Sarah was like a little sister to Stanley. He wasn't about to cheat on me and take her to bed. I swear you have a one-track mind! Sex is not the only thing that causes problems.'

'It can cause a whole hell of a lot of problems,' said Catherine, who then stopped walking and looked at Anita full on in the face. 'The only other thing people fight about like this is money.'

Anita sighed. 'Yes, that's true.'

'Your sister Sarah stole money? From who? From you?'

'From my parents,' said Anita. 'And I'm not just talking about sneaking twenties from my mother's wallet. She was a bookkeeper in my father's business, and she pulled some clever accounting.'

Catherine was blown away. She'd pulled lots of stunts in her own time, but embezzling from her parents?

'Sarah must be a horrible person,' she said now. 'Why would you want to find her?'

'She wasn't a career criminal,' said Anita. 'She was a young girl who felt desperate. Don't you see? I was her older sister and I should have helped her.'

Catherine knew enough to hold her tongue this time, and just let Anita explain.

'Sarah was in her early twenties,' said Anita. 'She was a lot younger than I was. I had three growing boys in the late 1960s, busy running a home. I had a drawerful of kid gloves – the circle-pin era died hard with me.'

Catherine smiled; she could certainly imagine this elegant woman in white gloves and pillbox hats.

'But my sister wanted to do and try everything,' said Anita. 'Even the tame things seemed shocking to us then.'

They waited for a stoplight to change, and Anita pointed to a teenage girl with curly dark hair strolling down the street with her friends. 'That's what she looked like,' she said. 'Always smiling.'

'Until . . .' prompted Catherine.

'Until she brought home a boy who my parents didn't approve of,' said Anita. 'That's what started things.'

'So I was right, though,' said Catherine. 'This really does come down to men.'

'All things end up being about relationships,' said Anita. 'We are driven by the need for power, or attention, or comfort.

'Sarah dated lots of boys, some not even Jewish, which was something my parents couldn't abide,' she added. 'And then, apparently, she settled on one fellow – his name was Patrick or Paul or something – and they got serious. I never even met the guy because she wasn't about to bring him around. But then she came and told me: They'd been together.'

'Your sister had sex. So, okay,' said Catherine. 'Wasn't she an adult?'

'She was twenty-two,' said Anita. 'Not so young, but not so sophisticated. She was very sheltered.'

'And you were shocked?'

'No, I wasn't shocked,' said Anita. 'But I was concerned. I didn't approve. How long had she known him, for example?'

'And you told her she needed to break up with this guy, and she wouldn't.'

'Not exactly,' said Anita. 'They hadn't used protection, she was worried, so on and so forth. On top of that, he'd been drafted.'

'Vietnam,' said Catherine.

'It was a terrible waste, a confusing time,' said Anita. 'But if you were called, you served. That's what my father thought. Stan, too.'

'And Sarah . . .'

'Their plan was to run, she told me,' said Anita. 'Draft dodge. Go up to Canada, I guess.'

'And this is the part where you give her money on the sly, Anita,' urged Catherine. 'Right?'

'This is what I always tell you about learning from bad decisions,' said Anita. 'You suffer for them, but there can be a lesson somewhere. Because that's not what I did. I berated her for letting everyone down. I told her she was a disappointment. I knew so much, with my happy marriage and my perfect children, that I wasn't listening carefully enough. I didn't ask the right questions.'

'And that's when she took the money,' said Catherine. 'So they could run away.'

'Over the next few weeks, yes,' said Anita. 'She wrote checks made out to cash and forged my father's signature. It was Stan who discovered it. My father was getting older by that point and he'd tried to balance the checkbook but couldn't figure it out. Stan came over to help and got suspicious . . . '

'And you turned her in to the police?'

'My own sister? Never,' said Anita. 'Instead, I ran straight to my father and tattled the entire story. What shocks me now is how virtuous I felt about doing so! But the surprise was on me: my father's blood pressure went so high that he ended up in the hospital with chest pains.'

'And then a heart attack?' They were close to a sidewalk

café and Catherine raised an eyebrow, questioning whether Anita needed a caffeine jolt. Anita nodded, gratefully, and followed her inside, sitting at a small round table and waiting for Catherine to bring over two espressos.

'Sarah came home in the middle of the night with her suitcase in hand, and there I was, staying up while my mother slept upstairs,' said Anita. 'They'd given her Valium or whatnot so she could rest.'

'You confronted Sarah?'

'Confronted her? I threw a ton of bricks at her,' said Anita, clarifying when she saw Catherine's look of alarm. 'With words, my dear. I told her, in no uncertain terms, that she was a waste of a human being. I told her she'd killed our father, who was dying in a hospital bed.'

'Well, you kinda had a point there,' conceded Catherine.

'I told my own baby sister that she should get on a bus and get outta there and never come back,' said Anita. '"You're dead to me," I said to her. "From this moment on, I never had a sister." And all she did was cry. You see, she'd given the boy the money, and he took it. Leaving her behind. She wanted to come home.'

'Oh my God,' said Catherine. 'She'd been used.'

'I don't think he was even drafted, not from this vantage point,' said Anita. 'He was a con artist, and she was a naïve girl. But I didn't know that forty years ago. I was still a kid in so many ways myself.

'But what I did know, I told myself, was that Sarah was a thief who was destroying our family,' said Anita. 'Well, I've had a lot of time to parse what took place since then, and I was hardly honorable.'

Anita grew quiet, gazing at her hands for a long while before looking up. 'I yelled for a while and then I gave her money,' she said. 'I up-ended the entire contents of my purse and threw it at her. "Is this what you want, you little thief?" I said. I told her that our mother had said she never wanted to see her in our house again. Only that wasn't true. I lied to her. But I believed I was in the right, you see? Protecting my parents.'

'I always figured you for perfect, Anita,' said Catherine as she finished off her drink. 'That you don't make the kind of big mistakes the rest of us do.'

'I wish I never had,' she said. 'It wasn't my place to tell her to leave. I took more power than was my right to have, and that made *me* a thief, as well.'

Anita undid the top button of her blouse; she felt hot, her cheeks burning at the memory.

'I followed my sister up the stairs, threw some of her clothes into a bag, and told her that I'd better not ever hear from her again: "Never forget that you are not welcome here,"' said Anita. 'Those were my last words.'

'So was she pregnant?' asked Catherine. ''Cause that seems like a big elephant in the room.'

Anita started weeping. 'I don't know,' she admitted.

'And the postcards?'

'They're from Sarah,' said Anita. 'I know it. I've always known it. What is she saying? It's anyone's guess. For years, I told myself she wanted to let me know she was okay. That she'd forgiven me. In darker moments, I've wondered if she's taunting me with the knowledge that I can't find her even if I wanted to.'

'Anita, you're human,' said Catherine, her tone thoughtful and more than a little surprised. 'I always thought of you as knowing all the answers.'

'Oh, I know a lot now, dear, don't be fooled,' said Anita, wiping her eyes with a tissue. 'I'm a lot smarter now than I was then.'

'You saw Georgia in the park,' said Catherine now, as realization dawned. 'You saw Georgia on the park bench, and she was your chance for redemption.'

'Yes,' admitted Anita. Relieved to say it out loud. 'And I did a good job with her. I loved her like she was my own, and I listened. Whatever she had to say, I listened first and put my judgments aside.'

'Anita, I have something to tell you,' said Catherine. 'Another postcard came. I misplaced it. And then I told myself I kept forgetting to tell you. But I just felt bad and I didn't want to deal with your disapproval.'

'Do you have it with you?'

'At the room, yes,' said Catherine.

'Well, we'll look at it sometime later, then,' said Anita. 'I don't think there's any stone we've left unturned. I don't think it'll do much good.'

'There are flowers on the front,' said Catherine. 'Camellias.'

'Not particularly helpful, I don't think,' said Anita.

'I just realized if you sell the San Remo, then Sarah won't know how to find you,' said Catherine suddenly.

'I know, dear,' said Anita. 'I've thought of little else this summer. Apart from the wedding, of course. But sometimes there comes a moment when we just have to accept and move on. It's not ideal, but it's what is necessary sometimes. And I've decided it's time for me to let Sarah go. I'm not going to look for her anymore.'

Several hours later, Anita was feeling a strong sense of relief. Other than Stan and Marty, she'd never shared her guilt over Sarah with anyone. But Catherine, who had made so many missteps of her own, understood. In fact, it seemed to Anita that Catherine was more relaxed around her than ever. She didn't seem as nervous, as eager to please. And Anita liked the change.

'So, just in case you're wondering, I'm not dating anyone,' said Catherine. Anita had tried on twelve dresses in seven different stores; Catherine hadn't just played bystander and also looked at twenty outfits for herself. 'Not even Marco.'

'Good thinking, dear,' said Anita, smoothing out some wrinkled silk.

'Why do you say that?'

'Because maybe you're a tad focused on men,' said Anita. 'A bit too much. Nathan told me about New York.'

'He did?'

'Yes,' said Anita. 'And it's fine, dear.'

'It is?'

'He's a handsome man,' said Anita. 'He told me you seemed to have a crush on him, often coming by the apartment when he was there.'

'I see,' said Catherine, starting to seethe. So what about her resolve to keep things to herself? Of course her natural instinct was to rat him out – she had to admire his sneaky strategy to test what his mother might, or might not, know – but who would that have helped? She thought of Anita and her story about Sarah. Giving her the real deal about Nathan wouldn't make Catherine feel better, and it would have only been one more issue to pile on Anita. She didn't need it.

'Maybe it was wishful thinking,' she told Anita instead. 'You see, I *was* seeing someone in the city around that time, but it didn't work out. So I think Nathan might have gotten things a bit mixed up.'

Anita seemed to brighten.

'Oh, wonderful, dear,' she said. 'I hate to imagine you pining away for something you can't have.'

A million sentences leaped into Catherine's mind: Your son is a cheater. Your son is a liar. Your son is so mad at you he slept with me in your bed. But instead she just took a deep breath and let it go. Oh, she was a quick study today, she complimented herself.

'So Lucie told everyone's favorite rock starlet, Isabella, that she could wear my Phoenix dress,' said Catherine, hoping to both change the subject and get a stamp of Anita approval to not loan out her dress.

'A bit presumptuous?' guessed Anita.

'Yes, exactly,' said Catherine. 'I paid a lot of money for that gown.'

'I do recall,' said Anita, a smile playing on her lips. Her eyes were still puffy, but she was recovering nicely.

'Well, I can't let her wear it,' said Catherine. 'What if she ruins it?'

'You could treat it like those diamonds they loan out at the Oscars,' said Anita, standing up, only briefly, in a pair of white four-inch stilettos. 'Send along Dakota and her new friend Roberto as bodyguards.'

'I don't want to,' said Catherine.

'And I'm too self-confident to need to torture my feet like this,' said Anita, slipping off the shoes. 'Maybe we should get married barefoot, on the beach in Hawaii.'

'What about your wedding coat?'

'Light enough for all seasons,' said Anita matter-of-factly. 'I like to be prepared. The only issue is that it's taking me forever to knit it up.'

'So you don't think I'm stupid for wanting to say no to Lucie and Isabella?' asked Catherine.

'If that's what you want to do,' said Anita. 'I mean, you display it in your store, so it's not like you hide it away. And why would you want to share Georgia's talents with the world? You should just keep them for yourself.'

Catherine threw back her head and laughed.

'Point taken, Anita,' she said. 'I'll take it under advisement.'

'Georgia would have loved to have her design in *Vogue*.' Anita was nudging but Catherine didn't mind. 'What about the second dress Georgia made for you?'

'The pink one?' said Catherine. 'It's also gorgeous, with that mandarin collar and the thigh-high slit, but I always objected to the fact that Georgia called it Powder Puff.'

Now it was Anita's turn to laugh. 'So rename it,' she said, softly touching Catherine's cheek. 'Change it to something more reflective of today's Catherine. I think you should call it "Blossom."'

29

One cry was for snacks, another for wet diapers, a third for being bored, a fourth for being too hot or cold. The babies had what seemed like a million sounds, each distinct, and yet they communicated in a language that no one else understood quite as fluently as Darwin. Not even her mother. Or her mother-in-law, who'd come for the second round to help care for the twins and to register her disapproval of all the decisions Darwin was making. A one-two punch.

And yet, thought Darwin, she had this private victory of knowing her children better than anyone. From a purely academic standpoint, it was fascinating stuff: instinct and primal conditioning conquering all. From an emotional standpoint, it was deeply satisfying.

Darwin breastfed on demand – and Cady and Stanton certainly were demanding – but Mrs. Leung was unimpressed. An imposing woman in spite of her tiny appearance, Dan's mother had given her daughter-in-law the option upon her marriage of calling her Mother or Mrs. Leung. Darwin chose the latter.

'You need a schedule, Darwin Leung,' said Mrs. Leung, knowing full well that Darwin had not changed her surname when she married Dan. 'Right from the outset, you must let the children know who's the boss. They're hungry? Well, they can just wait until feeding time.'

'That's a theory,' said Darwin, whose boobs leaked at

every sniffle. She had no objections to emptying things out. 'But it's not what we're doing.'

'You're going to find that a lot of your own little theories aren't much use on real kids,' said Mrs. Leung. 'That's what you get for reading all those parenting books: a whole lot of imagination. Tried and true is what works best. Parenting is not about innovation.'

'Maybe,' said Darwin. 'But that's the thing about having your own kids. You get to experiment on their psyche just as much as your own parents did to you.'

However, the arrival of her mother-in-law had been a bigger help than anticipated: Mrs. Leung annoyed Darwin so frequently that she often bundled up the twins – even in summer they needed layer after layer, to put on and take off per their internal thermostat – and took them on meandering walks throughout the city. *Thanks, Mrs. Leung,* she said in her mind. *I'm getting healthier and seeing New York with new eyes.*

The worry list remained tucked into her pocket, but she consulted it far less often as the summer drew to a close.

'I'm not such a newbie anymore,' she told Dan. 'I'm becoming a mom who knows what she's doing. Well, sort of. I'm building my own template for what kind of mother – and professor – I want to be.'

She wasn't the only woman with the feeling that her style of mothering made sense. Dan's mother came from the my-way-or-the-highway school of thought, and busied herself redoing anything and everything Darwin's mom had touched: and so once again, the kitchen was scrubbed down, the secondhand coffee table polished, and the cupboards rearranged.

'You really should fold your towels in thirds,' said Mrs. Leung. Darwin had strenuously avoided getting to know her mother-in-law for all the years of her marriage. Oh, sometimes she went with Dan when he visited, but mainly she stayed put or went back to Seattle to see her sister. And now, she realized with surprise, she'd be going happily to see her mother, as well.

Darwin's mother Betty had been a dynamo for the month she slept on the sofa bed, complaining, of course, but not for one second letting anyone put her in a hotel away from those grandchildren of hers. She had done anything and everything, even going so far as to buy a tiny chest freezer and plug it into the corner of the living room and then cooking endless dinner options. Darwin even caught her, late at night, reading the manuscript pages of the new book Darwin was writing. She wasn't going to finish it as quickly as her colleague on paternity leave, but she wasn't about to fall behind, either.

Darwin was fascinated by the return of the extended family and the potential impact of the aging baby boomer generation on women and their career opportunities. The idea was twigged by the changes in her own life, of course, becoming a mom and having to live the juggle. But so many people were – either by choice or by necessity – living with elderly relatives again. Was it a sign of a greater shift away from the nuclear family? Would it hamper all the strides women had made in the last forty years? *How are we to take all our experiences,* thought Darwin, *and build a paradigm that works? And how does one's place within a family constrain or embolden them?*

Darwin thought of the club: they were a family, too. A family of choice. And she, for one, missed her regular Friday night meetings, which had been put on hiatus through the summer. It had seemed like so much effort to get together for just KC and Peri and herself. But that, she realized now, had been a wrong attitude. The club wasn't only the club if they were all in the same room. They probably weren't always going to all be in the same city, she considered, especially now that Lucie's career seemed to be taking off. It was more than conceivable that someone would move away at some point – maybe even she and Dan, relocating to a small college town and riding their bicycles to work. And the club, she realized now, was not about the shop. It never had been. That was just the starting point.

And that's why Darwin decided it was the right moment to host a Friday Night Knitting Club meeting of her own. Dan agreed to take his mother out of the house – it was a protracted negotiation, since she insisted she had not come to New York City to have fun – and then Darwin would have the apartment for herself and her friends, assuming the babies stayed asleep.

She'd never had a dinner party before tonight. Never. Not once. Darwin was stoked.

Mushroom risotto, penne primavera, and caprese salad: Darwin ordered in a delicious three-course dinner from the Italian restaurant two blocks from her apartment. Just because half the club was lucky enough to go to the real deal didn't mean the other members had to miss out on a taste of Italy, right?

'Ladies!' cried KC as she arrived at Darwin's apartment. Peri was already there, nibbling on a plate of olives, cheese, and bread that Darwin had put out for appetizers. 'I brought the wine,' said KC. 'None for you, I know – the whole breast-feeding thing.'

'But I'll have,' said Peri. 'The beauty of living in the city is that the subway takes me home.' She popped a pitted olive in her mouth while simultaneously raising her right hand, as though asking the teacher to call on her.

'Yes, Ms. Gayle?' said KC. 'Do you have some news to report?'

'Yeah,' said Peri, chewing and swallowing quickly. 'You'll

never believe what happened this week. Catherine called me and, honestly, what she said made my jaw hit the floor.'

'She's joining a convent?' said KC. 'I worried she'd take things just that smidge too far. She always does.'

'No, I'm serious,' said Peri. 'She asked me to go up to her store and get the two gowns Georgia knitted for her and FedEx them to the V in Rome.'

'Okay, that's weird,' said Darwin. 'She's practically built a shrine to the one dress up at her store. Now she can't be without it for a summer?'

'Maybe she just wants to wear them, I guess,' said KC. 'Sometimes people form dependencies, you know?'

'We know,' said Darwin. 'Just remember this is a no-smoking household.'

'No, no, you guys, that's not it,' said Peri. 'She's going to loan the gowns to that pop star Lucie's working with.'

'You're sure you didn't dream this?' asked KC. 'I once asked her if I could try on the gold dress – with a push-up bra, of course, I'm not deluded – and she told me that "the Phoenix does not leave its home, KC."'

'Well, the Phoenix *is* flying right now, folks,' said Peri. 'All the way to Roma.'

'Why did she ask you to get it ready? She has a manager for her store,' said Darwin. 'A lot is expected of you, Peri, and sometimes I wonder if you're not asserting yourself enough. It's very crucial for women to learn to say no.'

Darwin left her with that thought as she ducked into the kitchen to get the salad, drizzled it with a little olive oil, and invited everyone to move to the table.

'I've felt that same way sometimes,' said Peri. 'Worried I'm underappreciated. But I understood Catherine didn't feel she could trust someone outside the club to handle that dress. And, frankly, I loved Georgia, too: she gave me a job, the chance to pursue my handbag business, and a piece of her own store. When Catherine said the dresses needed to go, I wasn't about to let just anyone touch them. They're true couture.'

'So an Italian pop star is going to wear Georgia's dress,' said KC. 'That's good. Georgia would have found that very amusing, I think.'

'Are you kidding?' said Peri. 'She would have laughed all the way to the bank. That woman was not afraid to demand what her work was worth.'

'Yeah,' said Darwin. 'She was no shrinking violet.'

'Actually, Isabella in that gown is great exposure,' said Peri. 'Just what a designer needs. That's what hit me: An errand for a friend – even an annoying one – could be the seed of an opportunity.'

'To do what? Make more of Georgia's dresses?' asked Darwin.

'Maybe, 'said Peri. 'But I figured why not toot my own horn.'

'Women rarely do enough of that,' seconded Darwin. 'So how?'

'I sent my entire collection to Isabella, with my compliments and on Catherine's tab for the shipping. One of each backpack, laptop case, hobo bag, evening purse, tote . . .' Peri reeled off the list of styles and colors.

'That is a fortune's worth of stuff,' said KC. 'Are you sure you can afford to give away all that inventory? Why didn't you call me?'

'Because sometimes a businesswoman needs to rely on her best friends to be advisers,' said Peri. 'And sometimes she needs to figure things out for herself.'

'That's true,' said Darwin. 'Sometimes your gut just knows.' She was very delighted by this club meeting: they were just starting the pasta and already the discussion had been some of the best she thought the club had ever had.

'For so long, I've just felt as though I've been stuck at Walker and Daughter,' confessed Peri, accepting a second glass of wine. 'But I was looking at my bags as I was packaging them up and I realized they are so much better and bolder than when I started.'

'Your bags have always been gorgeous,' said Darwin. 'I love my diaper bag. Each of the five times I've left the house since the kids were born, I've gotten raves from strangers. I always tell them about you.'

'That's exactly what I mean,' said Peri. 'A few years ago I never thought about branching into diaper bags. But now I am, and part of the reason is because I'm older. More experienced.'

KC nodded thoughtfully as she filled her plate with a helping of risotto. 'It gets easier to think long-term,' she agreed. 'That's why I'm quitting smoking.'

'Did the patch from Dan help?' asked Darwin.

'Hey,' said KC. 'Whatever happened to medical secrets? I was going to pretend I could do it on my own.'

'Sorry,' said Darwin.

'I wouldn't have believed it otherwise,' said Peri.

'Well, I know something else you wouldn't believe,' said KC. 'So let's go get the little monsters. I made a gift.'

'You mean you bought a gift,' corrected Peri.

'Nope,' said KC, as she whipped out a mobile with knitted triangles and circles and squares – some striped, some solid – hanging down.

'That's adorable!' said Darwin.

'Who made that for you?' asked Peri.

'I just told you, I made it on my own,' grumbled KC. 'Look, I'll even show you where I screwed up.' She pointed out several holes until she'd satisfied Peri.

'But where did you get the yarn?' asked Peri, and KC squirmed.

'No wonder sales are sluggish,' Peri said to Darwin. 'My own friends don't shop in my store.'

'Well, I doubt you were holding your breath for KC and I to keep the shop afloat,' said Darwin. 'It's taken us all these years to finally get any good.'

'Pretty great, you mean,' said KC. 'I'm genuinely amazed by myself.'

'Me, too,' said Peri. 'But if I ever see either of you with someone else's yarn, there'll be hell to pay.'

'Speaking of hell to pay,' said KC, 'I'm kinda peeved that half of the gang all went on some group adventure. Next time we should all take a trip together.'

'We could go somewhere exotic,' said Peri.

'Like Staten Island,' said KC, a diehard Manhattanite.

'Or Seneca Falls, where Cady and Stanton could see where their namesake signed the Declaration of Sentiments,' said Darwin.

'Or maybe just someplace with a beach,' said Peri. 'That might appeal to everyone.'

'Let's suggest it,' said KC. 'Part of the problem this summer is that Lucie got a darn job and suddenly all the self-employed folks tagged along. I mean, sure, I went to Europe after Barnard. But now I live in the real world. And the rest of us working schlubs have to put in requests for vacation with a lot of lead time.'

'Yeah, let's talk about it when we have our post-walk snacks at the shop,' said Darwin, who loved the idea of women coming together to save their sisters. That, too, might make a great research project. Walking to save each other. So simple and yet so effective, both at raising money and at feeling useful.

'I'm so going to turn in the most Georgia afghans and win the Walker and Daughter Golden Needles this year,' she continued. 'Anita's days as the reigning charity champion are numbered.'

'Let's call and tell her that, too,' said KC. 'Now works for me.'

'You mean now now?' asked Peri. 'It's not yet dawn.'

'Hey now, I didn't even have a drink tonight,' said Darwin. 'I'm not about to drunk-dial Italy.'

'You two are way too serious,' said KC. 'We'll call and have an impromptu club meeting, pretend we can't do the time difference.' She was punching in numbers before anyone could stop her. 'You have that Internet phone thing, don't you, Darwin?'

'Yes, but it's still late, even if the call's almost free.'

'True enough,' KC replied, undeterred from her plan. 'I'll call Catherine, and then I'm going to conference in Lucie. Okay, it's ringing. Go grab the other phone, you guys, or put it on speaker.'

'No speaker,' said Darwin. 'Think babies. Sleeping babies!'

'Hello?' Catherine's voice was sleepy.

'KC here!' shouted the ringleader.

'Do you know what hour it is? I just went to bed after a night at the opera with Marco and—' started Catherine, before being cut off mid-sentence.

'Hold the line, please,' said KC in her best operator voice, then punched in the number Darwin reluctantly gave her for Lucie.

'Isabella, it's the middle of the night!' moaned the voice that answered. 'Can't we get what you need tomorrow?'

'Surprise!' yelled KC. Peri and Darwin exchanged a glance, both feeling terrible for waking everyone up. No doubt Ginger would be protesting soon.

'Uh, who is this?' said Lucie, before answering her own question. 'KC? Is that you?'

'Damn straight it is,' said KC. 'And I'm calling because I've come up with a plan.'

'By the way, you forgot to punch Catherine back in,' whispered Peri as she stood in Darwin's living room.

'Oh, yeah,' said KC, pressing a button and getting everyone on one line. 'So what do you think about us taking a group vacation next year?'

'With you?' asked Lucie. 'Or from you? I'm exhausted here.'

'Sorry, Luce,' said Darwin. 'KC is a force unto herself.'

'What? You're here, too?'

'Surprise! It's a club meeting, brought to you by technology,' said KC. 'Now, who knows Anita's room number?'

'No!' said Peri, Lucie, Catherine, and Darwin in unison. Unlike the rest of them, only Catherine knew that although Anita put up a brave front, she was still coming to terms with finally letting go of Sarah. Even though she was probably awake with insomnia and working on her wedding coat, the last thing she needed was to be disturbed, thought Catherine.

'Well, what about Dakota, then?' said KC.

'You're not waking her up, either,' said Lucie. 'Though it sounds like I'm too late. I hear her stumbling out in the living room.' Muttering and complaining, Lucie slid into a robe and opened her bedroom door to let Dakota know she'd picked up the room phone. Hoping to press her luck and still not disturb Ginger, she didn't turn on the light.

'Oh my God,' she screamed into the phone.

'What?' yelled four voices in reply. 'Are you okay? What's going on?'

'There's a man in my living room,' she shrieked.

'Shit! Now what?'

In an instant, Lucie recognized the voice. She'd been hearing it often throughout the summer.

It was Roberto.

30

Was she or wasn't she? That was the question on everyone's mind. The phone call had been hastily ended, much to the chagrin of KC, who really, really wanted to stay on for the duration.

But no answer appeared to be forthcoming, and for that, Catherine had to admire Dakota. She'd rushed down from her room in her nightie and the pair of heels she'd worn to the opera, not even taking time to grab a robe. She wasn't sure, even as she hurried, if she was heading over to berate or to protect Dakota. All she knew was that Georgia would expect her to take care of things.

When Catherine arrived at Lucie's suite mere minutes later, Dakota was on the sofa with Roberto, and Lucie was pacing the room. She was obviously freaked out.

'What would your father think?' said Lucie. 'He's just down the hall. And it was such a challenge to get him to agree to you being here.'

'That's my problem,' said Dakota matter-of-factly. 'You are not responsible for what I do during my time off. If I went out and robbed a bank, no one would arrest you. Because it's about me. And so is this.'

Dakota apologized for scaring Lucie. She said she understood it wasn't appropriate to have Roberto over without permission because she was, technically, working for Lucie and the room was not her own.

'But as for any other details, I'll be honest enough to tell both of you,' said Dakota. 'It's not any of your business and I won't get into it.'

The conversation went around in circles until the sun came up, but Dakota remained absolute in her unwillingness to spill.

'You're overstepping,' Dakota said to Lucie and Catherine after hours of back-and-forth. Her voice wasn't sharp or sarcastic, but level and self-assured. 'I'm really not the club mascot,' she said. 'My life isn't a group project. And this subject is closed.'

Catherine had wondered to herself when she would know Dakota was truly becoming an adult. It wasn't whether she had sex, of course. Plenty of immature and unprepared kids experimented every day. It was when her concept of how she saw herself changed. Not the teenager's whining that she had her own life and wanted everyone to butt out, but the confident and quiet assurance that some of her life was public and a greater part of it was private and only to be shared at her discretion.

Certainly she had more to learn about life in general. But Catherine couldn't fault her for that, seeing as she was, in her early forties, only just now figuring out what made her feel best. And it was when she felt complete within and by herself.

She'd had a beautiful evening with Marco, going to a performance of *The Marriage of Figaro*, and finishing with drinks on the roof deck.

'So now you know where I hide out,' she'd told him, laughing. 'I've been avoiding you most of the summer.'

'Why?' said Marco. 'I'm hardly dangerous.'

'I don't know,' said Catherine, before looking him straight in the eye. 'No, I do. I haven't had the greatest luck with romance. Not lately. Not ever.'

'We have barely had time to get to know one another,'

said Marco. 'We don't even know what we'd be like in a romance. Not that I haven't been driving to Rome all summer trying to find out.'

'What do you think of the fact that I'm a divorcée?' she asked suddenly.

'Your husband must have been a stupid man,' said Marco. 'Or an unkind one.'

Catherine looked down.

'So now we know which one it is,' said Marco softly.

'Your wife,' said Catherine. 'You must miss her.'

'Every day,' said Marco. 'She told me I had better be a monk if anything ever happened to her.' He laughed heartily, caught Catherine's look of consternation.

'Don't worry,' he said. 'I spend a lot of time think-talking to her. She didn't mean it.'

'What do you mean?' asked Catherine.

'I pretend to talk to her in my mind,' said Marco. 'I try to imagine how she'd solve problems, or what she'd say. I'm sorry, this must not be very interesting to you.'

'No,' said Catherine. 'No, this is one of the most refreshing conversations I've had in a long, long time.'

She told him about Georgia, about the dinners with James, about her parents dying in a car accident years before, and about how it had taken her a long time to embrace her life as it was.

'I can't ruin things now, you know,' she told him.

He nodded, then graciously offered to host a wrap party at the Cara Mia Vineyard for Lucie's cast and crew. It was a drive into the country, he admitted, but it promised to be something truly special, and Marco told her he was going to call Lucie to extend the invitation. Everyone knew Isabella would be very interested, and it would make Lucie look very good, too.

'You're a very nice man,' she'd said, as Marco laughed.

'I know that American saying,' he said. '"Nice guys die first."'

'Something like that,' admitted Catherine. 'That's not what I meant exactly. I just mean you're not my usual type.'

'People aren't types,' said Marco. 'People are people. Unique. You and I, Catherine, are people who understand loss. But we can get lost in it. Maybe it's time we focused more on what can be gained.'

Isabella came over as soon as she got word the dresses had arrived, and she brought the photographer and the fashion editor from Italian *Vogue* with her. Ordinarily, of course, the dresses would be sent to them. But Catherine was adamant they not leave her side, and she made clear that if Isabella wore them, she'd be coming along on the shoot. As well as James and Dakota and Anita. It was a big moment for all of them, and for Georgia. It seemed right that they all share in her triumph together.

'Our friend Peri Gayle sent you a gift,' Catherine told Isabella, showering her with the knitted bags, much to the delight of the singer. She had hired two models to show Isabella the dresses. The first had a boyish figure and a very small chest, and Catherine put her in the Phoenix, which had been tailored to show off Catherine's curves and her very ample bustline.

'Oh, no, that's not what I'm looking for,' said Isabella, and Catherine felt as though she was shortchanging Georgia. But she knew what was to come.

'Well, the other one is my favorite,' she told Isabella. 'I almost don't want to show it to you.'

'I've come all this way,' demanded Isabella, who'd taken a taxi across town.

Catherine affected a deep sigh. 'Okay,' she said. 'It's called Blossom and it's the last dress this designer ever made.'

'I don't think you should show her, dear,' said Anita, intuitively picking up her cue.

'A promise is a promise,' said Catherine with great solemnity. 'We owe it to Isabella.'

She called to Lucie to send out the model – a dead ringer for Isabella, natch – with the dress pinned in certain places to fit perfectly. The blush pink of the gown against the model's light olive skin was stunning; the slit skirt paired with the mandarin collar provided a pleasing, vaguely exotic look.

'I must have this,' declared Isabella, standing up. 'Yes, it is decided!' And with that, she turned to rummage through Peri's giant box of knitted and felted bags, letting out little squeals of delight now and again.

'Tell me,' she said to Catherine without turning away from the box. 'Do people in America have personal knitters? You know, like a personal assistant? Someone who makes all your knitted couture?'

'If they don't,' said Catherine in a cooing tone, 'I'm sure they will now.'

Isabella pulled out an oversized green backpack with wide straps and grinned a devilish smile. 'Are you thinking what I'm thinking?' she asked the room in general.

'Of course,' said Lucie, who'd gotten accustomed to humoring Isabella. No need to change this close to the end of things.

'Me, too,' said Isabella. 'This dress and this bag are going to remake my image. In the dress, I'm the innocent awakening. With the bag, I'm going to be the naughty schoolgirl.'

'Huh?' said Dakota.

'Look at these straps,' said Isabella, sliding the bag on over her shirt. 'Perfect coverage. Like a string bikini. I'm going to pose topless with just the backpack.'

'Fabulous,' screamed the photographer. 'I love it.'

'I don't think that's what Peri had in mind,' said James.

'But then a good businesswoman knows all publicity is good publicity,' interjected Dakota. How much did she owe Peri for watching over the shop this summer? The past five years? More than could easily be repaid. But a nudge to boost Peri's clever initiative was the least she could do. 'Whatever Italian *Vogue* wants, Italian *Vogue* gets. And so that designer's name is spelled P-E-R-I . . .'

It was settled. Isabella was going to grace the cover in Georgia's pink dress, and the inside spread would include several provocative shots of Isabella hiding her body behind Peri's bags. Some of them quite tiny indeed.

Georgia's moment had arrived. Peri's moment had arrived.

And the Phoenix would be Catherine's, always and forever.

Lucie had seen a lot of Isabella during their weeks of shooting the world's most ridiculously complicated rock video movie, and during the *Vogue* photo shoot, to which she accompanied Catherine, she saw even more. And while she thought it was perfectly appropriate for Isabella, she knew she wouldn't want Ginger to see the photos. And Ginger loved all those girlish pop singers, bouncing around in their midriff-baring shirts.

She called Darwin.

'Hello, Professor,' said Lucie.

'Hello, Ms. Famous Director Sort Of,' said Darwin. 'I hear you talked Isabella into going topless.'

'Not true!' said Lucie. 'Seriously, though, I'm having a crisis of content. I keep thinking that I don't want Ginger to see what I do.'

'You're not making Wiggles videos, Luce,' said Darwin. 'You make music video movie things. They're all about sex but pretending they're about love.'

'I know that,' said Lucie. 'You think I don't know that? But I'm just saying to myself here that there ought to be a television channel for girls, you know? Something with cool science and a smart detective series and an appropriate fashion something or other. Something more . . . . not so shocking.'

'It's a perfect idea,' said Darwin. 'And you have the skills.'

'You have the background,' said Lucie. 'You could be my advisory board.'

The two women laughed, trading 'What if we really did that?' back and forth until they fell silent, imagining the possibilities.

'We'd need a lot of money,' said Lucie.

'And time,' added Darwin.

'And we'd probably fail.'

'It's a crazy idea,' said Darwin. 'But hey, I'm knitting up Georgia afghans like my fingers are on fire, and there was a time when I never would have done that. I think we ought to think about it.'

They made a deal: Each woman would work out a list of pros, cons – and worries, per Darwin – and then they'd decide just how willing they were to try something crazy.

'Talking about crazy,' said Lucie. 'I can't believe the summer's almost over and I haven't done half of what I'd planned.'

'Like contacting Ginger's father,' pointed out Darwin.

'Yeah, I know,' said Lucie. 'To be honest, I haven't thought about him that much since the night of the Roberto discovery. I thought for a while that I needed him. Then I wondered if any man would do.'

'Marco,' said Darwin.

'Yes,' admitted Lucie. 'But as nice as he is, and so attentive to Catherine, I've finally figured something out.'

'Which is?'

'That I have enough people to be responsible for,' said Lucie. 'I wouldn't mind the occasional friend for mature company, if you know what I mean, and Dakota being around has made me realize the value of a personal assistant. But a boyfriend or a husband? Not right now. Maybe never.'

'So Will never knows about Ginger?'

'Not for the moment,' said Lucie. 'It would affect a lot of people – Ginger, his children, his wife – and could lead to a lot of problems. For now, I'm going to close that door again.'

'You know I support you no matter what,' said Darwin. 'Even when you abandon me for Rome.'

'Ha! I might as well have been in a studio in Brooklyn,' said Lucie. 'I've seen nothing all summer. Not even the Sistine Chapel. Rosie's going to kill me.'

'How is she doing?'

'Eh,' said Lucie. 'Hard to tell. Mitch gives me long-winded stories about how she needs to be watched and then my mother tells me something else. The truth is somewhere in the middle. I'll be back in a week, though, and I'm eager to check in.'

'Well, Dan and I are finally free of the M-I-L,' said Darwin. 'I'm taking the kids to the pediatrician for a weigh-in but I could ask Dan to go get her on Saturday and bring her in for the afternoon. Frankly, I could use some help finishing up my Georgia afghans.'

'That's cheating,' said Lucie. 'You can't use my mother to finish your charity work.'

'Uh, yeah,' said Darwin. 'When you're in Italy, all bets are off.'

'I haven't finished a new one since April,' admitted Lucie.

'And that just makes you one more person falling in my wake,' said Darwin gleefully. 'I really liked Georgia, you know. We had our differences but we were alike in a lot of ways, too. So I think she's rooting for me this year, and I'm not about to let her down.'

*   *   *

'This is going to go down as the summer of no sleep,' mumbled Catherine to herself, as she dragged her body out of bed to answer yet another ringing phone.

'Catherine, I'm so sorry,' said Marco. 'So sorry to awaken you.'

'Is everything all right?'

'Fine. Better than fine,' said Marco. 'I have a few friends, you know, and I pulled a few strings.'

Catherine pulled off her eye mask, wondering what he was talking about. And then she remembered: Marco had promised her he could get her into the Vatican museums before they opened. Before all the crowds. At least an hour, he said, an hour to soak up the tapestries and the Sistine Chapel and the Egyptian artifacts, too. All sorts of good stuff.

'Oh, Marco, you know what would be wonderful?' said Catherine.

'I know, I know,' he said. 'Bring all your friends. Trying to spend time with you is like trying to spend time with a young virgin fifty years ago. The whole village comes out to walk with us.'

'Do you mind?' she asked tentatively.

'No,' he said. 'At least this way I get to see my son. He's been a hard one to find since he met your Dakota. She's his first real girlfriend.'

'Yes,' said Catherine, who'd kept her own counsel on the discovery of Roberto and Dakota, and advised Lucie to do the same. They'd told no one, not even James, determining that some things aren't necessary for fathers to know. Besides, Dakota had never given them a straight answer, had she? So they weren't even sure what they would tell James even if they did reveal all. 'Roberto is one of the only things I ever hear about from Dakota. So it must be love.'

'Ha!' said Marco. 'First love could only be this clean and simple. The rest of us have learned, haven't we? It can be more challenging as we go on. But, Catherine, no time to debate as we always do. You must be downstairs in half an hour if the taxi is to get you here on time.'

'I'll bring the group,' she said. 'I'd like you to finally meet Anita. She's been so preoccupied with this search for her sister and you hear us talk about her all the time . . .' Her voice trailed off.

'Marco?' she asked. 'We really do talk a lot, don't we?'

'Of course,' he said. 'We're friends.'

'No, we really are friends,' said Catherine, becoming more excited. 'You know about Georgia, about Adam, about the shop, about Anita and her sister, about my parents, about all those relationships that never work out.'

Marco jumped in as she paused for breath. 'We'll be late, my Catherine, and there will be a horde of tourists at the Sistine if we don't hurry,' he said. 'Get up, put on some clothes, and I'll see you soon.'

Catherine hung up the phone, feeling more energy than she'd felt in months. She'd had such fun with her friends from New York over the summer. And such fun by herself. Taking flowers to Julius Caesar. Reading. Writing. Eating. Walking. Sleeping (when someone wasn't waking her up). She'd put herself out there, helping Lucie. And she'd held herself back, with Marco. Not rushing into yet another quick romance that was full of spark and low on sustainability. Instead, she'd let herself just talk talk talk. And if he didn't like it, or her, he could just move on.

The revelation was that Marco seemed to really enjoy what she had to say. That he wanted to share opinions and ideas of his own. That he thought her store was a great idea, and not just the wine side of the business. He paid serious attention when she told him she was working on a book, and nodded in delight when she told him all the bad men were killed by a serial murderer in the novel.

'But of course,' he said. 'I wouldn't expect anything less.'

In short, he'd become a great buddy. A buddy from whom she wanted more, and who had made it plain he had more to give. But, for now, things felt just right.

She pulled on a light sweater and a pair of slacks, a tall pair of heeled boots, and a slash of lipstick, skipping the rest of her makeup routine. He listened to her stories, she figured, so Marco could at least see her eyes without mascara.

Catherine didn't need a mask anymore.

31

Dakota couldn't believe it as she opened her eyes and gazed out the window of her bedroom at the rolling hills of Cara Mia just outside Velletri, the bottles of wine yet to be produced from the endless rows of grapes.

All the New Yorkers had arrived the night before, making a caravan of convertibles and Smart cars as they drove out to the vineyard. Summer was drawing to a close, and as promised, Marco was hosting the wrap party for the Isabellastravaganza, installing white canvas tents close to the villa. The evening promised to be a night to remember.

As had the entire trip. Much had happened: Her nineteenth birthday was in a few days, and Dakota had found a chef to be her inspiration, told her father she wanted to sell the shop, and absorbed all the beauty – the art, the architecture, the smells of bakeries in neighborhoods near and far – that a person could in a few short weeks. She'd made a lot of progress.

Not to mention she'd fallen in love. Or maybe just super like. It was hard to say for certain, seeing as how she had nothing to compare it with. But one thing was clear: She had a boyfriend – a very cute boyfriend – and he was an excellent kisser indeed. She enjoyed thinking often about all the moments they'd spent together; she'd texted her friend Olivia after her first kiss with Roberto, thrilled and also grateful not to feel like the only college student in America who'd been left behind.

Roberto had a relaxed way about him and his easy laughter contrasted nicely with Dakota's natural seriousness. They made a good combo, she thought, and she'd figured out long ago that his English was fairly close to perfect already. Which had only made her like him all the more, the way he thought he had to come up with reasons to make her want to spend time with him. It was great to be pursued. To be desired. To be found beautiful. To have precious, private jokes with another person who could finally understand her in a completely new way. Different from anyone else. But she wasn't about to tell anyone what all transpired that night in Lucie's suite; that was hers and Roberto's alone.

'I know what I want and what I don't,' she said aloud now, as she stretched her remaining sleepiness away. This, then, is also what the summer in Italy had brought her: a deeper understanding. Of almost everything.

But there was still more to see: the grounds and villa at Cara Mia, and an afternoon in the kitchen. James had made special arrangements to bring out Chef Andreas from the V, and the chef was certainly eager to cook for the famous Isabella, and more than comfortable having Dakota function as his girl Friday.

'Thanks, Dad,' said Dakota when she found out.

'I always try, Dakota,' said James. 'You may not realize it, but I do.'

By the late afternoon, the guests were streaming in: cast, crew, and all sorts of famous friends of Isabella's, both American and European. But Dakota was far more interested in meeting Roberto's family. She especially liked it when he called her his girlfriend in front of his grandfather.

'And this is Allegra,' said Marco, introducing his shy, brown-haired elementary-school-age daughter to Anita and

Dakota. Allegra hid behind an older woman who stood beside her.

'And this is my grandmother,' said Roberto. Once again, a flurry of handshakes and head nods as Anita began a round of introductions to everyone in the New York group. Marco's mother – Roberto's grandmother – was a very petite woman with deep olive skin and wide-set dark eyes. *Aha,* thought Dakota, *now I know where he gets those gorgeous eyes.*

'Welcome,' said Paola Toscano. She, like Marco, seemed delighted to have a horde of guests descend upon their picturesque corner of the world. 'Cara Mia has been in my family for generations, and I'm so delighted to share it with you.'

'Thank you,' said Anita. 'You're very kind to open up your home.'

She'd had a wonderful rest the night before, her bed plush and comfortable. Anita had cried for several days, in her suite with Marty, feeling at a loss: everyone had found something she was looking for in Italy this summer. Except for her.

Acceptance sounds more graceful than it is, Anita thought to herself. It was its own battle, the challenge to let go, to recognize when grasping onto a dream had become its own curse.

So how to say good-bye to a forty-year-old burden? Anita took the postcards she'd loved, and hated, and kept in her junk drawer, and kept in her heart, and she gave them to Marty and asked him to burn them. He promised he would, and, finally, she slept.

Catherine went back and forth on the idea. To wear or not to wear. The photo shoot was done, the proofs on their way to the creative director. But one look at Catherine in the Phoenix, and Isabella would know she'd been had. In the end, though, she wanted Marco to know. 'Look at what my friend Georgia did for me,' she would say. 'She showed me how to bring myself back to life. She made me this dress with her very own hands and stitched it together with enough power to kickstart me on my journey.'

'You are ethereal,' said Marco as he saw Catherine enter the garden, the golden dress on her body and her blond hair piled high on her head, tendrils spilling loose. 'You are like a queen.'

'Thank you,' said Catherine. 'I've always been prone to flattery.'

'Flattery is fake,' said Marco. 'I tell you facts.'

And that's what they discussed, strolling through the vineyard, as the rest of the group sampled the food and the beautiful wine and even tried to dance to Isabella's DJ stylings.

'I came to Italy to run away from some mistakes,' admitted Catherine. 'But rushing into a relationship could very well just be one more.'

'Then we should not do that,' he said.

'I do this thing,' said Catherine. 'I bury myself in my relationships. I tend to lose who I really am, and I'm not sure I quite know how to stop doing that. But I'm learning.'

'I can wait,' said Marco. 'I'm a winemaker, for God's sake. I know enough to let possibility ripen in its own time.'

By midnight, Anita had grown tired of the party, and its loud Isabella music. She sampled all the pastries Dakota had participated in making, of course, and she kept an eye out for Ginger because Dakota was very busy charming Roberto's family. But soon enough Ginger was put to bed and Anita had had enough of the hubbub.

'*Buonasera,*' she heard Marco's voice boom just as she was sneaking away from the festivities. 'Come and meet my wonderful American friends.'

'I'm going to bed before I have to meet any more people,'

she whispered to Dakota. 'Tell everyone that at seventy, I have to get my beauty sleep.'

'But you're seventy-eight,' said Dakota.

'Never correct Anita when she's lying about her age, Dakota,' said Catherine, coming up to them and looking more relaxed than Dakota had ever seen her. 'And I thought you'd figured everything out this summer.'

'Good night, girls,' said Anita, before Catherine reached out and took her arm. 'One last drink with us, Anita. A toast to the summer.'

'Yeah,' said Dakota. 'Let's get Lucie and Dad over here, as well. Where the heck are they?' She scanned the outside area.

'They're on the dance floor,' said Roberto. 'The two of them are doing that old-fashioned robot dance.'

'Oh, I'm horrified,' said Dakota, not in the least serious. 'Why don't we go and have an Isabella-style dance-off with them?'

'And then we'll toast,' said Catherine. 'Right, Anita?'

Just then, Marco finally caught up with their group, escorting an attractive older woman on his arm.

'Nona!' said Roberto with enthusiasm. 'My girlfriend and I are going dancing.' Dakota turned, expecting to see Paola again. Instead, she saw a slim, silver-haired woman who looked vaguely familiar. Had she seen her at the party earlier in the evening? Catherine understood more quickly and immediately put both of her arms around Anita as the older woman began to shake and keen.

There, on Marco Toscano's arm, stood the woman who'd once been a New Yorker named Sarah Schwartz.

Anita had finally found her sister.

'I can't believe it,' said Marco moments later, looking from one woman to the other. They looked similar, but then again they were also women of a mature age. And men didn't always pay enough attention past a certain point. 'All this time looking for your sister, and she is my wife's mother. It's unbelievable. Now you are truly a part of our family!'

'It's like that game,' said Dakota. 'How if you know somebody who knows somebody who knows somebody, then you all know each other.'

'Six degrees of separation,' said Catherine. 'Because maybe what we look for is close to us all along.'

'Maybe I should have asked more questions,' said Anita, seeming at first to talk to the group but really meaning her words just for Sarah.

'You're finally here,' said Sarah, a petite and beautiful silver-haired woman, as she hung on to Marco.

'Thank goodness Anita's just my surrogate grandmother,' whispered Dakota to Roberto as they watched the two women hug and whisper to each other, forty years of conversation coming out all at once. 'Or you and I would have some real problems!'

Back in New York, Darwin and Rosie had a beautiful day playing with Cady and Stanton. They looked through Darwin's charity afghans, and Rosie knit several rows. They left the babies with Dan and lunched at Sarabeth's, stocking up on some good marmalade to take home, and then they popped into Walker and Daughter to select even more yarn for Darwin. Her maternity leave was drawing to a close, she was deeply tired, and yet she'd made great notes for her new research project. And then there was her charity knitting quest, which was going spectacularly well. All in all, it was a fabulous summer, even if she hadn't gone to another country and had endured an extended visit from Mrs. Leung.

Rosie, on the other hand, seemed tired, thought Darwin. She picked up coffees for the two of them and one for Peri, and walked upstairs to the shop, where Peri was just finishing up one of the lessons she taught on the weekends. She waved when she saw them come in.

'More yarn?' she asked, having already set aside a pile that Darwin had requested by phone.

'Yup,' said Darwin. 'I think I may officially retire once I win this year.'

'The greats never retire,' Peri observed, saying her good-byes to some of her students. 'They just live in their glory forever.'

'Girls,' said Rosie. 'Where did the bathroom go?'

'I took it out,' said Peri. 'The entire back office went during the reno.'

'Knitting shops aren't really using-the-restroom kind of places,' said Darwin. 'It's not a Starbucks.'

'Well, that's all well and good,' said Rosie. 'But I could use a little refreshing. Splash some cold water on my face.'

Peri pulled out her apartment key. 'For Lucie's mother, I couldn't refuse,' she said. 'The bathroom is the second door to the right. Don't look at the sink in the kitchen – my break-fast dishes are in there!'

'Breakfast dishes?' said Darwin. 'My kitchen sink is currently playing host to my breakfast, lunch, and dinner dishes from yesterday.'

'No more mothers, hey?'

'Just the one,' said Darwin. 'And she is me. No one pays extra for prompt service so I do what I can when I can.'

Ten minutes later, Rosie returned the key to Peri, and Darwin picked up her week's purchases. The shop telephone rang as they were about to leave.

Peri covered the handset with her mouth, a combination of ex-citement and surprise on her face. 'Italian *Vogue*,' she mouthed. 'Interview.'

Quickly, Darwin dragged over a chair to the corner and encouraged Peri to sit down. Then she took over trying to

run the register – a job she'd never done before – to help
the last remaining customers of the day. Rosie helped by
tidying the bins and sorting colors.

'Wowee!' shrieked Peri when she hung up the phone half
an hour later. 'They're doing a piece on me in the magazine.
My bags are in the pages, and then a mini-profile, too.'

'Let's celebrate,' said Darwin. 'I've got to get home but
let's pick up a bottle of wine for you and go back to my
apartment.'

'I'll make a little sauce,' said Rosie. 'We can have noodles.'

It was a date. They left as soon as the shop was empty.
There was no need for jackets on a humid August evening
in Manhattan, and so Peri didn't go up to her apartment
one floor above the shop. Which was unfortunate. Because
Rosie had turned the faucet on and then forgotten why or
how to turn it off. The water in Peri's bathroom sink was
filling faster than it could drain: Walker and Daughter was
about to drown.

It was only a matter of time.

32

'Just because I wanted to sell the shop didn't mean I wanted it gone!' Dakota had screamed as they packed; she didn't bother to hide her tears on the plane. The lazy weekend of celebrations had ceased for Catherine, James, Dakota, and Marty upon receiving Peri's call: an ocean of water had seeped from her apartment through the walls and the ceiling into the shop, leaking onto the yarn and the handbags.

'The floor is under a layer,' said Peri. 'I think the faucet ran for at least six hours, possibly more.' It hardly seemed fair: she spent so much of her time babysitting the shop and then when she finally enjoys an evening off . . .

They barely had a moment to thank Roberto and Marco before the group was racing for the airport.

'It's not gone, exactly,' said Catherine. 'It's just a little wet. A lot wet.' But of course she didn't know what they'd find when they got back to their beloved little yarn shop at Seventy-seventh and Broadway.

'I don't understand how Lucie's mother could just leave a tap running,' said Dakota. 'That makes no sense.'

'I know,' said Catherine, putting an arm around Dakota. 'It seems there's a lot more that's broken than drywall and pipes.' She didn't say anything further, knowing that Lucie's brothers were taking Rosie to the doctor on Monday in New York. Lucie had been blown away to learn of the incident, forced to confront some hard truths about her mother.

They didn't stop to go to their homes, but instead took two taxis – they couldn't fit all Catherine's luggage into one car – straight to the shop. From the outside, all looked fine: the sign was in the tall window, the hours clear. It was Monday, the store's regular day to be closed. And closed it was.

Peri was wearing gum boots and gloves when they arrived, gliding through a layer of still water that looked dirty, a sump pump going in one corner. KC was trying to lay out yarn in single rows of skeins to dry them out, or take stock of what was ruined by writing it down on a clipboard, her feet also in boots. Darwin was busy calling the service people on the phone and trying to dry business papers with a hair dryer at the same time. All around the store, streaks of dark water stains decorated the walls, leaving behind brownish rings. The wall of handbags was damaged more than any other, the clear acrylic shelves popping out of the wall in several places and floating around in the low layer of water in others. Most of the bags themselves – especially the newest computer cases that Peri had made – appeared to be wet, stained, or otherwise bloated. They were piled on top of the center table, wrapped in between layers of striped towels, waiting.

'What are we going to do?' cried Peri, as James, Catherine, Marty, and Dakota clambered up the stairs two at a time and hesitated, mouths wide open, in the doorway. All her hard work, her redesign, her bags, her years of looking after Georgia's shop, lay dripping. Coated in tap water, courtesy of Lucie's mom, Rosie.

But no one had the answer.

'Oh, Dakota,' Peri whispered, the exhaustion and upset clearly visible in her puffy eyes. 'What's happened to our store?'

And even James and Catherine were speechless as Dakota,

who had been unable to keep herself together for the entire plane trip from Rome, waded right into the now cold water and held Peri as she wept.

Anita called Marty every few hours to check on her beloved Georgia's store. She couldn't make the flight, of course, because of her phobia. And now was her time to sit with her sister and listen to all the details she'd missed for forty years. To commiserate with her on losing a daughter just like she'd lost Georgia, and to grieve for the niece she'd never had a chance to know. Roberto and Allegra's mother. And to reacquaint herself with Roberto not just as Dakota's pleasant boyfriend but as her own grandnephew. She had been looking only for Sarah but she found an entire family just waiting. Connected to her, waiting for her. Thanks to the Friday Night Knitting Club. It was a fluke, of course. But then again, thought Anita, maybe it wasn't. Maybe it was a bit of guidance from Georgia. After all, from Lucie's job to Catherine's wine connection to James's work at the hotel . . . everything had just fallen into place. Leading them here. To Italy and to each other.

'I went on to England initially,' Sarah explained. 'I sent the postcard and I figured you'd come for me. But then you didn't.'

Anita looked down and blushed. There would be a place for her to explain her actions and ask for understanding, but for now, it was Sarah's opportunity to share.

'I changed my name a long time ago,' she said. 'I figured if I'd been tossed aside, I might as well.'

'We didn't find those records,' said Anita. 'We looked all over Europe.'

Sarah looked thoughtfully at her older sister. 'Anita,' she said. 'I changed my name in New York.'

Anita was shocked. It had never occurred to her to look for records on her sister in her own backyard.

'Then I went to England after the name change,' said Sarah. 'There were different countries over the years, and then I met a good-looking Italian man while I was waitressing,' said Sarah. 'He was handsome, and sweet, and he gave me a home and a family.'

'Everything,' said Anita. 'Everything I took away.'

'Our only daughter married Marco over twenty years ago, and those were such beautiful days,' said Sarah. 'I've spent much of my time here at the villa ever since. Even after our daughter passed away and left us to worry along without her.'

'And your husband?' asked Anita.

'He's at home, in fact,' said Sarah. 'Probably asleep in his chair. Roberto could not convince him of the value of meeting the singer Isabella.'

'I am stunned,' said Anita. 'But I just don't understand why you always sent those blank postcards.'

'Why, Anita, isn't it obvious? I simply felt better believing I was still connected to you,' said Sarah. 'But we're getting so much older. I sent the last one from the village – it's practically a homing device. A picture of the famous camellia festival.'

Vaguely, Anita remembered Catherine mentioning something about flowers being on the postcard. All along, the clue had been there.

'Still, when I didn't hear from you, I thought that was its own reply,' said Sarah. 'Or worse.'

Anita leaned forward and giggled. 'I know. I thought you were gone, too,' she said, her face a smile of relief for a few moments. Then she became serious.

'It doesn't seem fair, you know, that people aren't around forever. Because when it's good, it's great.'

'And when it's bad . . .' Sarah let her voice drop off. 'I missed out on Mother and Father, of course.'

'I know,' said Anita, wishing they'd never have to talk about the hard stuff. The people who weren't there. 'My hasty decision cut you out of everything.'

'And the boys,' said Sarah. 'My daughter never knew her cousins. Nathan was always so stern!'

'He remains obstinate,' said Anita. 'In that regard, he's like me. He seems to think he's got the weight of the world on his shoulders. That he has to referee for everyone.'

'Do you still knit?' asked Sarah.

'I do,' said Anita, smiling. 'Maybe you could help me finish my wedding coat. That way Marty won't have to wait forever for the ceremony.'

'Of course. And I'll be there,' said Sarah. 'But we have a lot of catching up to do, Anita. I'm not a young girl anymore. We won't just fall into old roles, you know. You can't show up in Italy after forty years and begin telling me what to do.'

'I know,' said Anita, but inside she knew she didn't, really. She'd spent months looking at the photos of her first wedding, at that cute flower girl, and she knew well enough to realize that she wasn't entirely prepared to discover Sarah had silver hair. That she'd gotten older, as well, that time hadn't frozen her in place, waiting for Anita to be ready to ask for forgiveness.

Sometimes getting what is wanted only leaves more questions. But now, finally, they were ready to find the answers. Together.

They made runs for coffee. For mops. For paper towels, and cloth towels, and for garbage bags. And for tissues to sop up the tears.

The store was what her mother had left behind. Where she had seemed most fully herself. The photograph of Georgia and Dakota – the outtake from Lucie's film – was still hanging, chunks of drywall having fallen off all around where it had been placed. Behind what had once been the register.

Dakota felt angry, initially, with Rosie. With Peri.

'How could she just let her use the bathroom like that?' was one angry question Dakota had hurled at Catherine on the plane. She had all sorts of choice words she wanted to share with Lucie, demands and accusations. And then she thought of Ginger, little Ginger, born on the day Georgia died. Rosie's granddaughter. And she thought how sad it was going to be, for all of them, to watch Rosie get older. To adjust. To not know what to do to make it all better.

'She didn't do this on purpose.' That's what Darwin had come over and said shortly after they'd arrived, anticipated the question, when they'd pulled on their own hastily purchased rubber gloves and started on the mucking out. It would be easier to blame, of course, but that wasn't going to get the shop back. The store was gone – bits of ceiling had fallen to the floor and all of it had gotten stuck to the inventory – and everything was ruined.

What Dakota wanted was to order everyone out. 'Get out, get out,' she wanted to yell, so she could just perch herself on the counter by the cash register and spend some time – all day, weeks, who knew? – just absorbing what had happened. To close her eyes and walk herself through the shop in her mind's eye, seeing it as it had been when she was young, and how it looked after Peri's redesign. She wanted to make it go back. She wanted to make it all go back. Undo every bad thing. She'd give up all the good to make it so: Roberto, the summer in Italy, even that two-week trip when she met Gran for the first time. Too much had happened. There was too much to take in.

She bargained. With whom? With God?

'I just want . . .' was how she began every sentence. 'I just want the shop to be like I left it.' 'I just want the shop to be like it was when I was a kid.' 'I just want my mother to still be alive and for everything to be the way it once was.'

'Why?' shouted Dakota every so often as she cleaned, the rest of the crew deep in their own thoughts and leaving her to her own outbursts.

It all seemed so unfair. They confronted all this loss and back at Cara Mia, Anita was reconnecting with Sarah. Dakota knew she ought to be thrilled for Anita, of course. She adored Anita, who took all her calls, answered her texts, listened to her worries, helped solve her problems. But it was not fair! Why did Anita get to find Sarah? Why was she so lucky? Who wouldn't want to have a loved one come back from the dead, as it were?

Dakota wanted more chances, too. More time to be with her mother. To go back and apologize for all the moments she'd been a smart-ass, and maybe even to thank her for working in the store that Dakota could see now she'd never appreciated quite enough. What was she to do with the chunks of ceiling and the floorboards popping out? What was she to do with Peri's handbags mounded on the table, with KC running up and down the stairs trying to spare what could be saved, with Catherine cleaning and cleaning and never seeming to get anywhere – Dakota was certain she didn't really know how to use a mop but didn't want to take away her sense that she was doing something, anything, to stem the mess – and with the fact that James could not seem to stop walking around the walls of the shop, reaching out to touch the flaking paint as though trying to grab hold of Georgia.

All Dakota's mistakes came back to her now. Running off to Baltimore on the bike. All the mean things she'd said to her mother. Telling James to sell the store. Yelling at Peri. That was here, too, mixed up with everything else.

What was she to do with all the things she was finally old enough to make right?

'It's easy to look back and think how we could make only the good things happen to us,' counseled Catherine, still swishing her mop to and fro, spreading dirty water instead of soaking it up. 'But that's not how we become ourselves. You are made who you are by the bad stuff, the little things, as much as the great triumphs and big decisions.'

Even as Dakota saw her childhood reflected in the puddles, so Catherine saw herself, in her mind's eye, coming into Walker and Daughter to try to punish Georgia, to make her see how successful and happy she was in her life married to Adam. Only she wasn't. And Georgia hadn't recognized her. *Who am I?* That's what she'd wondered that day. It was a question she continued to ask but, more and more, she was starting to understand. Figure it out for herself. Accept that the answer changed, just as she did.

Because Georgia Walker never turned anyone away at all. That's what Lucie had said in her voice-over in the film about the shop and the club, the one that had gone on to the festivals. How true, thought Catherine. Georgia gave and gave, and they just messed up. Over and over.

She mopped, but she couldn't understand how the water seemed to linger, and her hands felt sore and blistered. *Only for you, Georgia,* Catherine thought, looking down at her fingers. How much her body had done in five, no, coming up on six years since that fateful October day. Right here in the store. Right where Catherine stood. *We knit and we sat and we laughed.* That's what Walker and Daughter had been: A place of laughter. A place of friendship. A place of renewal and reinvention.

It had just been a normal afternoon, the day that Georgia died. That's what always struck Catherine. There had been no warning label on the morning to let them know that something momentous was going to occur. She hadn't awakened in the San Remo knowing that she would return that night, heartbroken and lost. That there would always be a before, and an after, and they'd be left behind to sort out moving on without Georgia.

But what they'd always, always had since that day was the shop. All of Georgia's love captured in one place, made even more perfect when Dakota came to a club meeting. Where would they get together now? She hadn't thought about that until now. Catherine watched KC as she carted box after box of yarn downstairs to the deli, which was also closed to help speed up the cleaning operation. At Darwin, sorting through her paper, at Peri in her gloves, scrubbing away. Where would they go if they didn't have the store? What happens to a club when the club hangout has been washed away? She had no idea, and she worried.

She wished people did something other than cry. It was so messy, so obvious. But there it was: tears in everyone's eyes. No sooner would they dry up than someone would start again, that Dakota's muttering and James's aimless walking through the tiny shop would set someone off anew.

Catherine thought she was done crying. She believed that the counseling sessions she and James had attended were the final steps in a long process that was coming to a close. Now, she knew, fully aware as she looked at the destruction of Georgia's beloved shop, just how thin was the line between her life and the grief that flowed just under the surface. It wasn't only about Georgia, she knew. Her own regrets were mixed up with it all and, even as she moved forward, the sadness remained. It informed her. It reminded her how far she had journeyed.

★　　★　　★

After a day of cleaning, and crying, and cleaning some more, Marty and James brought in expert help to assess the damage to the store. The building was going to be fine, they were told, which was a relief. But then they looked around the shop and felt defeated again.

'Peri,' Dakota said, as she mopped the floor that had been refinished only months ago. 'You do a lot without getting enough in return from me. Thank you.'

'You're welcome, Dakota,' said Peri. 'You're like the little sister who drives me mental. Sometimes I hate you, but mostly I love you.'

'Same same,' said Dakota.

'Perhaps Georgia hated the reno I did,' said Peri.

'So much so she flooded her own shop?' said KC. 'She would have sent you a registered letter from The Other Side or something. No, this is a full-on of-this-world disaster.'

'Maybe it's a warning sign that we need to pay better attention,' said Catherine. 'To issues. To each other.'

'Maybe,' said Dakota. 'Maybe it's just something that is.' One thing was rapidly becoming clear to her as Darwin and KC and Peri and Catherine all pitched in and yet the room still looked a mess: Walker and Daughter was never going to be the same.

'Dad?' she asked. 'Can I talk to you and Marty privately?' The three went down to the deli.

'I wish I had a Scotch,' said Marty. 'I'd definitely offer you one, kiddo. It's been a tough few days.' He reached his arm around to pat Dakota's shoulder.

'I'm just nineteen,' Dakota reminded him.

'Oh, you've seen enough for one lifetime,' said Marty. His clothes were covered in flecks of drywall. 'I remember when your mom worked in here part-time to make extra cash – you were just a baby and she wasn't much older than you are now.' And then Marty leaned forward, put his face in his hands, and bawled. All James and Dakota could see was his white hair and his shaking body. In all this time, Dakota realized, she'd never once seen Marty cry for her mother, and the knowledge that he was also devastated – that he, like Anita, like Peri, like Catherine, like James – all had their own stories with Georgia that were in addition to her own moved and inspired her. She knew. Finally, she knew.

The store wasn't just about Georgia. It wasn't just about her. Or Peri. It was about all of them, as a group, being available to one another.

When they returned, Peri was on a ladder taking out stained ceiling tiles, Darwin was standing against the wall fast asleep, and KC was schlepping out bags of trash.

'Well, guys,' said Dakota, 'we have a plan. We're going to rebuild. Right here, the store my mother started. Because there will always be a Walker and Daughter. I didn't think I wanted that but this situation has helped me see that I truly do.'

'Me, too,' said Peri, still on the ladder. She reached up to adjust another tile, to add the stained ones to the pile she'd collected, and tried to tally in her mind just how much it would cost to replace the ceiling. Along with the walls, the floor, the yarn. Even the cash register, which wasn't opening as well as it might, not even ringing when the till opened. The cost would be astronomical.

But it was all fixable, she told herself. It could all be repaired. Would be repaired.

'Let's grab some coffee and rest our hands,' said Catherine, smiling. 'You made a good call, Dakota.'

'I'll say,' said Peri, her hands full of ceiling tiles as she balanced precariously on the ladder. 'Just one more and I'm done with this corner . . .'

She lost her footing, flailing at the ceiling as though to hold on, yelping as a flurry of white surrounded the room and Peri stumbled off the ladder with a thud. Followed, milliseconds later, by the ladder tipping over and a red binder falling right out of the loose section of ceiling, smashing into the warped wood just a few inches from her head.

'Are you okay?' yelled Marty, rushing over to steady Peri, who was bruised and shaking but otherwise fine.

'What the hell was that?' said James, stepping over the ladder to help Peri stand up.

Darwin came to with a start, utterly confused and exhausted at the sight of Dakota pumping her fist in the air just like she used to do when she was a little girl.

'Ha!' said Dakota. 'I've been searching the apartment for this for years!'

'What is it?' asked KC, just returning from dragging a trash bag to the street and seeing Peri, the fallen ladder, Dakota dancing. 'What's going on?'

'It's my mom's top-secret binder of original patterns,' said Dakota, reaching down and picking up the plump book.

'Oh, Dakota, it's going to be ruined,' said Catherine.

'No,' said Dakota, suddenly feeling calm. She smiled serenely. 'Think like Georgia Walker. Be prepared.'

She opened up the binder and there, in sheets of plastic matting, was page after page of Georgia's original knitwear. The launching of a career she never had the chance to have. Until now.

Experienced

You know enough now that you don't just have to follow someone else's pattern. Or keep repeating your own. You can break the pattern. Improve it. Perfect it. Change the plan. Adapt and improvise. Make what works best for you. Now your skills will take you wherever you want to go.

33

The day of the charity walk began, as it did every September, with a call from Scotland.

'Got your trainers on?' asked Gran.

'I'm ready to walk to the end of the world,' Dakota replied. 'How are you, Gran?' Her great-grandmother chuckled.

'As well as can be expected, I'd say,' said Gran. 'Now get out there and raise a million dollars, young lady.'

'I'm not there yet, Gran,' said Dakota. 'But I'm on my way.'

The plans were set in motion: the shop was being refurbished very simply so that it could reopen as soon as possible. In the meantime, Peri had scheduled a trip to investigate mass production: she had more orders coming in online from Europe than she could make herself. Even her slightly damaged bags had interested buyers, thanks to Italian *Vogue* and the power of Isabella. She'd already made her first hire: a lawyer named KC Silverman.

And she'd done something else. She'd decided to sign up for online dating, and get out there and find herself a guy if that's what she wanted.

'No use sitting around and wanting what you can make happen for yourself,' she told Dakota.

For her part, Dakota was working at dividing up Georgia's pattern book into her masterpieces and her more accessible concepts. Dakota planned to make her mother's hand-knit couture designs available for only a select few who could afford them, put together by a team she would personally hire. With the rest, she and Peri and Anita were putting together a pattern book available for sale, dividing the pieces into levels of difficulty so there was something for everyone, and then writing introductions for each section just as Georgia had once explained knitting sweaters to Dakota. And all the profits would be donated to charity.

'Your mother would like the idea that her own work is going to help save someone else from ovarian cancer that killed her,' said Anita. 'It's a very clever idea, Dakota. You make her proud.'

But Dakota had not abandoned her own dreams for her mother's, however. Quite on the contrary. With her father's full confidence, Dakota was doing one more year at NYU, and then she was going to start a degree in pastry making and management at the Culinary Institute of America in Hyde Park.

The arrangement suited everyone: in a few years, when Dakota was finished, Marty would be ready to retire – he had no intention of going anywhere before he turned seventy-five – and the first floor that was now the deli would become a knitting café, known as Dakota's Bakery at Walker and Daughter. Here, customers could eat all the muffins and scones and cookies they wanted while knitting with friends old and new. It would be the best of the club meetings. Reinvented as a business.

And on the second floor, all to its own, would be Peri Pocketbook. Couture knitted hand- (and diaper and computer) bags to the stars. And anyone else who could afford them.

The restructuring of the building was the initial project of a new concern, James Foster Architecture, which had come very well recommended, of course.

Dakota and Roberto kept up their correspondence via

text and the occasional phone call. He'd decided to spend the year working at Cara Mia alongside his father, just to figure out if his lack of interest was motivated more by a desire for independence than anything else. He still planned to fly, he told her, but there was time enough to wait.

And she saw Andrew Doyle, as well, at the end of the summer, while she was going with her pal Olivia to a concert at Jones Beach. He waved when he saw them, and Dakota waved back. He was still cute, she thought. But he was just a guy. She had a lot of goals to reach before she got serious. With anyone.

Darwin and Lucie were hard at work on a business proposal for a television concept they called *Chicklet*. It was everything they wanted all the little Gingers and little Cadys to learn about being smart and confident and believing in their own individual beauty. At the same time, Isabella's album – and the accompanying music movie – was climbing the charts, cementing Lucie's professional reputation.

Rosie was going through rounds of tests, and just as Lucie was confronting how to best help her, Dan and Darwin realized their small apartment wouldn't hold Cady and Stanton for long. The solution that worked for everyone and even made Lucie's brothers happy? Buy a duplex out in Jersey and coordinate all the different types of care – child and elder – that was needed. Darwin and Dan would take one side, Lucie and Ginger the other. And Rosie had a room of her own. Coming and going at her leisure, depending on who was at home. It was perfect research for her academic paper about women in the sandwich generation, thought Darwin. Not only that, but she'd submitted an early draft to a quarterly and had high hopes for its publication.

Anita and Marty's wedding planning resumed with full vigor, and Anita was well on her way to putting together a beautiful knitted wedding coat for the event they'd scheduled for the following spring. The ceremony would be outdoors, followed by a reception at the Pierre. Nathan agreed to walk her to the huppah, much happier since he'd reconnected with Rhea. And Anita, who once said she'd never move away from the city, now wanted to spend large chunks of the year in Italy to be near Sarah.

For her part, Sarah agreed to return to New York for a visit soon, and Marco promised to bring her. He hoped to buy the painting of Catherine wearing the Phoenix, though he was intuitive enough not to tell her so. The dress was back in its glass case now, more beautiful than ever. Catherine occasionally worked on her revenge novel from time to time, but only because it made her giggle. Instead, she hung out at her store most days and began writing a new story. A better one. About two best friends who met at a high school in Pennsylvania.

It was a crisp and clean September day; the scent of autumn was fresh in the New York City air.

'This is our fifth walk,' said Anita, wearing the pink sweatpants she put on only once a year. 'We've viewed a lot of scenery along the way.'

'Look at us,' said Darwin, pushing Cady and Stanton in the stroller she'd gotten at her shower. The babies wore the cardigans Anita had knit for them, although they were getting snug, and striped socks their mother had made. 'At how far we've come.'

'Far?' said KC, her hair pulled up in a scrunchie she'd knitted herself and that Peri had even complimented. 'We only go a few miles each year.'

'But at least we're moving,' replied Catherine, zipping up a red hoodie. 'At least we're not standing still.'

Dakota nodded as the grand marshal announced the start

of the charity walk, bouncing on her heels in her navy blue tracksuit, raring to get started. All around them, mothers, daughters, sisters, and friends of survivors and fallen fighters darted forward.

And arm in arm, the members of the Friday Night Knitting Club marched on.

Acknowledgments

Thank *you*.

To each and every reader who e-mailed me at katejacobs.com, who approached me at book signings, and who invited me to telephone your book group and then asked the question, when was I going to write a sequel? Your enthusiasm about the club was tremendous and much appreciated. And you know what? I never stopped thinking about Dakota and Catherine and Anita and the entire group, and sitting down to type out my thoughts was a delightful reunion with some old friends. So your encouragement was a wonderful gift.

My gratitude to everyone at Putnam and at Berkley, including Ivan Held, Leslie Gelbman, Shannon Jamieson Vasquez, Rachel Holtzman, and everyone in sales, marketing, publicity, editorial, production, and design. But above all, my sincere thanks to my brilliant editor, Rachel Kahan, whose good humor and support are particularly essential, and whose keen eye makes my books much, much better.

As always, I rely heavily on the support of my smart-cookie agent, Dorian Karchmar, of the William Morris Agency, who knows the answers I need before I even think to ask the questions, and to Dorian's assistant Adam Schear, because he happily handles all tasks, large and small.

Like the members of the club, I am fortunate to be surrounded by smart, independent women who come through for me whenever I need a helping hand. Much praise is deserved by my super crew of pals who are always on board to read early drafts, including Rhonda Hilario-Caguiat, Kim Jacobs, Shawneen Jacobs, Tina Kaiser, Alissa MacMillan, Robin Moore, and Sara-Lynne Levine. Thanks also to Dani McVeigh and Olga Jakim for keeping my websites up-to-date and looking spiffy.

And I couldn't forget my mother, who calls often to ask how many pages I've written (ummm . . . thanks, Mom?) but who also cleared off her desk so I could set up shop and finish up revisions while visiting my hometown. And to my father, who took over walking my dog, Baxter, so I could keep at it uninterrupted; my sister, Deenee Jacobs, who likes to talk knitting; and the folks who offered to adjust and taste the recipes, including Jackie Blonarowitz, my sister-in-law Shawneen (pulling double duty reading and baking), and my husband, Jonathan Bieley, who tastes all goodies to ensure their deliciousness.

You see, it's one thing to write about community and connection in my novels, but it's quite another to be surrounded by the same in my own life. I know that I am very fortunate indeed.

The Georgia Afghan

The original made by the club was quite generously sized and consisted of multiple panels. This throw is easily made all in one piece – which can make it a tad heavy as you get toward the finish, but it's still manageable – and is meant to be just the right size to keep one person toasty while napping or, better yet, reading a book!

needles: Your project will knit up more quickly if you use thick yarn and bigger needles. Opt for number 15, 17, or 19 circular needles.

yarn: Be sure to use machine-washable yarn that's soft to the touch. (Your fingers will thank you!) Visit your local yarn shop and choose something that appeals to your eyes, fingers, and Peri Pocketbook.

the pattern: A basic garter-stitch border kicks things off, and the interplay of knit 2 and purl 3 in the pattern creates a nice blocky texture and adds visual interest to the blanket.

Go to www.walkeranddaughter.com for detailed directions about basics such as how to cast on, how to knit or purl, and how to cast off.

Cast on 90 stitches.

Knit 10 rows.

Then follow the pattern like so:

Rows 1–10: Knit 5 (for border), knit 2, purl 3, knit 2, purl 3, knit 2, purl 3, knit 2, purl 3, knit 2, purl 3, knit 2, purl 3, knit 2, purl 3, knit 2, purl 3, knit 2, purl 3, knit 2, purl 3, knit 2, purl 3, knit 2, purl 3, knit 2, purl 3, knit 2, purl 3, knit 2, purl 3, knit 5 (for border).

Rows 11–20: Knit 5 (for border), purl 3, knit 2, purl 3, knit 2, purl 3, knit 2, purl 3, knit 2, purl 3, knit 2, purl 3, knit 2, purl 3, knit 2, purl 3, knit 2, purl 3, knit 2, purl 3, knit 2, purl 3, knit 2, purl 3, knit 2, purl 3, knit 2, purl 3, knit 2, purl 3, knit 2, knit 5 (for border).

Repeat the pattern until the desired length is reached.

Knit 10 rows, and then cast off.

Keep the afghan for yourself, or donate it to a worthy cause!

The Friday Night Knitting Club's Maple Apple Muffins

A quick and easy snack for any group meeting!
Makes 12 muffins.

Ingredients

- 1¾ cups whole wheat or gluten-free flour
- 1 tsp. baking powder
- ½ tsp. baking soda
- 1 tsp. cinnamon
- ¼ tsp. salt
- 2 large eggs
- ¼ cup oil
- ½ cup applesauce
- ⅓ cup maple syrup (Be sure to use real maple syrup, not artificial pancake syrup.)
- 1 tsp. pure vanilla extract
- ⅔ cup dark brown sugar
- 2½ cups peeled, cored, and coarsely chopped Granny Smith apples (approximately 4 apples)
- ½ cup chopped pecans (optional)

Directions

Preheat oven to 375 degrees F.

Line a muffin tin with paper cups.

Combine the following dry ingredients in a large mixing bowl: flour, baking powder, baking soda, cinnamon, and salt.

Beat the eggs in a separate bowl. Then add the wet ingredients: oil, applesauce, maple syrup, and vanilla extract. Stir, then mix in the brown sugar.

Add the dry ingredients to the wet ingredients and combine.

Stir in the apples, and nuts if desired.

Pour the batter into the muffin cups. An optional garnish makes things look even sweeter: place two apple slices on the top of each unbaked muffin, plus a sprinkle of brown sugar and cinnamon.

Bake in a preheated oven for 20–25 minutes; remove the muffins from the baking pan and cool on a wire rack.

Enjoy!

Catherine's Favorite Raspberry-Lime Granita

Delicious as a sorbetlike dessert, palate cleanser, or refreshing slushy.

Makes 6 to 8 servings, depending on size.

Ingredients

- ½ cup lime juice (approximately 2–3 limes)
- ½ cup superfine sugar or baker's sugar (or run white granulated sugar in the food processor to make smaller granules)
- ½ cup water
- 2 cups fresh raspberries (or frozen, defrosted)
- 4 tbsp. white sugar
- ¾ cup water
- Fresh mint leaves for garnish (optional)

Directions

Juice the limes and set the juice aside.

Add the ½ cup sugar to the ½ cup water in a pan over low heat and whisk together until the sugar dissolves.

Remove from the heat and add the lime juice; whisk again and set aside.

Puree the fresh raspberries in a food processor. Add the lime juice mixture, the 4 tablespoons sugar, and the ¾ cup water and blend again.

Strain the raspberry-lime puree through a sieve into a 13 x 9 glass pan, using a spatula to push the puree through. (Your goal is to remove as many of the raspberry seeds as you can! If straining seems like a lot of effort, then use strawberries. You can likely get away without straining, though the berry flavor won't be as intense.)

Cover the pan with cellophane and place it, flat, in a freezer.

Every twenty minutes, take a fork and scrape the just-forming layer of flaky ice crystals from the edges into the center of the pan. Do not discard, but leave the icy bits in the middle and return the pan to the freezer. Repeat until all the mixture is frozen and granular, about an hour and a half to two hours.

When freezing is complete, scrape the entire icy mixture with a fork until nothing is stuck to the bottom. Scoop servings into martini or dessert glasses, and garnish with mint if desired.

Spoon up!